CHARMED BY DARKNESS

Ruins of Rima Book 2

E. Abraham

DEDICATION

For everyone who stuck with me to the end. You're the true MVP. I hope
I gave you exactly what you needed…
Maybe not what you wanted, but definitely what you needed.

Author's Note

Please read this if you have any triggers or have seen the trigger warnings and need more information!

Charmed by Darkness is the second book of a spin-off for the Shadows of Synd Series. In Under the Shadows (Book one of the Shadows of Synd Series), you're introduced to the Guild. This organization is vile, depraved, and without moral regard. They steal people's lives for profit. They do not see them as humans, but merely a commodity to be bought and sold. They kidnap, rape, and sell these people with no regret. Because of this, it was very difficult to write about them and therefore I did not write about the inner-workings within the organization.

Charmed by Darkness delves even deeper into the world of the Guild. It deals with a lot of the heavy topics outlined in the trigger warnings. However, Dante does not participate in the trigger warnings listed.

One of the triggers listed is Dead Dove Do Not Eat. If you're unfamiliar with fanfiction (or *Arrested Development*), you've probably never encountered it before. It has morphed, but is widely accepted as a tag to indicate that the triggers are clearly labeled so you know what you're getting. Please take the trigger warnings seriously as this book is much darker than my previous works.

While the Ruins of Rima is fiction, an estimated 14,500–17,500 people are trafficked each year within the United States. Some of the atrocities within this book is a reality for those who are taken.

The National Human Trafficking hotline is open 24-hours a day, seven days a week.
888-373-7888

TIGGER WARNINGS

Anxiety/Depression
Assault (Sexual/Physical)
Murder/Death
Drugs (side characters-nonconsensual)
Emotional Abuse
Violence/Blood
Kidnapping
Human/Sex Trafficking
Misogyny
Physical Abuse
Sexual Abuse/Assault
Forced Prostitution
PTSD/Hallucinations
Sexual Harassment
Slut Shaming
Starvation
Torture: Chapter Eight & Ten
Hospitalization (brief)
Arson
Mentions of: dogfighting, gambling halls, brothels, suicide, drowning
Dead Dove Do Not Eat

Content Warnings:

Sexually Explicit Scenes (consensual)

Adult Language

Conversations on BDSM dynamics

PROLOGUE

Aelia

When I was small and afraid of the things that go bump in the night, I would climb into my brother's bed. I never ran to my father when I had a nightmare. He wasn't my safe place. Roman, on the other hand, always comforted me. He let me hide from the monsters—both real and imaginary, reassuring me he'd always be there to fight off my demons.

He lied.

The darkness swirling around me is a living being, threatening to suck me into a void I'll never be free of. I barely feel the cold anymore, though I'm sure it's freezing in here. The shadows keep me warm. At one point, they started whispering lies in my ear, but I ignored them until the voices vanished. I was afraid if I acknowledged them, they'd devour me whole. Or maybe bit by bit while I silently screamed into the nothingness.

I should be used to this—living in the dark. For years I've been walking the night, waiting for the soft kiss of the sun to brush my skin. The moments were few and far between, even after Dante came into my life. When I was with him, I allowed myself to dream of a new life. One filled with sunlight and dreams I thought were long dead. Even now, being locked away by the Guild deep in the bowels of headquarters, I'd do it all again. I'd choose *him* again. I'd choose the dreams and the sun and the happily-ever-afters. And love.

I'd choose love.

Over and over again, I'd choose love.

Every minute that passes in this hellhole, those dreams fade a little more. The darkness eats away at them, swallowing them whole while I cower in the corner waiting for the night it finally comes for me.

I should have made us run when I had the chance. I don't blame Dante. He did what he thought was best, even if it cost me what little freedom I had. I don't even hate him for not coming for me. It was never his job to save me. His promises burned away, the hint of ashes the only evidence left behind. I can't even muster up the rage I once had over the turn of events.

I'm slowly wasting away, forgotten. And I don't even care anymore.

ONE

Dante

One Month Later

We should have run when Aelia told us to. I blame myself. I thought I was doing what was right. I thought we had more time. And Aelia lost what little independence she had. I hate myself for leaving her—for not going back like Jag and Avery screamed at me to do. It was my job to save her. The promises I made to her burn within me, leaving the ashes of my heart as the only evidence. I can't even muster up the rage I had after I failed her.

"Pay the fuck attention, Raines," Shane King barks from the other side of the room.

I glance up, barely noticing the others. Their voices rise and fall, a gentle wave of nothingness. The room won't come into focus either. It's not like we've set up in a mansion complete with fancy conference rooms like King's house.

Part of me wishes we were back in Synd, fighting about who has the better plan to take down the Guild. In this abandoned restaurant with scorch marks running up the wall, the ideas run more toward what we're going to blow up first. I don't have it in me to participate.

"Dante?" MacKenzie, my sister, calls softly. Then her face floats in front of me. "Why don't we go for a walk."

It's not an invitation. Her soft hand brushes my wrist and I jerk away, regret and guilt flooding me instantly. I close my eyes, swallowing hard before I stand. Ryker Helms mumbles something to her, but the ringing in my ears drowns out his words. He wasn't talking to me, anyway. He's probably whispering for her to be careful. When I was holed up with the Guild I missed a lot.

I missed too much. New people, new relationships, tragedies, and heartache—the world marched on in the year I was gone. I barely knew most of these people before, and now I'm floundering as I attempt to navigate the changing dynamics. Everything is the same, yet different.

Mac's hand slides into mine, and my mind flashes back to when we were kids. She was always there. Always holding me together in a way no one else could. Every time a hit was too hard. Every time my father's lessons were too gruesome. Every time life put too much on my young shoulders. Every time she was there. And in the end, I left her. Just like I left Aelia.

"Tell me again," I whisper as we walk along the back alley.

She sighs, glancing at the lone pine tree rustling in the breeze. She shivers in her leather jacket—Helms's jacket, if the patches are any indication. As she pulls her dark hair over her shoulder, my eyes are drawn to the embroidered reaper. She never did like the viper one our club has. *My club.* She's fully made the switch back to Helms's MC and I can't even blame her. If I had the chance…no. I'd never go back to Synd. Maybe when I was younger I would have run back to the Reapers, but leading the Vipers is my priority.

"After you left, Maddox started talking, making plans and deals you never would have approved of. The Night Slayers were rampant, taking over Viper territory and killing…" She stops, pulling in a deep breath. "You don't want to hear this again, Dante."

"Tell me," I growl, tugging my hand from hers.

"Fine. He pawned me off to them. I escaped and ran to Ryker. Night Slayers followed and we stopped them. When I came back to Rima, nothing was left of them. Happy?" she spits out. Her use of the word pawned isn't accurate, but she's trying to protect me.

"You're missing parts. You didn't say anything about Ryker getting shot. Or them burning half of Reaper territory to the ground." I know what happened, but I keep asking over and over.

"It wasn't half," she mumbles, averting her gaze.

"You missed the part where you fell in love."

Her hazel eyes find mine and I'm struck again by how they're a mirror of our mother's. Nothing like mine and Maddox's which we got from our father. I wonder if things would have been different if our dad would have kept our mom alive. I push the thought away.

"Yes. I fell in love. And then Willow came to Synd and fell in love. And you—"

I pivot, walking away from her and her words. MacKenzie keeps bringing up Aelia, trying to get me to talk about her, about what happened, and where we go from here. I refuse to have a conversation about Aelia. I don't deserve to talk about her. Our story isn't one filled with first dates and flowers. It's not a tale of budding romance sprouting at the first hints of spring. No one will write our happily ever after.

"You didn't fail her, Dante. I wish you could see that," she calls, her voice riding the wind whipping through the darkness.

Thankfully, she lets me go. I stomp around the building, wondering if I should have told them to take over headquarters instead. The Vipers sure as shit aren't using it. There's a handful of members left and most of them are green. They don't have the history and skills to help us take down the Guild. I thought I was doing what was right, but everywhere I turn all I see is the consequences of my decisions. The fallout is massive and it's all my fault.

"You sulking again?" Alex's voice jolts me back to the present.

I whip around, searching for him in the dark. His blond hair is the only reason I find him leaning against the dingy building. It's another moonless night, the shadows matching my mood. They've been doing that more often than normal. I can't complain, since I'm sure Aelia is spending her time within that darkness—being swallowed alive by the evil surrounding her.

"What do you want, Alex?"

He gives me a soft smile before tucking his chin to his chest. "I've heard them. They're all telling you to suck it up. To focus on how we're going to take them down and get your woman back. How many times has Mac told you it wasn't your fault? Don't answer that."

"There a point to this lecture?" I ask, but there's no bite to my words. There's a void within me where Aelia once lived, and all my emotions have fallen into it.

"You know, when we couldn't find Sam, I almost lost my mind. And then she called. I mean, she called Ren, but she called." He shakes his head. "I thought she was dead. There was so much blood and the fire was consuming everything. And then she was fine. She was her same sassy self. And then it happened again. But there wasn't a call that time. There was just…silence. Even when we found her, there was this void. This deadened space where she used to be. It took too long for her to come back to us."

He shakes his head again, mouth parting as he exhales. "I know everyone keeps telling you to pull your shit together, but I just wanted you to know I get it. If you need to live in that void for a while, I get it."

Alex pushes from the wall, his mind clearly still reliving everything they went through. I wish I could sympathize with him. I wish I could tell him his words had any effect on me, but they don't. They're just words. Nothing more, nothing less.

"Except you had Shane and Ren." My eyes dart to him as he stops in front of me and rage erupts in my chest. "You had two other people who knew how you felt. They were willing to step in for you when you couldn't stand on your own two feet. And you got the girl in the end. Fuck you, Alex King. You have no idea what the fuck I'm going through."

He nods slowly, pressing his lips together. He claps me on the shoulder, squeezing before disappearing into the night. The burst of anger winks out as if it was never there to begin with.

I stumble toward headquarters. I don't have it in me for more plans. For more glances filled with pity. Shane is the only one treating me like I'm not about to shatter into a million pieces. I could seek him out, focus on something other than self-pity. Instead I keep going, ready for another night of staring at the ceiling. I'll relive the last few months and all the things I should have done differently.

Headquarters comes into view, swathed in shadows. We used to have it lit up, but that's just one of the many things that has changed. One of the double doors pops open and Blaze, my sergeant-at-arms, lifts a hand. He doesn't bother to stop me, knowing I'll brush him off. He's been doing my duties since Maddox went off the deep end. There's not much to do, though, since most of our supplies and suppliers have dried up.

A lot of the members that were here when my father ran things defected to the Night Slayers. I assume they're dead. Eventually, we'll need to rebuild, but I can't make any moves while the Guild has a foothold in our city.

I navigate the large space by memory alone, making my way to the back. My office had a layer of dust coating everything, but MacKenzie came through and cleaned it. Helms said it was her way of making things feel more normal. I didn't have the heart to tell either of them that nothing is normal anymore.

I collapse in the chair behind my desk, staring at the ceiling. Closing my eyes, I shut out the voice screaming at me to take my bike across town and blow up the Guild. And then I hear it—the scuffle of a shoe. A dark shadow in the corner of the room detaches from the wall, and my breath stalls in my chest.

Aelia. I shake my head, knowing it's not her. It can't be her.

"Sam, what the hell are you doing?" I grunt as my heart pounds in my ears.

She materializes from the dark, dressed in all black, per usual. I grit my teeth as she hops on top of my desk. Her foot hits the arm of my chair. The move sends a jolt through me, and I raise an eyebrow.

"I was going to do some recon, but then figured we should talk," she says as she pulls out a knife.

My muscles tense until she starts cleaning her nails with the tip. I've had a handful of interactions with Samantha Byrns, and all of them put me on edge. There's something about her that makes me feel like she's more than meets the eye.

"They didn't tell you, did they?" Her bottom lip juts out as she pouts.

"Going to have to be more specific. A lot of people talking lately without actually saying anything at all."

She tilts her head, then nods. "Gotcha. So, specifically, I was asking about Ren, Alex, and Shane."

"I haven't had the chance to have a sleepover with your boyfriends. Sorry," I grumble.

"And I'm guessing your sister isn't talking about anything other than how shit isn't your fault. Blah, blah, blah." She waves her hand around lazily, then tucks her knife away.

"Get to the fucking point, Sam," I grunt.

She leans back on her hands, legs swinging. "You heard of the Wraith?"

"Course I've heard of the fucking—" I groan when it hits me. "You've got to be fucking kidding me."

She grins, biting her lip. "I love seeing people's reactions. I mean, now that the guys know. It was a bit touch and go once they figured out I was the assassin they'd been hiring for years to do their dirty work."

Sam rolls her eyes and sits up to dive into her hoodie pocket, producing a bag of pretzels with a flourish. She holds it out to me, shaking it slightly, but I shake my head. I've barely been eating and I won't start with crackers that turn into dust as soon as I bite down.

"Your loss. Anyway, I need some info from you. Layout of the embassy the Guild is holed up in. Plus any other places they have throughout the city. Oh, and a list of the underground businesses they've got their shitty little hands in. Not to mention any contacts that might be able to help us." She squints, checking some invisible checklist she's made in her mind.

They've taken to calling the Guild's headquarters the embassy. It makes sense since it used to be one, but it throws me off sometimes. "Why exactly are you asking me?"

"No one else to ask. Plus, you seem like you could use something to do rather than wallowing in your own self-pity." She smirks, then pops another pretzel in her mouth.

"Ask Jag. He was skulking around that place more than I was ever able to." I lean forward, contemplating starting my computer. I don't have anything to do, though.

"Wow, you really have checked out. You know, you're better off just giving me the info. If Shane comes in here…"

"Is that a threat?" I growl, sitting back again and crossing my arms.

She hops down, circling the desk, and I breathe a sigh of relief. I didn't have the energy to deal with her before. Now I'm even more exhausted. My nostrils flare when she spins to face me.

"I get you weren't around for the last year and are probably beating yourself up over that. But honestly? We all have. It's been a shitshow of a time. We've been shot, tortured, kidnapped, and betrayed." She pulls in a deep breath as the shadow of a memory clouds her face. "But we kept going. We didn't give up just because shit got hard. We didn't let the nightmares overwhelm us. We learned how to lean on each other. I suggest you give it a try, because the only hope your woman has is you. And if you don't pull your head out of your ass and save her? Well, there's where you'll fail."

Her words echo through my mind long after she's vanished into the night. I should have asked her where she was going. Rima isn't the same as Synd. There's a lawlessness to the city that she's not used to. Mafia families don't control every official. MCs aren't keeping shit in line anymore. Not after Maddox's antics. Hell, even before, we didn't run shit. We were trying, but I failed in that area, too.

I wanted to build something here. Now I'm wondering if I should have cut my losses after my father died. No, Rima is nothing like Synd. I'd rather not be blamed by the Kings when Sam gets herself into a situation she can't get out of. I snort, shaking my head. Apparently, she's capable of taking care of herself. Unlike Aelia, who barely remembers the defense moves her brother taught her.

I want to believe Sam. I want to stop the vicious thoughts rolling through my head, threatening to suffocate me. I want to help the others bring down the organization that stole something precious from me. I just don't know how.

I'm slowly wasting away. And I don't even care anymore.

Two

Aelia

Sighing, I loll my head to the side. Not that I can see anything. It really is a desolate void down here. I'd like to say I'm handling the stress of being shoved into a cage, but I'm not. I thought I was apathetic before, but now I'm a shell of who I was. That wouldn't be such a feat, seeing as how I've been locked away for the last eight years. Then Dante waltzed his way into my life with his grand plans and bold promises.

A red light flashes down the hall and I scramble into the corner of my cage. Wrapping my arms around my legs, I make myself as small as possible. I can't hide from whoever is coming, but maybe they'll leave me alone this time.

A strangled sob echoes from the prison next to mine. The girl can't be more than seventeen, already skin and bones by the time they stuffed her down here. She's been crying on and off for the last two days. At least I think it's been that long. Time warps in a place like this.

"Hush. Bite your arm. Focus on the pain," I whisper, keeping my eyes fixed on where I know the door is, even if I can't really see it.

Every ten seconds, the light sends out a strobe, lighting the space for a split second before plunging us into darkness once more. It takes at least half a minute before I make out her form. I huff out a breath as she quiets, teeth sunk deep into her skin. I can't save her any more than I can save myself. My whispered words of advice are the only gifts I can give her. If she's anything like the last few women down here, she won't be here much longer.

"Get the fuck off me, asshole," a woman shrieks as the door pops open.

It's just as dark in the hallway as it is in here. The red light flashes once more, then a glow of red takes over the space. It's almost too much for me to take, and I bury my face in my arms. Whoever she is, she's fighting. That won't last. They'll beat her down or rape her into submission. Or they'll drag her out of here to do fuck knows what with her.

"Keep it up and we'll make you regret it, bitch." Grant's voice washes over me, and every muscle in my body tenses.

I haven't seen him since he threw me down here, supposedly on my father's orders. I'm not surprised Anders Drake couldn't do his dirty work himself. He never was one to get involved unless he had to.

Why waste my time when I can convince others to do it for me? It was one of the lessons he repeated to Roman, my brother, many times while we were growing up. Roman only made the mistake once of questioning whether that made my father weak. It did, but that didn't matter. My father lives off the fear of others, sustaining himself on the control he can exert over them.

The woman laughs sharply. "You sound like you're talking out of your ass."

I flinch when the sound of a fist hitting flesh pulsates through the room. It throbs through my body, a steady beat resonating in time with my heartbeat. Swallowing hard, I take the chance to peek at them. Grant stands over the woman curled into a ball on the concrete outside of my cell. The woman next to me pants, her panic overwhelming her.

She's too far away for me to reach her through the bars. Not that I'd risk it with my handler feet away from where I cower. The brush of my fingers against hers would be enough, probably. I'd think the Guild placed them this way on purpose, but that's not likely. Ever since they moved to Rima, it's been a slowly declining shitshow instead of the smooth operation they've been for years. I'd love to take credit for the Guild's current state, but I don't feel like I did much at all.

Grant grabs the woman's hair and drags her into the cage across from me. The bars clang as he slams the door shut, drowning out her whimpers. His soulless eyes, black in the crimson glow, bore into mine until I avert my gaze. I wasn't quick enough to miss his sadistic smile, though. I hold my breath until his footsteps fade away. As soon as the heavy metal thuds closed, the light winks off and darkness descends once more.

The woman next to me scoots across the floor, probably wrapping her cold fingers around the bars. I doubt she's searching for me. She tried to ask me questions when she first got here and I refused to answer. She gave up pretty quickly. If there's anyone else down here, they haven't revealed themselves. I don't blame them.

"Are you okay? My name's Nat. Well, Natalie, but everyone calls me Nat. What's your name?" Natalie sniffs, then clears her throat. "I know it's scary, but we'll get out of here."

"Don't," I grunt. "Don't fill her head with bullshit."

"Just because you don't have hope doesn't mean the rest of us have to give up," she hisses.

"Let me guess. You were snatched off the streets, right?" Bitterness weaves its way through my tone. It's not her fault, but I can't help but hate her optimism. Maybe I'm just too jaded.

Something hits her bars, probably her hand. "We all were taken. We're all in the same boat."

A humorless laugh bubbles out of me. Once I start, I can't stop. Digging my nails into my legs doesn't help. I don't even know if I care anymore. Let Grant come back in here. The darkness has seeped so far into my soul I just may be able to wield it to my advantage. I can drag him down with me, letting the demons that haunt me torture him for a while.

"What's so fucking funny?" the woman across from me snaps.

"I wasn't snatched off the streets. I wasn't taken at all. So, *Nat*, you can take all your platitudes and shove them up your ass," I snarl.

"Wait, how did you end up here, then?" Nat asks. Clearly, she can't take a hint.

The other woman snorts. "Bet she was sold. Who didn't love you enough to keep you, baby girl?"

"These people don't know how to love. They only know how to break things. Now stop talking before they come back." I bury my head again, trying to ignore them as they ignore my advice.

Within three minutes, I know more about the women next to me than I ever wanted to. Nat prattles on about her family, her job, her favorite color, and then she starts with the questions. The woman across from us, Nova, answers hesitantly at first, but warms up the longer they talk. Without the threat of someone coming in, I'm sure they think they're as safe as can be in this prison. They have no idea what's coming.

"Are you really going to ignore us? We need to stick together or we'll never get out," Nat says.

"We won't have to worry about escaping," Nova responds flippantly. "I've got people on the outside. They'll get us out."

She says it with such conviction, I almost believe her. Then I remember I have someone out there, too. He ran just like I told him to. And he's not coming for me. At least if he keeps his promises, he won't.

Tucked away in bed while the sun slowly rose over the horizon, I told him to leave me. I'd take care of myself, survive just like I have all these years. And if he happened to come back to burn them to the ground, I told him not to hesitate just because I might be inside. It's the only gift I can give to the world—sacrificing my life so others will never have to live under the Guild's thumb.

He didn't like it. He argued, mostly with himself, for days. Eventually, he gave in. Just like I knew he would. Because asking him to choose between me and eradicating the Guild wasn't fair. I had to take the option away from him or he'd be at war with himself. He'd be paralyzed by the decision and fail at both. Beyond Dante, my life doesn't matter. I have nothing else to live for, anyway.

"Do you know how many people have tried to take down the Guild?" I murmur, tipping my head back. The bars dig into my scalp, grounding me in the present.

"It doesn't matter. You don't know who I have backing me up," Nova sneers.

"Perhaps not, but they're not the first and they certainly won't be the last. One group can't do it alone. So unless you have a shit ton of friends, then you're up a creek without a paddle, honey." Even this small conversation has drained me.

A guard comes in every couple days with a pittance of food and water, but it's not enough. I'm better equipped than others to deal with the near starvation. This is extreme, though. The other two here will probably be put up in the Auction. Who knows what my father will do with me. I'd be surprised if Jenkins even knows I'm down here. Maybe Jenkins assumes I ran with Dante, which only puts him at more risk.

"How long have you been here?" Nat whispers as she shuffles around.

I sigh, kicking myself for opening the door. Now they'll think we're in this together and try to plan a way out. And I'll have to be the one to break their spirits. The Guild will do that enough. I shouldn't add more heartache on top of it. Breaking their hope isn't my job.

"Seven…eight years maybe. Don't worry. You won't be here that long."

Nat gasps, while Nova makes a sound in the back of her throat. I shouldn't have said anything.

"What are they going to do with us?" Nat's resolve is broken already. I can hear it weaving its way through her voice, in the desperation in her tone.

"If you're in here, probably put you up for the Auction. Vile, rich-ass men bidding for the privilege to break you until you're a shell of yourself or dead. I suggest rooting for death, personally." I bite my lip and close my eyes. No use breaking down when it'll only make things worse.

"So fighting that asshole wasn't a bad idea then, huh?" Nova's smug tone has rage boiling up in me.

No, not rage—jealousy. The number of times I wish I could have fought against Grant number in the thousands. Instead, I kept my head down. I took the beatings and the starvation and the abuse and the harassment for years. I thought if I was quiet, meek, then he'd leave me alone.

The shitty thing is it was working. Grant was losing interest. His insults were ever-present, but the heavy hand wasn't fun when I wasn't fighting back. Once Dante came along, threatening my handler's authority, all the progress I'd made was washed away. Not only did I not remember how to dive back into my apathy, but I also bought into the belief it would eventually end. I forgot that this darkness—this evil—never ends. I was a fool and I have no one to blame but myself.

I huff, checking out completely. I can't help one last comment, though. "Unfortunately, you just made yourself a target. Lucky you."

THREE

Dante

"We need a plan. Waiting around won't do anything," Shane snaps, running his hands through his dark hair.

The abandoned restaurant was once Nico's place. He moved locations and told us to use it, apparently. I didn't have the conversation with him, but someone called him. I never found out who, but I'm assuming it was Jag. He's been avoiding me since I refused to go back for Aelia. I don't blame him. He didn't understand I promised her to stay the course.

"Dante, if you aren't going to help, you should just get the fuck out." Shane glares at me from across the table they found from fuck knows where. It's a long conference table like the ones they have at home.

"Leave him alone, Shane," Sam says calmly, her gaze fixed on schematics of some random building.

His eyes soften when he looks at her, and he sucks in a shuddering breath. The dynamic between Sam and her men doesn't make sense to me. They move together like a well-oiled machine, anticipating each other's moves and shifting to accommodate one another.

Helms leans closer. "She's the sun and they're the planets merely orbiting around her. If she explodes, they'll gladly allow her to consume them."

"Kinky," I mutter.

MacKenzie leans forward, glaring at me as she mouths, "Knock it off."

I shrug, glancing around at the people summoned to Rima. The only one I hadn't seen since we were kids was Mason Byrns. Last I heard, he had just woken up from a coma after being shot in the head. The Guild really did a number on Synd before they were pushed out. Honestly, I'm surprised no one died. I still don't know how he hooked up with Nemesis, but apparently it was a whole production over the last few months.

Nemesis meets my gaze head-on, sending a shiver down my spine. She crooks her finger at me, then shoves to her feet. I've spent enough time with my sister to know I'm in trouble from that move alone. Not following her would be disastrous. Helms chuckles under his breath, and I slap the back of his head before I push back my chair.

"What's the fucking point of having any meetings if people keep disappearing?" Shane grumbles before the door shuts behind me.

Nemesis leans against the building next to Nico's, staring at the stars. There aren't many streetlamps in Viper territory on purpose. I follow her gaze, tracking the Big Dipper as it twinkles above our heads. I wonder if they're keeping Aelia in a cell where she can't see the sun, much less the stars. Shaking my head, I drop my chin to my chest.

"What do you want, Nemesis?" I ask after a couple minutes of silence.

"Lacey. But you already know that. Listen, I get it. Shit sucks and this is clearly not where you want to be. Problem is, I put my ass on the line for you and you fucked it up. Your sister practically beat the shit out of me. And the others followed suit. I almost skipped town because of it. And now you're sitting here like a lump of nothing. What the fuck are you doing?" Her desperation bleeds through the fog in my mind.

"Mac hit you?"

"What the fuck?" she breathes, rubbing her temples.

I glance toward the mouth of the alley we're stuffed in, then back at her. The lone streetlight across the street catches the edge of the scar running down her cheek. It's a stark contrast against her skin. No one told me what happened, and I didn't bother to ask. It's none of my business. She runs her finger along it, starting right below her eye and ending at her jaw.

"If Mac hurt your feelings, I'd assume Byrns would deal with it. If not—"

"I don't need Mason to fight my battles for me. Besides, it was all of them. I wasn't about to put him in the middle." She sighs, finally meeting my eyes again. "It's fine. We came to an understanding. But we need more from you, Dante. I was so close to getting into the Guild's system. I need to know if there's a way—"

I hold up my hand, shock flooding my system. "That was you?"

Her eyes widen and she flaps her hands, making an indistinguishable noise in the back of her throat. I rear back, wondering if I need to get someone. She comes at me, forcing me around, then pushing me through the door. I stumble along, trying to get away from her, but she's dancing behind me, anticipating every sidestep.

"Sit," she commands, smacking my arm when I don't immediately obey.

Alarm runs through me as conversations around us stop. She gestures for me to speak, but I have no idea what she specifically wants me to tell them.

"Kitten, there a reason you're manhandling Raines?" Byrns raises an eyebrow at her, and she rolls her eyes.

"So, I might not have mentioned it before…" She grimaces as Byrns groans. "It's not that bad. And I did tell Ren."

Sam's head whips toward Ren, who keeps his eyes fixed on his tablet as he pales.

"Will someone tell the rest of us what the hell is going on?" Shane growls.

Lacey tilts her head, widening her eyes at me. I'm already drained by the events of tonight and nothing has even happened. It's merely being here, surrounded by so many people. Couples in love who randomly touch each other or whisper in each other's ears.

I almost wish Jag would stomp through the door. Last I heard, he was trying to convince Avery to go back to Harris and she wasn't budging. Didn't help that Ghost refuses to give him an answer on what to do.

"About three months ago, Aelia—" My voice breaks on her name, sending shards of ice through my veins and I cough. "A random program popped up on her computer. She clicked on it and a code box was suddenly there. I don't know anything about code, but she took classes before she…when she was younger. She said someone was trying to hack into the system. And dropping a shit ton of f-bombs."

Lacey scowls as she drops into her chair next to Byrns. "If she would have clicked on the box instead of exiting out and trashing it, then I would've gotten in. I could have bankrupted their entire operation within minutes. It would have been glorious."

"Doubt it," I mumble, crossing my arms.

"Why do you say that, Raines?" Ren asks, speaking for the first time this evening.

"Because she was hacking into the wrong computer. Aelia's doesn't…didn't have full access. Even after I convinced Jenkins to give her more. You wouldn't have been able to get very far. And you certainly wouldn't have been able to bankrupt them. They don't just have offshore accounts. They have cash flow from several different streams, not to mention the satellite cities." It's probably the most information I've given them since they got here a week ago.

My stomach turns, realizing how long it's been since I've seen Aelia. I went from seeing her every day to nothing. I don't know how to move forward. I don't know how to make a decision without her. She became integral to my process. Running my ideas by her as she cuddled up next to me became second nature to me. I took it for granted, assuming we'd have more time.

The other's voices rise and fall as they start their own conversations. No one is yelling, but it's overwhelming. Helms grabs my arm and hauls me to my feet. Resistance is futile at this point. He won't lecture me like the others. Helms doesn't mince words and certainly doesn't push his ideas on others. He sits back and observes, waiting until whatever he'll say will make a difference.

"Why the fuck does everyone keep dragging me into the fucking cold?" I mumble. He ignores me, of course.

"Where's Jag?" Helms says as soon as we stumble into the freezing night air.

Winter won't give in to spring, plunging us into another cold snap. I haven't bothered to take my bike out, using the weather as the excuse. I could say it's because I don't want one of the Guild members spotting me, but I just haven't had the energy. I want the first ride back to be with Aelia. Even bringing my bike out of storage is too much.

"Dante." Helms shakes my shoulder and I focus on him. "Where's Jag?"

I shrug, staring off toward the south side of the city as if I'll be able to spot Aelia if I only try hard enough.

"He said something about taking Avery to Harris," I mumble.

His hand slides away. "You think he'll convince her to go?"

"No. She's a spitfire who can't keep her mouth shut. We were going to get her out as soon as I found her, but she refused. Said Aelia needed someone in her corner." I grit my teeth, remembering how much I fucked up by keeping shit to myself. Maybe Aelia wouldn't have had so many doubts about us if I would've opened my damn mouth.

"So she'll fit right in." He chuckles, shaking his head.

"Not sure if Mac and her will be best friends or hate each other. Either way, Avery won't give a shit. She does things her own way. Keeping her in the room was hard enough, especially when Aelia would come back with more bruises." The words stick in my throat, remembering each time another spot appeared on her skin. "I should have protected her more."

"Did you do what you thought was right?" Helms asks, crossing his arms.

I scoff, shaking my head. "Does that matter? Doesn't change the fact that she's gone."

"There it is," he murmurs.

"You expecting me to guess what the hell you're talking about?"

He glares at the skyline spread in front of us. "You're acting like she's dead. Like you're the one who put a bullet in her head. But she's not and you didn't. The sooner you figure that out, the easier you'll be able to see."

"See what?" I whisper, my chest tightening.

"The way forward. The way back to her."

Numbness steals through me, leaving my mind foggy once more. "If she'll even—"

"You know, when Kane was holding Kenzie, my only thought was to get her away. I didn't care what happened to me. I was more than prepared to die if it would give her a chance to survive." He faces me, shadows dancing in his eyes. "Her life was always worth more than mine. After, I thought she'd leave because I failed her. I didn't kill him."

I grunt, brows pulling low. Mac clearly didn't tell me everything. "Are you telling me he's still out there?"

Helms shakes his head. "She killed him, Dante. She stabbed him after she thought I was dead. She thought she was avenging me. Didn't even think about saving herself. You'll have to ask her the rest since it's her story to tell, but I thought she'd leave. I wouldn't have even blamed her. I failed to protect her like I promised."

"That makes two of us," I mutter.

"This story isn't about you, asshole. Stop focusing on what you think you did wrong and start figuring out how you can move forward. Because that woman—" He stabs his finger toward the Guild's headquarters. "She's waiting for you. Even if she doesn't want you after, does that matter? Because if it does, then get the fuck out of the way so the rest of us can save her instead."

"Like hell you will," I growl, dropping my hands to my sides.

He smirks, then glances over his shoulder. I follow his gaze to find MacKenzie's worried face framed by the window. She ducks to the side when our eyes meet.

"What the hell is she doing? She's not even hidden." I catch her peeking at us, and she whips around again.

"She's just worried about you. I'm going to give you a piece of advice. Don't get yourself fucking killed," Helms says, making his way back to the restaurant.

"I expected some wise words, but instead I get 'don't get yourself killed'? Seriously?"

He pivots, planting his hands on his hips as he scowls. "You didn't have to watch her breakdown every time you didn't pick up your phone. Or when you left that bullshit message with no way to reach you. If you die, she's going to go off the deep end, and I'll be the one picking up the pieces. I'll fucking bring you back just to kill you again. Don't fuck this up, Dante."

I face the city again, a chill snaking down my spine as a train's horn blasts in the distance. "Too late."

FOUR

Aelia

The crimson light beats in time with my heart as my head lolls toward the door. Every day, the red floods our space in a pattern, messing with our minds. Nat spiraled after two days, clutching her head and rocking back and forth. Nova's snarky comments stopped as soon as she found out how long I've been here. She tried to talk Nat through her panic attacks the first day. That didn't last long. It's been silent sobbing until now.

Nat wails, ripping her hair out at the roots. If they don't stop with the psychological torture soon, she'll lose her mind completely. She won't come back from this. She'll be another casualty—another life lost to the Guild.

They don't even have to possess people for them to deteriorate. All they need to do is brush against someone…no. They don't even need to touch them to corrupt every single thing in and around them.

The Guild doesn't just bleed people dry. It extends to the lifeblood of the cities they live in. I've seen the devastation when we pull out. It's all right there in the numbers.

Nat's breathing speeds up, sawing in and out of her lungs. She isn't doing herself any favors, but that doesn't matter. Common sense doesn't live here. Telling someone to calm down doesn't work in the real world, much less within this space. I just wish she would quiet the fuck down before she gets us all killed.

I jolt upright, chin trembling as it hits me. This is exactly how Jenkins turned us against each other. I've internalized all their fucked-up thinking. I thought I'd figured it out and gotten over the pain of being ostracized from the others, but apparently old habits die hard. Rachel and I were working together. A few weeks in the dark and I forgot how to sympathize with the ones who were suffering, just like me.

"Natalie, listen. I know it's hard, but they'll come for you soon if you don't pull yourself together. Just breathe and remember it won't last forever. Nova's got people on the outside," I whisper, trying to be heard over her sobs without being too loud.

"Keep talking," Nova hisses.

I can't think of anything else to say. Every time someone has a breakdown, Rachel takes care of them. She's their den mother. She takes them under her wing and helps them in a way I never could. In fact, she's usually the one picking up the pieces after I've delivered them to their twisted fate.

I'm just as much of the problem as the men in charge. My stomach cramps, trying to fold in on itself. Wrapping my arms around my middle, I double over, dry heaving between my legs.

"Seriously? We can't have both of you spiraling. Knock it off," Nova says, banging against the bars.

I inhale through my nose, letting it out slowly through my mouth until the nausea passes. The door at the end of the hall screeches as it opens. The light stops flashing, sending a steady red glow throughout the room. Grant's thunderous face appears, black eyes zeroing in on me. The nausea returns full force, not that there's anything in my stomach to come up.

Averting my gaze, I drop my chin to my chest, resuming my quest to calm my gut. Nat's sobs have faded into quiet sniffles, but it won't be enough. It's never enough. His footsteps echo like a death toll through the quiet. The metal door rattles as he opens Natalie's cage.

Relief floods me, followed closely by guilt. Nova throws herself against her cell, screaming at him to stop. She begs him to take her instead while I drown in my shame for not doing the same.

Natalie's shrieks ring through the air long after he's dragged her out by her hair. I doubt we'll be seeing her again. I thought this prison was for those destined for the Auction, but now I'm not so sure. When we were in the last city, there was a large warehouse for everyone who would be sold at the high-end event. The ones who needed to be broken, though, were kept in cages like the one I'm occupying. They were the ones most likely to attempt to escape. Natalie doesn't fit the profile—weak, the fight beaten out of her already. She was hopeful, not defiant. I don't understand why she was here.

I tip my head back, staring into the darkness. I assume there's a ceiling up there somewhere, but even with the light still on, it's too far away to make out. How many others have been kept down here, wondering who walks the halls above them with no knowledge of their existence? Not that they would care. They don't bother wondering where the people come from as long as they can use them for their sick and depraved fantasies. Disgust rolls through me and I swallow hard.

"You just sat there. What the hell is wrong with you?" Nova spits out, the venom of her words the lash of a whip against my already thin skin.

"It wouldn't have mattered. He still would have taken her," I say, closing my eyes.

"What the hell did they do to you that you don't care about anyone but yourself? What the fuck did they do to you?" She doesn't sound pissed anymore.

"I don't need your pity, Nova. I just know how to play the long game. I know how to survive. Sorry you don't like the methods I use in order to do that," I sneer, and our eyes meet in the gloom.

"I don't want to live like that."

I nod slowly, then force out a humorless laugh. "I'm not living. I'm surviving. Which is what everyone else who lasts longer than a week does here. We're not in a position to band together. Maybe at one point, but not now."

She scoffs, turning away. She didn't understand my words, but that's okay. If she follows my lead, we just might get out of here. Maybe in the future we'll get the chance to bring down the Guild, but not while we're locked up. Not while the Guild controls everything. Not while they can separate us, chain us up, abuse us. Biding our time is the only way we'll survive.

"Better find your patience, Nova. If you don't, you'll be next."

She doesn't respond.

Hours later…maybe days, I'm still thinking about Nat. Time has no concept in the dark. With the light blinking out a while ago, I can't even make out Nova's form. Last I saw, she was curled on her side, muttering to herself. She didn't bother answering when I asked what she was saying.

Another guard comes in, throwing bread between our cages, followed by a single bottle of water. The door shuts again, the lock thudding into place. Thankfully, red washes the room so we can at least see where they land.

"Don't touch it yet," I say when Nova scrambles toward the food.

"I'm starving," she wails, reaching through the bars. Her arms aren't long enough.

"Not enough to get beat," I snap.

I don't know if it's my words or my tone, but she sags, resting her head against the barrier.

"How are you not withering away?"

I sigh, shaking my head. "Because I've been through this before. Many, many times. I'm used to only being fed a couple times a week."

"These people are monsters." Tears muffle her voice, and I press my lips together to keep from snapping at her again. It's not her fault. I'm sure I wasn't exactly the calmest person when I was sold.

"Surprised it took you this long to figure that out." I glance toward the corner of the room. Right above the door, there's a camera.

It's how I knew they'd come for Natalie. I'm sure this room is soundproofed like the crimson chambers just one floor above us. At first I assumed they wouldn't be watching, like in the VIP room Dante brought me to the night he claimed me. I should have known better, but I was still overwhelmed by our plans falling apart.

After another minute I crawl forward and grab the bottle. I'd like to ration it, but they took the last one before we finished. I snatch up the dry roll next and tear it in half. As I stare at the crumbs dusting the floor, my chest tightens. Or maybe that's my stomach. The urge to stuff the whole thing in my mouth overwhelms me.

"Here," I call, tossing her the other half.

Slowly, I eat the bread. It's dry, crumbly, and tastes like sawdust. It's not even enough to be a ball of lead in my stomach. Drinking water doesn't really help and once the liquid mixes with the bread, it turns to concrete. Even when I'm done eating, it doesn't change, only weighing me down more. It rivals the exhaustion in my bones.

"Water," she mumbles around a mouthful.

I roll the bottle toward her, half-full. It barely fits through the bars, and the plastic crinkles as she tugs on it. Thankfully, I don't have to warn her about chugging it. She shakes the last drops from the bottle, giving it a forlorn look before tossing it into the corner of her cell.

"How long you think we'll be down here?" Nova's eyes close as she rests her cheek against the metal bars.

"I'd rather not discuss it," I murmur, glancing at the camera again.

"You really think they're listening?"

"My position within the Guild wasn't like the ones in the Pit. So telling you anything won't help you and will only hurt me. So whether they're listening or not doesn't really matter." I fix my eyes on the door, waiting for it to bust open again.

If Grant is monitoring us, he won't care if I say anything. He'll just add it to my list of supposed transgressions. I'm still not convinced Jenkins even knows I'm here. I wouldn't put it past Grant and my father to not say anything. I want to believe the Guild is falling apart without me. That Jenkins can't handle the accounts or his schedule. Do I want to return to the office and pretend like nothing happened? Obviously not. But it could give me the opportunity to escape.

If my father is spying, I'm sure he won't bother either. The Guild is merely a tool for him. Once they outlive their usefulness to him, he'll bolt. Having such a large organization at his back is convenient for now. Maybe for him it's habit and security. Jenkins might think differently, assume he holds the power over my father, but no one controls Anders Drake. The proof rests in his decisions over the past year. My father will never let go of his vengeance for the leaders of Synd. He'll never stop trying to destroy them.

Whoever it is, I'm not going to risk telling Nova anything. She can trust me or not. We'll probably be separated sooner or later.

"Are they going to sell me?" Nova's small voice barely carries through the silence.

I should lie. I should infuse hope inside her and allow her to live in a fantasy just a little longer. Or maybe it would be kinder to tell her like it is. I could spill everything about the Auction so she can prepare herself for the inevitable and damn the consequences if someone is listening.

I study her face, painted scarlet, her eyes swathed in shadows. "I don't know."

FIVE

Dante

"Sit down, Avery," Jag grunts, pushing her down into a chair.

He settles into the one next to her, then levels a look at me across the desk. Crossing my arms, I lean back and wait for him to break the silence. After a few minutes, my palms start to itch. Every time I'm around others I just want to be alone. The minute I'm alone though…the stillness overwhelms me. I want to do something, but I can't bring myself to actually take the first step.

"Are you guys in a staring contest or something? Because I'd rather not sit here while you two eye-fuck each other," Avery grumbles.

"Shut up, sunshine. You're not leaving my sight, so stop trying to slip away." Jag raises an eyebrow, daring me to refute him. I won't.

She scoffs, shaking her head. "Where the hell do you think I'm going to go, kitty cat?"

"Sure as hell aren't going back to Harris like I want. Get used to being attached to my hip for the next however long this takes."

Tipping my head back, I grit my teeth. I don't want to deal with the bullshit between them. When Aelia was with me, it was fun to watch them dance around the inevitable.

Aelia was convinced they'd end up tumbling into bed, then profess their love to each other. Jag is a stubborn ass, though. And Avery only seems to like pushing his buttons. I doubt either of them will cross the line, especially with her being Ghost's little sister. To Jag's old-school way of thinking, she's off-limits.

"There a reason you two decided to grace me with your presence?" I ask, cutting into their soft bickering.

"You're done," Jag says, crossing his arms. "You've had over a month of sulking and you're fucking done. We can't keep going like this, and it won't help Aelia."

I snort, gripping the back of my neck. "You don't really have a leg to stand on, Jag."

Avery sighs, tipping her head back. "Dante, we didn't exactly get off on the right foot—"

"Then keep your fucking mouth shut, Avery," I snap. I instantly regret the words.

I start to apologize, but Jag leaps from his chair. Defending myself isn't on the table. I deserve the beat down he's about to hand me. Leaning back in my chair, I drop my hands to my thighs and close my eyes. The hit never comes. When I blink, Jag has settled back, Avery's hand wrapped around his arm.

"I'm sorry, Avery. That was uncalled for," I mumble, pulling in a deep breath. This is why I've been avoiding everyone as much as possible.

"You're going through some shit. I get that—"

Jag's nostrils flare. "Don't fucking excuse his behavior, Ave. He's a fucking asshole. He deserves everything he's going through."

He pushes from his chair, then slams open the door to stomp from the room. His footsteps fade, leaving Avery and me staring at each other. She clears her throat, mouth parting.

"I miss her too," she whispers.

Her words rip through me, tearing apart the tenuous hold I have on my sanity. I cover my face if only so she won't notice how close to the edge I really am. Obviously I'm not fooling anyone by ignoring them. I've barely seen Avery the last month and a half and even she notices the raw emotions coursing through me. They're right. I need to get my shit together.

"I should have—"

Her hand slashes through the air. "No. We're not going there. It doesn't matter. She told me to run too. She told us all to run, and we didn't listen."

"She told you to run?"

Slowly, she nods, despair flashing in her dark eyes. "She dragged me to that closet. Said no one would look for me there but you. She knew she wasn't coming back. I could tell. I was supposed to wait, but if you didn't come by noon, then I should run. Couldn't figure out when noon was, but then you showed up, so it didn't matter. Dante, she knew she wasn't getting out."

"I should have done it anyway." I rub at the ache in my chest.

"What about me?" she snarls, slamming her hands on my desk. "You decided to get me out, which I am incredibly grateful for. So, let's just roll with your little thought experiment."

"What the hell are you talking about?" I snap. Jag may be able to decipher what the fuck goes on in her head, but I'm lost.

"You find me in the closet. We go on some wild goose chase trying to find Aelia even though she was probably long gone, thrown into some forgotten room that we'd never find. And then we'd be right the fuck next to her. Actually, *I'd* be next to her and you'd be dead. The only reason the guards hesitated to grab you and me was because they were still keeping up appearances. So don't give me any bullshit about going back. It wouldn't have mattered. They would have killed you. And then she would have raised you from the dead to strangle you with your own spine." She's panting by the time she's done.

My lips twitch, pulling at the corner of my mouth. A soft chuckle leaves me when I imagine Aelia's scowling face as she threatens me if

I die. My eyes dart to Avery and she snorts, covering a smile with her hand.

"Why did you refuse to go back to Harris?"

Avery rolls her eyes. "Because you were practically catatonic. All those other people were paralyzed. Oh, and Kitty Cat wanted me to go. So, yeah. I'm staying."

"You talk to your brother?" As soon as the words are out of my mouth, I realize my mistake.

Avery isn't the type of woman to defer to anyone, much less her brother. If their relationship is anything like Mac's and mine, she actively defies Ghost every time he gives her an order. Sisters live outside of the hierarchy within an MC. They grow up hard and fast and without an ounce of self-preservation. I doubt Avery is any different.

"I haven't. Not that I need his permission to go anywhere. But by the look on your face, you figured that out about two seconds after you asked that question, didn't you?" She smirks, brushing her dark hair over her shoulder.

The door pops open, revealing a scowling Jag. Avery tips her head toward him, and I swear pain flashes across her face before it vanishes.

"There a reason there's a dozen bikes blasting through Viper territory?" he asks as he throws his thumb over his shoulder.

"We don't even have a dozen members left. Reapers?" I push from my chair to follow him back through headquarters.

Pulling my phone from my pocket, I call Helms. The rumble echoes through the open space, and I curse. The last thing I need is Reapers taking over my headquarters. It'll destroy what little respect we still hold within Rima. I won't turn them away, though. I glance over my shoulder at Avery trailing me. If it isn't the Reapers, I'd rather she stay here until we figure out if they're allies.

"Don't even think about it," she hisses.

I hand her the phone. "Call Helms three more times. If he doesn't pick up, call Mac. If she doesn't, go through the others until someone does."

"I know how protocol works, Cruz…shit. I mean, Raines. Dammit. Just stop fucking staring at me," she snarls.

The front doors bang open as Jag shoves his way through and the noise overtakes the night. I glance at the sky, expecting a storm to be rolling in, but it's clear and bright, a half moon hanging above us. Jag slips his gun into his hand, waiting for the headlights to turn toward us.

"You sure this isn't just the Phantoms?" I ask. I still pull out my gun as well.

"Fuck you, Raines. I'd know if Ghost was coming."

"Or I would," Avery chimes in, sliding between us.

Jag steps in front of her. "Get back in the building, Avery. It's not safe."

She pokes him in the back, then leans around him. "I'm as safe as I can be in hell, Kitty Cat."

Pain stabs at my temple and I wince. "Don't repeat Aelia's sage words of advice."

"That wasn't advice, toots. It was a fact. Rima is a cesspool. A living, breathing, hellscape. Just because I got it from Aelia doesn't mean it isn't true," Avery says, eyes fixed on the headlights steadily coming closer.

"Don't be an ass, sunshine," Jag mutters. He's still trying to shove her behind him until she skips to my other side.

I catch black hair streaming behind a woman with a bandana wrapped around her face at the head of the pack. Shaking my head, I tuck my gun away.

"You won't need that. It's Raven," I say to Jag, and he scowls.

"Who's Raven?" Avery's voice holds a tinge of jealousy, and I smother my grin.

I've smiled more in the last thirty minutes than since we left the Guild. The thought is quickly followed by an extra dose of guilt.

"She helped us that last night. Didn't realize she was sticking around Rima. Her crew bounces around quite a bit." I lift a hand to Raven as she pulls up along the curb. The rest fan out around her, blocking the street.

Avery tucks herself behind Jag, sticking her tongue out at me when our eyes meet. Raven waves away one of the women who tries to stop her from approaching us.

"Put your damn gun away, Jag. You're freaking people out," I mumble.

He scowls, but tucks it into his holster, brushing Avery as he does. I swear she shivers, but I'm not getting in the middle of that. They'll have to deal with shit themselves. When Ghost gets here, it'll only get more complicated.

"Raines, we've got a problem," Raven says as she plants her fists on her hips.

"Good to see you too, Raven."

She waves away my greeting. "We don't exactly have time for pleasantries. The Guild is searching for you. And they're not doing it subtly."

I thought I'd done a good enough job of treating Aelia like she was nothing to me in front of others. It wasn't easy, but apparently it didn't work. Otherwise they would have assumed I left Rima.

"I know what's going through your head, Raines, but it's not logical," Jag mutters. "They knew you were trying to take them out. They didn't have concrete evidence before, but they do now. Of course you wouldn't leave her behind."

I glance at him, grinding my teeth. "But I did."

"Except they know you'll be back. Which is how I know she's still alive." He turns to Raven, gesturing her to continue.

Raven rolls her eyes. "They're burning down sections of the city. A lot of them have squatters, but some of them…heard a rumor they might hit one of the clubs later."

"Which one?" The opposite end of the street fills with more headlights, and I breathe a sigh of relief.

"Top Notch. The fancy one. Might want to call up any connections you have to head them off," she says, eyeing Helms as he climbs from his bike.

"We're going to need all the help we can get, Raven."

We don't have enough people as it is. The Kings and Mason might be able to pull some of their people, but they can't leave Synd unprotected. Helms left Hawk and Willow in charge of Reaper territory. Their numbers are already depleted from their run-in with the Night Slayers. Ghost has some, but it's still not enough. It's never enough. We're going to fail from lack of numbers unless we figure out something soon.

"We're not in the business of sticking our necks out for people, Raines. You know that. I helped you before to settle the debt, but we're out. We've got enough shit to worry about without the Guild on our asses too." She crosses her arms, gaze still fixed on the Reaper's president.

"Raven?" MacKenzie tumbles from a car, followed closely by Sam. "Seriously? You come to town and don't call? What the hell?"

Mac's grin spread across her face as she takes in the others. Raven likes to pop up at random times, flitting in and out of town as she sees fit. Every time she has new women in her crew. They come and go as they please, but there are several who stick with Raven. Her core group took Mac under their wings whenever they were in Rima, doing what I couldn't.

"Kind of busy saving your brother's ass." The corner of her mouth twitches. It's the closest I've ever seen her come to a smile.

Mac turns to me, raising her brows. "Is that so? Why don't we go inside and you can tell us all about it?"

SIX

Aelia

"Ah, my illustrious daughter. How far you've fallen." My father's nasal voice jerks me awake.

Blinking, the red light washes over my vision and distorts his face. My hope that it was merely a hallucination bleeds away. I've been expecting him. I'm surprised it took him this long to come gloat.

I clear my throat. "What do you want, Father?"

Nova's soft gasp rebounds off the walls. There's nothing down here to dampen the sound. No hum from air conditioners. No buzz from lights. No noise from the crimson chambers above. It's a concrete block that allows the slightest sound to reverberate around the room. It's how I knew she was crying last night. The plink of her tears hitting the floor rang in my ears long after she pulled herself together.

"I thought after all these years you'd learn to keep your mouth shut. Must be your mother's genes." He sniffs as if thinking of my mother is distasteful.

I smirk, rolling my head toward him. "You're the one who married her."

He tips his head back and lets out a braying laugh. It sounds foreign and forced all at the same time. I don't think I've ever heard him display any type of joy. He wouldn't know it if it slapped him in the face. I don't know what's so funny about what I said, though.

I never met my mother. She died giving birth to me, which I assumed was why he always resented me. He may not know how to love, but I thought she was the one person he cared for as much as he could.

When I can't take it anymore, I huff. "What's so fucking funny?"

"My wife was not your mother. But that's a story for another time." He waves his hand lazily like he didn't just drop a bomb on me. "It's time to do what should have been done when I gave you to the Guild. Get up."

"Fuck off," I mumble. I wanted to shout it, but the old fear of him creeps up, stealing my resolve.

His chest expands and his nostrils flare. "Excuse me?"

I struggle to my feet, the lack of food making me dizzy. Wrapping my numb fingers around the cold bars, I lean closer.

"Fuck. Off."

A tightness in my chest stalls my breath. I straighten even as my knees threaten to give out. I've been starved before. I've been beaten and degraded and harassed, but I've never been this weak. I'll never be able to fight him off. Not that I care. I fully expect to die in here. If I could take him down with me, I would. From the way my limbs refuse to cooperate, I doubt I'll be able to.

His shoulders jerk as he gains control of himself. "Very well."

He pivots, then marches for the door. The heavy metal thuds as he closes it, and I slump against the bars. Sliding to the floor, I groan. The adrenaline that kept me upright flows away, seeping into the concrete, never to be seen again. I doubt I'll be able to stand up to him a second time.

"*That* was your father?" Nova asks quietly, and I nod. "What an asshole. What did he mean?"

"I believe he was saying my mother wasn't my mother. It's not exactly surprising. I never knew her anyway. But if my brother was alive, well…" I sigh, not sure how to finish the sentence.

I wish I would have told Dante more about Roman. I spent so much time fighting my attraction to him. I was too broken to trust him. I'm still too broken.

"How'd he die?" Nova's question pulls my thoughts away from Dante.

"I don't know. Which is probably worse than knowing the truth. My father…well, he obviously isn't a sharer."

"You don't exactly look like your dad. What about your brother? Did you look like him?" Her excitement bounces around the room. I wish it was infectious, but I'm too exhausted to feel anything.

"Roman looked a lot like our father," I mumble.

The door swings open before she can respond. She scurries into the back corner of her cell, tucking her knees to her chest. Her wide eyes find mine in the low light and I shake my head.

My father's heels click against the stone as he approaches, ringing through the silence. I know what's coming. There's nothing I can do to stop it even if I had the strength. I'll get out of this cage, but the place he'll bring me to will be so much worse. So much darker. So much harder to endure. It doesn't even matter where I go. All roads lead to death in this place. At least I'll be at peace. Anything is better than this hell.

"Bring her." His voice rings out from the doorway and I whip my head up.

It wasn't my father's footsteps but Grant's. A chill rolls through me, the only fear I can't suppress. I close my eyes when they start vibrating in my skull, creating waves in my vision. All that's left is the sharp tang of copper invading my nose and the sounds—the jingle of keys against metal, Nova's breath fluttering past her lips, my heart throbbing in my ears, the slight buzz from the light I never noticed before. All of it threads together into a tapestry of discordant noise, weaving with my veins as it slowly chokes the life from me, and my blood shivers in resistance.

Grant doesn't bother giving me instructions. He merely grabs me by the hair and drags me from my cell. A whimper catches in my throat, but

I refuse to let him hear my distress. Nova isn't as stoic, her cries crashing over me, severing the cord to the other sounds that were choking me alive.

"Don't damage her too severely. She needs to be intact for the event," Anders says, though there's no regret in his tone. No remorse for damning his daughter to a fate where death would be the merciful option.

"You'll have to take that up with Molly. She can't wait to get her hands on the Mistress." Grant laughs as if he's on his way to a party.

I have no idea who Molly is. There are several women who are members, but I don't keep track of them. Rarely do they stick around for long. Usually, they're harassed to the point where they'd rather not deal with the men within the Guild. Molly sounds like she's got personal issues with me, though. On the best of days, I doubt I'd know her. With how weak I am, I can barely recall Dante's face.

Grant hauls me to my feet, his hand gripping my arm. I've lost so much weight over the last few weeks his fingers overlap and grind my bones together. I wish I would have packed on more pounds when Dante was feeding me, though it probably wouldn't have made much of a difference.

I trip up the stairs behind Grant, almost pulling him down with me. He snarls, muttering curses as he keeps up the grueling pace to the next level. When we reach the top, my breath stalls in my lungs.

Soft lights glow overhead, reflecting off the crimson walls. Black doors on either side of the hall disrupt the flow and send a chill down my spine. I was ready to starve. I was ready to be sold. Hell, I was ready to die. I'm not ready to be tortured.

"Is that fear I spy in your eyes, little bit? I was afraid we'd beaten it out of you," Grant hisses as he twists my arm behind my back.

"Grant." The warning bounces off the walls, seeping into me.

I'm not naïve enough to believe Anders is concerned for my wellbeing. He just doesn't want damaged goods. I wince as Grant yanks at my arm and my muscles scream in pain. When he releases me, I collapse to my knees, an ache spreading from my shoulder to my fingers. I flex them, gritting my teeth as pins and needles stab at my hand.

Anders cups my chin, fingers digging into my jaw as he tilts my head back. "If you damage her, she won't be able to withstand Molly. As much as I'd love to be rid of her once and for all, she's a means to an end. As always."

He shoves me back and my head hits Grant's shins, then he kicks my side. I have nothing left in me to fight them. Grant may as well put a bullet in my head for all the good I'll be to my father. I'm weak as it is. All the strength Dante attempted to instill in me has faded away with the shadows. The smirk on Anders's face confirms it. I'm too weak to survive what he has planned.

Grant grabs my upper arm, digging his fingers into the bruises forming there. The marks staining my skin will last long after the redness fades. If I'm alive long enough to witness them heal. I doubt I will be. The scars will seep into my soul, scarring it for eternity. Not that they care. I'm merely a means to an end for them.

Perhaps he really does mean to sell me off. I doubt Jenkins has approved, but Anders is resourceful, if nothing else. He'll find a way around my former boss. Maybe he'll bring me back to Synd. I can't figure out if that would break me more or finally set me free.

Memories of my childhood flash through my mind, most of them starring my brother. He was my only friend for a long time. My only solace in an otherwise bleak existence. Synd is also the place I lost my freedom. No, I don't think I'd like to see it one more time.

"Make sure she's fed. And hydrated. One week, Grant. That's all you get." My father pivots, stalking away on the hunt for his next victim.

Glancing over my shoulder, I try to track his retreat, but he's already disappeared into the darkness. I wish I could slip away as easily.

"Just us, little bit." Grant's sadistic grin cuts into me as he shakes my limp body. "Nothing to say? No begging? Too bad your master ran off."

Grant shoves me against the wall, rattling my skull as it bounces off the concrete. I refuse to give him what he wants. My dignity might have been stripped away long ago, but I won't give him the satisfaction of seeing how broken I am—how close to the edge I truly am.

Dante's voice echoes in my mind. *You're a lot less broken than you think, Aelia.*

I shake my head, closing my eyes. He was right when he said those words. I wonder what he'd say to me now. Probably the same thing. He'd want me to fight, to run, to show them I'm more than just a piece of property. Personally, I think I've done remarkably well given the circumstances, but it never ends and I'm tired of fighting.

Grant's hand wraps around my throat, squeezing as my eyes fly open. My fingers scratch at his wrist, and he merely tightens his hold. I kick out wildly, connecting with his shin. He tips his head back and laughs at my pathetic attempts. Every defense Dante taught me flees in the wake of my terror at not being able to breathe.

My vision darkens at the edges until all I can see is Grant's face, evil carved into every groove. Just when I'm sure my life is about to flash before my eyes, he drops me. I collapse into a heap, coughing and gasping. He doesn't give me time to recover, merely grabs my arm again and drags me forward.

At least he's not dragging me by my hair anymore. It's a small consolation as he pulls me in front of an ornate door complete with a metal ring dangling from the mouth of a horned demon. Grant lets it drop, sending a ripple through the air, and I shudder. Almost immediately, the door swings open, revealing a dark room. I've grown used to the red glow from my cage one level below. The soft white light inside is jarring and does nothing to alleviate the terror coursing through me.

A woman's sigh echoes from somewhere deep inside. "Hello, Aelia. Welcome to your worst nightmare."

SEVEN

Dante

Raven is sulking. And she's blaming me. I'm not surprised, since everything seems to be my fault these days. I'll take the guilt along with their disapproval over how I handled things. How I'm the one who got Nova, one of Raven's riders, supposedly caught by the Guild isn't clear. Raven is holding me personally responsible, though.

"Raven, I'm sure she'll be okay. She might not even be there. And if she is, well, they're gearing up for the Auction, so they'll keep her intact." Mac's voice wavers and she grimaces.

I've told her enough about the inner workings of the Guild that she's practically an expert. At least as much as I am, which arguably isn't much.

I wish Aelia was here. She'd be able to see the pattern in the chaos. The map of Rima spread out in front of me doesn't lend much insight into where the Guild will hit next. Raven's convinced it'll be the nightclub, but not everyone is on board. The conversations of a dozen people swirl around me, buzzing in my head. It's hard to concentrate and my vision blurs.

Ren leans over the map, catching my eye and raising his brow. I shake my head, focusing on the paper again. He sighs as he rounds the table.

"Come on," he mutters, jerking his head toward the back door.

I throw down the marker Raven used to mark the hits and stomp after him. No one notices when we slip out the back. There's no forest like there is in Synd. Just more houses and eventually a small river. If I went far enough, I'd hit trees, but it's not in our backyard. I miss the quiet. I never fully settled in Rima. This city doesn't live in my soul like Synd.

Mac was the only reason I came here. Our Dad wouldn't let her stay with the Reapers, and I wasn't about to abandon her. Now that she's back in Synd, I doubt she'll ever come back. And I'd never ask that of her. Merging with the Reapers would be the wise thing to do. Defeat the Guild and cut our losses. Rima can burn for all I fucking care.

I shove the thought aside. Give it a day and my opinion on that will change. Just like it does with everything else. Settling on one path is too hard right now.

"There a reason we're out here? Again?" I ask after several minutes of him stargazing. I never took Ren for one to contemplate the universe, but here he is with his gaze firmly fixed on the few lights blinking in the sky.

"Figured you could use a break from the noise." His hands clench into fists over and over.

"Apparently I'm not the only one," I mutter, glancing down the tight alley.

Usually only bikes come this way, funneling to either side of the building. The layout has saved us more than once. I wish the old embassy had the same design instead of being surrounded by vast amounts of barren space for the most part. We won't be able to sneak up on them, that's for sure.

"Did you hear anything I just said?" Ren asks, but his voice is devoid of emotion. I'm still getting used to the way his mind works.

"No, but then again, you weren't really talking to me, were you?" I raise an eyebrow as our eyes meet and the corner of his mouth twitches. It's probably the closest I'll get to a smile from him.

"Fair enough. I need to know what Nemesis did for you." He turns to face me, leaning his shoulder against the building.

"Why? You looking to start a new life?" I don't really care, but I assumed he'd ask Nemesis—not me.

His nostrils flare as he tucks his chin to his chest. "Unlike you, I don't leave behind those I love."

Rage flows through me, then trickles away, leaving only an echo behind. I don't have it in me to argue with him. I lean against the brick, resting my head against it. Ren scowls, stomping away, only to pivot and prowl back. He's not much taller than me, but the frustration on his face as he looms over me is palpable. I eye him, tilting my head as I wonder what he'll do. Ren isn't the type to settle shit with his fists.

"What the fuck happened in there?" he growls.

"In where?"

His eyes narrow. "Inside the Guild. Because this shit is more than just leaving her behind. You said yourself she wanted you to go, so what the fuck is it?"

"When Sam was taken—" I grind my teeth when he looks like he'll interrupt. "Did you hesitate? Did you stop yourself from finding her because she was capable of taking care of herself? I didn't think so. You rushed to save her. It's one thing to know what the Guild is doing. It's entirely another thing to experience it. To watch them get dragged away, knowing you couldn't fucking save them. So don't fucking lecture me on my choices. I did the best I fucking could."

I'm panting by the time I finish. This is what I was afraid of every minute I spent in that building. That once I got out, I'd be different. I'd change into someone I didn't recognize. And that everyone would blame me for the mistakes I made. Going into the Guild was a miscalculation—one that very well might be fatal to us all.

"And your best wasn't good enough, was it?" Shane's voice resonates through the alley, bouncing off the stones.

I bite my tongue, knowing I don't have a defense, though I sorely want to pound them both. They have no idea what it was like. They can't even fathom. They think seeing several dozen people rounded up was bad. They think the hits they took, the supplies they lost, the men who defected were enough. Being immersed in that world was completely different. And then I fell in love. Meeting Aelia changed everything. She made the situation personal.

"Ren, go inside. Sam needs you." Shane crosses his arms, waiting for him to move.

With one final glare, Ren stomps through the door. Sighing, I resign myself to another lecture. Part of me wishes I'd never called them. I can't bring down the Guild by myself even when cashing in all the favors owed to me. If it was just me, I could sneak back into the embassy and find Aelia. I could save her.

"You can't save her," Shane mutters, leaning next to me.

"She needs help. I told her I'd get her out and I didn't. But I intend on fixing my mistakes."

I spent all those months convincing her how strong she was. Yet every time she needed me, truly needed me, I left her to battle everything alone. The last time was merely a culmination of my hubris. I thought I could do it all. No wonder she didn't stay with Avery. She probably didn't think I'd ever come for her.

Shane scrubs his face, sighing. "I hesitated."

"What?" I glance at him, brows pulled low. He looks like he's locked in the past, reliving the worst parts of his life.

"When Sam was taken, I hesitated. Not my finest moment, but I was pissed at her. And we'd both said shitty things to each other we didn't mean. But that's not why I waited. I didn't want to fuck up whatever she was doing." He shakes his head. "How foolish is that?"

"Is that the only reason?"

"No. I was being pulled about a thousand different ways. You were there when Emma busted in, sobbing about them taking her and Sam being gone. There were people counting on me. How the hell was I supposed to choose between them?" He glances toward me as if he's still searching for the answer and I might have it.

"You chose her. Bet she doesn't regret that you did," I murmur.

"You don't get it. Sam was strong enough to save herself. It didn't matter whether we were there or not. Not at the end. When she was shot, well, that was a whole other story." He lets out a sharp laugh, then sighs. "Raines, is Aelia strong enough to save herself?"

"Yes." There's no hesitation now. When I was getting Avery out, doubt plagued me, but I never thought Aelia wasn't capable.

"Then why are you beating yourself up over it? We'll go back and get her when she's done bleeding them dry from the inside." His hand lands on my shoulder. I'm sure it's meant to be reassuring, but all it does is set another weight on me.

I grit my teeth, forcing the argument down deep. Shane won't understand any more than Ren. Or Helms. Or Mac. None of them were in there. Aelia is strong, but she's not in a position to use that strength for anything other than surviving. Unless, by some miracle, we're able to distract the Guild enough to stop them from focusing on the Auction.

"We need to hit them," I whisper, a plan forming in my mind.

"What the fuck you think we've been doing at all these meetings? We get Nemesis in and she'll take down their security, their finances, then we can—"

I push from the wall and pace back and forth in front of him. "No, she'll never get in. Not with the way their shit is set up. I had a plan to have them hire her, but that's fucked now. We need to stop more of their cash flow, hit them harder. We've already wasted enough time sitting around in those damn meetings. We lost any momentum we had when Jag and I took out the dogfighting ring."

He snorts, and I pause before continuing my pacing. "Raines, I hate to break this to you, but that wasn't the big trigger you thought it was."

"I laid the groundwork. There are people waiting for us to strike. We just need to—"

Shane steps in front of me, blocking my path, and I skitter to a stop. "Slow down. Anything that needs to happen has to be brought to the group. You disappearing and going rogue was what got us into this in the first place."

"Mr. King, I believe it's time for you to go back inside," Avery says from behind me.

Shane snorts, leaning around me to eye Avery. "I don't know if you understand the hierarchy. Maybe you should see yourself out of this conversation."

I cover my grin with my hand, wiping it away. I've seen him go up against Sam, but Avery is another level. Sam puts him in his place, but there's a layer of love to her words. Avery doesn't have to worry about hurting his feelings. I glance around, wondering how far away Jag is. I doubt he'll let her flounce around Rima by herself.

Avery smirks, planting her fists on her hips, "I'm not one to care about hierarchies, much to the dismay of my brother. Perhaps you should take up any issues you have with him."

Shane's phone buzzes, interrupting whatever retort he was about to sling at her. He scowls down at the screen before stomping away.

"We should get back inside before Jag comes searching for you," I mumble as I face her.

She rolls her eyes. "As if I care. Why are all the men around here so fucking protective? Never mind. Don't answer that."

"Was there something you wanted?"

She gestures toward the back door. "People are yelling in there. You don't want to go in right now. But I was wondering what the plan is for getting Aelia. We can't wait for them to decide she's a priority, so I figured we'd go rogue and find her."

"There's no way I'll be let back in. And I'm sure they've discovered all their weak points."

I already snuck away to check the alley doors where Aelia and I kissed. Where I threatened Grant's life. I should have taken him out when I had the chance. Maybe things would have gone differently.

"What about—"

"No, Avery. We just have to wait for an opportunity. We'll draw attention by blowing shit up and see if that helps."

I don't like it any better than her, but there's nothing else I can do. If I die attempting to rescue her, then she's dead. Or worse—broken beyond repair.

EIGHT

Aelia

I've never been tied to a chair before. I thought it would hurt more. Then again, I'm not struggling like they do in movies. Plus, I think the ropes are made not to leave marks.

Grant probably would have done more to hurt me, except Molly stepped in, garish red curls bouncing around her shoulders. I don't know why he deferred to her. I've never seen her before in my life—though that doesn't mean much. Thousands of people have flitted in and out of the Guild over the years. And I spent most of that time in a fog.

I've been trying to find that indifference ever since Dante left. Yet it evades me. Something tickles at the back of my mind, but I chalk it up to my inability to get out of here.

Closing my eyes, I concentrate on the low hum in the walls. I swear they were vibrating the last time I checked. In this room, I wouldn't be surprised. It's jam-packed full of items ranging from a riding crop to an array of knives. Some of them are torture devices, but others are probably supposed to be fun in the bedroom—like the collar and leash I wore not long ago.

As soon as Grant tied me up, Molly ordered him out. She checked the knots, then smiled at me before flouncing out herself. Time warped again, just like in the cages. I searched for a clock, but my heart started pounding with each new object I found. Eventually I gave up.

My stomach folds in on itself, grumbling for food. I cough, my chest heaving with the force. Swallowing does no good, since my throat has a layer of sand coating it. I don't know how many hours I've been here, but the tips of my fingers are numb. My feet are fucked. I wish I could ignore the lack of feeling, but it itches at the back of my brain.

The door opens and I tuck my chin to my chest. A shiver of terror skitters up my spine. Digging my nails into the wooden chair, I feel them crack one by one—the pain finally registering through the numbness.

I swallow hard, concentrating on easing my muscles one at a time, but it doesn't do much good. As soon as my neck relaxes, I move onto my shoulders and my neck bunches up again. There's no relief, only more dread.

"I'm so excited to spend some time with you, Mistress," Molly purrs, running her sharp red nails across my shoulders.

My muscles twitch even though it doesn't hurt. The anticipation is almost worse than anything she can inflict upon me. I've seen others use this tactic. It's part of the reason I was so wary of Dante. Lull me into a false sense of security, then break me down. Apparently, it's more fun that way. Even the thought in my mind rings with sarcasm.

"What? No greeting for me?" Her face comes into view as she crouches in front of me, a pout painted on her lips lined in crimson. "That's too bad. Do you not remember me? Is that it?"

I narrow my eyes, trying to place her. I don't think I've ever seen her, but her voice—there's something about her voice that knocks at the back of my brain. She *feels* like she should be familiar, like a childhood friend long since grown up. It's there in the curve of her cheek or the tilt of her lips. Maybe it's merely the sadistic gleam in her bright blue eyes. Their color wars with the garish makeup adorning her face, yet still there's something there.

The realization hits me suddenly that they're the same shade as Roman's. It's disconcerting to discover the similarity gracing the face of my abuser. She may not have hit me yet. She may not have tied me up. She may not even have threatened me. But she's the abuser, nonetheless.

If I live through whatever vicious schemes she has planned, she'll haunt me for years to come. She'll burrow into my brain, seep into my blood, and drill into my bones, refusing to let go. And I'll never be rid of her, not anytime soon at least.

"You won't be able to stay silent forever. Eventually, you'll crack too." As soon as the last word leaves her, I'm flooded with recognition.

She tips her head back, letting out a sultry laugh, and I shiver. I know her. I wish I didn't. Molly didn't come from the Pit. She was never in Rima, as far as I know. No, she was in the last city we were in, way up north over a year ago.

Jenkins thought it would be a good idea to bring in some women who didn't mind being treated like the others. Ones who didn't care about the people who were kidnapped and forced to perform for the scores of members.

I didn't find out until later that most of them were lied to. They were told they'd be paid. That the Guild was an upscale brothel. The problem was, Jenkins preyed on the desperate, the weak, the struggling.

He went after single mothers and left orphans in his wake. He went after the young homeless women, promising them a place to stay while they got back on their feet. He went after the runaways, telling them he'd hide them from those searching to force them back to their abusive households. So many of them thought the Guild was their ticket to a better life.

Of course, he lied.

Molly, though, wasn't like any of them. She was one of the few who was chosen to teach the others how to behave. If she would have taken another path, she could have been like Rachel—someone to look up to and who prepared the women for the harsh realities that were now their lives.

Instead, she chose to give into the evil, assuming Jenkins would keep her around and give her a higher status rather than that of another bit. She thought she could replace me. When Jenkins sold her to the highest bidder, she raged. I watched as it took three guards to subdue her. She scratched and clawed her way out of the room. Not even the music could drown out her shrieks of outrage. It wasn't the act of being sold that upset her, but the fact that she wasn't informed. And that she wasn't being claimed by Jenkins.

She didn't look like you. He'd whispered in my ear as he tugged on a strand of my dark hair.

As our eyes locked before the door closed, I realized she knew exactly why she'd been handed over to a man three times her age. Because she wasn't me and never would be. Molly blamed me for her fate instead of the people who were really at fault.

I don't know how long I've been lost in my thoughts, but clearly my mask hasn't slipped since her nose wrinkles as she sniffs. Her nails dig into my arms as she pushes upright, leaving deep grooves in their place. Droplets of blood seep from several of the half-moon cuts. I tilt my head, wondering why I can't feel anything. It may be from the cold, but more likely it's because I've finally achieved ultimate numbness—both inside and out.

"You know, when I first came to the Guild, I saw you and I thought, 'That's the dream. That's someone who's made it.' Imagine my surprise when I found out you were sold to them. You didn't appreciate the opportunity you were given. You didn't see the *power* that was within your grasp if only you'd reach out and take it." She wanders around the room, trailing her fingers along the whips, floggers, and riding crops hanging on the wall. "I wanted to kill you then, but Grant told me to wait."

Of course, this all comes back to Grant. I wonder when he started taking orders from my father. It couldn't have been very long. Perhaps when Dante claimed me. Otherwise, this whole plan would have gone into action months ago. I wonder how much time Dante bought me by making me his to command. Probably more than I deserved. He saw something I couldn't. I still don't know if I fully believe in myself the way he did.

"Patience isn't my strong suit. Although, there is something poetic about picking away at someone. Slowly breaking them down bit by bit. It's a finesse I'm afraid I'm still learning." She shoots me a smirk over her shoulder before she lifts a flogger from its peg. "Too bad we won't have that much time together. I'm hoping you'll be open to receiving the gift I'm so graciously giving you."

I swallow down the questions, giving her a bored stare in reply. The longer she prattles on, the more memories flood my brain, reminding me of her quirks. The complaints from the other women trapped on the ranch the Guild occupied were vast.

Molly had many victims, but they couldn't retaliate. They had to suffer in silence, as usual. No one would have stood up for them, anyway. I was too far into my own apathy, just trying to survive, and Rachel hadn't been taken yet. I doubt it would have mattered either way. Fighting against the Guild is a losing battle—not without outside help.

Which circles back to Dante. He's our one hope. There's only so much I can do from the inside. Actually, there's nothing I can do. I'm as much of a victim as the others now. The only hope I have is escaping.

Then I'll find Dante, join whoever else he has on our side, and the Guild will fall. I have no idea how that will happen, but I don't have it in me to delve too deeply. At least not while I'm tied to a goddamn chair.

My attention snaps to Molly as she flicks the flogger and a crack ripples through the air. She frowns, fingering one of the strands. The soft light catches on something sharp embedded into the end and I shiver. Nails or pins stab through tip of the leather on each strap. When our eyes meet, she grins.

"This is going to hurt. Grant may have said to keep you more or less intact, but that doesn't mean we can't leave a few scars behind, right?" Her giddiness invades my pores, making my blood curdle in my veins.

I fix my gaze on her face instead of the torture device she's wielding. Her tongue darts out, then runs along her teeth as if she can't wait to sink her fangs into my skin and rip me apart bit by bit. Anders may want me alive, but I doubt I'll survive what she has in store.

"Let's get you more comfortable, hmm? Should I call someone in to help me or are you going to take your punishment like you've taken everything else in your life?"

I have no idea what she's talking about, but I clamp my lips together anyway. I don't even bother biting my tongue. She doesn't deserve any more of my blood than she'll get at the end of the flogger.

I blink slowly, basking in the glimpse of shadows behind my lids. I don't fear that darkness. There's comfort there. Dante lives in those shadows, and I refuse to let go of him. Savoring those images, though, isn't a luxury I can afford.

Molly's ruby-red heels click against the concrete as she saunters closer. She leans, running the butt of the handle from my knee to my thigh. I clench my teeth, imagining all the ways I'll tear her apart if I get out of here. Dante may have told me it wasn't possible to rip someone's spine from their body, but I certainly could try.

She tilts her head, narrowing her blue eyes and whispers, "I know that look. Give up, Aelia. You'll never win against me. My power far outweighs your own."

She slams the end of the handle into my thigh, and I choke on my cry of pain as my body attempts to curl forward. She smirks and shakes her head, her red hair creating a curtain around us as she leans closer.

Her lips brush my cheek as my breath stutters in my chest. "Beg me to stop. Tell me how much you want me to let you go—how you don't want me to hurt you. Plead with me for mercy."

I swallow hard and tip my chin up. "Fuck off."

They're the last words I speak for a long time.

NINE

Dante

"I don't know where the fuck you got your info from, Raven, but it sucks dick," Shane spits out, stomping into Nico's.

The rest trail after him as Raven seethes next to her bike. Her fingers brush the handle of her knife tucked in her belt, and I wonder if I'm going to have to get in between them. I sigh, tipping my head back, and Avery pinches my arm.

"What are the chances of them getting along?" Avery mutters.

"A lot of people set in their ways and used to running shit. Plus, the others have spent the last year showing up for each other. We're the odd ones out." I don't like making that assessment, but it's the truth.

Sam emerges from the darkness, and I squeeze my eyes shut, the image of Aelia dancing behind my lids. For a moment, I thought it was her standing there. Sam sidles up next to Raven. They exchange a flurry of words I barely catch. I'm pretty sure Raven is demanding Sam force Shane into line. Soon enough they're laughing as if they've been friends for years, and I turn away. Avery huffs as she follows me, tripping over my heels. I snarl over my shoulder and she rolls her eyes before stepping next to me.

"So, what do we do now?" She stuffs her hands in a sweatshirt three times too large for her. It's probably Jag's. Not that I'll ask about it. She'll bite my head off like every other time, and I don't have the energy to deal with that.

"Where's Jag?" I ask as we round the building.

I'd like to go home, but I'm pretty sure we're about to have another fucking meeting. I'm sick of having them. All they do is bitch about the Guild and come up with a million scenarios with no actual solutions. Not that they're qualified.

From what I saw, they were mostly flying by the seat of their pants in Synd. No one could agree on what the best course of action would be. I don't blame them. They were fighting a ghost they couldn't find—a foe they couldn't hope to understand.

Even after spending almost a year embedded with the Guild, I can't claim to be an expert. There are so many threads tangled together I doubt anyone fully knows what's happening within the organization other than Jenkins.

"He keeps disappearing. I tried to follow him once, but he caught me." She seems more upset that she got busted rather than the fact she doesn't know where he's going. "You could just text him, you know. He'd answer you."

"Bitter much?" I glance at her, popping my eyebrow up.

She purses her lips, shaking her head. Avery might talk circles around Jag, but she has no argument for the truth. I push through the back door to the restaurant and the muffled voices of the others overwhelms me. I can't even make out what they're saying, yet I break out into a sweat.

"Do we have to go in? We could just run." Avery shoots me a sad smile as exhaustion lines her eyes.

I lean against the doorframe to the main area. "Wouldn't do any good. Someone would find us. My money is on Jag."

"I suppose he could come with. We'll grab Aelia, then ride off into the sunset. Then we'll—"

"Live happily ever after?" I snort, crossing my arms. "That's not how the real world works, Avery."

"Now who's the bitter one?" She saunters into the room, then throws a cheeky grin over her shoulder.

Reluctantly, I follow her, plopping into a chair around the large table next to Ren. I can count on him not to mindlessly pull me into a conversation neither of us wants to have. His face is buried in his tablet, anyway. Whatever anger he harbored before in the alley fled with the dying moon. We pretend it didn't happen now.

Avery settles next to me, then drops her head onto her arms. Shane keeps prattling on about ways to infiltrate the Guild's headquarters. None of them will work. Everyone keeps interjecting, getting louder and louder the more time passes. My head pounds and I crack my neck to relieve the tension building up, but nothing works.

"If we come from the forest, they won't be able to launch a defense," Byrns says, pointing to the map of Rima spread out in the middle of the table.

"What about the flood lights? We'll have to take them out before we get there, which defeats the element of surprise." Shane runs his fingers through his hair.

"What about the alley Dante told us about?" Mac's eyes meet mine before quickly darting away as she continues. "Sure, there's not a lot of room, but it'd be easier to take out the cameras and pick the lock and sneak in that way."

"I still think I should just go in and deal with it. I can take out Jenkins and be gone before they even know I'm there." Sam waves her knife leisurely at the round of protests that ring out, then she goes back to picking her nails with the blade.

Glancing behind me, I heave a sigh as Raven and Jag slip through the front door. Neither of them look worse for wear, except for the matching annoyed looks on their faces. I'm sure Jag was talking Raven down from gutting Shane after he insulted her.

I squint into the dim light. I'm pretty sure Raven's eyes are red. We may not be very close, but I've never seen her cry. I've always known her to play her emotions close to the chest.

Avery smacks me in the arm, and I whip around. She rolls her head to peek at me, then gestures toward the others. I didn't notice the conversation dying around me and now all eyes are on me.

Shane's nostrils flare and Helms shakes his head, but it's Mac I'm fixed on. It's the pity in her eyes that hits me. I'm no longer the older brother she looked up to. Now I'm someone to be ashamed of. How am I supposed to live through this and give Aelia a chance at something outside the Guild when I couldn't even keep our brother in line and protect my little sister?

Avery hits me again, and I turn to find a dangerous glint in her eye. The others begin to argue. They may say it's strategizing, but no matter what fancy words they dress it up as, they're fighting.

They battle about where to go, what to do, who should do it. The men are constantly trying to protect their women without offending them. The women are demanding a seat at the table, though none of the guys are used to it. They're all trying, yet it all ends up with no decisions getting made because there's no clear leader. Or maybe there's simply too many men used to being in charge.

"What?" I hiss, clenching my hands in my lap.

"You love her?" Her tone holds an accusation in it, though what she's accusing me of, I have no idea.

"She's my sister. Of course I love her."

Avery makes a noise in the back of her throat. "I mean Aelia, dumbass. Do you love her?"

My brows pull low and I snarl, "Yes."

"Then perhaps you'd like to get off your fucking ass and put a plan in place that will save the love of your life, hmm?"

I rear back, the reality of her words hitting me harder than any of the others before. Shane and Mason are in each other's faces, yelling about perimeters and how many men they need to call in. Ryker leans into Mac, a pained expression on his face. Lacey and Ren have twin masks covering their features as they pour over their tablets, desperately trying to hack into the Guild's systems.

Alex's head lands into his hands as the rest fight over the scraps of what is left of their ridiculous plan. Behind me, Jag growls and Avery shoves away from the table, probably to stop him from starting more shit. Or maybe she just realizes how close to the fucking edge I am.

I stand slowly, scanning them as they continue to argue. No one notices. They're so wrapped up in their own worlds convinced their ideas are the ones that will ultimately win. I've spent too long living with my regrets. Avery's words play on repeat in my head.

The best plan would be to bring down the Guild no matter the cost—even if it meant Aelia dies. Pain stabs at my heart at the thought. That's what a better man would do. Good thing I'm not a better man.

The only way I'll be able to ensure her safety will be to take over. And they'll just have to fucking deal. I slam my palms on the table, then lean forward. Nobody even pauses or flinches. It's as if I'm a ghost—a phantom haunting their meetings with no more substance than a shadow in the corner.

"Shut the fuck up," I bellow and still nothing changes.

I hang my head, staring at the scars gouged deep into the wood. Part of me wishes I'd never called them. Too many chefs in the kitchen and all that. I could have gathered the people who owe me favors and used them to at least get Aelia out, then faded into the background and allowed them to take over. Shaking my head, I wonder how many more times I'm going to fuck up before we're done.

A gunshot echoes over the shouting and everyone drops to the floor except Sam and me. She's in full Wraith mode—a bored expression plastered on her face as she eyes Jag. Glancing under my arm, I take in the smoking gun pointed at the ceiling and his flared nostrils as he bares his teeth at the others, daring them to start up again.

Shane climbs to his feet, then throws his chair from his path. The wood splitters as it skitters into the wall. Sam steps in his way, her blade lying forgotten on the table. If this was any other situation, I'd laugh at the scene of the great Shane King being cowed with merely a look from a woman who barely comes up to his shoulder.

"You all are going to sit down and shut the fuck up," Jag growls, stepping next to me and taking Avery's vacated seat. He sets his gun on the table, a clear warning.

I heave out a sigh when no one moves. "None of your plans will do a goddamn thing other than getting most of us fucking killed. This shit may have worked in Synd, but now it's time to step the fuck back. Either you let me lead or you go home."

"You can't do this without us, Raines," Shane sneers as he leans his fists on the table.

"Maybe not, but we need a clear leader. We need someone who knows what the fuck they're talking about. And correct me if I'm wrong, but the only one who's qualified is me. If you can't handle that..." I spread my hands out, giving them the option of walking away.

None of them will. We all understand the consequences if we fail. I doubt any of them will fuck off to Synd and leave the rest of us to fend for ourselves. From what Mac told me, they didn't even hesitate to come to Rima. Deciding who would stay behind might have taken some time, but they all answered when I called. I meet Mac's eyes and she nods.

"I hate to interrupt this little...kumbaya moment you all have going on, but we're staying to help," Raven says, and I spin.

"Thought you had other shit going on." I shouldn't push her, since we could really use them. But I don't want them here if they're forced.

"The Guild took Nova. Just got the confirmation. Guess the whole it's personal thing really does apply." She grimaces, glancing away.

I nod, turning again to address the group. "Obviously if I knew how to bring them down by myself, I wouldn't have called you. I'm the one who's been on the inside, so I can tell you none of this shit will work. Jag and I worked out a tentative plan before we were forced out, so we'll be doing that. I don't give a fuck what you all want at the end of this, but I'm getting Aelia out. She's my priority, whether you assholes like it or not. You don't like that, again—get the fuck out."

No one says anything, but Avery snorts and I clench my teeth together. Shane looks like he wants to blow my head off and I'm pretty sure Alex is holding back laughter.

"Alright then. Mac, order some food. We're going to be here a while."

TEN

Aelia

A timer dings and I tip my head back. My limbs might be numb, strapped to what I'm pretty sure is a Saint Andrew's Cross, but my body needs water no matter in what form it comes. The bucket positioned above my head tips, dumping water over me.

A few days ago, at least I think it was a few days, I thought I could drown myself. There wasn't enough liquid, though, and I just ended up wasting what little water I could have consumed.

It splashes over my face, dousing my naked body. One mouthful is all I get before the bucket tips upright. It's not nearly enough. My stomach cramps, and I drop my head between the wooden slabs. The constant dripping starts over as the bucket begins to fill once more. I don't know how long it takes before it will empty again, but it's not nearly soon enough.

My back screams in pain and I moan. My toes scramble on the thin block of wood attached to the bottom of the cross. I can't imagine if I was left hanging. The blood loss alone is concerning without having to worry if I'll lose my feet as well. She's only released me three times and she muttered about pushing her luck—whatever that meant.

Molly left hours ago, leaving me to mull over her questions. None of them makes sense. I can't tell if that's because I'm delusional from what she's done, the lack of food and water, or because she's speaking in riddles.

My brain feels fuzzy, my head disconnected from my body. Shadows lick at the edges of my vision, and I close my eyes. I wish I could disappear within them—fade away, detached from the pain Molly inflicts on me. I lost count of the devices she's used. The only time she stops is when I'm on the brink of passing out. Apparently, it's no fun after that. I've used it as a tactic when I can't take any more.

"Wakey, wakey," Molly calls in a singsong voice. The door thuds closed behind her. "No use pretending you're asleep. You can't hide from me."

I lift my head slowly, attempting to focus on her wavering form. All I make out is her lips painted bright red, her dress matching. She explained the color hides the blood, though it really doesn't. Not that I asked. I never speak. I haven't since I told her to fuck off.

It wouldn't make a difference, anyway. Her blows would still sting. Her voice would still ring in my ears. Her image would still haunt me in my dreams. I keep waiting for the day that someone else walks through the door.

No one ever does.

"Aren't you glad we've been granted more time together?" She steps behind me and I tense. "I want to etch our time into your skin."

Her nail traces the wounds she's carved into my back. I gag, my stomach rebelling. She does it again, digging deeper, and a sob escapes me. Blood trickles over the curve of my waist, leaving an itchy trail in its wake. I haven't seen my skin, but being flayed alive is sure to leave scars. Molly has already accomplished her goal. I'll carry her marks on me for as long as I live, though I doubt I'll have to deal with the aftermath of this particular trauma for long.

Her breath ghosts across my ear. "Where's the den? Who will find it?"

I hold my breath, waiting for the blow. It whooshes from me as her bloodred heels click away. She's back to speaking in riddles. I think she's doing it on purpose. I'm sure she's talking to Grant, and possibly my father.

They probably want information on Dante, though I don't know the things they're searching for. He was right to keep so much from me. If Molly was asking coherent questions, I'm sure I'd have already broken. But she's clearly skewing her inquiries so she can tell Grant I'm uncooperative, which leaves her more time to break me.

I'm close. My mind fractures a little more each day, pieces splintering off and spinning into the void. Once the last bit of my self vanishes, I'll be lost for good. Not even Dante will be able to find all the fragments to put me back together. I'll be irrevocably damaged.

My father may have warned Grant to not break me, to keep me fed and hydrated. He failed. It may have been through Molly, but he still failed. And Anders doesn't accept incompetence. Maybe he'll take care of Grant and Molly for me. It won't save me in the end, yet the satisfaction will be worth it.

"Your inability to answer me tells me you were no more than a bit. I wonder why I craved your life. I'm much better off in this position."

There's a crack of a whip and I flinch. It doesn't land on my already ravaged back, but that doesn't matter. It's no longer the pain I fear.

"You're no fun when you're not screaming," she whispers in my ear.

I jerk in my holds, the bindings cutting into my wrists. I never even heard her move. Maybe I blacked out and didn't realize. She slides her fingers into my hair, gripping the strands and forcing my head back. My neck cracks, the sound reverberating through my skull.

Her teeth graze my earlobe and I jolt, hoping she doesn't start ripping off body parts. She's broken all the other rules Grant set out, or rather the ones Anders put in place. I wouldn't put it past her to start sawing off my fingers. Not that I can feel them, so it won't matter to me.

What little terror was left in my body flees and I shut down. My eyes fall shut and my breath comes out in gasps. Whatever strength I was drawing from is gone, along with most of the sensation in my body.

I can't pour from a dry well, just like my brother always warned me. He probably didn't think this would ever be a situation I'd be in, though. I'm sure his advice would have been different had he known where I would end up.

I shudder as Molly steps back. A buzzing fills my mind and I grit my teeth. I slam my temple into the wood. I'll do anything to get it out of my head. My body vibrates in a steady pulse. It might be my heartbeat, but it's slowing down. Sinking my teeth into my lip, I use the pain to center myself again and the world comes back into view.

"What the fuck did you do to her? She has to go on the auction block in less than a week. Goddamn bitch. How the hell am I going to explain this to Drake?" Grant continues to rant and rave, though his voice is muffled again.

Molly cries out, snapping me back to the present. I crane my neck around, finding her sprawled on the floor with Grant towering over her. I never thought I'd be thankful for that waste of a man. A sob escapes me, and I bite my lip again, holding back the scream that begs to be let loose. Molly whimpers behind me as Grant rips a riding crop from the wall.

In one sweeping move, he brings it down across her face—again and again without faltering. The thin wood splinters and a rage-filled growl leaves him. He throws the broken crop at her, then stalks around the room as he searches for another weapon. He passes several, but he's clearly set on a specific piece.

My body sags under the exhaustion. Now that there's no more pain, the adrenaline that keeps me conscious gradually fades. Molly's light eyes find mine, her fear finally shining through. Her mouth moves, but no words come out. She wants me to help her. She wants me to stand up for her. She wants me to save her. Slowly, I shake my head and despair bleeds from her eyes, mingling with the blood streaking her face.

Grant seizes the flogger she used on me not so long ago and stalks back to her as she cowers. Unintelligible pleas fall from her lips as she covers her head. He only hits her a half a dozen times, a fraction of the number she inflicted upon me. From her wails, I'd think she was dying. She's not, based on the welts forming on the exposed skin of her back.

Of course she wore a blood red dress that dips to her waist, showing off her unblemished flesh. I suspect she did it on purpose to rub salt in my wounds. The gashes on my own back twitch with the remembered pain of her dripping lemon juice over them.

"Get the bitch off of there and bring her back to the cages. And you'd better have her cleaned the fuck up or I'm giving you to Drake. No fucking way am I taking the blame for this." Grant stomps out the door, leaving Molly a blubbering mess on the floor.

I jolt when her trembling fingers fumble with the buckle at my ankle. I don't know how long I was passed out, wading through the shadows between life and death. Enough time has passed for Molly to pull herself together, though the bright red welts streaking her face haven't faded.

She doesn't speak for once. Her taunts drained away with every one of Grant's blows. I drop my head to the wood as she unbuckles my other ankle, barely holding myself upright on the thin strip of wood. She doesn't bother to catch me when she releases my wrists and I crash to the ground.

I curl into my body, wrapping my arms around my head as I convulse with pain. Every muscle screams, and the wounds on my back stretch, sending bolts of rage through me. She did this to me and has the audacity to cry as if she's the victim here.

I don't even have the energy to scream at her, much less kill her, but the urge is there. It's not even buried all that deep. If Molly hadn't ravaged my body so thoroughly, I could stand up and use any of the tools available at my fingertips to beat her to death. I could electrocute her. I could attach her to the cross and stab her over and over and over…a sob escapes me.

Molly's fingers wrap around my arm, ruby nails digging into my skin as she hauls me to my feet. I collapse to my knees, my stomach rebelling against the movement. She doesn't wait for me to be done and she ends up dragging me from the room. I'm still naked, praying no one else is in the hall. The cages are freezing as it is. I won't last long between the wounds and the cold.

The bright lights in the hallway blind me, sending a stabbing pain through my already pounding head. Molly's nails leave scratches behind as she drops me to the ground again. Blood seeps through the streaks, mingling with the dirt and sweat coating my skin. It's just one more transgression to add to the list.

"This is your fault, you little bitch. If he comes after me because of you…" Molly mutters as she returns.

She tucks a small bag under her arm, then reaches for me. I flinch, jerking away, and shame floods me. Her smirk is back, taunting me. Without a word, she crooks her finger as if she'll share a secret with me.

Pushing to my feet, I lift my own finger, though she's already marching away, the click of her crimson heels echoing around us. I follow slowly, hunched over as I protect what I'm sure are more broken ribs. I swear I heard a crack when she used the paddle on me several days ago. At least I think it's been that long.

The stairs prove to be an almost unsurmountable obstacle. I end up rolling down the last few and she leaves me groaning at the bottom. Thankfully, no one is around, but Molly is still there, standing witness to my downfall. I fucking hate her.

Pulling in deep breaths, I grasp at the apathy I once swam through. My head swims as I push to my hands and knees. Molly's overpowering rose perfume wafts around me, infiltrating my senses, and I cough.

"Crawl," she snarls.

The heaviness in my bones pulls my head down as I shuffle after her. Molly swings open the door to the cages and leans against the metal.

Her toe taps out a steady beat, reminding me of the plink of water in the bucket, and my muscles seize. A soft sob floats from the darkness beyond Molly, and I renew my efforts. Whoever is back there doesn't need to see me like this. Maybe my mind made it up.

I make it through the door, my lungs burning with each inhale. She snatches me up and drags me to the cage Nova occupied before. It's empty now, but the red light still blinks steadily overhead. Adrenaline floods my system and I scramble away. Her hold on me doesn't falter, no matter how I twist. I'm just not strong enough anymore. Even her recent beating doesn't slow her down.

I'm thrown into the empty cage, the small bag landing next to me. The metal of the door clangs shut, locking me inside once more. I curl into a ball, resigning myself to dying alone in the dark. My only regret is not telling Dante how much he meant to me. Maybe I'll get my chance in the afterlife, but I'm not holding my breath.

Eleven

Dante

Sweat drips down my temple, mingling with the blood seeping from the cut under my eye. I swipe it away with my sleeve before heaving out a sigh. Several blocks away, flames lick at the sky while sirens blare in the distance. They'll never make it in time to save the building. Good fucking riddance. By the time they get here, we'll be long gone and so will another dogfighting ring.

Jag sidles next to me, eyes fixed on the two vans driving off into the night. I don't know where he found an animal rescue willing to come to the seedy part of Rima, but at least they'll help the pups. The last couple times we've broken these rings up we haven't been so lucky. I'd rather set them free on the streets than let them burn with their abusers.

"I got them all out. Did a headcount when they were being kenneled." Jag tips his head back against the brick building of the alley we're currently hiding in. Leave it to him to care more about the animals than the people who probably died.

"Anyone missing?" I ask as I slip my phone from my pocket.

The plan was to divide and conquer. If it doesn't work, I'm sure I'll hear about it from Shane. He hasn't made any asinine comments since Sam told him to shut the fuck up at the last meeting. Everyone else seems to have fallen in line.

This is our first big move, hitting all the dogfighting rings we could find. No one from the Guild showed up here, which only makes me worry the others ran into problems.

"Everyone is missing. We're kind of in the middle of the shit, Prez. Technically, we're missing too." Jag smirks, glancing at me from the corner of his eye.

I send a quick text to Helms with an update. He doesn't respond, so I move to the next on my list. It isn't until I message Mason that I finally get through to anyone. His reply is clipped, which isn't surprising, but it still annoys me. My fingers tremble and I shove them in my pockets. It's like my bones are vibrating, pushing me to do more—to find Aelia.

Jag's hand lands on my shoulder. "Don't rush. We're doing what we can. One of these hits will catch their attention, and you'll be able to bust in there and get her. Right now, you'd end up dead and I'd have to take over."

"Like hell you will," I growl, and he grins.

I drop my chin to my chest, pulling in a deep breath. Aelia is smart. She's lived in that world a lot longer than I had to. And she survived. The fact she even had it in her to trust me...

It hits me again how I failed her.

"You didn't fail her," Jag mumbles, and his hand falls to his side.

I whip my head up, wondering how the hell he read my mind.

He shakes his head. "It's written on your face. For someone who's been living a double life for a year, you're incredibly easy to read, Raines."

He pushes away, leaning around the corner to peek at the fire in the distance. I check my phone again, seeing messages from the others and their intentions to meet back at Nico's. The last thing I want to do is have another discussion tonight.

It's almost three in the morning and I'm fucking exhausted. Flipping back to sleeping during the night after spending so much time with Aelia on her nocturnal schedule has been a struggle. Not having her next to me probably doesn't help. Neither do the nightmares.

I shove off the wall to stroll farther into the darkness. Jag will catch up and Raven's gang will circle around. I shouldn't have insisted on walking tonight. It's not far, but my bike would have been faster. I still haven't touched it. I told Mac she could ride it while she was here if she needs. Based on the horrified look she threw me, I doubt she'll take me up on it.

Jag falls into step next to me, and we emerge onto a quiet street lined with boarded up businesses. Traffic has died, leaving nothing but the hum of the city to fill the night. We make it several blocks before he snorts.

"Spit it out, Jag, before you choke on whatever the fuck is eating at you."

"Avery's been getting close to Sam. What are the chances Sam can convince her to go back to Harris?"

"None. I don't know Sam that well, but she's not the kind of woman to discourage another to stand up for herself."

He grunts, his nostrils flaring in frustration. "This isn't standing up for herself. This is pure stubbornness. She's got it in her head she's invincible, and she's going to get herself into trouble or worse."

"Ever think she just trusts you enough to help her if she gets herself into a bind?" I smirk when he scoffs.

My face falls when I remember talking with Aelia about whether he and Avery would ever get together. They bicker like an old married couple. Aelia probably isn't thinking about them right now. She probably isn't concerned with what's going on out here.

Hopefully Jenkins has gone back to ignoring her. From what I saw, he's not able to function without her. It's the only protection she has against Grant. And even if Anders tries anything, Jenkins will shut him down. At least that's what I'm banking on.

"I can't keep her safe," Jag mutters.

I sigh, running my fingers through my hair. "Then you're just going to have to trust that she can take care of herself. You realize she's an adult, right? She's not a kid anymore."

"I know that," he snaps. "Doesn't mean she's…"

I wait for him to continue, but he just stomps along. "So she runs her mouth sometimes. And not every decision is the best but look at the shit we're in the middle of. We all fuck up, Jag. Doesn't mean we're not smart."

"I didn't say she wasn't smart. And I didn't say she couldn't take care of herself. But I can't keep her safe and do what we need to. She's not like these other women. You know I saw Sam leaping across the rooftops the other night? And your sister was using Helms as target practice yesterday. How the fuck he just stood there while she chucked knives at him…never hit him once. I don't know what the hell Lacey does. Probably be able to take out an army of zombies with a flamethrower or some shit."

"Uh, Lacey is a hacker. And carries a Taser. I don't think she does well with weapons."

Jag whips his head around. "Is that why they call her Nemesis sometimes? I kept thinking they were talking about someone else but fuck if I was going to ask."

I chuckle, shaking my head. "Maybe having Avery here will help. She can learn a thing or two from the others. Then you won't need to worry about her so much."

He stops at the mouth of the alley, gazing at the boarded-up windows of Nico's. "Like you don't worry about Aelia? Even though she's way more qualified at surviving the Guild than both of us put together?"

His gaze bores into me, but I refuse to meet his stare. I grit my teeth, keeping my retort—and my fists—to myself.

"If I knew she was in the same position now as when I first came around, then maybe I wouldn't worry as much." My heart clenches as he scoffs. "Avery learning how to throw a punch isn't the same as Aelia being locked away in that shithole. We have no idea what's happening to her. I have no idea if she's even alive. Don't try to compare our situations, Jag. Besides, I love Aelia. Avery's just a woman you feel an obligation for. So shut the fuck up."

I walk away, leaving him to do whatever the fuck he's going to do. I shouldn't have said that shit to him. It's getting harder to keep my mouth shut, though. I'm sick of everyone commenting on things they don't understand. Which is exactly why I need to be in charge.

Worrying about Aelia, fighting the urge to storm in there and snatch her away, doesn't help me get any closer to actually saving her. Blowing shit up will only work if they pay attention. I wasted enough time waiting for them to get here, then wallowing when I should have hit the ground running.

My feet stutter as I spot a shadow from the corner of my eye. Whipping my head around, my heart skips a beat. I peer into the dark, then run my hand over my face when a small tree wavers with a gust of wind. I won't admit, even to myself, I'd hoped it was Aelia emerging from the dark.

I push through the front doors and scan the space, trying to dispel the ache in my chest. Helms and Mac aren't back yet, but the rest are scattered around the room. They're as dirty and scraped up as me.

"Where's Mac?" I call as Jag steps in behind me. He shuffles off to the corner and drops into a chair. I'm surprised he didn't go straight to Vipers headquarters to make sure Avery was okay. I'd assume it's because he trusts Lacey to keep an eye on her, but it's probably because he knows Avery won't leave Rima.

"Her and Helms took a detour. Someone was following them. They'll be here in a few—said we can start without them," Sam says as she leans against Alex. They all look exhausted and we haven't even gotten started yet.

I take the place I've claimed for myself at the head of the table. Staring at the map, I try to concentrate on our next hits, but my eyes blur. Until Mac returns, my focus will be split. My concentration at the tasks we have to accomplish is already wavering because of Aelia. I can't afford to slip up now.

Until we can lure some of their forces outside of headquarters, I can't go in for her. If I thought just blowing shit up would help, I'd do it. Mac keeps reminding me that isn't an option if we want to defeat the Guild. It takes everything in me not to scream at her I don't give a fuck about them. She can tell, which is why she keeps saying it.

"Can we start? I'm fucking tired and my ass hurts," Alex whines, then drops a kiss on Sam's head. Jealousy turns my stomach and I avert my gaze.

"Why the hell does your ass hurt? You let Sam peg you or something?" The question would be funny if it wasn't coming from Ren and delivered with his usual stoic tone.

Alex smirks, raising his eyebrow at Ren, then bursts out laughing.

Sam's elbow digs into Alex's side. "He tripped over a lip in the sidewalk and landed on a chunk of concrete. I almost had to carry his ass back here, he was whining so much."

Alex tips his head back against his chair. "Aw, Bug, why you gotta do me like that?"

The door to the kitchen pops open and Mac stumbles through, annoyance stamped on her face. The tension in my muscles bleeds away and I heave out a heavy breath. I may trust Helms to have her back, but I'll never be completely comfortable with my baby sister putting herself in danger.

"We need a better plan other than divide and conquer. Those assholes were fucking persistent. If we'd taken a car instead of my bike, we'd be halfway to Synd, still trying to shake them," Helms growls.

"If you've got a better plan, let's hear it," I say, spreading my hands out as I gesture to the map. No one speaks up. "This is the best way to disrupt their cash flow. We don't have the manpower *or* firepower to hit them directly yet."

Jag clears his throat. "Ghost will be here with some guys soon. Raven said she'll help, but only if it'll—"

"Don't put words in my mouth, Jaguar," Raven snaps as she busts through the door. "Headquarters—their headquarters—is locked down. Something is happening though."

"We're calling the Guild's headquarters the embassy. And you're going to have to be more specific, Raven," Shane says.

She huffs, narrowing her eyes at him. "If I knew I would have said. There's whispers about an event coming. They're setting it up off-site, I think. Haven't figured out where yet."

Raven pivots, then pushes out the door again. She didn't want to stay in Rima in the first place. With Nova being taken, Raven doesn't seem to know what to do. It took several of us to talk her down when she tried to go after Nova. I don't blame her. Jag had to do the same thing for me while we were waiting for the others to get here.

"I think we're going to have a problem if we keep going at the pace we are." Mason catches my eye, gesturing with his chin to Mac, who's fallen asleep on Helms's shoulder.

"We've barely gotten started," I grunt. "We slow down and that gives them time to regroup. We have three days before we hit the gambling halls, so everybody better get their shit together by then."

I shove to my feet, planning on making a grand exit. Alex tentatively raises his arm, wiggling his fingers in the air and I curl my hands into fists.

"I know you've got your whole 'let's blow shit up' thing going on, but I may have an idea that'll move things along a little."

I sink back into my chair and cross my arms. "I'm all ears."

TWELVE

Aelia

"They look better," Nova whispers as her eyes dart to the camera in the corner of the room.

No one has bothered us other than Grant. He hasn't done anything other than leave food for us. There's an edge of fear in his eyes now. Good. Hopefully, that fucker gets exactly what's coming to him. I don't know what he told Anders, but I'm pretty sure it's been over a week since Molly made me crawl back to my prison.

When Molly tossed me in this cell, I thought I was alone. Thankfully, she put me in here with Nova this time. I would have died otherwise. Molly was probably terrified she'd be held responsible if that happened.

My eyes track Nova as she digs in the bag Molly chucked in with us. The cream for my back eases the pain at least. She slathers it on, then takes the time to apply the bandages that are almost gone. The last thing I need is an infection to set in. I'm surprised I didn't get sick after how weak I was.

Facing forward, I swallow the rage that's been riding me since my mind cleared. "Are they closed?"

"Yes. These deeper ones will scar, but some of the smaller ones will probably disappear. How are your ribs?"

"Better. Doesn't feel like I'm being stabbed every time I breathe." I press a hand to my side as if I'll be able to tell if they're truly healed.

She sighs, dropping the thin robe Molly was kind enough to supply. I settle against the bars, hissing when they hit a particularly sore spot. Grant dropped off a blanket as well, but it's not enough to ward off the cold. He wants me to be weak, not dead—easily manipulated, yet not well enough to fight back. Not that I have the strength to do more than eat and sleep. Nova insists on waking me when she thinks I've been out for too long, terrified I'm going to die in my sleep and she'll be left with a body instead of a patient.

"You think he'll care?" she murmurs as she repacks the bag, refusing to meet my eyes.

I narrow my eyes as I study her. "Who?"

"*Him.* Will he say anything about the scars?"

"Probably," I admit, and her head whips up. "We'll have a whole, 'who did this to you' moment. Hopefully by that time I can say she's dead, and he'll call me a good girl."

Tipping my head back, I close my eyes. Dante's face emerges from the darkness, the intensity of his eyes sending a shiver through me. The vision is fading, becoming blurrier every day. I'm forgetting the way his lip tips up when he finds something funny but won't admit it. Or the tilt of his eyebrow when he's questioning my latest scheme to kill Jenkins.

My memories of him are slowly disappearing, which doesn't seem possible. It's only been a few months, maybe less, since I last saw him. When I noticed, I started whispering stories to Nova as we huddled under the small blanket.

"Did you tell him?" she asks after several minutes.

"Tell him what?"

She leans closer, afraid to be overheard. "That you love him."

I school my face into an emotionless mask, yet my body lights up. My heart skips a beat while my stomach flips, an eruption of butterflies taking flight and leaving me lightheaded. Since I was brought back, I've stoically ignored the despair burrowing deep within my soul whenever I think about Dante's and my conversation about love.

I shake my head, swallowing the bile climbing up my throat. "Love doesn't exist here."

She tilts her head, and a rueful look overtakes her face. "Until he came."

I don't bother to respond. Explaining to her that even with Dante, love still didn't exist within these walls would take too much out of me. She'd never get it anyway. Maybe he thought he'd found love, but until we exist outside of the Guild, we'll never truly know if it's love or something else.

I told him I was too broken and that fact hasn't changed. I'm teetering on the edge of losing myself. Dante may have claimed that he'll love me through the process, but actually living with a shell of a human being, someone he once cared for, is exceptionally harder. At least I assume it is.

I can't think about a future that may never exist. I'm not even living day-by-day. Every second is a fight to stay on this side of the living. And I don't even know if it'll be worth it.

The sudden flash of crimson across my closed lids jolts me awake. I don't know how long I've been out, but several more days have passed. I blink rapidly, whipping my head toward the door. A sliver of light appears as someone cracks it open and I turn to wake Nova. Except she's not there.

Pushing to my feet, I scan the space, then the other cages. The shadows obscure the corners, but I don't think she's here. I would have jolted awake had they come to take her. She would have screamed or at least woken me up once she knew someone was here. Panic floods my body and I drop to my hands and knees as I attempt to pull in a full breath. I made promises in the darkness—to protect her, to keep her safe, to keep their attention off her as long as possible.

I failed.

I keep failing. Over and over. Dante kept pushing me to stand up to the Guild and take risks. What's the point when everything I touch crumbles in my grasp? I don't know if I saved or condemned Avery. I don't know if Jag made it out. I don't know if Dante is suffering in another forgotten place. Nothing I do changes the outcome. The Guild always wins. Always.

Foolishly, I believed Dante when he said we could change that. Nothing changes. Nothing goes right. Nothing…

I gasp, rage replacing the despair. I spent long enough within the darkness, shying away from the shadows of this world. My head rises as I jut out my chin, my body heaving with the weight of my wrath. Fixing my eyes on the door, I grin when long red nails wrap around the frame. My neck pops as I roll my head.

By the time Molly steps into the dank space, I'm resting against the back bars again, a bored expression plastered on my face. She smirks, assuming I'm still weak and controllable. I track her movements, subtly scanning her for weapons as I do. Nothing other than a leash and collar. Clenching my teeth, I tuck my chin to my chest.

"Did you miss me?" Molly coos and my head whips up as her fingers wrap around the bars. "Oh, don't be like that. We had fun, didn't we?"

She tips her head back, a throaty laugh leaving her. My body vibrates with the effort to hold back the barrage of insults filling my mouth. I'll choke on them before I allow her to see how affected I am. As much as I'd like to fold my hands around her neck and end her, I can't. I won't be able to leave a trail of dead bodies in my wake if I'm locked up still.

Molly slips the collar through the bars and the metal lands at my feet. It's not the same one I wore with Dante, thank fuck. I wouldn't be able to force myself to wear it then. It's not until I pick it up, the chain still linked back to Molly, that I realize it's pronged. Teeth line the inside, filed into points sharp enough to draw blood if she's not careful.

Glancing at Molly, I catch the sadistic edge in her eyes. She'll definitely use this to her advantage. I wonder how Grant will take it—unless he's the one choosing. Actually, I'd be more inclined to believe this gift came from Jenkins, just like the first one. I wonder if it's a message straight from him—that he knows where I am and what I did.

"Put it on." She shakes the chain, the clinking grating on my nerves.

I slip it over my head, the chain sliding through the ring as she yanks on the leash. It's cold and rests on my collarbones until she tugs on her end, cinching it tight against my windpipe. I choke, resisting the urge to jerk away.

"Perfect," she purrs, and her red lips pull into a grin.

Producing a single key, she unlocks the door, then runs into a dilemma she didn't anticipate. The leash is strung between the bars, preventing her from dragging me out without passing it through. Her eyes dart between the problem and me, probably wondering if I'll take advantage of her mistake. I won't get this opportunity again.

The toe of her red stiletto heel beats out a rhythm as she contemplates what to do. I tense, planting my hands on the damp ground, the cold seeping into my feverish skin. When the leash slips from her fingers, I launch my body toward hers. I hit her lower than I planned, striking her thighs instead of her stomach, but it doesn't matter. At least we're outside of my cell now. Her scream cuts short when she hits the ground, forcing the air from her lungs.

Crawling up her body, I wrap my fingers around her throat, squeezing as she twists underneath me. The chain swings wildly as I grit my teeth and she snatches it. Her blotchy face swims in my vision and I realize I'm crying. Tears of pent-up rage splash on my hands and stain her skin. I growl, renewing my efforts to extinguish the light in her eyes.

She bucks underneath me, wrenching the chain as hard as she can. The teeth bite into my neck, but the rage overshadows the pain. Just when I think she's given up, her fist swings around, smashing into my barely healed ribs, and I crumple.

She bats my hands away, snarling at me. It's enough for her to roll us until she's straddling my barely healed body. The veins on her neck stand out as she strains for control. My back screams as I pull my knee to my chest, then wedge my heel under her arm.

A feral cry leaves her when I kick her chest. I don't know what I hit, but clearly she was injured when she came in. I take advantage of her weakened state and do it again. There's not enough room to push her off me, and I focus on the chain. She slaps me with it and a ringing invades my left ear. Shaking my head back and forth, I let my hands fall from her, and she hits me again.

My vision darkens, Dante's face floating from the shadows once more. His mouth is moving, forming words I can't hear, and I close my eyes as Molly whips the chain across my chest.

Don't hold back.

Over and over he mouths the words. My vision morphs from black to red, dousing me in a crimson rage. I explode upright, shoving Molly off me. She falls back, the bars ringing when her head slams into them. Her eyes cross, red hair covering her face. When she scrambles away, crawling toward the main door another wave of rage crashes over me. She screams for help as I pounce on her back and she collapses on her stomach.

"No one's coming to save you," I hiss in her ear.

She rolls sideways, and I slide off her back. Crouching, I wait for her to make a break for it. Instead, she seems to shake off whatever fear enveloped her. Slowly, she pushes to her feet, and I mimic her movements.

She pivots to face me and I grin, letting all the mania shine through. No use hiding how much I loathe her. Only one of us will walk out of here alive. Internally, I snort. I refuse to throw out cheesy lines like

Molly did the entire time she was whipping me, abusing me—even in my mind.

"You little bitch. You forgot—" She straightens, throwing her shoulders back. "You're not in control here."

She leans forward, snatching for the chain, and I throw it over my shoulder. She stumbles toward me, leering at my half-naked body. Bruises mar my skin, red gashes on full display as my robe gapes open. She's admiring her handiwork. I raise my eyebrow, refusing to cover up. I'm done cowering before her. Edging toward her, I end up kicking one of her shoes she lost in our scuffle.

"I think once you're sold, I'll find that delicious morsel you were attached to and offer him my services. I'm sure I'll satisfy him more than you ever could."

Her taunt does nothing. I don't know if that's because I trust Dante or the fact I fucking hate Molly so much. Her words lost their sting long ago. She's shuffling forward, probably thinking she's sneaky. I shake my head, chuckling. If she gets her hands on me, she might leave a few more bruises, but nothing more.

"Did you fall in love with him, little lamb? Did you think he would save you?" She tilts her head, pursing her lips. "Clearly, he didn't care enough to bring you with when he left. He took someone else instead."

My heart skips a beat. She doesn't understand what she's revealing. I didn't even know Dante got out. And he found Avery too. A sob catches in my throat, and I struggle to maintain my mask of indifference.

My distraction costs me when she launches herself forward and grapples for the leash. She's so focused on getting the chain she doesn't see my knee until it's buried in her stomach. I push her back as she doubles over, and she lands on the ground again.

Dropping down, my fingers brush her abandoned shoe. Her foot snaps out, catching my arm, and the entire limb goes numb. We grapple again, my strength flagging now. I'm too weak, too wounded, to do this much longer.

I end up on my back, her straddling me again. She wraps the chain around her hand as I hit her again and again. My punches are weak, like I'm stuck in a dream, and no matter how hard I try, nothing works as it should. She leans down, her hair brushing against my flushed cheeks.

"If I could, I'd take you back to the crimson chambers and carve you up. Are your insides as scarred as your back?"

My hands fall to my sides as I turn my head, closing my eyes shut as my body freezes. She nips at my jaw, then presses her lips to my cheek. A shudder of revulsion overtakes me.

Molly shoves off me, yanking me upright by the collar. She leans down, tilting her head to gaze at me.

"Why are you smiling? You can't honestly believe you'll survive being sold," she scoffs.

"Welcome to your worst nightmare," I sneer.

She forces out a laugh, peering at the door. When she glances back, I bash the heel of her shoe into her eye socket. She rears back, a guttural cry leaving her as she stumbles away, hitting her head on the cage I used to occupy.

Instinctively, she drops the chain, clawing at the stiletto still stuck in her eye. A squelching noise follows, turning my stomach. Blood seeps into the heel, staining the red fabric.

I could leave her here. The door hangs open, tempting me with freedom. It's a false snapshot, the way out laden with pitfalls. I doubt I'd make it, especially after Dante and Avery fled.

Molly's sobs fill the background of my decision and I push to my feet. I grab her other shoe, adjusting my grip as I approach her. Blood weeps from her damaged eye, streaking down her face and neck before pooling into her red dress.

I flip the shoe around, glancing from the sharp heel to her. Terror flashes in her remaining eye. She holds her hands up, warding me off, but I will not be waylaid. She deserves no mercy. Retribution will be mine, and I refuse to yield any longer.

THIRTEEN

Dante

My office is stuffy, yet I'm loath to open the window. I don't honestly think someone will try to slip through and slit my throat, but I'm not taking any chances. The words blur on the paper and I toss it on the pile on my desk.

Rubbing my hands over my face, I wonder how long the MC has been neglected. Maddox clearly didn't care about maintaining our trade relationships. Now we have no money coming in, not that it matters. It's not the cash I'm concerned about. We need firepower, though.

Shane refuses to pull any of his men. Byrns outright laughed in my face, citing the fact they put a reformed enemy in charge. Apparently, Byrns isn't as confident in the man they installed in Synd or his commitment to leading the city as some of the others. I suspect Lacey had something to do with that decision.

Alex bursts through the door, not bothering to knock. He collapses in the chair across from me and heaves out a sigh so heavy I'm surprised he doesn't slither off his seat.

"Something I can do for you, King?" I ask as I pick up another stack of papers. They're filled with numbers I don't bother tallying.

"I'm bored. I hate nights off. Especially when it's not *truly* a night off." He slouches, resting his head on the back of the chair.

"What the hell does that mean?"

He tilts his head, giving me an incredulous look, then sobers. "Sam's out hunting. So, not really a night off."

I nod once, then feign scanning the sheet. My vision blurs as I wonder if Aelia and I will ever get to a place where we can complain about not being able to spend time together. It's such a mundane thing. With the lives we lead, I never really understood standing still and enjoying the moment. There's always something else that needs to get done.

"Well, if you're actually bored, I might have something we can do together," I murmur, not quite sure I want him tagging along. Logically, I know it's better to have backup, but I've been operating mostly on my own for the past year. Bringing someone else into my side quests is still a hard pill to swallow.

"I'm not letting you paint my nails," he snaps. "Unless you have black."

I roll my eyes. "It's a little more dangerous than that. But I'm sure Mac has some nail polish in her old room if you want to do that after."

"After danger comes ice cream. Come on, Raines. Everyone knows that." Alex smirks before shoving to his feet.

He follows me out of the office, and I head for the back door. "You realize I'm not going to be a substitute for your wayward girlfriend, right?"

Alex chuckles as he falls into step beside me. "You couldn't handle stepping into Sam's shoes. Even temporarily. Oh, and maybe don't let her hear you call her wayward. She'll rip your dick off and make you thank her for doing society the service."

I shake my head as I head for the SUV parked at the end of the alley. I don't know what strings Nemesis—Lacey—pulled, but the same driver keeps pulling up every time I call. One of these days I'll ask what his name is. He doesn't exactly encourage conversation. I can't blame him. The last time he picked me up, we were running for our lives.

"Where are we going?" Alex asks, climbing into the backseat after me.

"There are a couple labs I want to check out. I think they're making Oracle." I turn off my phone. I wouldn't put it past Lacey, or hell, even Ren, to track me. "Turn off your phone."

"Oh no. I'm not doing that. They want to track me, they can go right ahead. Saved my ass at least once." Alex taps a rhythm on his leg as he watches the dark buildings fly by.

"They pull your ass out of the river or something?"

"Nah, though someone did set the river on fire. That was a bitch to deal with since Nikki didn't want anyone down there. Pretty sure I'm still banned after 'the incident'. And no, I don't want to talk about it."

"I wasn't going to ask," I mutter.

He sniffs as if I was grilling him about some mysterious event. "Anyway, after Shane said Sam couldn't stay, I kind of went rogue. Her uncle Victor caught me skulking around the Depot. To be fair, I wasn't being very sneaky. Too tore up over the fact I couldn't get through to Shane and Ren about Sam. My phone was the only way Ren was able to find me."

"Maybe this time you should try to be sneakier."

I honestly don't know what else to say to him. Every time I think about the shit they've told me they lived through, it gives me hope that Aelia and I might have a chance. I don't have the full story, but I know enough. It's too hard to focus on the future with our present so dismantled.

He sighs, glancing at me. "I get you're used to doing shit alone. But there's a reason you called us."

"Because I needed the manpower," I mutter and cross my arms.

"Oh, so it had nothing to do with the fact you were completely destroyed? And that you had no idea how to bring the Guild down alone? Or because your half-brother destroyed your club?"

I grit my teeth, turning to gaze out the window. "Thought you were the one who said I could live in that space. Whatever the fuck that means."

He snorts. "Sure, but you calling us doesn't have anything to do with manpower. I mean, it does a little, but I think a lot of it has to do with loneliness. But we don't have to talk about that shit. You're probably not ready."

My mouth drops open, no words coming out. Honestly, I don't even know what to say. I'm not lonely. People like me don't *get* lonely. At least that's what I was taught. Maybe it's because we never talk about it. Being in an MC doesn't exactly scream "let's talk about our feelings." No one cares anyway. Alex can spout about his bullshit theories all he wants.

"While I can sympathize with what you went through…" I grit my teeth as he snorts, then continue. "Our experiences are vastly different. I'm not fucking lonely. I'm—"

I search for the right word, but it eludes me. I'm exhausted. I'm overwhelmed. I'm just fucking done. None of them truly encompass what it's like being away from Aelia. The guilt still eats at me, day and night. My world won't be right until she's free from them. Even if she chooses not to stay with me, at least I got her out.

"You're terrified," he whispers.

I shake my head, not willing to admit he's right. Alex may not be one to rub shit in, but the minute I say it out loud, it becomes real.

He waves his hand, brushing away his statement. "Again, you're not ready to admit it. That's okay. I'll be here when you're ready."

"Why?"

I don't understand why he cares so fucking much. We're not exactly besties. Even Helms has been avoiding me, sighing every time someone comments on Aelia or about getting her out. The last few years we've been trying to rebuild the relationship we had, but it's not the same as when we were kids. Now that he's practically my brother-in-law, I should make more of an effort to bridge the gap. After we've dealt with the Guild. Maybe.

Alex sighs and leans his head against the window. "Because I know how it is. Feeling like you're missing something. Even with Shane and Ren, I still got lonely. No use going through that shit alone."

We pull up to the mouth of an alley a few blocks away from the drug lab. I nod to our driver, then climb out and Alex follows. His grin is back in place as if we didn't just have a mini therapy session.

I scowl as we dip into the dark alley. I swear if he could get away with it, he'd be whistling. Alex seems to have the ability to turn off his happy-go-lucky nature and tap into some secret mafia part of his brain. His steps switch mid-stride from an easy lope to that of a barely contained killer.

"Easy there, King," I murmur, my hand landing on his shoulder. "We're only here to check shit out. We'll burn it down later."

The vein in his neck throbs. "Don't know why we're waiting. Might as well take them out while we're here."

"Except we're not equipped for that level of destruction."

He grumbles the rest of the short walk, randomly clenching his hands. The way his mood swings from one extreme to the other tells me there's something else going on with him. The last couple months I've gotten to know him pretty well, and this isn't normal behavior. It's then that I notice the stress lines around his eyes. There's an exhaustion there I didn't see before—probably because I was too far gone myself.

They probably thought they were done with all the bullshit. And I dragged them straight back into the fire. From the hesitancy Jenkins displayed, I'm pretty sure the Guild never would have gone back to Synd. No matter how much Anders pushed for it. He's probably still going off the rails and harassing Jenkins.

The decrepit building looms out of the darkness and we both stop. Light filters out from the gaps in the boarded-up windows, shadows cutting it off every once in a while. It's not a large space, but it's enough if they're making Oracle. The drug they've introduced into Rima is potent, deadly, and addictive. People black out, unable to recall anything while in the throes of a trip. It's the last thing we need on the streets. The Guild makes a shit ton of money from it as well.

"How many of these places do they have?" Alex murmurs as he crouches to peek in one of the cracks.

"At least a dozen. If we're going to blow them at the same time, we'll have to time it perfectly. This isn't like the dogfights."

He glances over his shoulder at me. "Except this time, we're not getting anyone out. You don't think they've brought kids in there, do you? They didn't in Synd, but you never know."

"Nah. They wouldn't trust kids with something like this. No animals either. This is still low-level gang shit."

He nods slowly and taps his finger against his chin. Someone opens the front door, spilling light into the night. He can't be more than twenty. Alex and I duck back into the shadows, tracking the figure as he lights up a smoke. Not the smartest idea with a bunch of highly flammable drugs around. He pulls out a phone, and the sounds of a woman moaning fill the air.

Alex rolls his eyes, then jerks his head back the way we came. We only retreat to the other end of the alley, and I lean against the brick wall. Alex steps in front of me, leaning in. I jerk back, hitting my head on the stone, and he rolls his eyes again.

"Stop being weird. That shit they're making burns in water. At least the stuff in Synd did. You don't think they'll pull a what's-it-called and dump it in the water supply, do you?" He shudders as he pulls back, his wide eyes finding mine. I can't tell if he's being serious.

"No. I think they're going to sell it and make a shitload of money so they can fund their sadistic operation. And I'm not being weird."

He retreats to the wall on the other side and leans against it. When he cranes his neck to spy on the drug dealer, I sigh. He won't be able to see him from here, but he keeps trying. I don't think I was acting strange. Asshole practically jumped me. I was bound to react, especially in such a tense situation. In reality, it's probably the closest anyone has gotten to me since I left Aelia other than the occasional pat on the shoulder.

I push the thoughts from my mind. Nothing good will come from lamenting the fact I'm touch starved. Something glitters at the other end of the alley and I jolt. Squinting into the dark, I hold my breath. Nothing appears. We're the only ones out here. I press my fist against the pulse of pain in my chest.

Glancing toward Alex, I realize we've been skulking around for too long. Someone is bound to do a sweep and then we'll have to come up with a cover story. I don't have it in me to deal with any of that. If we kill them, it'll tip off the Guild and we really don't want that.

With a gesture, I lead Alex back the way we came. Tonight was a bust, mostly because I didn't want to get too close. I was hoping we'd figure out how many men they have, or if they have a patrol. With this location, though, it's too hard to tell without exposing ourselves.

"So you get what you were looking for?" Alex asks as we slide into the SUV.

"Not exactly. I'll have to find another lab before we set anything into motion." I turn on my phone, and it buzzes for a good minute with all the notifications. I don't bother looking at them since Alex had his on the whole time.

"Don't you have a list of them or something?"

"They didn't exactly hand them out as party favors at the Guild."

"Don't get snippy with me because they didn't reveal all their devious plans to you, Raines." He bites his cheek, then snaps his fingers. "We need to start establishing ties to the inside. Or maybe just blowing shit up. I bet if we take out the labs, it'd give us an in with the lower gangs."

The seed of an idea sprouts at his suggestion, and I stare out the window at nothing. It's not perfect and could get some of us killed, but it might be just the push we need to set things into motion.

FOURTEEN

Aelia

I should be running. The heavy metal door sits open, the light filtering in tempting me. I roll my head away from the scene, and my gaze lands on the bloody mess across from me. Molly didn't scream very long after I started beating her with her other shoe. I waited before I took her other eye.

It might make me sadistic, but I wanted her to watch while I dismantled her slowly. She may have passed out at some point, but I didn't notice. Once I went for her remaining eye, though, the gurgling became too much. I blacked out after that.

I didn't lose consciousness, but I might as well have. My entire body went on autopilot, slamming the heel into her over and over. My own sobs snapped me out of whatever rage-induced mania I was stuck in. Then the apathy flowed in. It's probably the only thing protecting me at the moment.

My mind has split, half residing in my blood-stained body and the other hovering overhead. I'd like to say the spectral part is protecting me from the horrors of what I've done, but I'm not so sure. I've tried not to think about it too much.

The scuff of a shoe reminds me I'm not alone. I never truly am. In this bubble of chaos, though, it certainly felt like I was. At least now I know the camera never was working. Not that it mattered. We weren't going anywhere, anyway. They knew that.

I assumed they were spying on us, waiting for me to drop some information. The more I think on it, the more I realize they assumed I was used by Dante. Just like they use the women around them. It didn't cross their mind he would confide in me. I'm nothing more than a bit—a profitable bit, but a bit, nonetheless. They're still operating under the guise that all men are like them. Never in their wildest dreams would they confide in the whores they use. We're property—nothing more.

Spending so much time with Dante made me forget that fact. I never had to cover for him. I never had to protect him. Even Molly's questions make sense now. She never truly wanted to know anything. It was a distraction and nothing more. Yet I was too broken to see it.

A meaty hand wraps around the door and pushes it open, making the hinges squeal in protest. It mimics the small part of my soul still fearful of the men who have run my life for almost a decade. The rest of me hushes it, soothing it back into the dark space that's more sanctuary than prison.

Grant's disheveled hair pokes through first. I expected to feel something, whether it be terror or rage, when I saw him again. Yet there's nothing. He doesn't scare me like he used to. There's a certain peace that comes with knowing one's fate, I suppose. I'm about to be sold. Grant can't touch me any longer.

"What the fuck," he breathes as he takes in Molly's mutilated body.

It's not all that bad, the damage mostly concentrated in her face. I glance down at my own body and notice the scratches for the first time. They run up and down my arms, and gouges cover the backs of my hands. She must have fought back. I didn't notice. I turn my head, scanning him slowly.

"You have got to be fucking kidding me. Now I have to deal with a goddamn body, too?"

There's something there, in his eyes, right before he spins away. It's not pity or compassion, of course. He knows neither of those emotions. No,

I'm pretty sure it's relief. Probably because he won't have to deal with her now. Though why that would be an issue for him, I'm not sure.

Grant has killed many people over the years—mostly women. I was forced to watch several times at Jenkins's insistence. Something about escorting the women from birth until death. I didn't understand until later that he considered their birth to be when they came to him. They were reborn at his hands, then broken and eventually disposed of.

Ah, there's that rage I was missing.

"Dumb bitch was supposed to shower you. Fuck that," he mumbles, more to himself than me. "Drake can suck a dick if he thinks I'm doing more."

My only hope is one of these days Anders will get sick of Grant and kill him. Even sitting next to the body of someone I just stabbed to death with a stiletto heel, I don't know if I'd be able to get rid of Grant as well. I used up all my strength. After all the things he's done to me, he should be six feet under. I should be enraged by his very existence. I should be attacking him as he bumbles around the space doing absolutely nothing.

Yet I can't. Maybe it's shock. It's been so long since I've felt anything other than pain. Dante may have affected me, woken me up, but his influence is wearing off in the wake of his absence. I wish he was here with me. He could take care of Grant. Actually, I should have let Dante kill him all those months ago.

"What the fuck," I breathe, closing my eyes. If I'm in the business of wishing, I'd wish my ass out of here.

I jolt forward from the pressure on my neck. My eyes fly open and I scramble on my hands and knees to keep the prongs from digging into my skin. He stomps toward the door, clutching the chain and still muttering to himself. Finding my feet, I stumble in his wake, almost crashing into his back. I shudder, pushing down the revulsion when I spy the blood coating my hands.

I didn't think this through, too caught up in stopping Molly. Now I'm covered in blood, wounds, and bruises. It's not much different from when Molly tossed me in the cell with Nova, but the freshness of it all…another shudder rolls through me, and I lose my footing.

Crashing to my knees, I cry out as one of them pops. Grant snarls and yanks on the chain. The sharpened prongs dig into my skin, sending sparks of pain through me. My hands hit the cold concrete when he heaves on the leash, attempting to pull me to my feet again.

"I don't have time for this, bit. We have five minutes or I'm killing you myself and dumping your body in the dark. No one will ever know what happened to you. And no one will care." His taunting gives me a small reprieve from being hauled around and I'm able to push to my feet.

Tears track down my face, and I bow my head. I hid my tears from Grant for years. I hate that he's seeing them now. It's ridiculous since it gains me nothing. I thought it made me stronger, but it doesn't matter now. None of it matters anymore. All the grand plans I had slip through my fingers, spilling at my bare feet. My battered body moves without volition, leaving the remnants of my strength behind.

"Shit, shit, shit. Snap out of it, Aelia. We don't have much time." Rachel's voice cuts through the fog in my mind.

I glance up at her from my kneeling position with dull eyes. Her brows pull low and she peeks over her shoulder toward the door, then back at me. Her hands flutter around me as if she's afraid of doing more damage to my already mangled flesh. The curtains surrounding us ripple, casting shadows across the floor. I've mostly blocked out the low murmur of voices of the crowd seated on the other side of the drapes. They're tucked away, waiting for the show to begin.

"Can you stand? I can get you out."

I let out a breathless laugh and the corner of my lip twitches. Even I can hear the lie in her voice. She can't get me out any more than she can escape herself. The truth rests in the jerkiness of her limbs, the despair in her eyes, and the paleness of her skin. Hard to believe just six months ago we were sniping at each other. The gap dividing us seemed insurmountable until Dante stepped in.

"I am getting out, Rachel. Just not the way we expected."

"In a body bag?" She huffs, shaking her head. Sorrow drips from every line in her face, threatening to drag me down into the depths of her despair.

"They giving out body bags now? How generous." I smirk, but she doesn't return the gesture. I don't blame her.

"At least fight back. Isn't that what we were supposed to do? Fight?"

I tilt my head, contemplating her words. A small voice in the back of my head screams at me, but it's smothered under the weight of years of abuse. It's too tiny, too weak, too broken. Just like I always thought. Add in the fact I just killed someone, and that last bit of hope has almost flamed out.

"You should fight. Rage against the dying of the light and all that. I won't be here to do it, so you'll have to take up that mantle."

She opens her mouth, then snaps it shut when the curtains twitch. Between one blink and the next, she's gone, slipping out the door. I tuck my chin to my chest, intent on retreating into my mind.

My thin robe gapes open, highlighting the bruises marring my ribs. I should tie it closed, but what's the point when they'll rip it off me as soon as I hit the stage? The men out there want to inspect the goods. Wouldn't want to buy damaged merchandise. Although, some of them probably prefer us a little bit broken.

Grant stalks in, scowling before seizing my arm and dragging me to my feet. He hauls me to the back door, then freezes as he takes in all the other women gathered. I spot a flash of Rachel's hair disappearing around the corner. There's only about twenty of them, but in this small space it feels like there's more. Grant growls and the crowd splits, revealing a makeshift setup at the back with a tarp laid out and a bucket full of water.

He tugs me around him, then pushes me toward the area. A hard-bristled brush rests inside the bucket, and I balk. If he's wanting me to be clean, tearing open my barely healed wounds won't help. Grant shoves me to my knees and gestures to the water.

"Wash your fucking face. You look like an extra in a horror movie," he grumbles, none of his usual vitriol present.

I dip my hands in the water and scrub it over my cheeks. He grips my chin, forcing me to meet his eyes. He nods once and grabs my arm again. My mind shuts down with each step closer to the curtains. Music swells and I flinch at the sudden change. Grant's hand drops to his side, confident I'm sufficiently cowed to follow him. He's not wrong.

Fingers brush my arm, and I whip my head to the girl. I recognize her, though I don't know her name. As I focus on the other faces, I realize I know most of them. There's no pity in their eyes, thank fuck. My gaze catches on one who looks eerily like me. She presses her lips together and tips up her quivering chin. I mimic her as I face forward and glide toward my fate.

By the time I'm at the curtains, whatever confidence she lent me has fled. There is no dignity here. No compassion. No escape. Grant sweeps the dark fabric aside and I wince at the bright light. His hand lands on my lower back, though he doesn't push me like I expect. I don't like this new side to him. Maybe he's just leery of how he'll be punished for the state my body is in.

My bare feet skid across the wooden floor as the music lowers. The murmur of men's voices washes over me, sending my limbs trembling.

My entire body tenses. I wish I would have tied the robe. A shadow beyond the harsh lights detaches from the darkness and approaches the side of the stage. My stomach flips when I catch the familiar silver hair of my father. He whispers into Grant's ear, not bothering to even glance my way.

I don't know what I expected, but it wasn't for Grant to shake his head, gesturing wildly as Anders's face becomes redder by the second. Maybe he's learning of Molly's demise. Or the myriad of trauma painting my flesh. Nova was right, they'll scar. Anders can't possibly be happy about that.

My gaze sweeps around the room, waiting for the announcer. The Auction always has someone presenting the men and women up for sale. It's all very civilized, with men holding numbered paddles in the air as they bid on the "items," as Jenkins called them. It was always jarring to witness rich people dressed up looking like they were going to bid on some dead person's painting and instead be met with screaming and crying people on the stage.

I threw up the first few times I was forced to attend. My mind skips back to when I tried to climb out of the box hanging high above the others, thinking I could save the girl who wasn't much younger than me. My fingers wrap around my throat, and I trace the scar from my punishment for that stunt.

No one will be jumping out of their chairs to save me. I wouldn't expect them to. This faceless mass conveys all that is evil in my world. There are no knights in shining armor.

"Sold." My father's deep voice echoes through the silence.

My stomach tightens, and I tip my chin up as I gaze down at him. I didn't realize he had moved back to his seat. Front and center—just the way he likes it. His mouth twists into a sadistic grin as if he's finally reaching a goal—tying up a loose end that's taken too long to unravel on its own.

Rage floods my system, overriding what good sense I have left. I've already been sold. What does it matter if they kill me now?

I launch my body off the stage and crash into him. My hands find his neck as the room explodes. Men scramble away as I let out a guttural scream. No one jumps to interfere. They're more concerned with spilling their drinks than the man whose eyes are bulging. I'm not strong enough to actually kill him, but I can try. I wish I would have kept the heel to gouge out his eyes. He doesn't deserve to have them.

The temporary shock wears off and he rips my hands away. As he tosses me to the ground, I cry out again, this time in pain. Anders looms over me, baring his teeth.

"Do it," I hiss.

He grins that same smile from before, and tears fill my eyes. He'll never kill me. Hands paw at me and I'm dragged away. One thought echoes through my mind as the darkness overtakes me.

I failed.

FIFTEEN

Dante

I tip my head back, trying to wrap my mind around the concept Raven is attempting to explain. She's not making any sense. It could be because she's drunk, but I suspect it's more the fact she doesn't know what to do. She's always been so sure of herself—confident in a way I never felt as a leader.

Without many members of the Vipers left, I'm not exactly in a position to judge. Blaze, my third in command, took the remaining men to investigate our missing supplies. I doubt he'll have any luck. They've been gone for weeks now with no word.

"But if we go *down*…Can you imagine their faces when we pop up from the pipes?" Raven says, wide eyes staring at Alex.

His lips twitch and he glances away. "I'm going to say they'd be able to smell us coming. But it's a good option to put on the list."

I don't know how he was able to say any of that shit without cracking a smile. He's the only one still entertaining Raven's wild plans for sneaking into the Guild's headquarters. A hand lands on my arm, and I whip my head up.

Mac stares down at me, her eyes searching mine. She sighs and walks off to sit next to Helms. She's been doing shit like that more often than not these days. I don't know why she doesn't just spit out whatever is eating at her.

"Raines," Shane calls from the front of the restaurant, and I spin.

He jerks his head toward the door, then disappears into the night. Heaving out a sigh, I follow him. No one notices. They're all working on their individual plans for dismantling the Guild. Alex has been sneaking glances at me from the corner of his eye for the last hour. I'm pretty sure he's still stuck on dealing with the Oracle labs. I'm waiting for him to ambush me and convince Shane it needs to be done.

"What's wrong?" I ask as soon as I step through.

Shane leans against the building and cracks his neck. "Fuck, I wish I smoked."

"What kind of smoking?" I ask, leaning next to him, and he raises an eyebrow. "Weed would calm you down at least."

"Neither one of us has access to that shit anymore, unfortunately." He crosses his arms. "I get you want to be in charge, and I won't railroad you..."

"This you talking or Mac?"

"Neither. Though I'm pretty sure Mac talked to Sam and then Sam talked to me, so take that for what it is. We both know you can't do all this shit on your own, but I'm not going to say that in front of everyone. We're all used to being in charge. It's too easy to get carried away when we're in a pissing contest with one another."

"And you think excluding Byrns and Helms is going to help?" I snort, shaking my head. "Pulling this type of move with Byrns didn't work, so why do you think we'll breeze through it now?"

"What the fuck are you talking about?" He swings to face me, confusion stamped across his face.

"You pushed Byrns out, refusing to include him, and it almost cost you Synd. You sure you want to do this shit again?"

Mac told me all about the issues they had before I called. She wasn't very impressed with how Shane acted, but there was a hint of shame in her tone. I suspect it had something to do with Nemesis. Mac hasn't talked about it a lot, but I've noticed how she and Sam hover around Lacey now.

Shane scowls, resuming his place on the wall. "I'm not pushing anyone out. I'm just saying maybe let the rest of us figure some of these things out. Share a little more about what the Guild is like on the inside. You've given us barely anything."

"What the hell you think is happening in there?" I throw my thumb over my shoulder. "And I didn't expect you to be chomping at the bit to tell you about my love life."

I've tried to ignore the terror that floods me every time I think about Aelia. There's nothing I can do for her right now, and worrying about her won't help. Locking up my feelings for her in a box until I'm lying in my bed as the sun slowly rises is the best I can do.

"You're not the only one scared for the people we care about, Dante. Just remember, we're on the same side," he murmurs before pushing from the wall and disappearing through the door.

I flex my fingers, smothering the urge to put my fist through the brick behind me. Breaking my hand right now wouldn't be a good idea, but the desire is there, if only to relieve the tension riding me. Ren materializes from the dark, tablet tucked under his arm, and a small vial of liquid flashing in his hand.

"Raines." He nods, slipping the bottle in his pocket. "We need to discuss whether Jenkins ever leaves the embassy."

"Not that I know of. Others do, but he's pretty heavy-handed when it comes to the day-to-day operations. You won't be able to snipe him or something."

"Barring the fact I don't know how to snipe, that's not why I asked. If we could set up a meeting between someone he hasn't encountered before—"

I hold up my hand. "He doesn't meet with people he hasn't vetted. He doesn't dine with anyone. He barely leaves his office unless it's to engage a bit. And I doubt anyone will be volunteering to put themselves into that situation."

"Who would you pick to try to get close to him in that way?"

My mouth drops open, then snaps shut. For a minute, I forgot who I was talking to. Ren wouldn't put any of the women with us in danger like that, no matter what their opinions on it were. He merely needs an explanation. He'll file away the information until he can use it or discard it.

"Sam. Her and Aelia could pass for sisters. And Jenkins is obsessed with Aelia for some reason. I don't know if it's because she's worked for him for so long and he's curious to see what will make her break or if it's a game for him. I doubt it's because he's attracted to her. He's more concerned with how much he can hurt them." I swallow down the bile creeping up my throat.

Ren nods, staring over my shoulder at nothing. "You say they look like sisters? Could Sam perhaps be a diversion?"

"Doubt it. The women are brought to the Pit and sorted. I don't know how often Jenkins picks women or whether he's alerted when someone new comes in. It's pretty unlikely. The only way you'd be able to get Sam in front of him would be to stage her as a patron." His eyebrow pops up, and I shake my head.

"I believe we should keep that information to ourselves for now. Samantha will most likely try to exploit it." Ren's jaw twitches. The Kings trust Sam to take care of herself, but that doesn't mean they like her taking risks.

The others spill from the restaurant and gather in small groups. Jag scowls as he drags Raven back to Viper headquarters to sleep off her drunkenness. I'll feel better having him stay behind with Avery, Lacey, and Raven. As long as Avery stays put, he'll be able to keep them safe.

Sam hugs Mac before skipping down one of the alleys. I have no idea what she's doing most of the time, but Mac said to trust her, so I leave her be. Shane scowls before rushing after her. Sam's giggle echoes through the night, then dies away.

Mason steps next to me as Ren wanders off to join Alex. "Ren and Alex are going to check out the rest of the labs. Shane convinced Sam to stake out some of the clubs, see if they could waylay someone. Helms and Mac are making sure they haven't started up the dogfights again."

"I was in the meeting, Byrns. In fact, I was the one who handed out the assignments."

"Except you didn't say what we'll be doing." He levels me with a stare. "Unless you're planning on skipping off into the fucking night to play vigilante."

"Seeing as how I'm not the Wraith, no. I don't plan on doing that. We're going to visit an old friend."

I lead him to the SUV that's been waiting at the end of the block for the last half hour. My reliable driver sits behind the wheel, and I breathe a sigh of relief. I keep expecting him to turn on us or skip town, but it hasn't happened yet. We climb into the back and head toward the south side of the city. It didn't take me long to find the address.

"Who's this friend of yours?" Mason asks as he fiddles with his phone, probably texting Lacey.

"He's the one who got me into the Guild," I say, smirking when his head whips around. "Friend may be a misnomer. Last time we saw each other, I tried to break his kneecaps. Though he had that coming by trying to take Aelia from me."

I sober, remembering what happened after that incident. Aelia's bruised face floats in my mind's eye and I shake the image away.

"You're not going to see if he can get you back in, right? They'll kill you."

"I'm well aware. If I was going to test the waters, I would have done that before you guys showed up. Too much time has passed now to pretend I was away on business. Plus, I can't explain Avery's disappearance."

I check my gun at my waist. After a year without carrying one, I'm still getting used to having a weapon with me again. "We're not going to talk to Byron. We're just going to case his place. If I can use him in some way, I'd like to know what type of security he has."

He glances behind us, then smirks as he faces me. "If we're not going to take him out, why is there a shitload of bombs in the trunk?"

"One can never be too prepared, Byrns."

"Is he high enough up they'll care?"

Digging my nails into my legs, I remind myself I can't keep doing shit alone. No matter how much it annoys me when everyone asks questions.

"Not unless his status has changed in the last three months. I used him once, though, so we might be able to use him again. We need options beyond what we're doing. Blowing shit up and disrupting their capital is all well and good, but it won't stop them from setting up shop somewhere else."

"You still care about that?" he murmurs, staring out the window.

"Why the fuck would you ask me that?" I snarl.

"Settle down, Raines. I wasn't insulting you. I just know how it gets. There's a lot of shit going on, your woman is still there, and you don't know what the future is gonna look like. I wouldn't blame you if your only goal was to get her back and disappear."

"You speaking from experience?" I spit out, curling my hands into fists.

"Yes. Which is exactly why you know it's a valid question. Others might blame you for being selfish, but our world encourages it. What we're doing in Synd—working together—it's not done. No one outside of our world would understand what the hell we're doing. We're supposed to be fixated on our own families, our territories, our little slice of the city. We saw what that type of thinking did to our fathers. They practically burned it all to the ground rather than lean on each other."

We sit in silence as the dark houses pass by. The residents of Rima are tucked away in their beds, safe and sound without a care in the world. They don't realize a mafia boss and an MC president are driving by. Or that a heinous organization is stealing people from the streets and selling them. Their lives are largely unaffected by everything in our world. It seems strange to imagine them going about their normal lives. I wonder who I'd be if I hadn't grown up in a club, surrounded by the mafia and drugs and death. If my life wasn't dictated by where my loyalty lay, who would I be?

I shake my head, refusing to think about the what ifs. I can't even fathom what their lives are like, so what's the point of dreaming about it? I wouldn't have my family. I wouldn't have my club. I never would have met Aelia. I'd never give any of it up for a normal, boring life. My heart clenches in my chest, the lies clinging to me, dragging me down.

I'd give up everything for her.

SIXTEEN

Aelia

I didn't think I'd be back in this fucking cell. Yet here I am, in this cold, damp prison. I ripped some of my wounds open. My robe sticks to my back every time I move. I'm hoping it's sweat and not blood, but that's wishful thinking. Actually, Grant was gentler than I thought he'd be. I'd love to believe he's scared of me after what I did to Molly. In reality, I think it's because I'm someone else's property now.

He didn't even bother to lock the cage. Molly's body is gone, but the blood splatter remains. I can't seem to pull my eyes away from the dark stains. The knowledge that I put them there eats away at what little sanity I have left.

Dante warned me. He told me killing a person, even someone who deserved it, wasn't easy. I didn't believe him. I thought since I'd seen others shot or stabbed or both, I'd be able to handle it. With how out of it I am, I'm learning the hard way, though I can't bring myself to regret it.

Raised voices outside the cracked door have me rolling my head around. It's like the bones in my neck have vanished, leaving me bobbing around in a sea of indifference. The rage that consumed me when I attacked my father flowed out of me as Grant dragged me away, his grip tight around my upper arm.

"I don't know what you're playing at, Drake, but I'm not paying full price for a subpar product. You told me she'd be just as Cruz left her.

Then you parade her around as if she's exactly what I ordered. But she's not. The only reason you were able to sell her at all was because I was there. No one else would have touched her. Unless she attacked you *before* the bidding." The man's voice is younger than I expected—closer to my age. Familiarity wraps itself around my mind, whispering in my ear to remember.

I swallow hard as dirty blond hair comes into view, followed by the broad shoulders of someone I'd hoped to never see again. Byron hasn't changed in the few months since we last saw each other. I shouldn't be surprised by that, but I am.

I'm used to the people in the Pit who age years within a few months. It took a while for Jenkins to figure out why their hair was greying so quickly. That's about the time he brought in someone to dye the strands to whatever the clients desired. Such a high-scale operation for something so despicable.

The lop-sided smile he shoots me drips in condescension. I'm sure he believes he's hiding his cruelty, but I've learned to spot these types of men. Reading people is probably the only thing I've learned in here that would translate to the outside world. Not that I'll be able to execute that particular skill.

"Time to go, doll," he says jovially.

He doesn't open the door, just stands there and grins at me. His eyes rake over my body, and I wrap my arms around my waist. When he licks his lips, my body tenses, the trembling from before returning in full force.

My thoughts spiral as the metal screeches when he opens the cage. The sound echoes through my mind, over and over and over. My vision blurs, distorting his wide frame. There are no tears as shadows dance around the room, and I gasp when his hand grabs my arm.

"Don't be like that. We're going to have so much fun together," he whispers, his hot breath rushing into my ear.

I shiver as I gag, and he chuckles. Bastard probably thinks he's turning me on instead of sending me into a full-blown meltdown. He pulls me upright, and I sway as the blood rushes from my head. Byron brows pulling low as he scans my body again. For some reason, it's different this time, almost like he's assessing me. I tucked the information away, wondering if he'd let me go with just a little pressure.

He shakes his head, huffing before his hand trails down my arm and his fingers grip mine. As he tugs me from the cell, I glance away from the blood splattered across the concrete. I doubt they'll clean it up. They probably don't even use this area for anything other than the problems they need to deal with later.

"We're not going out the front door. Wouldn't want anyone else seeing you like this, now would we?" He grins over his shoulder and an idea wiggles its way through my mind.

What if he's helping Dante? What if he's getting me out?

Once we reach the top of the stairs, the area becomes familiar. Turn right and we'll eventually come to the stairs that will take us to the upper floors—to the main sections of the Guild. Turn left and we'll come to the Pit. I'm confused when he turns right, tugging me behind him. I stumble, and my toe scrapes across the concrete. A burning sensation rolls across my foot, and I hiss.

Byron stops, then spins as he crouches. His touch is gentle as his finger brushes over the angry red mark that still smarts. I catch the edge of a scowl as he stands, then gathers the ends of the sash and ties it in front of me before grabbing my hand again.

"They shouldn't have touched you. We'll get you cleaned up when we get home," Byron mutters as we continue down the dark hallway.

The closer we come to the stairs, the more noise filter through. Random thuds of a bass, the occasional scream, and the rush of water through the pipes hanging overhead overwhelm me after so much silence. I grip the edges of the robe in a failing attempt to ward off the chill as well as any prying eyes that might happen by. No one would give me a second glance—not in this place. I cough as bile climbs up my throat.

The stairs loom ahead, and I tip my chin up. My strength may have abandoned me long ago, but I'm getting out. Even if Byron isn't in league with Dante, I'm getting out. It'll be different than the alley with Dante. I'll be free. I'll feel the wind against my cheek again. Maybe I'll even get to dance under the rays of the sun after so long spent locked away in the dark. All the possibilities swirl through my mind. All the things I thought were unattainable are right there within my grasp. I just have to reach out and seize it—even if it is only for a moment.

At the last second before we reach the stairs, Byron veers to the left, taking us further into the dark. A door swings outward as he pushes through and the night slams into me, overwhelming my senses. Between one blink and the next, tears streak down my face, and I bite my cheek. The door to a black SUV pops open and my moment is gone as Byron ushers me inside. The click of the lock when he crawls in after me sends a shockwave through my system.

He smiles, then faces forward as we pull from the shadows. Clamping my lips shut, I hold back the questions building up in my mind. I don't know if he can be trusted. I need the wariness I've held all these years. Buildings flash by too quickly to take in. Not that I'd know where we are, anyway. The last time I was in a vehicle was with Dante, and I was close to losing it then. I wasn't enjoying the scenery.

I turn my head, trying to keep an eye on both where we're going as well as Byron. His hand rests between us, bridging the gap as if he's subtly throwing me a lifeline in case I need it.

I don't. Even if I did, I wouldn't take it from him. Dante's arms are the only ones I'll tumble into. His strength is the only one I'll borrow from. Tucking my trembling hands in my lap, I lean away from him.

The moon hangs overhead as we pull up to a moderately sized house. At least I think it's average. My idea of a house is unusually skewed by how I grew up. Throw in my years in the Guild and I have no concept of what normal is. There are only three floors as far as I can tell.

Byron opens my door and I jerk back. I didn't realize he'd gotten out, I was so intent on studying the grounds. If I need to run, there won't be many places to hide. Large swaths of lawn separate one property from the next. Trees ring the property several hundred yards away, blocking the view. Even if I disappeared between the trunks, I wouldn't know if there was another house to run to. Couple that with the fact I have no idea if they'd help me, and my hope dwindles again.

"Come on, doll. Let's get you inside. Then we can clean you up." His lip twists the slightest bit when his eyes sweep over my face.

He holds his hand out as if he's a gentleman escorting me to a fancy gala instead of locking me in his house. I'm still not decided on whether he's someone I can trust. He hasn't done anything to make me think he's going to act like he has the previous times we've been in the same room. Then again, that could have been a front just like Dante's.

Between my mind attempting to slot everything into place and my body slowly shutting down from exhaustion, I practically fall from the car. Byron catches me before I hit the ground, swinging me into his arms, and I cringe. My skin crawls, though he isn't doing anything wrong.

He sets me on my feet when we step through the door. I should have run as soon as the car stopped. I should have bolted even if I wouldn't have gotten very far. I spin, intent on rectifying my mistake, but he blocks the way, cutting off my way to freedom.

"I'll show you where you'll be staying, doll." His hand settles on my lower back, deftly pivoting me before guiding me further into the dark house.

He ushers me down a hallway, then another, passing several closed doors. Stairs march up into the shadows and another shiver skitters down my spine. A left turn and we finally enter an open space. The moonlight filtering through the curtains isn't enough to do more than give the vague idea of furniture scattered around what I assume is a living room.

His hand folds over mine, tugging me after him. I expect him to turn on a lamp, but he navigates around obstacles easily until he reaches the far corner next to an ornate fireplace.

All it takes is a press of a disguised button and a hidden door popping open to send me into a spiral. I stumble back, tearing my fingers from his. I trip over a table in my haste to escape the looming darkness and fall on my ass.

They're living things, those shadows. They sit at the entrance, loath to breach the invisible barrier between the living world and the abyss buried beneath the floorboards. Once I pass over that line, I'll cease to exist—every bit of my being eaten away by the beast of nothingness within.

Byron's form floats over me, his face covered in shadows with only his black eyes shining in the glimmer of moonlight.

"Don't be like that, doll. Gotta keep you safe, just like Dante."

He reaches down and I shriek. My head hits another table as I scuttle away from him. No way am I going down there. I didn't go through all that just to be locked away again. I flip to my hands and knees before pushing to my feet. Byron curses as I attempt to flee, hitting every piece of furniture along the way.

I'm not even halfway to the hallway when his arm slides around my waist and he picks me off my feet. I kick and squirm, but he never loosens his hold. He's snarling something I can't make out over my wailing. Tears crash down my face as my throat closes and I dissolve into a coughing fit. My breath saws in and out of my lungs while the surge of adrenaline ebbs from my body.

The darkness swallows me whole, and I let out an ear-piercing scream. It's as if we're swimming through a sea of oil. Not oil—blood. It coats my flesh and I frantically swipe at my skin. I can't see it, but it's there, running down my body in rivulets while Byron carries me down the stairs. Lights flicker on once we reach the bottom, and I gag as I take in the space he's created. It's a replica of the VIP rooms at the Guild headquarters.

My eyes dart from the bed to the false window next to it. A chair sits underneath the painting of a bright blue sky framed in wood, the same rings attached to the arms. Doors to the left hang open, revealing a white tiled bathroom and a nearly empty closet. Dresses take up one wall, the sequins glittering in the light. Nothing could have prepared me for this.

My feet hit the ground, and he eases away from me. I spin slowly, attempting to wrap my head around what I'm seeing. Everything is the same, down to the stain of blood on the carpet. I left it there after Grant locked me in the room. How did Byron know? Did he go in after Dante fled and I was taken? Did he catalog everything just to copy it here?

"Why?" I breathe, not realizing I asked out loud until Byron smiles.

He glances around the room, surveying his work. "For you, doll. Transitioning can be difficult. Figured you'd want a place that was familiar. Somewhere you could make new memories."

I don't know what to say or how to take what he's done. Nothing about what he's stating is particularly nefarious. Something about his actions turns my stomach, though. But he keeps saying "we" as if there's someone else working with him. I assumed it was Dante, but putting me in the basement, locking the car doors, nothing screams that I'm safe.

"You know where the bathroom is. And the closet." He gestures to the rooms, then runs his fingers through his hair. "I'm going to get dinner. I'm sure you're hungry."

With that he leaves, closing the door at the top of the stairs behind him. I don't bother to run up there and see if it's locked. I assume it is. If he thinks I'm going to shower, he's out of his fucking mind. Instead, I use the time to rinse off the blood from the wounds that I can reach.

The bandages Nova applied have almost fallen off, the tape no longer sticking to my skin. Flecks of red pepper my flesh, and I resist the urge to gouge my nails in to scrape them away. I use the pristine washcloth, leaving the pink mess in the sink. Of course there's no sweatpants in the closet, but there is one dress a little looser than the rest. It'll keep the fabric away from the many cuts I have.

And then I wait. There's no clock, just like the other prisons I've been in, so I have no idea how much time has passed when the door at the top of the stairs swings open. I stand as he clomps down them, making a racket the whole way. I doubt it's for my benefit.

A scowl turns his mouth, but he wipes it away. He waves me up, then pivots to clomp upward once more. I follow him slowly, keeping a healthy distance between us.

He's already seated on the couch when I emerge, soft lamps casting light around the room. He pats the space next to him, but my feet refuse to move. I've left a piece of my soul behind with every step I've taken. Longing stirs in my gut to turn around and gather up the pieces. If I can shove them back inside me, perhaps one day I'll be whole.

He sighs, shaking his head. "It doesn't have to be like this, doll. I can take care of you. Not like he did. I'm sure he promised you all sorts of things, but…" He sighs again, a pained expression on his face. "He left you behind. What kind of man does that?"

He stares at me, eyes imploring me to understand. I tip my chin up as I fold my arms over my chest. The fabric pulls, slicing across the wounds on my back. I use the ache to center my thoughts and remind me what to say. Dante and I prepared for this eventuality. I'm sure he didn't think Byron would be the one I'd be protecting him from, but here we are.

"I was his bit, Mr. Michaels. Nothing more. Everything you saw on my end was what was expected of me in that role." The words burn as they roll off my tongue. Every lie lodges in my heart, shattering it a little bit more.

"If you were acting, then I'd say you pursued the wrong profession, doll." He chuckles and rubs his hands along his light grey slacks.

I narrow my eyes. He must be joking. There's no way he's delusional enough to think we're with the Guild by choice, much less getting paid. Byron may have a more jovial disposition than the other members, but he can't seriously assume I'd stay after they beat, starved, and abused me. After what I'm sure he witnessed, he can't truly believe there was any form of consent within those walls.

He pushes to his feet, and I lean back as he approaches me. I flinch when he lifts his hand to tuck a strand of hair behind my ear. The scent of his overpowering cologne invades my nostrils and I hold my breath.

"We could be good together. You just have to be a good girl and listen." His fingers brush down my bare arm, and my knees lock up.

My pulse races as a voice in my head screams at me to move. Yet I don't. A roaring fills my ears and drowns out the words he's whispering. His hand continues his journey along my skin and nausea rolls through me in waves. Once it crashes over me, I'm afraid I'll be sucked under and pulled deeper into the riptide he's creating with just one finger.

My hearing switches back on as he steps in my eyeline. His smile turns sinister, probably taking my silence as consent. I swallow hard and my eyes dart away from him. He reaches for me, and I jolt away.

One step back. That's all it takes for his face to morph, the grin dropping away and frustration filling his eyes. I shake my head, terrified of opening my mouth. I have no idea what will come out.

"You'll fuck him but not me?" he snaps, crowding into my space.

My knees bump into something hard—probably an end table. Wrapping my arms around my waist, I dig my fingers into my skin. I glance to the side, searching for an escape route. I'd have to weave through the random pieces of furniture to get out through the front door or a window. Neither option is feasible. Not with the way he's tracking my movements.

He steps into me again, pressing his body into mine, and a choked sob leaves me. He snarls, sweeping away only to pivot to face me again. At least there's some space between us now. It's not enough.

"You should be grateful. I got you out of there." He jabs his finger in my face and my eyes cross as I focus on it. "The least you can do is pay me back. You fucking owe me, stupid bitch."

"I just want to go," I whisper, my voice wavering. "Please…let me go."

I hate that I have to beg. I hate that I can't just leave. I hate that my entire life has been controlled by others. Every decision has been made for me. All I want is to decide something for myself. My world has never afforded me that luxury. Even with Dante, I never had a choice. Our circumstances established where we would go and what we would do. My heart made the other choices for me. I really didn't stand a chance.

His hand cuts through the air, his frustration clear. "I deserve this. You denied me before and I understood why. But you need to see reason."

I shake my head again, stumbling around the table. The last thing I want to do is fall into the fireplace behind me. Flames within the grate flare as if they're mocking me—begging me to trip into them. I glance at them as they lick at the ash-laden bricks.

The distraction doesn't last long as Byron's heavy footfalls echo behind me. Whipping my head forward, I gasp, then scramble to the side. His foot hits mine and I crash to the ground.

His body smashes into the table, and he groans as it collapses. My foot gets caught underneath him until he pushes to his feet. I crawl away, yelping when he grabs my ankle. He yanks me toward him with a roar.

Sobbing, I kick at his face. He yells at me to stop, but I struggle harder. My heel connects with something hard, and it crunches under the force. A grunt leaves him and warm blood splashes across my calves. I shudder, then do it again and he lurches to his feet.

Flipping on my back, I suck in a deep breath. I freeze as he looms over me, a feral look stamped across his face. He leans down, hands outstretched, and I kick him in the balls. If I wasn't terrified, I'd probably find the scene comical when his eyes bulge and he clutches his junk. He moans through gritted teeth, and I lash out one last time. He drops to his knees in slow motion, and a manic bubble of laughter escapes me.

Forcing my body to move, I scramble upright, swaying when I reach my feet. I scan the space for anything to defend myself. I should run, but I'd rather end this now before he's able to carry me back downstairs.

Adrenaline is the only thing keeping me standing and I know I won't last much longer. My eyes fall on an ugly vase resting on another table running the length of the couch, and I wrap my hand around the neck.

Swinging around, I smash it over his head, and he tips slowly to the side as his eyes roll back in his skull. I stutter back, my body vibrating with the need to flee. Making sure he's passed out is more important to my survival. I huff out an incredulous laugh as his temple collides with the edge of the fireplace. Blood splatters across the brick, the small crimson specks standing out against the white.

He doesn't move. And neither do I.

SEVENTEEN

Dante

"Change of plans. We need to stop by the club Shane and Sam went to," Mason murmurs as he stares at his phone.

He knocks on the glass separating us from the driver and gives him the new address before I can question him. I don't know who told the man behind the wheel we needed a bullet-proof vehicle with a partition, but my money's on Lacey. She has a tendency to anticipate our needs. I didn't question the change since the driver was the same one that's been carting me around for over a year.

"Did something happen?" I ask, slapping my phone against my leg.

Something is driving me to get to Byron's place, but I can't put my finger on it. I haven't seen him for months. There's no reason to rush since we have all night. Yet I can't help the irritation at the detour. We make our way toward the city lights, and I bite my tongue.

"King said we needed to meet someone."

I sigh, tipping my head back. "We don't exactly have the time to fuck with some random asshole King picked up."

Mason's head whips to me, brows pulled low. "Shane wouldn't fuck around on Sam. Plus, she's there."

"What the fuck," I breathe. "I wasn't...we don't have all night to do their job as well as ours, Byrns."

"Because we have so much planned. Casing out a house isn't exactly hard or time-consuming. We'll be fine."

We pull onto club row, which isn't nearly as fancy as Synd's. Most of the buildings are run down and sorely in need of more security. One man owns most of them and he's done a piss-poor job at the upkeep. I had plans to exert some of the Vipers' authority to take over. I never got the chance.

Maybe if we take out the Guild, I'll be able to revisit all the ways I wanted to help Rima. Unless Aelia doesn't want to live here. We never talked about the future. She never thought we'd have one.

"Snap the fuck out of it, Raines. Get your shit together and put your goddamn mask on," Byrns snarls before shoving from the car.

I didn't even notice us pulling into the alley, much less that we stopped. Shaking my head, I follow him.

"What's up?" Sam's voice floats from the shadows, and I glance around for her. "Dude. Look up."

She's perched on the edge of a windowsill, eyes fixed further into the alley. Her gaze darts to me, then back to where I'm sure Mason disappeared.

"There a reason you're up there and not down here?" I'm not pressed on joining them either.

She sniffs, then stares at her phone. I doubt it's even on. "I got kicked out for being 'unsupportive.' Whatever the fuck that means."

"Uh, you want to fill me in on what's going on? Or maybe we should just switch and you come with me and your brother can help Shane."

Her eyebrow pops up before she swings down. I step back, though she lands far enough away. Leaning against the SUV, I feign nonchalance at the fact she just dropped fifteen feet without even stumbling. She smirks, making me scowl.

She tips her head back, staring at the thin strip of sky. "You ever think this will never end?"

"What do you mean?"

"Just feels like one damn thing after another. Like it will never end. Once the Guild is taken care of, I'd really like a break. I wouldn't go back to before since it fucking sucked, but sometimes I wish we didn't have to go through all the shit to find happiness," she says.

"Wouldn't know. I wasn't really a part of any of the things you guys were going through." I keep to myself the fact that I haven't found happiness. I love Aelia, but that's not the same thing as being happy.

She nods and her bottom lip slips between her teeth. I glance away, not wanting her to call me out on shit. Sam's perceptive, though she usually doesn't say anything. I can tell in the way she holds herself when she wants to call someone out on their shit but knows it won't make a difference.

"You know Roman?" she asks after a few minutes.

"No. Mason already asked me. So did Helms. I didn't hang out with you guys when we were kids. Why?"

She huffs, crossing her arms. "Everyone seems to think we should trust him. Or at least trust him enough to keep Synd from falling into disrepair. I'm not so sure. I keep getting this feeling in my gut that something bad is coming. Can't figure out if it'll happen there or here."

I tuck my chin to my chest, trying to place why the name Roman feels familiar. It's more than the fact he grew up in Synd. I feel like I've heard his name recently.

"What's his last name?" I cross my arms, mirroring her stance.

Sam tilts her head and narrows her eyes at me before opening her mouth. She snaps it shut when Shane calls from deeper in the alley for her. Shooting me an apologetic smile, she hustles toward him, leaving me to follow or not. I suppose this isn't the time to have this conversation, anyway. We have bigger things to worry about other than who Roman is to me.

"Raines! Get your ass over here and help. We need to get her back to Raven," Byrns calls, and I launch into action.

Raven's scattered her gang around the city, using them mostly for surveillance. She sent them out in pairs to make sure none of them go missing like Nova did. Hope blooms in my chest, wondering if it's the missing woman. It dies just as quickly when I remember Aelia said no one escapes the Guild. If Nova really did get captured by them, there's no way they found her in the back of a dank alley.

Shane emerges from the darkness carrying a woman in her twenties with lank, dark hair. Dried blood coats half of her face and her eyes are closed. She certainly looks like she's been held captive. I swallow down the bile, wondering how much life is left in her eyes.

"Is her hair dyed?" I ask, then clear my throat when the words stick.

"Seriously? She's fucking unconscious and *that's* the question you ask?" Byrns spits out and his hands curl into fists.

I just stare at Shane, never taking my eyes from his. Sam rushes to the woman's side and slides the strands through her fingers. Byrns throws up his hands, then pulls out his phone and turns on the flashlight. I don't need Sam's confirmation, but she turns to me and nods.

"Bring her to headquarters. Set her up in one of the prospect's rooms and tell Raven." Shane moves around me, but I hold up my hand. "Actually, call Avery. Raven's in no condition to help her. Avery...she's been there before."

"You really think she was there?" Byrns asks as he slides next to me, tracking Sam and Shane as they move toward their vehicle.

"Yeah. I do. They dye their hair, wax their bodies…"

"You think she ran into your woman?"

I don't have an answer. The likelihood of them crossing paths would have been high before. Now? I have no idea. With the woman's condition, I almost hope they didn't. If Aelia is half as bad as the woman looked, with bruises covering most of her exposed skin…rage flows through me and I stalk to the SUV.

If they've touched a single hair on Aelia's head, I'll tear them apart bit by bit, then make them watch as I burn their world to the ground. Then and only then will I step aside for Aelia to decide their fate.

"Get in the car, Byrns. We have some bombs to explode."

My palms are itchy. Not the little annoyance that goes away with a quick scratch. No, this one is all encompassing. The sensation takes over, consuming my every thought no matter how much I try to ignore it. I scrub my palms against my jeans, hoping the denim will ease the feeling of ants burrowing into my skin. It doesn't help.

"Would you knock it the fuck off?" Mason growls.

He's still pissed we didn't cancel the trip to Byron's. Why he wanted to go back with them is beyond me, but I couldn't. My hands wouldn't let me. Something is coming and it isn't good. Some people get gut feelings—I get itchy palms.

I had them when Maddox accidentally shot Mac with a BB gun when I was ten. I suspected it wasn't an accident, yet Mac defended him so fiercely I dropped it. The pain kept me up for three nights before the attempted coup in Synd over ten years ago. No one believed me, not even Helms, when I told him we needed to prepare Reaper territory. It happened again when I decided to infiltrate the Guild.

"Something's wrong," I mutter as I dig my nails into a particularly sore spot.

"No shit, Sherlock. We're in the middle of a goddamn war zone, fighting a battle no one else knows about—not even the opposing side. We could all fucking die. Of course something's wrong."

I grind my teeth instead of responding. I didn't expect him to magically put two and two together, but his sarcasm is a bit much. Aelia would listen. She'd notice the tension in the air, the strain in my body. She did it when Anders showed up. That knowing feeling welled up, telling her something was coming. I wish she was here. The ache in my chest pulses, but it doesn't distract me from the incessant itching of my palms.

Mason exhales sharply, pulling me from my thoughts. "Why are we still doing this? Shouldn't we be going back with that woman? If she did escape from the Guild, she'll have more information than we'll gather from watching some asshole's house for an hour."

"She won't wake up tonight. And even if she does, she'll be in no condition to talk to us. She's malnourished, dehydrated, and was clearly abused. The last thing she needs is a bunch of strange men looming over her as they grill her for info. She deserves rest. In the meantime, we can do what we planned."

Concern flashes across his face before he turns to gaze out the window at the houses slowly giving way to trees. Byron lives on twenty acres outside the city limits. The farther we travel, the larger the houses become. Eventually, the mansions will take over, their massive, manicured lawns hidden among groves of dense forest.

I liked living on the edge of Synd with the trees butting up against Reaper territory. Out here there's too much space and nowhere to run. Country living is a contradiction I never could wrap my mind around.

"Fire," Mason says, a warning in his tone.

Rolling down the window, I pull in a deep breath. Smoke tints the air even though we're still a mile away from the nearest house. Orange dances in the dark sky and my hands stop itching. Here it is—the reason I've felt like there's a live wire attached to my senses the entire night. I can only hope Byron got caught in the blaze.

Mason rolls his own window down, trying to get a clearer view through the trees. "You don't think the Guild did it, do you?"

"Don't see why they would," I mutter.

"He did bring you into the Guild. They have to be salty about that. Maybe they took it out on him."

I nod, even though I don't agree. I tap on the glass and the partition disappears. "Cut the lights. Then go to the rendezvous point."

"Are we meeting someone else?" Mason asks, and I meet his wide eyes.

"No. We're taking a service road to a specific spot. Figured it was the easiest way to explain it when I texted him." I gesture to the driver since I still don't know his name. "No one will be able to see us unless they take the road, which is unlikely. We'll have a bit of a trek, though, before we'll be able to see what's going on."

The next couple minutes are spent in silence as we make our way down a bumpy road. The closer we get, the thicker the smoke becomes, and we roll up the windows. Rummaging through a bag from the back, I pull out two bandanas and we tie them around our faces. It's the best we can do in these circumstances. Mason checks his gun before pushing from the vehicle, and I follow.

Heat billows through the trees and I wonder if we'll be able to get close enough to spot anything. I doubt Byron is home. Most likely he's holed up at headquarters, enjoying his latest victim. Mason points to the right and we swing that way, dodging trunks and fallen logs as we go.

Finally, the half-burnt house comes into view. Flames lick at every available surface, the crackling the only sound for miles. No sirens or men running around attempting to curb the blaze. We work our way around until the front of the three-story comes into view, and Mason shoots me a look. I nod, just as worried about the lack of activity.

It's then that I see the lone shadow outlined by the flames, long hair whipping around. My breath catches as I take in the lithe figure. My feet move before I register what I'm doing. Byrns tackles me from behind, wrestling me to the ground. His hand slaps over my mouth before I can scream her name.

"Don't. We don't know what's going on. She could be bait," Byrns hisses, then groans when I drive my elbow into his stomach.

I struggle all while keeping my eyes trained on her. She doesn't move, but the edges of her frame waver. Headlights cut across her form, and she turns. We're too far away to make out her features, but it doesn't matter.

I see her face every time I close my eyes. Her image is stamped on my mind, consuming every waking minute no matter how much I attempt to focus on the shit I'm doing. It's all for her. To get her back. To save her. To set her free.

"Dante," Mason's voice cuts through the roaring in my ears. "Who is that?"

My eyes dart to the dark SUV stopped a dozen feet from Aelia. A man's broad frame emerges from the open door, and I squint into the shadows. I shake my head, confusion swirling through me. Could it be Byron coming home? Maybe it's the person who set the blaze, checking to make sure there are no witnesses left behind. They step closer to Aelia and the headlights illuminate their face.

"Jenkins. Nolan fucking Jenkins," I spit out, renewing my efforts to get away from Byrns. He pins my arms and locks his legs around mine.

"More," he hisses, and more headlights round the corner of the house.

Jenkins brought reinforcements. There's no way we'd be able to fight them all off. Even if we had the others with us, we'd be overpowered within minutes. Aelia would be caught in the crossfire, people would die, and it would accomplish nothing. I can't just let her go, though. I have to fight for her. I failed her before. I can't do it again.

Aelia takes a step toward Jenkins, then another. The lights flash off something in her hand. I roll to throw Byrns off, but he keeps hold. We struggle until finally I break free. He grabs my ankle as I stumble to my feet, and I crash into a tree trunk. My palms burn as they connect with the bark and a snarl rips out of me.

Jenkins presents the way for Aelia, ushering her closer to the open door. If he gets her inside…

"Angel," I bellow, the wind carrying my voice to her.

Her head whips toward me, and I open my mouth to scream for her to run. The butt of a gun hits my temple and I sway, then drop to my knees. As my vision darkens, I watch as she climbs into the SUV. The flames flickering across the night sky are the last thing I see before the world goes dark.

Eighteen

Aelia

"You'll be happy to know Anders is gone," Jenkins says as we pull into an underground parking garage at the Guild I never knew existed. "I assume back to Synd since he's so obsessed. Perhaps someone will take him out for us."

I nod as I clutch the knife I took from Byron's kitchen before I set his house on fire. I should have left then, but I needed to make sure he didn't make it out alive. At least I have the opportunity to do something from the inside. Dante's voice echoes in my ears as if he's still yelling from miles away.

He was right there and I walked away. Jenkins might have caught me before I reached him or shot me in my attempt to flee. From the way Jenkins is acting, I don't think he heard Dante calling to me. A blessing wrapped in a curse.

"I should have listened to Cruz when he told me to get rid of your father. Hindsight," he says, then laughs ruefully as I attempt to school my face.

Does he really not know? Could he believe Dante just disappeared on business or something? According to Jenkins, he didn't know Grant had taken me. He didn't even know about the mini-Auction they put on.

There weren't very many men present, but I'm still surprised they were able to keep an event like that quiet. Especially from Jenkins. He always seems to know everything that happens within the Guild. Perhaps Dante did more good than we realized.

I clear my throat as Jenkins opens his door. "Did he come back?"

"No. Bastard just disappeared, though I expect he'll be back soon. One of the satellite cities has had contact with him. Apparently, he's been dealing with personal matters. In light of his departure—" Jenkins stops, and I hold my breath as he scans me up and down. "You'll be reinstated in your previous position and kept waiting for him. Your room is ready, though I'm sure you'll be spending some time in the Pit as well."

He shoves from the car, leaving me to follow as he knows I'll do. Jenkins never questioned whether I would do what he said. His stubbornness is one of the few advantages I have now. He assumes he holds the same control over me as he once did. And the asshole still believes Dante is on his side. I file away every scrap of information I can gather, just in case. Now that I know this garage exists, maybe I can escape this way when I'm done.

"Mistress," a familiar voice calls from the far wall as I stumble from the vehicle.

I bite my tongue to keep my tears at bay. Rachel's eyes shine in the muted light, pity lining them. She didn't expect to see me again. I don't blame her for assuming I'm here under duress. My stomach flips and nausea bubbles up my throat.

I took the time to eat the dinner Byron had laid out in the dining room before I set his house on fire. Now my meal is threatening to make a reappearance and all because I have no idea how I'm going to pull off the half-baked plan I came up with.

"This way," she says haughtily, tipping her chin up as she turns to lead me up the dark stairwell.

She takes two turns and another set of stairs before spinning around to face me. Her hands brush over my body, and I stand still for her assessment. I've seen her do it before to the women who make it back to the Pit after a session. Once she's done, she leans in and studies my eyes.

"I'm fine," I whisper. Even I can hear the lie in my voice.

She makes a noise in the back of her throat, then scowls. "What happened?"

I glance behind me before answering. "Byron Michaels bought me. Took me to his house."

"Where?" she breathes. I can see the gears turning in her mind, and I shake my head.

"Focus, Rachel. He had a replica of one of the VIP rooms in his basement."

She shudders, her revulsion clear. "Why would he do that?"

"He wanted me to feel more comfortable or something. I think he wanted me to choose him. He was always jealous of Dante. When he didn't get what he wanted, he was…not happy."

"Tell me he's dead."

I nod, and relief floods her face. "Then I set his house on fire. Jenkins showed up and said he didn't know Grant took me. Is my father really gone?"

"As far as I know. Listen, we don't have much time, but why did you come back? It didn't look like he was forcing you." There it is, that kernel of doubt. If I can't convince her I came back to fight, she'll kill me herself.

"I had to. We didn't finish."

It's not enough. I know it's not, but I don't know how else to explain things without jeopardizing everything Dante and I started. Every time he withheld information from me, I was upset, assuming he didn't trust me.

Now I see it was to protect me. He told me, yet I couldn't believe him. He didn't know I would be able to withstand the torture. Just like I don't know if Rachel would be able to stay quiet if they steal her away.

Instead of pushing my ass down the stairs, Rachel nods before spinning around and continuing upward. I should have trusted her long ago. Following her into the Pit is a surreal experience. I spent too long in the dark, and then in the crimson chambers. It's jarring to return to a place that is unfortunately familiar.

"We've had an influx of assets," she sneers, her mask in place now that there are guards around.

I tip my chin up. "When will the Auction be?"

"Figured you'd know something like that, Mistress. Why ask someone as lowly as me?" She smirks over her shoulder, and I return the favor.

Benjamin snorts from his usual place in the cage, probably seeing right through our act. I glance at him from the corner of my eye. He's largely the same, though his cheeks are sunken. I wonder if they're running out of food.

The supplies were never great down here. Jenkins gave them the bare minimum to survive, but it was always more than I received. I doubt Rachel knew that. For all the perks I had working in Jenkins's office, there were downsides as well. I'd take being intermittently starved over what they had to go through, though.

"We'll get you cleaned up. I suspect he'll want you back sooner rather than later," Rachel says, cutting through my thoughts.

She leads me to a crowded makeshift tent and grabs a mesh bag filled with toiletries. I'm surprised they allow them to keep that shit down here. At the ranch, they had everything under lock and key after several of the women tried to drink the products. They thought death would be a better path than living there. The toiletries merely made them sick, though, which didn't stop anyone from consuming them, searching for a way out of this life. My chest throbs as I wonder how many lives the Guild has destroyed. Too many to count.

This is why I came back. Even if I could have gotten to Dante, I doubt I'd be able to do much to help him. He'd spend his time protecting me and he'd end up getting hurt or worse. I can do more here, hopefully. And if I sacrifice my life in the process, so be it. At least I'll have done something with my existence other than merely surviving.

One floor up and we enter the bathroom. It's not much, just three walls hastily constructed with spouts jutting near the ceiling. They weren't built with luxury in mind.

I shower quickly, trying to avoid the spray when it comes to my wounds. It's not easy with the water shooting everywhere. Rachel steps in, gently peeling the remaining bandages from my back before cleaning the gashes.

"These are deep," she murmurs so the guard at the doorway won't overhear.

"Most of them were from the flogger. I'm sure some are from the whip, though."

She inhales sharply as she applies an ointment to them, then moves to cover them again. "Who?"

"Molly. I doubt you knew her," I mutter. Rachel wasn't at the ranch.

"So she's dead. Good." She hands me a short skirt and a loose blouse. Where she got them, I have no idea, but I'm grateful all the same.

She leads me from the bathroom and up more stairs. The adrenaline from burning Byron's house is wearing off, and my feet drag the farther we travel. Jenkins didn't say whether he expected me in his office tonight still. I'll end up passing out before I even get there.

I wish I would have asked more questions on the ride back. Yet I fell into the old habit of silence. It's what's kept me safe all these years, but now I have no idea what to expect. The unknown sends chills down my spine.

Thankfully, Rachel takes the service stairwells. I can still hear the rumblings of music and hundreds of voices, but I don't think I'd handle the sensory overload right now. We come out to a familiar hallway and panic seizes me. I stutter back, the urge to flee overtaking any common sense I possessed a moment ago.

This was a mistake. Why the fuck did I think I could come back and do what Dante did? Why the hell did I assume I'd be perfectly fine? I'm not fine. My mind spirals until Rachel seizes my wrist, gripping me tightly. The pain filters through the panic and I gasp.

"Get your shit together. It's a closet. It's your own fucking space. Do not fuck this up, Aelia," Rachel hisses, then tugs me forward.

It's the first time she's ever used my name. Usually it's Mistress or nothing at all. I haven't heard my own name in weeks, maybe months. I still don't know how long I was locked up. Before I know it, she's swinging open the door. It hasn't changed, the old thin blankets making up a makeshift bed, an old skirt with sequins unraveling from the hem, a pair of worn flip-flops I forgot were in here. Nothing has been touched.

Rushing inside, I throw the blankets around, searching for my old pajamas. Nothing. Tears fill my eyes as I drop to my knees, my body screaming in pain from the inside and out. Dante probably left them in our old room. They must be long gone by now. A sob escapes me, and I shove my fist in my mouth to stop the pathetic sound. They were just some ratty old clothes, but they were mine.

I pull in a shuddering breath to calm my racing heart and stop my tears. Nothing good will come from crying over things I can't change. I made my choice to come back here for a reason. The longer I hold on to that, the stronger I'll be.

"I heard him," I breathe. "He called to me and I went with Jenkins anyways."

"He'll understand."

I doubt he will, but I keep that to myself. I don't need Rachel's reassurance. Keeping my mouth shut would have been better for both of us. It's bad enough she saw my breakdown.

The crimson chambers broke something in me. A piece of my soul will forever wallow within the bloodstains on the concrete, in the nails of the flogger, in the water droplets soaking into the wood of the cross. I'll never be whole again.

I don't know how to live missing a piece of my soul. After all these years of surviving, I finally broke. If I see Dante again, will he notice I'm not complete? Will he notice how many bits of myself I've left behind?

"Even if he does, I don't think it will be enough."

NINETEEN

Dante

One, two, three, four, five. Pivot. One, two, three. Pivot. Repeat. I've been pacing the perimeter of the cell in the basement of Vipers' headquarters for the last fifteen minutes. I spent twice that long cussing and demanding to be let out. No one came. I know why I woke up here, but I still don't have to like it.

My head throbs and I wish I had more water. There were four bottles by the mattress on the floor. I already drank them. I won't be down here much longer, but the silence is eating away at me. The rattle of the door at the end of the hall makes me freeze. Mac's dark hair appears, and she marches toward me, a sour expression stamped across her face.

"You done freaking the fuck out? Because we have other shit we need to deal with. And you running off to find your girlfriend isn't going to help with any of that." She leans against the opposite wall and crosses her arms.

I grind my teeth to keep from blasting my sister at her tone. It only serves to make my head throb more.

"Open the cell, Mac."

She shakes her head. "Not until you can promise me you won't run back to the Guild. You'll get yourself killed and then you won't be good to anyone."

"There's no point in going back there. I know that. Which means we need to speed up our plan so I can get her out faster. Now open the fucking cell," I snarl, my patience holding on by the thinnest of threads.

"Mason's spouting some shit about her going with them willingly. Figured I'd tell you before you hear him and shoot him in the head."

Wrapping my hands around the cold bars, I tuck my chin to my chest. "I'm sure that's what he perceived. She wouldn't go back. Not by choice."

I'm lying, but not entirely. She wouldn't trust Jenkins, but she would definitely go back to the Guild if she thought she could do more good from the inside. I have no idea how she got to Byron's house. Or what's happened to her. But she was standing on her own. She was walking by herself. She was whole, more or less.

Until I talk to her, hold her in my arms, I won't be able to truly rest. The image of her body outlined in flames will haunt my dreams. It'll merely be added to the procession I've been subjected to for months now.

"Did the others come back?" I ask since she hasn't moved to free me.

"All but Alex and Ren. They said they were making a detour." She sighs, glancing toward the open door. "The woman Shane and Sam found? It's Nova. She hasn't woken up, but there are bruises all over her body. We called Ink. He said he might know someone who can come by and check her out."

"Raven see her yet?"

She nods and her lip slips between her teeth. "She sobered up pretty quickly. Hasn't left Nova's side. I'm pretty sure she's sleeping next to her now."

"You gonna finally let me out of here?"

"Full disclosure, some people are with Mason. Prepare yourself for pushback. Or just ignore it. Either way, it's a fight you're not going to win right now." She pulls out the key and unlocks the cell.

The pressure in my chest eases as I step into the hallway. I didn't realize how wound up I was at the thought of being locked away. Even when I was embedded with the Guild, I could mostly come and go as I pleased. There was always the fear that someone was following me, but I was still free to leave. I can't imagine what Aelia felt like standing in that open space after years of being trapped. Something must have driven her back.

"Don't fly off the handle," Mac calls as I rush up the stairs.

I wave over my shoulder, though I won't make her any promises. When I reach the main area, Ren and Alex are among them. Food is scattered across multiple tables, mumbled conversations rumbling through the air. It reminds me of when my men were still here, filling up the space. After my father died, there was laughter too. Based on the despondent looks on all their faces, I doubt there'll be any of that anytime soon.

"Dante, we need to talk," Lacey mutters, waving me toward the office next to mine.

She's taken over the space with two long desks and a plethora of monitors. Some of them I understand, like the cameras canvasing Viper territory. Others are a mess of letters and numbers that look like code. I wonder if she's still trying to hack into the Guild's system.

"Listen, Mason told me about your little sojourn to the south side of Rima. I already know what you're going to say, but I need you to consider that perhaps Aelia played you," she says, plopping into her chair.

"Why do you say that? Because if your only evidence is Byrns's take on the situation, I'd advise you to come up with something else." I drop into my own chair across from her. I'm pretty sure Ren's been using the computers set up behind me.

"I'd never make a statement with so little to go on." She sighs, her brows pulling low as she studies me. "I've been thinking about her kicking me out of the system. While I can understand her panic, if she has any knowledge of code, she'd be able to see what I was trying to do. And even if I wasn't connected to you or everyone from Synd, wouldn't that be a good thing? Wouldn't she *want* to let me in?"

"Listen, Nemesis." She winces, and I push to my feet. I don't really give a fuck what she wants to be called. "I appreciate everything you did for me. I realize you didn't have to take the job, especially knowing it could potentially put you at risk for exposure. You kept me alive for a fucking year in that place. However, in this instance? You have no fucking clue what you're talking about."

She opens her mouth, and I cut her off with a swipe of my hand. "Save your arguments. No one here understands what goes on in there. No one saw what I saw. Not one of you can fathom the sheer horror it's like living in that place as a pawn. They're not even cattle headed for the slaughter. They're toys to be used and discarded. Aelia endured for almost ten goddamn years between the Guild and her father. So unless you're willing to volunteer to go through all that, then you're not qualified to make a fucking judgement on anyone. And neither is your fucking boyfriend."

I shove out of the room, almost taking Ren out with the door. He slides to the side, raising his eyebrow at me. Alex steps up next to him and his gaze bounces between us. We can't afford to be at each other's throats, but I'm not going to sit here and let them talk shit about Aelia and her choices. I don't know why she went with Jenkins. Doesn't mean she didn't have a good reason.

"Raines, I need your help with something," Alex says after a minute.

Ren just slips around me, shutting the office door behind him. I lead Alex into my office. He collapses into the chair across from my desk, but I opt to stand, staring out the window. The last thing I want to do is have another conversation that ends with more tension.

We don't have fucking time for this. Plus, my head is pounding. There's a weight sitting on my chest and only having Aelia in my arms will alleviate it.

"You going to start talking? Or can I go to bed?" I rest my forehead against the glass, letting the coolness seep into my skin.

"Byrns really cracked you, didn't he?" There's a tinge of laughter in his voice, but it's subdued.

"Not really. I'd be dead then. The adrenaline…" I roll my body around, leaning my head against the wall to stare at the ceiling. The stains peppering the white tiles pulse in time with my heartbeat. Maybe he hit me harder than I thought.

"You know what they used to call pistol whipping? Buffaloing. Dates all the way back to the Wild West."

Dropping my head, I narrow my eyes at him. "Why the fuck do you know that?"

He shrugs, glancing away. "Ren and I got a good look at some of the drug labs they've got set up. They're all making Oracle from what I could tell. One place was making Molotovs in the next room."

"So we don't have to worry about that one," I snort.

The corner of his mouth twitches and concern worms its way through me. Even when I came to Synd a year ago, Alex was cracking jokes and dropping random facts. This restrained version of him is freaking me out. I wonder if the others have noticed. Not that I'll say anything. If Alex is going through some shit, there are plenty of other people who are closer to him he'll talk to instead of me.

He leans forward, linking his hands together and resting his elbows on his knees. "Here's the thing. We need a man on the inside. Everyone else has a role. They know what they're doing and how to do it. I mean, except for Shane, who's still trying to be sixty-nine things at once. The thing is, you'll need him when the time comes."

"Let me guess. You want to infiltrate the lower gangs and bring them down from the inside. But Sam won't let you go off on your own like that."

He shakes his head. "Sam's not the problem. She knows I can take care of myself. It's actually Ren. He keeps saying I take stupid risks and it's not fair to Sam. That she'd be devastated if something happened to me. Whatever. I'm not here to discuss that shit."

"Are you looking for my permission? I'm not your dad, Alex."

He sits back, eyeing me before sighing. "If you want to be in charge, then you should start acting like it. I'm telling you my plans so you can veto them in case they interfere with the bigger picture. You *do* have a bigger picture, right?"

I scowl at the insinuation. It may be rough, but I have a fucking plan. And I've been fighting against my better judgement to keep it to myself. I've gotten so used to only sharing shit with Jag that I forgot I have other people to lean on now. And Jag has been MIA lately. I've led the Vipers alone for half a decade. Maddox was no help. Mac was dealing with her own shit. And the other members were a mix of young blood who couldn't handle the responsibility and the old guard who only wanted to see me fail.

"When do you plan on leaving? And are you going to tell the others?" I ask as I glance out the window.

A shadow detaches from a building and my heart leaps. I catch the flash of Sam's face and scowl. She lifts her hand and wiggles her fingers at me before disappearing into the night. I wonder if she's sharing her plans with anyone and whether Alex is busting her balls for it like he is me.

"Gotta tell Sam or she'll come searching for me. I'll let her tell Shane and Ren. Otherwise, I'm leaving the rest up to you. Might take a bit to find an in, but I'll be gone by tomorrow." He pushes from his chair. "Try not to beat Byrns up before I get back. I wanna video that shit."

I wait a few minutes after he leaves to make my way to the bedroom I've been using at headquarters. I let Jag and Avery stay at my house, and while I'm not upset that they're sleeping there, I'd rather not have them hear me when I wake up yelling from the nightmares. My room here is bare and looks slightly like a dorm room, but the mattress is comfortable.

Collapsing fully clothed on top of the bed, I resign myself to staring at the ceiling until the sun rises. Aelia was right there, in my reach. And she chose to go back. She may have had a reason, but it doesn't stop the guilt from swirling through me that I failed her again.

I sigh, closing my eyes. Hopefully, the world doesn't burn while I sift through my memories of Aelia and relive every time I let her down.

TWENTY

Aelia

I feel like I've traveled back in time. Once again I'm seated at my desk in Jenkins's office, staring at a computer screen while he silently works on whatever it is he does.

I never did quite figure out what the pile of papers in front of him are. I assumed they were numbers from the satellite cities, but he started handing those off to me last week. It took at least that long for me to recover from the injuries Molly gave me.

After Rachel left me in my closet, I thought I'd crash since I was exhausted, both inside and out. Instead, I stared at the ceiling, reliving all the mistakes I made and second-guessing myself about going with Jenkins. Dante shouting my name echoed through my head for most of the day.

Sitting here, biting my lip while I sift through the dues, or lack thereof, from the outposts, I'm more confident in my decision. There's still an ache resting in my chest, making it hard to breathe at times. I wonder how Dante found me at Byron's house. I'm pretty sure Anders didn't put out an announcement, since Jenkins had no idea it was going on. Not that Dante would get an invitation. Then again, my father is an asshole. I can see him trying to find Dante just to gloat.

Thankfully, Anders has stayed away this time. Grant apparently went with him, so I doubt I'll have to deal with them anytime soon. They'll be back, though. If they think they can get away with what they did, they'll slink back to the Guild when their latest scheme fails.

"We need money transferred to the Auction," Jenkins calls, his voice jarring after so much silence.

"Where would you like it to come from?" I ask quietly to hide the waver in mine. I'm still terrified he'll revert to his old ways if I question him.

He sits back, tapping his finger on his chin. "One of the offshore accounts. I'd hoped to use the money from the fights, but they're not making as much lately. We'll need to look into moving on soon. This place is cursed."

He buries his head back in his papers, then spins in his chair when his phone buzzes. I can't make out the conversation, just Jenkins's low mumbling. My heart ends up in my throat and my stomach has little men doing a tap dance in it as I push to my feet. I never approach Jenkins unless commanded. The closer I get, the clearer his voice becomes, and I slow my steps as I clutch a random piece of paper.

"What do you mean the gambling halls got shut down? The police in this town are a joke." He pauses, listening to the response. "Then buy them off." Another pause and I drop the paper on top of the others. "What the fuck do you mean, we don't have the money? Find some."

I pivot, tiptoeing quickly back to my desk so my heels don't click on the floor. I'm halfway when his chair squeaks as he spins back and I slow to a normal pace.

"There a reason you're out of your chair, Aelia?"

I tense when I hear my name falling from his lips. He's been dropping it more and more instead of his usual insults. It's jarring every time. I turn, folding my hands together in front of me, and nod to the paper.

"Current numbers for the dues, sir." I spin, retreating to my chair.

"Did Cruz mention a trip or issues?"

"He wasn't exactly a sharer," I say, then bite my tongue. He doesn't comment on my blatant sarcasm.

Jenkins's change in demeanor is throwing me off. I don't know how to respond to him, how to act, how far I can push things. I'm waiting for the moment he snaps. Although he seems more stressed than anything.

Maybe he passed more off to Dante than I thought. The fact Jenkins broke Guild rules that have been in place for years was wild enough. Then he kept piling more decisions onto Dante. The loss in Synd was a blow the Guild couldn't afford. Jenkins may have brushed it off, but numbers don't lie.

The Guild is hemorrhaging money. The influx they saw when Dante came in has long since dried up. Now with the fights being affected, not to mention whatever issues Jenkins was talking about a minute ago, I have a feeling they're worse off than we thought.

I pull up one of the offshore accounts, yet there's nothing there. I haven't had time to go through everything from when I was gone. Jenkins probably moved things around in my absence. I access another and another, then one more. All of them sit at zero.

The more I look, the less I find. Three are closed, another four are scraping the bottom of the barrel, and one has about ten thousand in it. None of it is enough to fund the Auction.

Glancing at Jenkins, then back to my screen, I access the domestic accounts. I won't be able to do a deep dive into what's going on, but hopefully I can get an idea.

Massive amounts of money are flowing out in the way of food, toiletries, and liquor. With all the people they're bringing in for the Auction, I'm not surprised the cost of everything is rising. With the dues not coming in, the Guild is struggling to survive.

I wish I had a line of communication to Dante. If I could warn him that Jenkins is talking about moving, he could act now. At least it's a production to move. It usually takes months to put things into place. I doubt we have that long.

The door pops open and Reynolds stalks in. Before Dante came along, he was Jenkins's go-to man. He's always been kept at arm's length, though. Jenkins prefers to do things himself. Which makes it all the more interesting that he relied on Dante so much.

"We need more revenue streams. Someone raided the gambling halls. They were all hit at once. Half of them burned down." Reynolds rests his hands on the back of the chair facing Jenkins. I don't blame him for not wanting to sit.

"Excuse me?"

Apparently Reynolds doesn't feel the tension rising in the room since he sighs. "No idea. But between that and the fighting rings—"

"What the fuck happened with the fighting rings?" Jenkins growls, leaning on his elbows.

"The dog fighting rings were raided. They released the dogs and blew up the buildings." Reynolds straightens, looking like he's about to bolt. "Did no one tell you?"

The vein in Jenkins's forehead ticks and he laces his fingers together, his knuckles turning white. I duck down in my chair, hiding behind my hair. Maybe I can slip out with Reynolds so I don't become the target of Jenkins's wrath.

This is the moment he'll snap. The tension in the air is palpable. My body responds, my muscles tightening the longer the silence stretches. My wounds ache, the tension pulling at the still-healing skin.

"What else is going on that no one has told me about?"

Reynolds blanches, then swallows hard. "The area for the Auction flooded."

"And is anyone cleaning it up? We're supposed to be doing that in two weeks. We have members coming from all over the country. They're used to a specific caliber for this event."

"We're working on it," Reynolds says in a strained voice.

"How exactly are you working on these things?" He pushes to his feet and leans on his fists.

His suit falls open, revealing a gun strapped to his belt. I wonder when he started carrying. I'm not naive enough to think he didn't have any weapons, but wearing it out in the open sends a message. If the guards will have them as well, it'll make things more difficult. My hands tremble at the thought of Grant having a gun. I curl them into fists, reminding myself Grant is gone for now.

A shiver rolls down my spine as my gaze darts between the two men. Part of me wants to flee, even if it draws attention. The other screams at me to stay put and gather as much information as possible.

My screen flashes and I focus on it. The last time this happened, someone was trying to hack into the system. Without knowing who it is, I'm leery of helping them. The last thing I need is Jenkins catching me messing with the security. He'd put a bullet in my head for sure, regardless of whether his demeanor toward me has changed.

"A cleaning crew will come and fix the flooding. I'll send someone out to scout more locations for the fights. I'll contact the police commissioner myself. Merrick—"

Jenkins hand slashes through the air. "Merrick is dead. He has been for a while, so get what Merrick would do out of your head. What else has happened?"

"Some of the supplies have dried up," Reynolds mutters as he takes a step back, finally noticing the weapon. "No one is running into Rima anymore."

The screen distracts me again as a timeout box pops up. I didn't realize I was still logged into the offshore accounts. Closing the box, I pull up another program. It was specially made for the Guild by the hacker who put the security in place and allows them to find the best location for the next home base.

I take notes, ignoring the ones that would actually be lucrative for the Guild. If they move before Dante has a chance to bring them down, then at least I can make it harder in the next city. Maybe someone else can finish what we started.

"So let me get this straight." Jenkins's voice cuts into my thoughts as he rounds his desk. "The Auction is falling apart—again. All of our cash flows from lower levels are drying up. We have no guns or drugs or assets to sell—"

He punctuates every statement with another step toward Reynolds and my muscles coil tighter. The other man retreats until he's almost backed against the door. If they're out of assets—people—to sell, they've bled Rima dry in record time. It's not as large as Synd, but I can't believe how quickly things have turned in merely a year. We were at the ranch for close to three before Jenkins decided to move.

"Sir, Rima is a cesspit of darkness. If we'd been able to take Synd…" Reynolds spreads his hands, then his eyes widen as he realizes his mistake.

In a blink, Jenkins has the barrel of his gun pressed to Reynolds's forehead. My mind shifts, no longer afraid of what will happen. I watched my father pull this move countless times, no matter how much my brother tried to protect me. I got used to being surrounded by violence. It's calming, in a way. At least compared to the constant unpredictability of living within the Guild's clutches. I'll take this scenario any day.

"Aelia," Jenkins calls softly, and I straighten.

"Yes, sir?" My voice doesn't waver, and relief flows through me.

"Tell Reynolds why going to Synd would be a poor choice for the Guild." Jenkins's gaze never leaves Reynolds and sweat beads on the older man's forehead.

"Synd is held by several mafia families, as well as a prolific motorcycle club. They work in tandem to allow for better protection within the city limits. Those within are loyal to the families who run things. They prosper under their rule and, therefore, are unlikely to be swayed by something as paltry as money or assets. Those at the top will remain at the top, regardless of what the Guild could offer."

"Principles. Reynolds. They have principles even though they're criminals. We're lucky they didn't do more damage than they did when we attempted to take over the first time. The man *you* suggested was weak. Easily manipulated, but weak. And while you may have assumed he was willing to switch sides and betray his family, you judged wrong. So why would I trust you to pull us out of the hole that you landed us in?"

Reynolds's throat bobs, his entire body vibrating as Jenkins digs the barrel into his flesh. With a sneer, Jenkins retreats, slipping his gun back into its holster. Reynolds's eyes find mine and I tip my chin up.

I'd rather not make an enemy of him, but my boss has already done that for me. Reynolds will blame me regardless. With Dante gone, he'll take his jealousy and rage out on me. Unless he's convinced Jenkins will castrate him for it.

"Get the fuck out before I change my mind about replacing you," Jenkins snarls.

Reynolds straightens his suit, his fingers slipping on the buttons before stalking from the room.

"Get back to work, Aelia. We don't have much time."

I nod absentmindedly while my mind whirls. All we need is a little push and the Guild will implode. I just have to figure out how to light the match without going up in flames myself.

Twenty One

Dante

"I'm not saying you shouldn't inform the Reapers, Helms. I just don't think it's wise to tell him how slowly things are going." I grind my teeth as I stab another sausage off my plate.

Helms insisted I come over for breakfast, which is actually an early dinner. Our sleep schedules are all fucked up, but it's been easier for me to function than the others. Mac is practically tipping out of her chair as she dozes. Helms scoots his chair closer and guides her head to his shoulder. My heart pulses and I rub my fist to my chest.

Helms points his fork at me. "That shit won't go away until your woman is back. Just so you know."

He smirks as he stuffs a large bite of waffles into his mouth. I scowl, shaking my head before concentrating on my food. I'm sure it tastes fine, but everything is ash in my mouth these days. It's been a long time since I've sat at this table. It used to house the entire Raines clan when my father was alive, not that Mac liked that very much. Guilt eats away at me as I remember some of the shit I turned a blind eye to.

"She doesn't blame you."

My eyes dart to Mac before settling on Helms. Of course he could read my face. "Didn't think she did. Doesn't change the fact I should have seen."

His eyebrow pops up. "Exactly what are you letting get to you? The fact she was sold to the Night Slayers or that Maddox treated her like shit for years?"

"Both. But you can't have one without the other. If I would have taken care of Maddox before, he wouldn't have been able to sell her." I drop my fork on my plate, my appetite fleeing in the wake of the conversation.

"I didn't do anything either. You know she begged me to stay after the coup?" His eyes take on a faraway look. "Crawled through my bedroom window and begged. I told her no. Actually, I mocked her, broke her heart, and *then* told her no."

"That explains a lot," I mutter, crossing my arms. "How'd you get over it?"

He lets out a humorless laugh. "I didn't. I just spend every day making it up to her."

"And her?" I nod to Mac, who's snoring softly now.

"She says she doesn't think about it. Don't know if I believe her." He sighs, resting his cheek on her hair, then turns back to me. "You realize I'm going to kill him, right? When Maddox pops back up, I'm going to put that bastard six feet under."

"We'll draw straws. I have a feeling you're not the only one who wants a piece of him."

He picks up his plate and resumes eating. He doesn't even jostle Mac as he does it. I wonder how many times he's let her sleep on his shoulder while going about his business.

My heart clenches again, and I realize how jealous I am. Their problems are dealt with. The Night Slayers are gone. They could be in Synd, holed up in Reaper territory, and making up for lost time. Instead they're here, helping me fight my battles. I'd tell them to go home if I thought Mac would actually leave.

"Stop it," Helms grunts.

"Stop what?"

He glares at me, setting his empty plate down. "Stop feeling guilty that you called us. We show up. That's what we do. You and I didn't talk for five years and the next five were superficial at best. But I called and you came. That's what family does, Raines. We show up."

Gently, he wakes Mac, whispering in her ear. I avert my gaze, not wanting to intrude on their moment. Or maybe it's because it hurts too much.

Glancing around the room, I notice there's nothing on the walls. Nothing to make it a home. Maddox never kept shit. Possessions merely tied him down. I took everything with me when I moved into the house closer to headquarters. Blaze sent Mac's things to her when she decided to stay in Synd. There's no legacy in this house. It's a shell waiting for someone to fill.

The front door slams open, crashing against the wall, and Shane steps through. He scans the area until his eyes alight on me, and I raise my eyebrow.

"Where the fuck did you send him?" he growls, prowling toward me. Sam slips through after him, closing the door quietly.

"Nowhere. He saw an opportunity and took it. Although he was supposed to inform you of his decisions." I cross my arms, refusing to be cowed by Shane fucking King.

"Who are we talking about?" Mac asks. Sam slips into Helms's vacated chair and whispers in her ear.

Shane stops, widening his stance as his hands curl into fists at his side. "He goes off on his own and he'll make reckless choices and get himself killed. And you approved that shit."

"We have to ramp things up. Taking out the gambling dens and fighting rings might have jumpstarted shit, but it won't bring down the Guild. Alex took it upon himself to deal with the lower gangs. And he's the best person for the job." A sound of disgust leaves him and I clear my throat. "He's charismatic. He'll probably have them eating out of the palm of his hand within a week."

"He's capable of taking care of himself, Shane," Sam murmurs, but worry lines her dark eyes. "Though I *did* advise him to take someone with."

Shane rounds on her, his mouth dropping open. "You fucking knew?"

I push from my chair, not ready to be involved in a dispute between two lovers. It's awkward enough being around my little sister while she's in love with my once-best friend. I wish we were still as close as we used to be. I'm not part of their family, no matter what Helms spouts. I'm like the weird cousin who shows up every couple years to the family reunion who no one really knows how to talk to.

"Where the hell are you going?" Helms calls.

"Gotta check on Nemesis." I wave over my shoulder as Sam corrects me. Half the time they still call her Nemesis and I haven't quite figured out their system yet.

I walk to headquarters as the sun slowly sets, casting the neighborhood in shadows. Winter had its last gasp and has given way to spring finally. It's the perfect night for a ride, but I won't be taking advantage of it.

We have plans that could make or break our overall strategy to hit the Guild. The shit before was small annoyances, designed to disrupt their cash flow. Bringing down the brothels and torture centers they've set up will hit them in more ways than one. The risk of taking on places with more security worries me.

"Lacey would like to see you, but Mason is with her right now. Give it five minutes and you'll miss him." Ren sidles up next to me, tucking his tablet under his arm.

"There a reason I need to avoid him?"

"Perhaps it's because he believes your woman played you and is working for the Guild and she will kill you should you ever cross paths again. I assumed you wouldn't be very happy with that."

"Does anyone else agree with him?" I've been avoiding the conversation with everyone else other than Lacey. Mac keeps trying to get me to talk, but there's nothing to talk about.

"I'm sure if things go sideways, they'll be persuaded to his way of thinking."

I run my fingers through my hair. "What about Nemesis…Lacey?"

We may have talked before, but if her inklings have turned to full-on certainty we'll have a problem.

"Lacey has a mind of her own. She doesn't just blindly follow Byrns's lead. However, I believe we all wonder if you're making a mistake."

I round on him, glaring, and he holds his hands up. "I lived with her for a fucking year. You don't think I would know if I was being played?"

"You also were able to convince Jenkins you weren't a mole. It's entirely possible she's as good of an actor as you were."

I deflate, not willing to refute him. I'm exhausted by the sleepless nights and constant worry. As much as I know we need to see this through, I'm tired. There's no clear path without massive loss of life on both sides. I wish I could just bust into headquarters and snatch her up. Then we could disappear and leave someone else to bring them down.

"Until we have more to go on, no one is going to act on the assumption. But also, I don't believe it matters either way." He rolls his eyes when I snort. "To the rest of us, it truly doesn't. Clearly, you have a more personal stake in whether she is actually in love with you or was just pretending. However, the rest of us will still do what we came to do. And we'll still save her if possible. Her fate lies in your hands, Raines."

He pivots and walks toward the Raines house. His words ring in my ears all the way to headquarters. Her fate hanging in the balance isn't something I wanted to think about. I already know how badly I fucked up. His words feel like another stab in my already wounded heart.

Byrns nods to me as he exits the front doors, but says nothing, thank fuck. I'm pretty sure if he did I would end up punching him like everyone expects of me. I don't really care what he thinks he saw. In the end it won't matter.

"You wanted to see me?" I ask, dropping into Ren's empty seat in Lacey's office.

Lacey swings around, leveling me with a look. "Here's the problem. I've been infiltrating their system on a surface level, but my attempts keep getting deleted from the inside. It's not a program or bug taking it out. Someone is manually going in and deleting all my efforts."

"There a question in there? I'm not a hacker, Nem. I have no idea how any of this works." I swing the chair back and forth, my leg jiggling rapidly.

"First of all, don't call me Nem. That's weird. Second of all, you have to admit it's suspicious. I know you've got a hard-on—"

"I'm going to stop you right there. I don't have a 'hard-on' for Aelia. I'm in love with her. And I will do everything in my power to get her out of there, even if that means giving up my own life so she can live. If you'd like to reword your statement based on that information, I'd advise you do that now." I'm done pussyfooting around this. Better to draw the lines clearly now rather than when we're in the thick of it.

Her nostrils flare, then she nods. "I'm just saying that looking at the data, and all the evidence, we have to be careful. Did you tell her what our plans were?"

"No." My jaw ticks as she stares at me with pity. "And not because I didn't trust her. The likelihood that she would be discovered should I make it out and she was left behind was high. I wanted her to have deniability. I didn't want her to have to endure the torture while trying to hold all my secrets."

Her eyes soften as they stare over my shoulder. She reaches up and traces a scar on her cheek unconsciously. I still haven't asked her what happened and I don't plan on it. Byrns has been tightlipped about the entire saga of how they found one another. Alex said they were still in the possessive phase. When I told him I had no idea what the hell he was talking about, he just laughed and clapped me on the shoulder.

"I'm sorry, Dante."

I jolt and I narrow my eyes. "For what?"

She sighs, focusing on me again. "For everything. I did as much as I could to set you up, but I feel like I should have done more. I'm sorry you had to leave her behind. It's never easy to walk away. Especially when you understand the consequences. And even more so when you know it's because they told you to."

"We have a plan," I whisper. All the early morning conversations Aelia and I plotted run through my head.

"Then here's hoping it works. Because if I can't get in, you're all on your own."

TWENTY TWO

Aelia

"They stopped feeding us," Rachel hisses, glancing toward the door of my closet.

She snuck up here in the middle of the day while everyone was sleeping. She's still terrified someone is going to bust through and catch her. I don't blame her, but no one has come in the weeks I've been back. I can feel the complacency taking over the longer I'm here. The risks don't seem as risky anymore.

"Did you ration the food like I told you?" I flip through the small pieces of paper I've managed to smuggle out of the office.

"Yes, but even that is running low. Some of them won't make it to the Auction."

I don't know what she wants me to do about it. As much as I'd like to save them all, I know I can't. Some of them will die even if I put shit into action right now. Tonight. I smother a yawn behind my hand. The lack of sleep is getting to me.

Once the building goes quiet and most of the members have left, I go hunting. For information and people and anything that I can pass on to Dante when I see him again.

"Did you find her?" Every day I ask about Nova. She's disappeared, though she could be stuffed in the Pit somewhere.

Rachel shakes her head. "No one even recognizes her. I wonder if she got out."

I scoff, rolling my eyes. She shrugs, giving me a sympathetic smile. No one escapes. No one leaves. No one makes it out of here whole.

Even if I succeed and find my way back to Dante, he'll have a broken woman. I don't know if he'll be prepared to handle the trauma I'll carry out of this place. I shove the thoughts away. I'll cross that bridge when I get to it. It doesn't change what has to happen now.

"I checked the way to the parking garage. Guards aren't at the door to the Pit and it's not locked. But there's at least a dozen milling around the vehicles. They're coming and going at all hours. If we use that way to get the others out, some of them won't make it." Rachel leans against the wall, tipping her head back.

"Die, Rachel. They'll die." I don't understand why she avoids the obvious, finding new ways to skip around the truth. "But if they stay here or get sold, they'll die anyway. Most of the members don't care about keeping them alive. They laugh about it."

Closing my eyes, I pull in a deep breath. I wonder how long I would have hidden away, never acknowledging my reality. Until Dante came, I was focused on surviving. I didn't have it in me to worry about the others.

Guilt swirls in my gut, and I press my fist to my stomach. I could have saved them. Not all of them, but some. I don't know if Rachel feels the same way. She's been stuck in the Pit with little freedom.

"Do you ever wish you could have gone back?" Her slitted eyes meet mine.

I shuffle the papers, avoiding her eyes. "Back to what?"

"Before? I don't know. I made silly mistakes—took risks that put me on this path. Do you ever regret the decisions that led you here?"

"Does it matter? It won't change where we are. Doesn't seem like a worthwhile thing to think about."

She huffs and my eyes dart to her. "I'd think you of all people would answer honestly. I know what *I* did to land myself here. And what I would change if I could."

I tilt my head, scanning her face. "If you want to know about my past, then why don't you just ask instead of skirting around the question?"

She straightens, crossing her ankles and arms. "Fine. How the fuck did you get here? I know your father sold you, but why?"

I weigh the risk of telling her. The more she knows, the more she can reveal if she's ever in a position like I was with Molly. I'd rather spare her the extra burden of keeping my secrets.

My mind skips a beat as I stare at the wall. Dante told me the same thing in not so many words. I thought he was protecting himself and his mission and using lies to cover it up. Instead, he was protecting me. Somehow I forgot. Then again, I've been going through some shit that's sure to leave my memory spotty.

Rachel waves her hand in front of my face. "Where'd you go? If you don't want to talk about it, that's fine."

I shake my head, giving her a sad smile. "No, it's fine. Just working shit out in my mind. I grew up in the mafia. I mean, it was weird because my father was the head of the family, but we didn't really have a lot of territory. It's a long story. Anyways, Anders went to settle some debts in another city and I followed him, chasing a boy."

She laughs, then claps her hand over her mouth as her eyes dart to the door. Nothing moves and there's no sound from the hallway. Crawling over, I peek out, but no one is there. I shake my head as I ease the wood closed and settle onto my blankets.

"Not my best decision I suppose, like you said. Father lost that war, killed the boy." She scowls and I press my lips together. "Don't feel too bad. He was an asshole. I thought we'd go home, but Anders faked his own death, my brother died, and eventually I was sold. I don't know if

I'd decide to not chase after the boy, though. I can't even fathom what life would be like out there. And Dante..."

I don't have an answer. If I hadn't gone to Synd as a teenager, I probably never would have met Dante all these years later. But I don't think I'd be able to relive all the horrors just to find him again.

I sigh, closing my eyes. "I'd like to think we'd cross paths even if I wasn't here."

"Fate," Rachel murmurs.

"Seems silly. Or cruel. If fate exists, she's a real fucking bitch."

"Fuck fate. If she led us here to live through this shit? Fuck her."

I giggle, nudging her foot with mine. "Pretty sure fate's a dude if they're pulling our strings and leading us here."

She sobers, glancing at the door again. "Evil really does live everywhere, doesn't it?"

"It certainly does."

"Aelia, fix this," Jenkins demands as he shoves away from his desk.

I sigh under my breath and make my way over to his computer. It's been on the fritz for the last few days. Every time he touches it, something goes haywire. The problem is, I don't have the skills to fix it. Usually I just turn it off and back on again. I even tried blowing in the fan, but that didn't work.

Jenkins stalks to the window, muttering to himself. I glance at him before sitting, but he's not paying attention to me. He's been slowly unraveling day by day. I keep waiting for him to fly off the handle and take his frustrations out on me. Reynolds seems to be his target as of late. As soon as he kills Reynolds, though, I have no doubt I'll be next.

The screen is a mess of fractured lines and pixels bouncing around. Whoever is fucking with the system really did a number this time. I decided to let them continue on their quest to get in without interference. Too bad I don't have that option for Jenkins. I wish I could communicate with them, but they've blocked me somehow. I'm not skilled enough for this. I should have paid more attention in those classes I took on coding.

My mind drifts back to the best friend I left behind. I wonder if she's out there still. Does she ever think about me? Maybe she thinks I ran off with Chad and left her behind. I wouldn't blame her if she hated me. When I get out of here, I should find her. Maybe she wouldn't even remember me.

Jenkins grunts and I focus on the task. I need to stop letting my thoughts on the future take over. When I shake the mouse, nothing happens. Not that I expected anything different. Turning it off and on again, I tap my finger against my bare leg. It's slow and I told him he should buy a new machine, but he insists on using this one. He's afraid of the securities not transferring or something. I stopped listening to him rant and rave since he never said anything new.

"Well?" he demands, swinging around.

"I restarted it. Takes a bit. Perhaps—"

"Don't. I'm not getting a new one. Is yours working?" He narrows his eyes at me.

"Yes, sir. I believe this one is just old." The screen comes to life, as crisp and clear as a ten-year-old computer can be. "It should be working now."

I slip around his desk as he stalks to his chair. He's been keeping his distance since I've been back. I wonder if it stems from the way Dante treated me. I'm not naive enough to believe Jenkins trusts me, but maybe he trusts the way Dante trained me. Or at least how Dante *said* he trained me. I snort softly as I sit.

"There a problem, bit?" Jenkins growls, and my breath stalls.

"No," I croak, then clear my throat. "Sir."

I peek at him through my hair. He's focused on his computer, squinting at the screen. I don't think he even realized he called me a bit instead of my name. It could be a slip of the tongue or a subtle move to remind me of my place. Either way, I've become too complacent.

It's strange I survived so long here by living on the edge. The minute I came back…no. The minute I stabbed Molly something changed within me. I was too numb at the time to notice. The problem is my newfound indifference. I just don't care if I survive as long as I take him with me. It'll be worth it.

"Go down to the Pit. Pick someone," he grunts, and I stiffen.

I push from my chair, and another box pops up on my screen. Code appears, one line at a time, and I glance at Jenkins. I can't leave this up for him to find. He may not be tech savvy, but he'll know someone is fucking with the computers. Nausea bubbles in my stomach as I kill the box, then shut down my computer. The feeling stays with me all the way to the Pit.

TWENTY THREE

Dante

The silence is crushing, weighing down on everyone.

Raven sits with red eyes in the back, avoiding everyone. I don't blame her. Nova still hasn't woken up, though the doctor thinks it's her brain protecting her. Once she feels safe, she'll wake up. That answer wasn't good enough for Raven, but there's nothing she can do about it.

Sam purses her lips as she fiddles with her phone. She's probably trying to track Alex, though he's fallen off the grid. I warned her not to go after him. Of course, Shane blames me for upsetting her. Even if she could find him, which wouldn't be that hard, he wouldn't want her to. It's an unnecessary risk and she knows it.

"Everyone have their assignments?" I ask, my eyes falling on Byrns.

"There a reason you want me here with Lacey?" Mac asks, and I glance at her.

"She needs someone who's observant. And capable of protecting her should the rest of us...if shit goes sideways." I've developed as many contingencies as possible. I can't account for every way this could go wrong.

"One more time, Raines," Ren says as he stares at the map spread out on the large table.

The edges are littered with the remnants of the meal Nico dropped off. He tried to say he'd fix up the inside, but I told him not to worry about it. We only use this space for things like this. Once this whole cluster fuck is settled, maybe I'll help him reopen. He has a daughter ready to take over the family business, but maybe she'd like to branch out on her own.

"Mac will stay with Avery and Lacey. Jag and I will set the bombs at the rest of the gambling halls. Ren and Shane are going to the brothels. Helms and Sam are heading to the crimson chambers. Raven's crew will split with each of us. Clear the innocents out as much as possible. Mason will be at the rendezvous point to receive them and get them to safety. Set timers to go off at five-thirty. Any later and we'll get caught by the rising sun. Any earlier and it'll be too crowded."

"Why do we care if it's crowded? Those assholes should burn," Jag says, crossing his arms.

"Because we won't be able to get the bits…others out," I respond through gritted teeth. We've been through this countless times, but they're still questioning me. Jag's face sours at my choice of word. I didn't do it on purpose, but it's hard to break the habit.

I wish I could do this all on my own. This is my plan, and if any of them are hurt or killed, I'll be to blame. It's hard enough being an MC president, knowing the fate of my members rest on my shoulders. These people are family, even if I feel like I'm on the outside looking in. Mac may be my sister, but she's part of Synd now. I no longer am. Not truly.

"Be back here by seven. That should give you enough time to get the victims out and to the rendezvous points. If you get waylaid, call in. Keep calling or texting until you get ahold of someone. You know the drill if you're compromised."

No one moves, the weight of the situation blanketing the room. The other things we've done seem like harmless pranks. Surface level annoyances that the Guild probably doesn't even notice. Or they attribute their issues to the incompetent police or something. This plan will severely impact their revenue. It will disrupt their supplies. It will hurt them in a way they can't come back from. Hopefully.

My phone buzzes as I pivot. I wait until I'm outside before I look at it. Another satellite city calling me. I've been stringing them along, using them as a small gateway into the inner workings of the Guild. If Jenkins was on better terms with them, he would have told them I went rogue.

Every time they contact me, I wonder if Jenkins is in the dark, thinking I disappeared for other reasons. I'm smart enough not to test my theory. If he doesn't know, I'd be able to walk back in there without consequence. Unless I ran into Grant or Anders.

"Hold up, Prez. I want to swing by headquarters before we take off," Jag says, falling into step next to me.

"We don't have time. Whatever you want to say to Avery, you can do it over text."

"Who the fuck says I'm confessing anything to her?" he sneers, and I press my lips together.

Clearing my throat, I glance at him. "Confess?"

"Oh, fuck off. I just want to make sure she's not going to try to follow us." He straightens his jacket. He probably shouldn't be wearing his leathers, complete with Phantom patches. It's not my place to dissuade him, though.

"She won't. I made it clear. Then Sam talked to her and she promised."

"Good to know I'm not the only one she doesn't listen to," he grumbles, pulling himself into the backseat of the SUV.

The ride to our starting point is silent, both of us lost in our thoughts. I try to keep my mind on the present, but Aelia keeps popping up. I can't afford to be distracted. Reminding myself of that fact doesn't work.

Several of Raven's crew mill about, talking in small groups when we pull to the curb. Our driver opens the back and we climb out. Handing out the C-4 should come with instructions, but the women take the packages in silence, tucking them in the saddlebags attached to their bikes. The engines flare to life, creating a cacophony of sound in the dark alley. As the rumbles fade, the anxiety in my chest rises. They're set to hit all the smaller gambling dens.

"I think seven of these suckers is a bit excessive. We might take out the whole goddamn block," Jag says as he slams the trunk.

"Good. This town could use a clean slate."

"Setting half of Rima on fire will result in a bombed-out city. Not a clean slate."

"Not like that, asshole. Like a forest. The burning makes way for new growth. Which is exactly what this city needs."

"You gonna be the one who rebuilds it? Won't be easy without a crew."

I glance out the window as we head for the next stop, refusing to answer. I don't know how to. Ghost would let me join his club. Helms would expect me to return to Synd. But I'm not about to oust one of his members just because I want to come back to the Reapers. I wish I'd never left. I could have fought harder for Mac and me to stay. Or sent for Mac once she turned eighteen. Then I'd be VP of the Reapers right now.

You wouldn't have met Aelia then.

I close my eyes, pushing the dark voice down deep inside. Locking it away until she's with me. Then it'll disappear and everything will fall into place. If she leaves, so be it. But at least I'll have gotten her out. If I keep repeating the words, maybe I'll actually believe them.

"Let's go," I murmur when we pull into another dark alley.

I feel like I've lived half my life skulking around the shadows, with the smell of dumpsters filling my nostrils. Rima really needs a fresh start. I just wish I wasn't the only one here to salvage what's left.

Envy wraps another thread around my heart, cinching tightly as I unload three packages. The driver takes off as soon as we're done. He'll wait at the next spot for us to return—*if* we return.

"You sure this guard is on our side? I'd hate to catch a bullet because we were double-crossed." Jag's ragged breaths heave from him with every step we take. I can't tell if it's from nerves or exertion. Probably both.

"He's solid. Risked his life for this. But I also don't want you inside. You take care of things out here. I'll go in."

We duck into yet another alley, the deep bass from inside infiltrating into the night. I pass a package to Jag before tucking the other two under my arm. My heart is in my throat as I knock on the door. Jag mumbles behind me, pissed off I'm taking a risk without him. Testing my pull within the Guild is one of my goals.

If Jenkins doesn't know, I'll be let in without a word. It's the only reason I wore a suit this evening. Shane gave me the side eye, but Jag understood. He doesn't like it, but he got it. Ripping open the packages, I stuff the explosive bricks in my pockets, then line the door with the rest. Jag vanishes around the building to set his own charges and I knock.

Cracking my neck, I wait for it to open, apprehension swirling in my gut. This was not smart. This might rival the ridiculous decision to infiltrate the Guild. By myself. The door swings open, a familiar guard on the other side. He ushers me in, checking the alley before he closes the heavy metal behind us.

"I've got most of the women in the back. There's a few on stage, but I should be able to get them to your man," he mumbles, leading me along the dark hallway.

This place is much louder than the previous gambling halls I've been in. I pass several bricks to him as we walk. He'll place them backstage. Hopefully, the building will be demolished enough that no one will notice there aren't any bodies back there except for the few handlers who make sure the women get on stage.

He glances over his shoulder, determination in his eyes. "We have fifteen minutes. Make them count."

I nod, then slip into the main salon. Men linger at the round tables, placing bets and watching the gameplay. Others cluster at the bar, laughing over the loud music blaring through the room.

Only three women are on the stage, a familiar brokenness on their faces. Fear laces every line of their bodies as they half-heartedly sway to the beat. Shock collars hang around their necks, keeping them in line. Thankfully, they're easy to remove unless Jenkins upgraded his products. I wouldn't put it past him to have trackers in them. I thought about stashing them in trucks leaving the city, but we didn't have enough time to set something like that up.

"Cruz!"

I whip toward the sound of my name carrying over the noise. A man I can't place approaches, a grin gracing his face. I don't have time for a chitchat, but to snub him would give me away. Then again, I wasn't exactly friendly with the other members. I earned a reputation while in the Guild. I scramble for the part I played not very long ago.

The man reaches out his hand and I shake it firmly, resisting the urge to wipe my palm on my leg when he releases me.

"You disappeared. Everyone will be so glad you're back," he shouts, attracting attention from several others.

"I'm only in town a day or two. Can't allow my businesses to fail or Jenkins will take me out." I smirk and tuck my hand in my pocket. It's a tight fit with the explosives that I momentarily forgot I'd stuffed in there.

"Will you miss the Auction then? They keep touting it as the largest one yet." He leans in closer, not bothering to wait for a response. "Personally, I'll be surprised if they have it at all with the many issues they're running into."

I raise an eyebrow, weighing the risks of finding more information versus getting the fuck out of here as quickly as possible. Lacey won't wait for a call to activate the charges. I'd rather not blow myself up for some gossip from a mid-level member.

"I've been off the grid for too long it seems. Perhaps I should swing by headquarters. We certainly want the Auction to go off without a hitch. When do they have it planned for?"

"Next week, though no one's received an invitation. At least not at the embassy. If you find anything out, you'll let me know, right?" He wiggles his eyebrows at me and I nod.

I don't bother giving him a farewell. Rushing toward the edge of the room, I slip into the bathroom. I check my time as I press the explosives in hidden places, then tuck a blasting cap in them. One room after another, I repeat the process methodically.

I don't have enough time to put any by the bar since there are so many people stuffed around it. If it was a simple timed charger, I might be able to pull it off, but this device requires more assembly. Even with Shane's insistence that C-4 isn't sensitive, no one was willing to push it. Too much rides on this to fuck with explosives.

I check the time and blanch. I have less than three minutes to get out. The women are missing from the stage, but no one seems to notice. The man from before lifts his hand as I make my way toward the exit. I was supposed to go out the back, but I don't have time for that. I'll barely make it as it is.

Blasting out the door, I suck in deep breaths of night air. I glance left, then right, and don't hear or see anything. Adrenaline pumps through my system, heightening my senses. I swear there's a ticking in my ears, counting down the seconds until Lacey initiates the sequence. I have no idea how large the blast radius will be. We set a shit ton in there, so I assume it'll be massive.

I take off toward the quiet street, pushing my body faster with each step. A muffled explosion shatters from behind me and my muscles scream. Pumping my arms, the next detonation rings through the chilly air, followed by another, then another.

I race across the street, attempting to put as much distance between me and the building as I can. It's not enough.

As the front of the gambling den blows, I'm knocked off my feet. Heat sears across my back. Another wave hits me and my ears fill with a roaring whine. Curling into a ball as another shockwave rolls over my body, my head swims, and memories lick at the edges of my mind. I grasp at the image of Aelia as it dissolves, and I fall into the darkness.

Twenty Four

Aelia

A consistent beep rings through the air, penetrating the walls of my closet. I jolt upright and throw on my clothes from last night. Once I open the door, the tone cuts off, but an alarm blares from the floor below. The window at the end of the hall is dark with the moon still filtering through so the alarm isn't a lockdown, thank fuck.

I rush to the back stairwell, taking the steps two at a time. My back protests, still healing from my time with Molly. The skin pulls and stretches with each leap. It's a constant reminder of how I'm broken both inside and out. I shove the thought away as I push the door open to the next level.

Guards hurry back and forth, yelling and running into each other. It's chaos incarnate. No one seems to be in charge or knows what the fuck they're doing. It's not my place to take over, especially since I have no idea what's wrong.

The lights start up, the strobe adding more chaos to the scene. I rush back into the stairwell and up to the office. I don't know where Jenkins is. The upper levels are quiet, so I doubt there's actually a fire. Slowing to a stop, I smooth my hands down my skirt. There's no way to get the wrinkles out. Not that anyone will notice.

Stepping into the office, I scan the area. No Jenkins. No light. Nothing. Even the camera in the corner of the room is off. A flutter starts in my stomach, then moves to my chest.

I trip on my way to my desk, hoping my computer still works. The bright glare of the monitor sends a rush of relief through me, and my leg jiggles as I wait for it to boot up.

"Come on, you piece of shit," I mutter.

The desktop icons appear, and I let out a shuddering breath. My eyes dart to the door, then the camera, and back to the screen. My first order of business is to drain the remaining funds.

I yelp when I pull up one after another, finding them flush with cash. Where Jenkins got it all from, I have no idea. It wasn't there last night and I don't have time to follow the trail back. I transfer them to a dummy account I set up months ago at Dante's insistence. Jenkins will still have access, but only if he can find it.

There isn't much else I can do except print off the list of current assets trapped in the Pit as well as those being sent to the satellite cities. The printer lights up, moving at a snail's pace. I should get on Jenkins's computer and see what damage I can do there.

If he comes in though, I'll be hard pressed to come up with an excuse. Maybe he'll buy that I'm trying to get the fire alarms under control. He's been distracted and ignoring me mostly, so it just might work.

I tiptoe to the door and peek out. It's blissfully empty, the thud of rushing feet and light echo from the alarms filtering up the stairs. Once at his desk, I slam into his chair and shake the mouse to wake up the monitor. He never turns it off, citing some archaic knowledge about bugs in the system infiltrating while the machine is off. It's a blessing tonight.

I flex my trembling fingers before searching file after file for anything that might be useful. Jenkins never took away the privileges Dante convinced him to transfer to me. Which helped, but now I have no idea what I'm supposed to be looking for. I open every program I can, half of them leading to error boxes.

"What the fuck were you doing?" I whisper as my fingers fly across the keyboard.

Finally, I reach one that works. A code box pops up and my heart thunders in my chest. I only know the basics, maybe a bit more, but I also haven't used those skills in a very long time.

My brain short-circuits as line after line appears. I still don't know if this is something that will hurt or help us. The cursor hovers over the box and the code stops. I didn't even do anything, but clearly they can see my movements.

A pain stabs behind my eyes from glancing at the door so often. The brightness of the screen doesn't help. I hold my breath, then move the cursor again, slowly inching toward the x in the corner. I cough as the arrow flashes from white to blue to pink. It cycles through colors faster than I can keep up with.

The box fills again, but not with lines of code. No, it's merely one word. Over and over. Faster and faster.

Angel.

I shove away from the desk, covering my mouth with my hands to keep my sob from echoing through the quiet room. Even if this isn't Dante, which I highly doubt it is, it's clearly someone who knows him.

Wheeling myself closer, I click on the box and the messages stop. I type one code sequence I remember when Ember and I were taking the class. It's the only thing I remember, actually. I'm hoping this doesn't come across as strange, but I don't know enough to convey what I need. I smile as dots appear, creating the image of a hippo. Is there time for this shit? No. But I don't know what else to do.

The lines of numbers and letters start up again and I let it roll. There's nothing else I remember how to do in terms of code without fucking something up. I bring up the admin for the system and open it up to remote control. The last thing is to turn off the monitor. It will slow down Jenkins enough. Hopefully that will help.

Snatching the papers from the printer, I rush from the room. As soon as my foot hits the first stair, alarms ring out. The shriek weaves through the air and spears into my head, leaving a throb behind.

It cuts out after a minute, but as I pass through a landing, the doorway to the main ballroom bursts open. Men stream outside, hands covering their ears. I catch a glimpse of Jenkins's blotchy face roaring at some guards.

Ducking around the corner, I sprint to the door leading to the Pit. After what I did upstairs, my time has finally come. Maybe I can convince Rachel to run with me. She's adamant that she'll stay here and protect the others. Personally, I think she could do more good on the outside, but at least I'll have a contact within the Guild.

The guard taps the side of his nose and widens his eyes as he pulls open the door. I don't know what the fuck that's supposed to tell me. Adrenaline is the only thing keeping me going at this point.

My heart thuds, protesting how hard I'm pushing my body. I ignore the stitch in my side telling me to slow down. I can rest when I'm far away from this place.

Skidding around the corner, I slow, the cold concrete biting into my bare feet. I didn't think this through. The Pit is chaos, mirroring the floors above. There has to be at least two hundred people, mostly women, packed in the space. I'll never find Rachel in this mess. I throw my shoulders back and tip my chin up.

"Get the fuck out of my way," I bellow, channeling all my rage against the Guild into my tone.

The people closest to me whip around, eyes widening when they spot me. They may not know who I am, but they know what I come down here for. They scramble out of the way, pushing others back as they do. A path clears and I pull in a shuddering breath. I hate being the Mistress, yet I can't deny it's useful in this situation.

"Where's Rachel?" I sneer as I scan the crowd.

A hush falls over the crowd in a wave, punctuated by wailing with a backdrop of anguished sobs. Rachel's light brown hair appears, weaving through the masses until we're in a face-off. She smirks, planting her hands on her hips.

"Something we can do for you, Mistress? We're a little busy here." She gestures around her before piercing me with a hostile stare.

"Inspection time." I purse my lips and swallow down the bile inching up my throat.

Her shoulders stiffen and she nods. "This way, Mistress. Even in a crisis, we're ever your puppets."

She leads me toward a door tucked in the corner—the same one I came through several weeks ago. The rumble of arguments and panic take up again in our wake. I've put them at risk coming here. It can't be helped. Maybe the chaos will save them from being interrogated when Jenkins finds me missing. Or maybe he won't suspect me at all. He's clueless about Dante. Perhaps my fate will be the same.

"What the hell is going on?" Rachel hisses as she tugs open the door and shoves me into the dark.

"I have no fucking clue. The fire alarms are going haywire. I went to the office and implemented—"

"Dark Horse." I can hear the grin in her voice, though I can't see her face.

"I never agreed to calling it that. But I doubt it matters since we're in the middle of executing it anyway. Now, what's happening in the Pit?" I'm suddenly very glad for the number of times Jenkins has sent me down here recently. It gave Rachel and me time to plan at the very least.

She holds up a hand as we come to the stairs, then creep down them. "The holding cells flooded. Water was leaking from the ceiling, then it came out of the vents. There's at least three feet of standing water in there. Good thing it's sunken or the whole Pit would be fucked."

"Did you find anyone to ferry me out?" I ask as we sneak around the last corner, the parking garage coming into view.

"No. You're going out the main door or the vent. Since I'm not confident in your ability to recognize cardinal directions, the vent is out and we're winging it," she whispers.

I turn wide eyes to her. "You expect to wing this when I'm wearing this?"

"I'm going to create a distraction." A sound of protest erupts from me, and she holds out her hands. "It's the best I could come up. Don't fail, Aelia."

Searching her face, I find nothing but determination. There's no way to dissuade her. Even if I called it off, I'd be signing my life away. And Rachel would still proceed full steam ahead, dragging me kicking and screaming the entire way. She levels me with a glare until I nod.

"Okay, give me three minutes, then make a break for the door. Do not turn around. Do not try to help me. Do not stop until you find him."

Tears fill her eyes and I pull her into a hug. As we separate, sharp alarms blare through the parking garage. Men bellow from somewhere, their voices echoing off the concrete and making it hard to decipher where they are. She glances at me one more time before scrambling around the corner.

Tucking my body behind the door, I close my eyes and count. It's the longest three minutes of my life, and that's saying something with what I've been through. Waiting as voices bellow, alarms reverberate, and finally an engine revs is the worst. I'm not about to peek out in case one of the many feet thundering past sees me. Once the time runs out, I pull in a deep breath and center myself before easing open the door.

Tires screech as I slip through, and my jaw drops. Rachel flies by behind the driver's seat of an SUV. Several guards shoot at the tires, their bullets pinging off the windows and embedding into the back. One of the taillights explodes, plastic ricocheting everywhere.

I shake myself from my paralysis and sprint for freedom. Rachel's intent is clear, but I can't follow behind her. Not with the guards still attempting to take her out. I skirt the edge of the area, weaving around pillars. My heart thuds and my head throbs the more exposed I become. This was not a good plan. Every second I expect a bullet to rip through me. It's a pain I never want to feel again.

A man shouts over the others, his words drowned out by the chaos swirling through the air. I slide across a hood, knowing I'll relive that moment later—if I make it. The engine revs and I whip my head toward the vehicle. Rachel's eyes meet mine a split second before she crashes into the metal garage door.

Time slows and the air bags explode, shoving her head back even as it pillows her face. The front of the vehicle crumples, bits of metal, plastic, and glass pinwheeling through the air.

A ringing invades my ears, even as my body flies toward the opening she's created at the bottom of the gate. I pivot at the last moment and rip at the door handle in one motion. My feet trip over each other when it bounces, only opening halfway.

"Rachel," I cry, just now realizing the heaving sobs leaving me.

She shakes her head, eyes finding mine. And then she's falling into my arms. All of ten seconds have passed, but it's too long. We don't have time to assess her injuries. Men yell from behind us as I drop to my stomach and squeeze past the tire. The gap is barely wide enough for my shoulders and Rachel shoves me through, a jagged piece of metal catching me at the hip. It cuts down my leg as she pushes, and I bite my tongue, copper flooding my mouth.

Once free, the cool night air slaps me in the face. I spin on my stomach, reaching my hand through the hole.

"Rachel, grab on," I yell over the havoc raging on the other side.

Her fingers latch onto my wrist and I yank her back as hard as I can. My strength wanes—I pushed myself too hard. I refuse to leave her, though.

Staggering upright, I crouch and latch onto her arm again. She glances over her shoulder as her body scrapes against the metal, and I scream at her to help me.

Her wide blue eyes find mine, her mouth making a perfect O before she's ripped from my grasp. I fall back and my head bounces on the concrete, forcing the air from my lungs. I gasp as black spots swim in my vision, blocking out the stars twinkling overhead. My stomach clenches. My muscles scream.

A single gunshot rings through the night.

Wheezing, I roll to my side and glance at the gap spilling jagged light onto the pavement. Rachel's lifeless eyes stare through the hole, blood trickling from the corner of her parted mouth.

Another gunshot and the world goes black.

TWENTY FIVE

Dante

"How long?" I croak as I blink grey spots from my vision.

My entire body is on fire, burning my lungs with each pull of breath. The scratchy fabric brushes against my cheek as I twitch. I attempt to roll, but multiple hands stop me.

"Don't move. We're almost done with your wounds," Jag grunts.

"You're fucking lucky, Dante. If you would have been any closer, your back would have been shredded." Avery's voice cuts through my muddled thoughts.

The events from last night…I think it was last night…crash into me. My head throbs and I close my eyes as nausea rolls through me.

Jag clears his throat and I peek at him through slitted lids. "You've been out two days. Or rather two nights. Between your back and hitting your head, you've been a little disoriented. Everything can wait until you're fixed up."

"Tell me."

He shakes his head, glancing at someone by the door, then back at me. Worry lines his eyes, none of the usual gruffness present. Something happened and him not telling me only ratchets up my anxiety.

"Alex still isn't picking up. Raven's crew got the women away. Only a handful of men were among them. They opted to stay. We put them up at one of the safe houses."

"Say it," I groan as someone pokes at my wounds. He's dancing around what went wrong and I don't know how long I'll stay conscious. With the waves of pain radiating from my back, I doubt long.

"Helms and Sam went off grid. We're pretty sure they're alive, but they were being followed by the Guild. Mason is still on the road. He took the women west because some weird shit is happening in Synd." He glances over me again, the vein in his forehead pulsing.

I don't know why he's pissed off. Jag isn't prone to nervousness, so someone must have fucked up. Maybe it's me he wants to blast, but since I'm injured, he's holding back. As if I couldn't take him lecturing me for my decisions while my body is slowly melting.

"Just fucking spit it out, Jag," I wheeze, flexing my fingers over and over.

He tucks his chin to his chest. "Shane's missing. Ren said he got a text from Sam and then she stopped responding. Shane was inside still, setting the charges. But she sent it to their group chat or some shit. Shane never came out. Ren almost ran in there, but one of Raven's crew held him back. He's pissed at her."

"So let me get this straight. Ren and Raven are the only ones who came back. And everyone else is either missing or possibly dead. And you're fucking concerned over whether my back heals properly?" My voice rises the more I get out.

I struggle to get upright, panting. Having this conversation while I'm trapped on my stomach is degrading and doesn't hold as much weight. Avery steps into my line of sight, shoving Jag back, and getting in my face.

"Listen here, buddy. You're going to lay the fuck down and let Nova finish patching you up or so help me I will drown you in the lake," she hisses.

My arms give out, and I fall with a groan onto my stomach again. "We don't have a damn lake."

"I'll fucking find one, asshole. It was hard enough to get your ass back to headquarters. You're not going to go all hero complex and try to run off to save everyone. Not to mention we don't know where half of them are. Once Nova says you're good to go, you can run off and risk your life all you want. By then, you'll have to answer to Aelia." She smirks, crossing her arms as if she knows she won.

She did. But I'm not going to admit it. I scowl, breathing my way through the last bit. My mind floats, never fully settling on one image.

Several minutes, hours, hell maybe days, later a familiar face fills my vision. Her dark hair sways as she sits. Bruises grace half her face and a cut below her eye stands out, garishly red. We've only met a few times and never without Raven, but she was in the Guild, like so many others. It's like I'm staring at every person I wasn't able to save in the year I was there.

"Are you okay?" I ask, instantly regretting the words. "I'm sorry."

She waves away my apology, then sucks in a deep breath before leveling me with a look. "We don't really know each other, but I think we have someone in common."

"Raven stuck around just to get you back. She was going to—"

Nova holds up her hand, smiling just a bit. I wonder when she smiled last. I wonder what the fuck happened to her in there. Asking would not be wise. Light still shines from her eyes and I refuse to be the one to extinguish it.

"When I was first brought in, one of the catchers—I don't know what else to call them—handed me off to a man named Grant. I was brought to a small room where an older man told Grant to take me to the cages. I didn't know what that meant, but soon I was stuffed into a prison. They lined the walls of a long room." She swallows, tipping her head back as my heart thunders in my chest.

I push upright, wincing as the tape pulls at my skin. It's like they've attached a water-logged blanket to my back. It's wet and sticky and disgusting. I swing my legs over the side of the makeshift hospital bed that's nothing more than a long table lined with padding. Bracing my hands on my knees, I breathe through the pain.

"They weren't canvas tents? Or a big room that was blocked off with bars?"

She shakes her head. "There were two other women in there. Natalie, who wasn't exactly strong enough to withstand the darkness, much less anything else they planned on doing to us. And another woman. I believe you know her."

"Aelia," I breathe.

Every emotion I've shoved down deep wells up within me, and I drop my head in my hands. Guilt and shame war with the need to race out of here and rectify every mistake I've made.

No matter what I do, for as long as I live, I'll never make it up to her for leaving her behind. I justified my decisions with excuses. She told me to go, we had a plan, she would have stayed with Avery, I never would have survived if I stayed. Every single one sends another spear through my heart.

"She never said your name. But she talked about you. Raven didn't share why we were here in the first place, and believe me, we've had a conversation about communication. It was just a series of random missteps that no one could have predicted. But I thought you should know she's not upset with you. She doesn't blame you for leaving."

"We found you the night she went back," I say, my voice muffled by my hands.

"Ren told me what happened. Told me his theories, or rather, Mason's theories. They were wrong, which I'm sure I don't need to tell you."

I raise my head, meeting her steady gaze. "What happened to her? Is she okay?"

"I don't know. They took her away for a while. When they brought her to the cages again, she was…not okay. I cleaned her up the best I could. She was better by the time they took me away. I mean, as good as she could be. I did my best." Her chin trembles as if I'm going to yell at her for not doing enough.

"Where'd they take you?"

She sighs and rubs her palms on her leggings. "I think they drugged us. I don't remember them coming, but when I woke up, I was in a room. It looked like a supply closet that was converted into a makeshift bedroom of sorts. I won't go into the details since I'm pretty sure we'd both lose what little we have in our stomachs. They weren't exactly gentle when handling me. For some reason, they never raped me. I don't know why not.

"A guard found me. I don't know his name or why he did it, but he got me out. I wandered away into the woods and eventually found myself in that alley. No one bothered to help me. Truthfully, I'm surprised your people stopped."

"And then Aelia went back. How did she get to Byron's?" I'm not even asking Nova. She doesn't have answers.

"I believe she was sold. I don't know anything after I was moved, but she was convinced that was her father's plan."

It makes sense, even though I didn't want to admit it. Still doesn't explain why his house was on fire. Unless she killed him. Pride wells up inside of me, drowning out the shame. I hope she killed him.

And I hope it was brutal and satisfying and healing in a way I could never give her. His death belonged to her. Along with Jenkins's and her father's. But none more so than Grant's. If I can hand him to her trussed up and ripe for the killing, all the better.

"If anyone can get out of there, it's her."

Raven stomps into the small room, nostrils flaring, but at least she's not glaring at me. I sit upright, distancing myself as much as possible from Nova. Raven steps in between us and plants her fists on her hips.

"Why the hell are you out of bed? You were supposed to patch his ass up and go rest." Underneath the annoyance is a layer of concern.

"Rae, I'm going to need you to take it down a notch. I've dealt with enough shit without you going all protective mode on me. Now, instead of scolding me in front of an audience, why don't we go back to our room." Nova tilts her head and Raven presents the way, not willing to give an inch.

Jag steps next to me, offering me his shoulder. It's a struggle to gain my feet, but I manage with minimal grunting. He leads me toward the main hall, probably set on the room I've been using here at headquarters.

"Byrns is on his way back," he mutters, nodding to Ren, whose eyes dart away from me.

"Any word on Helms?" I grunt as I shuffle my way forward.

He sighs, nodding to a man who looks familiar. I narrow my eyes and he smirks. Fuck. I don't know his name, but he kept harassing Rachel when I'd visit her in the Pit. He ducks his head, digging into his food again. My stomach grumbles, making Jag snort.

"Helms talked to Mac. I think he called Hawk too, whoever the hell that is."

"His VP. Doesn't matter."

The rumble of a bike echoes through the quiet space. Whipping my head to the front door, my heart races. It's been too long since our territory has heard those sounds. I tug Jag toward the noise, and he grumbles the whole way. I'd go alone if I thought I wouldn't pass out halfway there.

"Slow the fuck down before you hurt yourself. They'll still be there."

Spring air hits me as the doors pop open, and I suck in a deep breath. Helms kills the engine and Sam hops from the back. I didn't realize they were taking his bike when they went to deal with the torture chambers. Hopefully, they were able to get the victims medical care before they passed them over the Byrns.

"Where's Shane?" Sam demands, eyes darting around as if he'll magically appear.

Her steps falter, then she's racing past us and throwing herself at Ren. He wraps his arms around her, and his face softens as he buries his face in her neck. He spins them and she links her ankles behind his back.

"Should have known you'd run away, Princess."

Ren pivots, scanning the dark, and a sob leaves Sam. Shane steps from the shadows around the corner of the building, looking like he's been through an explosion. Helms stops in front of me, scanning me up and down.

I try not to watch the King's reunion, but it's hard to keep my gaze away. Sam drops from Ren's arms and flies into Shane's. I never understood their dynamic until now. Shane envelops her and before long, she's sandwiched between the two. It's a raw moment I'm afraid to see, yet terrified of looking away.

"What the fuck is wrong with you?" Sam cries, her voice muffled by their bodies.

"I could say the same of you, Princess. I'm fucking starving." They untangle from one another and make their way inside.

Helms clears his throat, running his hand through his hair. "We took out a few of the Guild's men. Took a while to lose the rest. We hunkered down for a bit to make sure we'd lost them. Rode the long way back. Would have called, but Sam said they might have hacked our location since they kept showing up wherever we were."

"You should tell Lacey. See if she can figure it out." Exhaustion hits me hard, almost bringing me to my knees. I struggle to stay upright, even with Jag holding me up. "Did she get in?"

"There's a lot we need to talk about, but it'll wait until after you've slept," Jag says.

Helms hand stalls halfway between us like he was going to clap me on the shoulder, then thought better of it. I huff, nodding. We've been in a bad way before. We'll get through this too. Eventually. In the thick of things, it's hard to see the finish line. Helms steps past us, probably to find Mac. I don't blame him. My heart clenches as I stare into the night.

"I keep waiting for her to step out of the shadows. Like she'll just magically appear if I wish hard enough," I murmur.

Jag glances behind us and his arm slides against my back, creating pinpricks of pain, and I pull in a deep breath. I close my eyes, focusing on the fact that Aelia's still alive. I didn't get the others killed. They're walking and joking and giving each other shit. We saved a lot of people and hit the Guild where it'll hurt. We finally did something. Yet it's still not enough. It'll never be enough until she's here with me.

I open my eyes, opening my mouth to tell Jag to help me back inside, and I freeze. Squeezing my eyes shut, I shake my head, then open them again. Aelia steps out of the darkness, emerging from between two houses.

A mirage. My mind conjured the one thing it needed to heal. She's a false hope, dangled before me. Or maybe it's my guilt manifesting to torment me some more.

I've been glimpsing her form every time I lie down to sleep. Every time I step into a dark room. Every time I spend more than five minutes alone. She's been haunting me, reminding me of all the ways I failed.

When the figure takes a staggered step, my breath whooshes from my lungs. Shoving away from Jag, I sprint toward her. She stops in the middle of the street, tears cascading down her face.

I drop to my knees, wrapping my arms around her waist. It's not until her fingers slide through my hair I'm convinced she's real. A choked sob leaves her, and I glance up.

"Hello, angel."

TWENTY SIX

Aelia

I'm floating, both from the exhaustion and pain, but also being with Dante again. I'd hoped for so long, the wish became smoke, slipping through my hands. Being with him again was a dream I no longer thought would happen. Now that he's here, clinging to me, I can't wrap my mind around reality.

I grip the back of his neck as he presses his face into my stomach. When he stiffens, I yank my hand away.

"Sorry," he mumbles, his body swaying.

Glancing up, my eyes meet Jag's, and he prowls toward us. "Raines, let go."

Jag's hand lands on Dante's shoulder, attempting to tug him away, but his arms tighten around me. He hits a sore spot on my back, and I hold my breath until the ache passes.

Swallowing hard, I press my lips together. Jag narrows his eyes as I sway. The adrenaline that kept me going the last two nights has long passed, leaving me a shell stumbling around Rima.

Everything was too bright, too busy, too terrifying. I hid during the day, though that probably wasn't smart. I wonder if I have a concussion from hitting my head. It would explain the confused state I found myself in. Every face I came across was twisted, morphing into an enemy.

Convincing myself I was free wasn't an option. Even now, I can't seem to grasp that I'm safe. Especially with the way Jag is studying me as if I'm a wild animal that will rip Dante to shreds at the first sign of distress.

"Raines, you're going to pass out. Let her go," Jag growls, his eyes darting from Dante to me and back again.

My nails dig into Dante's arms as I ease back. Eventually, he drops them to his sides, head hanging. I don't know what to say or how to say it. I can't even trust my own voice at this point.

The front door to the large building pops open and several people spill out. Of course I don't recognize any of them. From the hostility painted on their faces, I doubt I'll be welcomed into the fold.

Gazing down at Dante, I wonder what he told them. Or Jag. Or Avery. I thought we were on the same page, had become friends. Maybe I was wrong.

I take another step back, my leg aching with each step. I cleaned it up the best I could, but it wasn't easy. The restaurants I passed as I walked wouldn't let someone like me in. Not only am I dressed like a hooker, and not the kind who chooses the profession, but also I'm dirty, bloody, and look like I've run into more than one fist. Not exactly the clientele they're hoping to attract.

I found a gas station that handed over a key to their bathroom. The attendant's eyes lingered a bit too long, though, and I rushed to get out of there.

Standing in front of this group, I realize I made a mistake. I thought because of Dante I'd be accepted. Shame flows through me as I glance down and take in my appearance. I bite my tongue to keep the fresh round of tears at bay.

Clearing my throat, I fix my eyes on Jag. His lips part as if he's going to placate me, and I subtly shake my head. I get it. This isn't my family. These aren't my friends. The last thing they need is another mouth to feed. Another liability. Another person to protect.

Even if it's more than that, it doesn't matter. I don't want to know. I'll give them the information and then…I have no idea what I'll do, but I won't jeopardize Dante's mission or his friendships.

"I moved the funds to the dummy account." I pull the papers I stuffed into the waistband of my skirt. "These might help with current counts. The holding cell in the Pit flooded as well as the Auction ballroom. The fire alarms went haywire. And the door to the parking garage is damaged."

I brush my fingers across the deep cut on my thigh, the image of Rachel's lifeless eyes staring at me. Shaking my head, I focus on Jag again. I can't think of anything else to tell them. I'm sure there's something, but I'm too tired—deep in my bones tired.

I've spent so long waiting to be free, hoping to find a place I belong. Dante's promises wormed their way into my heart, no matter how I tried to protect myself. I don't think he anticipated the backlash from these people.

"Anything else?" Jag asks, and I shake my head as I shuffle back another step.

Dante's frozen figure shivers and his hands drop to the pavement. I don't know what happened to him, and I doubt Jag will tell me. I reach for him but tuck my hand around my waist instead.

Jag leaps into action and several of the others rush forward. They surround him, blocking my view. Terror floods me at no longer being able to see him—to touch him. No one pays me any attention as I stumble over the curb. Within the span of a breath, I duck into the shadows between two houses.

My mind screams at me to run. To find a place where I'll be safe, but my feet refuse to move. I watch from the darkness as they haul him up. His head lolls around, eyes blinking sleepily. The vise around my heart squeezes, stealing the air from my lungs.

Avery appears in the large doorway, the light outlining her figure. She scans the area, taking in the group slowly moving toward her with Dante stuck in the middle. I can barely make out her eyes narrowing.

"Where is she?" she demands as her fists plant themselves on her hips.

A woman who could probably pass for my sister glances over her shoulder and her face morphs from hostility to confusion.

"She was right there," a man says, waving at the street. "Must have taken off. Not surprising."

"Are you fucking kidding me? What the hell is wrong with you people?" Avery shouts, throwing up her hands.

Jag steps in front of her, letting the others carry Dante inside. His voice barely carries on the wind to me. "She went back with them, Avery. That says something."

"For fuck's sake. Did anyone bother asking *why*? Or was that just too fucking much for you?" She glares at them, then slides past Jag. "Never mind. You all are assholes and will rot in fucking hell for it."

Jag spins as she stomps past him. "Where the hell are you going?"

"To find her, jackass. You think Dante will be happy...no. Do you think he'll be *functional* when he realizes she's gone again? And because of you?" Tears fill my eyes at her defense of me. I knew going back was a risk, but I didn't think they'd believe I was the enemy because of it.

Jag has the good sense to look ashamed as he glances away. "Let me get him into his room and I'll go with you."

She nods, but as soon as they disappear, she marches toward me. I lean against the dark house, then plop down. No use trying to keep my feet underneath me. I won't make Avery chase after me. That would only get her hurt or killed. She steps into the darkness and scans the space until her eyes alight on me, and she heaves out a sigh.

"Didn't get very far, did you?" she whispers before sitting next to me.

"I wanted to make sure they got Dante inside. What happened to him?" I swipe at the tears, frustration flowing through me. I didn't cry until I met Dante and I blame him for the fact I can't keep my shit together anymore.

"Well, when he saw you at Byron's, Mason had to pistol whip him to stop him from chasing after you. Couple nights ago, though, was merely poor time management. They blew up a building and he was too close. His back isn't bad, but he hit his head on the way down so he's been out for a bit. I mean, he'd wake up, but he wasn't making any sense." She sighs, leaning her head against the wood. "He kept calling for you."

They blame me for his injuries. "They think I'm a mole, don't they?"

"It's been tossed around. Honestly, I just think they're all a little high-strung right now. They're a family and half of them were missing. They showed up like minutes before you did. It's just been a lot piled on top of the stress from the Guild." She rolls her head toward me. I refuse to meet her gaze.

"I can't stay, Avery. Even if Dante wants me here, my presence will only complicate things. He'll be able to function just fine without me. At least for a little while. Once the Guild is taken care of, maybe I can come back." The words burn as they leave me.

"Yeah? And where the hell you think you're going to go?"

"Back to Westmont? Or maybe Synd. I don't know. I could just find a place here in Rima to hide. Just need some clothes." I gesture to my tattered attire. It doesn't leave much to the imagination.

"Fat fucking chance. Not about the clothes, obviously. Dante needs you. Are you really going to bail on him?" She raises an eyebrow.

"Can you smuggle me in? I'm too tired to deal with the stares."

"Well, that was fucking easy," she mutters.

I snort, then push to my feet with a groan. "I learned pretty quickly not to argue with you unless I was sure I could win. And I don't want to leave. I just know it's probably for the best in these circumstances. But if I can hide out in a room that isn't locked, then I'll take that."

She stands, leading me from the shadows. "We've got a lot to catch up on. But we can save it for later. Right now, we need to get Dante better and clean you up. Then we can deal with the Guild."

She hooks around the front of the house, and I follow her across the street, then around the corner of the building they all disappeared into. An emblem painted on a side door stands out, a large viper wrapped around a sword taking up the length of it.

I search my limited memories of motorcycle clubs and realize this is their headquarters. I wonder how many bikers are tucked away inside. The people who snubbed me were probably the help Dante called. They didn't look like bikers, but then again, not all of them wear leather.

"The bed in Dante's room is a queen, so there should be enough room for both of you," Avery says over her shoulder as we make our way down a muted hallway.

"He stays here?" I assumed he'd have a house. There's so much I never learned—couldn't learn—that I'm second-guessing whether I made the right decision despite the points Avery made.

"Helms and Mac took over his house. He needed distance, I think." She sighs as she stops in front of a closed door. "I know you don't know these people, but you will. They just need a little reassurance. They've been burned a lot from what I've gathered. Just don't slip away without a word. I don't think I could take it."

She waits until I nod before she swings the door open, stepping back. A single lamp by his bedside illuminates half his face. How he's able to stand lying on his back, I have no idea. I step in, taking in the barren space.

Nothing hangs on the walls, no papers or devices other than his phone charging on the tiny desk shoved in the corner. Even the armoire is empty, other than the pile of clothes he was wearing earlier. He clearly hasn't been doing anything else in here.

I jump when the door shuts quickly behind me, then whip around when Dante groans. I rush to his side, hands hovering over his body. I don't want to hurt him more, but his pale face winces and I drop to my knees next to the bed.

The cut on my leg rips open, sending warm blood trickling to my ankle. I should deal with it, but there isn't even a towel in here. Resting my forehead on the mattress, I breathe slowly, closing my eyes to focus on anything other than the pain. It's nothing compared to what Molly put me through. I'll be fine in a minute. The lie rests in my brain, mocking me.

Dante groans again as he rolls on his side to face me. I prop my chin on the covers, staring at his chest rising and falling rapidly. As it eases into a steady rhythm, my muscles relax.

I won't last long kneeling on the tiled floor with injuries peppering my body. But I can't pull myself away from him. Deep grooves form between his eyes, pulling his brows low, and I trace them gently with my finger.

"Aelia," he breathes, and I bite back a sob.

My leg pulses, each heartbeat forcing more blood from the wound, but I refuse to move. I'll stay a little longer, watching him sleep. He spent so long watching over me, it's the least I can do. My eyes grow heavy and my chest tightens.

I don't know when I fell asleep, but soon strong arms lift me, and my body eases into a mattress that feels like a cloud. Warmth invades my flesh and I shiver before succumbing to sleep once more.

TWENTY SEVEN

Dante

"They did what?" I hiss, not wanting to wake Aelia.

I glance down at her sleeping form tucked next to me. She puffs out steady breaths through parted lips. Every few minutes my heart pounds and my palms become itchy and I have to convince myself she isn't a hallucination.

I glance back at Avery, who glares, but I doubt she's upset with me. From what she's been telling me, everyone, including Jag of all people, were shitty to Aelia. I don't remember much, but I do remember her slight smile when she heard my voice.

"Listen, you don't have to kick their asses or anything. I already did that. And more than a few of them are *very* ashamed of themselves. I just thought you should know that they haven't seen her since that little encounter. So, when she finally wakes for good, it might be smart to go in short bursts with them." She leans back in her chair, eyes darting to Aelia.

I sigh, rolling on my back as I run my fingers through my hair. I wince as the tape pulls my still-healing skin. Nova took the bandages off the smaller wounds yesterday, leaving most of the flesh exposed. My head hurts more than my skin, though. Pressing my thumbs to my temples, I attempt to ease the pounding. Avery makes a sound in the back of her throat.

"Here," she snarls, and I peek at her.

I struggle to sit, gingerly leaning against the wall. Aelia rolls, her arm tucking around my thigh. She sighs as I rest my hand on her hair before taking the meds and glass Avery's holding. I don't want to face the others. They can keep their judgements to themselves. Once we're all in the same room and hash everything out, they'll be fine. And I'll have Aelia.

"Why hasn't she woken up?" I ask, threading my fingers through her hair.

"Her body has been running on high alert for weeks. She wasn't merely maintaining anymore." She glares and I scowl at her. "She's exhausted, Dante. Now that she's here she knows she's safe. So her body is recharging. Just make sure you're here when she wakes up. And for fuck's sake, do not lock her in."

"Stop lecturing me, Avery. I'm not a fucking child." There's no bite behind the words. Our conversation drained me, though I feel like I've been sleeping for weeks.

"I'm going to harass Sam into teaching me how to gut a man. Oh, and they've got a meeting scheduled for tonight. I'll make sure you're there."

She walks out without bothering to wait for an answer. Tipping my head back, I close my eyes. My mind won't settle, all the worries pile up alongside the list of shit we still need to do. We can't make any more moves until Ghost gets here. Or Alex comes back—if he comes back. Definitely not before Aelia and I talk. As much as I don't want her to relive what happened while we were separated, we don't have a choice.

"Dante," she whispers, and I glance at her.

"Hey, angel. Go back to sleep," I murmur, brushing my thumb over her forehead.

She grumbles, though I can't make out the words. Scooting down, I swallow a groan as her hand brushes over my length through my sweatpants. I'm not even wearing underwear. This is not the time for that reunion. My cock doesn't seem to care. Her hand settles on my heart as she tucks her body closer and fits her leg between mine.

"This is real. You're here. And we're safe."

I don't know if she's asking or stating, but I hug her tighter. "This is real, not a dream. We're here together. And we're as safe as we can be."

I won't lie to her. She'd see right through it, anyway. There are so many things I had to hide from her before—things I wanted to share but never could. I want to shake her fully awake and tell her everything. I press a kiss to her hair instead.

"I'm sick of sleeping," she murmurs, then gasps, shooting upright. "You're hurt. And they needed you. You should be at…"

Her face blanks, mouth parted as she searches for the word she lost. I sit up and cup her cheeks until her eyes focus on me.

"I'm okay. Still not fully healed, but it looks worse than it feels. If someone needed me, they'd be knocking on the door. And there is a meeting later, but it's not right now."

"Meeting. That's what it was. My brain is fuzzy, but not hurt fuzzy." She shakes her head, then widens her eyes. "I'm okay. Sorry. This whole getting enough sleep thing really fucked with my head."

She leans forward, resting her forehead against my chest, and I run my hand up and down her back. "I should have known you'd steal my shirt the instant you came back."

"I'm lucky I found this one. Your room doesn't exactly look occupied. I think they still have your clothes at headquarters. I was too worried about getting caught to check."

I chuckle as I lie down, pulling her on top of me. "You just wanted the sweatpants, didn't you?"

"Duh," she says, resting her chin on her folded hands on top of my chest.

She wiggles, straddling my stomach, and sighs. Running my hands up and down her sides, I close my eyes, relishing the feeling of her being in my arms again. After so long, this moment doesn't seem real. If I open my eyes, or stop touching her, she'll disappear.

"Why'd you go back?" I whisper, and she stiffens.

She rubs her nose on my chest, then rests her cheek against my skin. "I didn't know where you were. What you were doing. If you were hurt or had run. I kept reminding myself to trust you, so I figured you were still out there. But with only Jag? Not exactly much you could do."

"So you started doing the Guild's dirty work?"

Her head snaps up, her lip curling. I grip her waist to stop her from launching off of me.

"What the hell is that supposed to mean?"

"Byron's house. You were watching it burn. Then Jenkins showed up and you went with him."

The tension leaves her body, and she relaxes on me again. "Anders sold me to Byron. I thought…doesn't matter. The point is, he brought me to his house. We fought. I kicked him. He fell and hit his head. I don't think he was dead, but I'm assuming he is now because I set his house on fire and didn't bother to pull him out."

Her recounting of events is a mixture of emotionless rhetoric with a dash of defensiveness. As if I'd ever fault her for protecting herself. As if I'd care if she killed someone. She's still the woman I met in one of the hardest situations I've ever come across. She's still the woman who fought me and helped me and saved me more times than she realizes. She's still the woman I fell in love with.

"Tell me why you went back. That's all I need to know," I murmur. "Then we'll go take a shower."

"Are you saying I stink?" She smirks and her lip slips between her teeth. "Don't answer that. I went back because I thought I could do more good in there than out here. And I didn't know if you were alive or dead. And I didn't know where you were. I thought I heard you calling for me, but

I couldn't trust it wasn't my brain tricking me. So, I figured I'd weaken them enough for the next person if need be."

I nod, gathering her up in my arms before sitting up. Swinging my legs off the bed, I slide my hands under her ass before standing. She wiggles until her head rests in the crook of my neck. I don't know if I'm going to make it through this shower if she keeps doing shit like that. I'm loath to let her go, though, still afraid she'll disappear.

"You're not going to carry me in front of other people, are you?" she mumbles, her lips brushing against my bare skin, and I shiver.

"The showers are down this hallway, so we won't have to go through the main area. Everyone should be sleeping. No one will be down here."

She hums, digging her fingers into my neck. I should take her back and let her sleep, but we'll both feel more human once we get clean. Stepping into one of the bathrooms, I've never been happier that I remodeled them a few years ago.

It used to be one large room with several shower heads, like a locker room. I hated it, and Mac kept complaining that she didn't feel comfortable, but the water got hotter here than at home. Single showers are much more convenient.

I set her on her feet, making sure she's steady before I step away. Flinging back the curtain, I start the water, the spray hitting the tiles and drowning out her sighs. There's a chair in the corner I could post up in while she showers, but she always closed the door before. I assumed she liked the idea of privacy since there was no lock on the door at the Guild.

"There's a lock on the door. No safeguard, so someone will have to break down the door to get to you." I step toward the exit, resting my hand on the knob as she glances around, confused.

"Where are you going?"

"I'll be right next door showering. I'll leave my door unlocked in case you need me."

She snorts as she gathers the hem of her shirt and tucks her thumbs in the waistband of her skirt, then shoves it down and my cock twitches. "No. We've showered together before and I'm afraid I'll tip over if you're not here."

"So, I'm here as your safety rail?" I smirk, crossing my arms and leaning against the door.

She peels off her shirt, then mirrors my stance and my mouth goes dry. It's been too long since I've been inside her. I'm capable of keeping my shit together, but the way she's pushing her tits up, I'm pretty sure she's doing it on purpose. I don't know where we stand now, and I'm hesitant to ask. I don't want to push her.

She sobers, staring at my chest or maybe at nothing. I can't read her and it terrifies me. She's clearly been through things I can't even fathom. We're in new territory, stumbling around without a clear view.

Whenever I thought about her being here, I focused on the things I would show her, the adventures we would take, and how I would convince her to stay. I didn't think about this part—the awkward conversations about where we stood and what the other wanted after sharing so much while trapped together.

"This is new. We've never had the choice to *not* be in the same place. And while I'm fucking terrified right now because I *really* don't want to leave, I think you should know." She bites her lip, then lets out a shuddering breath. "I don't want to talk about what happened yet. And I don't want to plan anything outside of this room. And I don't want to—"

I hold up my hand, and her lip ends up between her teeth again. "Instead of telling me all the things you *don't* want, why don't you tell me what you *do* want."

She nods, a blush traveling from her chest to her cheeks. It's a sharp contrast to her paleness. The lights in the Guild were always so muted, hiding the dark rings and sallow skin. They must do it on purpose. Rage bubbles up within me and I shove it down. I don't want her thinking I'm upset with her.

"You want a list? Fine. First, I want to shower. With you. Second, I want to do…things. Three, I want to eat. And four, I don't know yet, but I'm pretty sure it's swimming around somewhere in here." She gestures to her head as she avoids my gaze.

I shove down my sweatpants, kicking them off. She purses her lips, eyes fixated on the pants.

"You can wear them later. Get in the shower, Aelia."

Her eyes dart to my crotch, then away again. I'm hard as a fucking rock, but until she makes a move, I'm stuck. She may say she wants to do *things*. Doesn't mean she'll act on it. She steps into the shower, water splashing across her skin.

She turns her back to me, and my heartbeat pulses in my ears, drowning out everything else as my vision tunnels, focusing on the scars marring her flesh.

A growl builds in my chest. "Who the fuck did that to you?"

TWENTY EIGHT

Aelia

I freeze, closing my eyes before slowly turning to face him. When I open them, his nostrils flare as he scans my body. I didn't think about the consequences of undressing in front of him. It was my poor attempt at seduction. Not that I know how to do that, but it worked in the book Avery gave me.

Every time the love interest would start an argument, the heroine would whip off her shirt and they'd get down and dirty. I should have thought through how my body has changed since he saw me last. Now I'll have to relive the memories—all of them.

"Answer me, Aelia."

I swallow hard, and his nostrils flare as his eyes catalogue each fading bruise. "There was a woman named Molly…"

He spins, latching onto the handle and ripping the door open. My feet slip as I attempt to chase after him and I yelp, throwing my hands out. Suddenly, he's there, arms catching me as I fall. He sets me on my feet, and I cling to him when he tries to step away.

"I'm going to fucking kill her. Let go, angel," he growls.

"You can't," I gasp, my heartbeat still pounding in my throat.

"The hell I can't. She hurt you. She tried to break you. She doesn't deserve to breathe." He grips my wrists, not enough to hurt, but enough to pry my grasp away.

"Dante Reginald whatever-your-last-name-is, since all I know is Cruz."

He leans back, still gripping my wrists. "That's not even close to my name."

I huff, glaring at him. "Well, I don't know your middle name, and until I said it out loud, I didn't realize your last name probably isn't Cruz, so I went with what I had. While we're on the subject though…"

The corner of his lip twitches. "My last name is Raines. I don't have a middle name."

I narrow my eyes and his gaze darts away. He's lying, but now isn't the time to call him out on it. I'll badger him later. Lacing my fingers with his, I tug him toward the shower. It's like trying to move a brick wall.

"You realize I have a list and the water is going to get cold, right?"

"Your list of demands? Yeah, I heard them, though the water won't get cold." He smirks, then it falls from his face. "I'll be back and I'll bring you food."

"She's dead."

Shit. I didn't mean to blurt it out like that. I still don't know how to feel about what I did. Not having regret for taking someone's life seems very unhealthy. I'm not worried about how he'll react. Dante understands the world I grew up in. He understands what the Guild is like, too.

How do I explain the emotions swirling through me whenever the image of her bloody body flashes through my mind when I don't have the words? How do I erase her from my memories without forgetting how powerful I felt after it was done?

He stops trying to get away. Lips parting, he scans my face, and I glance away. He cups my cheek, his thumb forcing me to meet his gaze, and I brace myself for the questions he's sure to ask.

"Did you?" he whispers, and I nod. "Good girl."

He dips, kissing me hard and fast. His hand slides into my hair and he tilts my head, deepening the kiss. His tongue sweeps in, dancing with mine, and I moan. My body responds long before my mind catches up as he presses into me.

Before I realize we're moving, my back hits the wall of the shower. Steam swirls around us, encasing us in our own little bubble. His cock rests between us, and I squirm as I cling to him.

He pulls back, resting his forehead on mine as we catch our breath.

"Shower. We need to shower," he pants, even as his hands slide up and down my skin.

"We're in the shower. That's good enough," I murmur, pulling his mouth to mine and biting his bottom lip.

He groans, tipping his head back as his hands grip my hips. "You're going to be the fucking death of me."

I pout when he retreats, then tugs me under the spray. If he's insisting I wash first, I'm going to at least give him a show. He deserves it since he's making me wait. I lick my lips as he bends over to grab a bottle from a low shelf. As my gaze slides up, though, all thoughts of seducing him flee.

He straightens, and I rest my palm against the pink puckered streaks on his back. He glances over his shoulder, but I can't tear my eyes away from the burns. I trace a tattoo of a scythe, the skin raised and puckered. I haven't thought about my own scars since I can't see them. Seeing his, though, sends a flash of outrage through me.

"You stayed too long. You didn't get out when you should have," I murmur, and he turns.

His arm wraps around my waist, hauling my body into his. "I did what I needed to do. Just like you."

His lips brush over my cheek, and I tip my head back. He moves to my jaw, nipping at my skin. I shiver as I run my hands up his chest. My nipples brush against his skin, sending a bolt of pleasure through me. It's like all the desire I've been repressing floods in, sweeping me off my feet.

"We should—"

"Stop talking, angel," he growls in my ear. "I need to be inside you, now. Everything else can wait."

"Please," I gasp. Even I'm taken aback by the hunger lacing my tone. I didn't realize how much I missed him—missed this—while we were separated.

"Needy little thing, aren't you? Did you dream of my hands on you?" He slides his palm between my legs. "Did you miss my fingers stroking you?"

His thumb presses against my clit, then circles slowly before his finger dips to my core. My knees go weak, his arm the only thing holding me upright as he continues worshipping my body. He stops and my eyes fly open. He raises an eyebrow, waiting for my response.

"Probably not as much as you did," I say, smirking.

He growls as he picks me up, and I wrap my legs around his waist. His cock presses against my clit, sending another flare of pleasure through me. My back hits the wall and his mouth descends on mine, devouring me. I cling to him as he grinds his hips. His lips graze my sensitive skin, and I yelp when he licks my nipple.

His hand slides under my ass, kneading the flesh as I rub against him. I grip his hair, keeping him in place as he nibbles and sucks from one bud to the other.

"Dante, please. I need…" I can't even finish my sentence. Desire erupts inside me, overflowing the walls I carefully constructed when he left. I can't wait for him any longer.

He nips at my nipple one last time, and my legs go numb, slipping from his waist. A noise in his chest rumbles out of him. I doubt I have enough strength for him to fuck me against a shower wall unless he can hold me the entire time.

"Use your words, angel," he murmurs against my skin as his hand delves into my pussy again.

He strokes me, humming as I stutter out incoherent words. He slips two fingers into me, then slowly pulls them out. Over and over, he repeats the move and I whimper.

He ducks his head, nipping at the spot behind my ear. "So fucking wet for me. Your cunt missed me just as much as you did, hmm?"

I grab his hair, forcing his eyes to meet mine. "Stop teasing and fuck me."

He grins, joy shining from his eyes. "All you had to do was ask, angel."

I squeal when he hoists me up again, his arm around my waist. I lock my ankles around his back, hoping I don't hurt his wounds. It's my last thought before my mind empties as he lines up his cock and eases into me.

I suck in a shuddering breath, and he groans when he's fully seated. I close my eyes and rest my head against the wall, basking in the feeling of being with him again. He presses kisses across my collarbone, up my neck, then seals his lips to mine.

"Never again," he murmurs, and I stiffen, my pussy clenching around him. "I'm never leaving you ever fucking again."

A single tear falls from the corner of my eye, and he catches it with his thumb. I smile, gripping his arms. I don't want him to think he's hurt me, but forming sentences is out of the question. My mouth refuses to do anything except make needy noises every time I open it.

"I've got you, Aelia." He pulls out of me slowly, then plunges back in. I should have known he would understand.

My eyes dip down, mesmerized as his cock disappears again and again. My orgasm builds as he surges into me, harder and faster each time.

"Eyes on me. I need to see you when you come all over my cock."

His words send a shudder through me, and his thumb circles my clit. I explode, moaning his name as I spasm around him. He thrusts into me, drawing out my orgasm. My muscles tense, then relax as I fall back to reality. Too long and not enough. He kisses me sweetly, rolling his hips, and I squirm.

"Again," I gasp.

"Demanding," he grunts, though his voice is strained.

I giggle and his nostrils flare as he stops. I nip at his bottom lip, meeting his dark eyes as I pull back.

"I'm not going to last long if you keep doing shit like that," he says through gritted teeth.

I smirk, but before I can respond, he slams back into me, and my retort turns into a moan. He buries his face into my neck, our bodies molded together as his fingers dig into my ass, and he thrusts into me. With each move, his stomach rubs my clit, sending sparks of pleasure through me. My name falls from his lips like a prayer.

He plunges into me twice more and I sail over the edge into oblivion, stars exploding behind my lids. He groans out my name into my skin, branding me in a way I never knew I needed. I cling to him, basking in the blissful aftermath. Peace flows through me as his lips skim across my body, whispering promises into my flesh. For once, I actually believe them.

He eases out of me and my legs drop to the ground. His arm snakes around my waist when my knees give out and he snickers.

"Something funny?" The snark I intended is lost in the waver of my voice, and he laughs.

His face fills with joy as he grins. I can't help but smile back, awe welling up inside of me. He hugs me close, then pulls me under the still warm spray. He tips my head back gently, the water running down my hair.

My muscles relax one by one as his fingers knead away the ache. He guides me around and then his hands are in my hair, working shampoo into the strands. I can't hold back my groan as he massages my scalp.

Closing my eyes, I let him take care of me. I don't know if it's more for me or for him. The gentleness with how he handles me tells me he needs this just as much as I do. I sigh, leaning against his chest. His arms wrap around me, holding me as we sway under the water.

"How is it still warm?" I mutter as steam billows around us.

"I put in the biggest water heater I could find." He presses a kiss on my temple.

"I, for one, am grateful for that."

"I'll replace every one of them for you," he says.

I burst out laughing. "Seriously? If that's your best pickup line, we might have problems."

Dante snorts, tweaking my nipple, and I squeak. "I don't think I'll be using many pickup lines anymore."

"Did you use them before?"

"No, I didn't." He tips my head back, his eyes meeting mine. "I think I was just waiting for you."

TWENTY NINE

Dante

Nerves bounce around my body. Shane wanted to meet at Nico's, but I insisted we gather here. Aelia hasn't left headquarters yet, barely even leaving our room and the bathroom. I'm not about to introduce her to a bunch of people who snubbed her in an unfamiliar place.

Even now she's hovering in the shadows of the hallway, refusing to sit next to me. The others filter through the front door, coming from fuck knows where. I haven't been keeping track of them for the past few days.

Nova comes in, glancing around until her gaze alights on me. Grooves appear between her eyes, and I nod toward the hallway. A squeak from the shadows tells me Aelia has spotted her. Nova rushes across the space and launches herself at Aelia.

Glancing away, I meet Sam's eyes. She weaves her way around the tables, avoiding Shane's hands as he tries to pull her into his lap, and drops into the chair next to me.

"Shane doesn't like you fraternizing with me," I mutter, my eyes darting from the mafia leader to the hallway and back again.

She waves her hand, dismissing my concerns. "Like I give a fuck. He's just pissed that everyone went off the grid. He's trying to find a way to blame you even though he knows it's not your fault."

"Might have something to do with him thinking Aelia is a mole for the Guild." I grind my teeth, crossing my arms as I lean back in my chair.

She snorts, finally pulling her eyes away from the pair still crying in the hallway. "No one actually believes that. There was a shit ton of emotions the night she showed up. And none of us knew who she was or how she got away. Plus, we all talked to Lacey, so we're good."

"What the hell does Lacey have to do with her?"

"You didn't hear about the hippo? What the hell have you two been...you know what? Never mind. I don't want to know. We'll go over it in the meeting. Now, I'm going to introduce myself to your woman. She's going to need someone who can stab things on her side." She bounds across the room, then slows as she gets close to them.

Byrns drops into the chair across from me, blocking my view. I scowl and he rolls his eyes. Whatever he wants I don't fucking care. I've avoided him so far since I don't want his apologies or his excuses. Looking at it from his point of view, I see why he thought Aelia might be aligned with the Guild. Doesn't excuse the fact that he spread it around like wildfire.

"I'm not here to argue, Raines."

"Then maybe you should get the fuck away from me, Byrns," I grunt, fixing my gaze on him.

He sighs, dropping his elbows on the table and lacing his fingers together. "I talked to Lacey before we went on the last mission. I told her to try to hack in again. And I told her to try to get through to Aelia. I won't apologize for cracking you over the head. You would have gotten yourself killed."

"You think I'm pissed you stopped me from getting shot? Fuck, Byrns. I'm not even pissed you had your doubts about her. The fact you spread that shit around and turned everyone against her before they'd even met her..." I dig my nails into my arms to keep the rage at bay.

His head pops up. "What the hell are you talking about? No one was against her. In fact, most of them bitched me out when I brought it up. Lacey told me to pull my head out of my ass."

"Then why…" I can't even remember who talked to me about it. My memories are a bit muddled. Nova said it probably was the concussion.

"I don't know, man. But when she showed up, we were more concerned with the fact you were passing out in the middle of the street and there were gunshots in the distance. When I turned around, she was gone. I wasn't about to leave Lacey unprotected. Jag was going to go after her once he got you inside."

"Then why'd you'd say it wasn't surprising that I disappeared?" Aelia asks from behind him, and he spins in his chair.

I tip my chin at the seat next to me and she stalks over, Byrns tracking her as she does. A blush paints her cheeks. She may be calling Byrns out, but she clearly isn't used to it. I slide my hand to her thigh and squeeze as pride wells up in me. Sam sits in the chair between them, propping her chin in her hands and her elbows on the table as if she's getting ready to watch a tennis match.

"You were clearly frightened by the lot of us rushing out of the building. Most people in your position would run," he mutters, avoiding her gaze.

"People in my position?"

He grips the back of his neck as Sam snorts. "Ya know, someone used to…not…uh, trusting people."

"That's a nice way of saying I'm basically terrified of people because I've been locked away with a bunch of sex traffickers."

Shane chokes, doubling over, and his hand slaps the table next to Sam. The ghost of a smile graces Aelia's face, and I relax. I didn't think I'd need to protect her. She's capable of taking care of herself. I just didn't know how long it would take for her to feel comfortable enough to actually do it. Apparently, I didn't need to worry.

"We should get started," I say loud enough for the others to hear. "Unless you want to bust Byrns's balls some more."

I smirk at Aelia, and she shakes her head before tucking her chin to her chest. A strangled noise leaves Byrns, but Sam slaps the back of his head and quietly scolds him. I can't make out her words, but I'm sure it's similar to the shit Mac tells me off for.

Helms and Mac are missing tonight, off trying to find Alex. He's still not answering anyone's calls or texts and the others are getting antsy.

The meeting lasts longer than I expected. I knew we'd have a lot to discuss, especially telling them what Aelia went through the last few months. After a while, I steer the conversation away from her experiences. The questions are valid, but nothing I can't answer. I'm not about to put her through the trauma of reliving the shit she went through. Sam's eyes rarely leave Aelia.

As the others disperse, Sam stays behind, waving Ren away when he posts up next to her. He brushes his knuckle down her cheek before stalking for the door. I'll have to fill Helms in once they get back. I don't know if I'll make it that long, though. I push up, holding my hand out to Aelia.

"I have some questions, but if you're not ready for them, they'll keep," Sam says, and I sink into my chair again. "You're not exactly needed for this conversation, Raines, but I'm not about to kick you out of your own headquarters."

"How thoughtful of you," I mutter, and she smiles sweetly at me.

She fixes her gaze on Aelia again. "Are there any windows not monitored?"

"I don't know what you mean by monitored, but they're all rigged for a lockdown. It was the first thing Jenkins had installed, even before we got there. The lower windows have locks on them. The upper ones have alarms, but I don't know how they work. Mostly it's so no one gets thrown out."

I whip my head toward her, my brows pulling low. "What?"

She inhales deeply, her fingers lacing with mine. "At the ranch, there was a member who liked to throw the women he used off the roof after. Then there were the bits who tried to jump, hoping they'd get out that way. They put in precautions after that. Couldn't be losing assets."

Bitterness laces her tone and she purses her lips. Sam nods, her mind a million miles away. Her eyes dart back and forth, probably picturing the blueprints of the Guild's headquarters. Or maybe she's already staked out the embassy. She slips away randomly, only telling one of the Kings where she's going. And they're not about to rat her out.

"Is there a rotation for the guards on the outside of the building?" Sam asks, her gaze still out of focus.

"Not that I know of, but there's one stationed at most of the exits. The farther up you go, the less of a presence they have. Oh, and Jenkins has started carrying a gun." She grimaces at me. There's so much that's happened, it's hard to remember everything. I have a feeling this won't be the last thing we've forgotten to share.

"Only him? What do the others carry now?"

"Mostly Tasers and batons. A few have knives, though I've never seen anyone use theirs." She snickers, covering her mouth with her hand. "There was one guy who tried to carry a sword around. He ended up stabbing his foot."

Sam rolls her eyes. "Of course he did. I had a guy jump on his accomplice's blade once. I can laugh about it now, but Alex tried to step in and 'save' me. It was a whole fiasco. I ended up having to kill him. The guy, not Alex, obviously."

Aelia's eyes meet mine, confusion swirling in them.

"Alex is one of the Kings. And one of Sam's boyfriends. He wormed his way into the lower gangs so it'll be a bit before you meet him. I think you'll like him."

She nods, forcing a smile at Sam, who wrinkles her nose. "You don't have to do that. I'm not going to be offended because you don't know who he is. Or that you don't think you'll fit in. This shit is intimidating. And I'm not about to make the same mistakes I did with Lacey."

Aelia's eyes widen. "What exactly happened with Lacey?"

"She was a bitch and blamed me for shit that wasn't my fault. Sound familiar?" Lacey calls from the doorway of her office. She didn't bother to attend the meeting, trusting Byrns to relay any information she needed.

Sam scowls, dropping her forehead to the table with a thunk. "I made up for it."

"Making, Sam. You're *making* up for it," she snaps, but there's laughter in her voice.

"At least I learned from my mistakes. Some people just keep fucking up over and over and over. They just don't like to listen. Now—"

"I know you want to interrogate her more, or can I borrow her?" Lacey asks, and my stomach tightens.

We've been here for over two hours, most of them focused on Aelia. She's swaying in her seat, her body pushed beyond exhaustion. Between the injuries she sustained and the concussion, she needs more sleep. I stand, pulling her up with me.

"Tomorrow, Lacey."

Lacey opens her mouth, ready to argue, then scans Aelia. She nods and pivots to retreat to her temporary office. She only makes it a few steps before she's turning back.

"Aelia, we didn't go through the same things, but if you need help with the scars, I have experience." She gestures to her face. "And if other shit starts happening, we've all been through some trauma. Whatever hits you, we probably have a way to get through it."

Sam raises her hand, a sad smile gracing her face. Aelia sinks back into the chair, and I wonder if I should leave. This doesn't seem like the type of conversation I should be a part of. Sam pins me with a glare, then gestures to my seat with a pointed look and I sit.

"What exactly have you been through?" Aelia asks in a small voice.

Sam sighs, drumming her fingers on the table. "Well, I was kidnapped. Actually, all of us were kidnapped, weren't we? Huh. Mac and Willow's story are their own, but Mac was sold by her half-brother to a rival MC, then ran to Helms when she escaped. The leader went after Mac and she ended up killing him. Willow, who is still in Synd, had a stalker and a shitty stepfather. She ended up killing both of them, actually."

"Don't forget her getting kidnapped again, though that was more of a misunderstanding than anything," Lacey chimes in.

"How is a kidnapping a misunderstanding exactly?" I ask, but Sam waves away my question.

Lacey snorts. "And then there's me. I was sort of, kind of obsessed with Mason, but not in a creepy way. Turns out he had some enemies and they snatched me. Gave me a souvenir before Mason saved me. There was a lot of other shit too, but you're about to pass out."

"How much other shit?"

"Let's just say if they wrote a book about me getting involved with Mason fucking Byrns it'd be a long-ass book." She grins as Sam smothers her laughter behind her hand.

"Maybe one day I'll get the story," Aelia whispers.

Lacey glances at Sam, then back to Aelia. "It's a date."

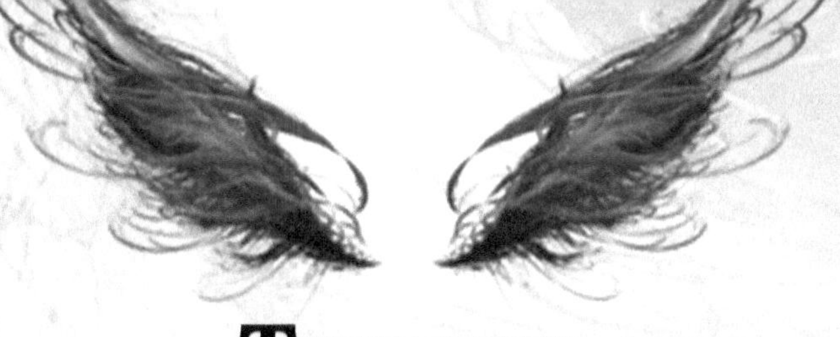

THIRTY

Aelia

"Do you think Helms is avoiding me?" I ask, cuddling close to Dante's side.

"No, I think he's got work to do and you two just keep missing each other." His sleep-laced voice rumbles through me, and I brush my hand over his tattoo.

"I want to help." This makes day three of asking what I can do. I hold my breath, knowing what his answer will be. It's a rote response for him at this point, and I mouth the words as he says them.

"Just focus on healing." He leans away, narrowing his eyes. "Are you mocking me?"

I sigh, shuffling until I'm straddling him. His hands grip my hips and his cock hardens underneath me. As much as I'd like to ignore everything else and let him seduce me, I'm sick of being shunted to the side. I slap my palms on his chest, and his eyes find mine.

"You're pushing me away and not listening. I realize when we were inside, I couldn't do much. And I fought you every step of the way, but that doesn't mean I can't do shit." I glare at him. It's hard to be stern when I'm completely naked. Especially when his thumbs keep circling my hip bones.

"Okay. What do you want to do?"

It feels like he's placating me. Like I haven't been through hell and back. Like I don't know what I'm asking for. The shit I've been through—that I've dealt with—it has to count for something. I have to *do* something to make them pay. They stole my life. Thousands of lives. They tore apart families and didn't care how they infected the world around them. As long as they got their cut. As long as they were able to exert their particular brand of torture.

"Anything," I breathe.

"Well, that might be a hard position to fill, but…Aelia?"

My mind blanks as my vision darkens. I can feel his hands on my skin, but his voice cuts off. Unless the sudden silence from him is merely the thrashing of my heartbeat in my ears. I swallow down the bile in my throat and close my eyes. Byron's face floats up from the void and my body vibrates. As I open them, a strangled cry leaves me. The VIP room Byron built just for me comes into view. Did I imagine it all?

Byron not dead.

His house still standing.

No fire alarms blaring.

No chaos within the Guild.

No freedom.

Did I dream Rachel's death? Her sacrifice to get me out a mirage my mind fabricated. Did I need to escape that badly that my brain could no longer function? Am I truly broken and have no idea?

Hands. Arms. Fingers. They burn as they touch me, ripping a scream from my throat.

A high keening noise takes over the roaring in my ears, and I thrash away from the pain. And then it's gone, a numb coldness taking its place. I blink over and over, hoping it goes away. I'll be back in Dante's room. In his arms. I'll be safe.

"Stop," a firm voice commands, and the noise cuts off. I realize it was coming from me all along. "What happened?"

A low rumble echoes through the air, and I curl into a ball. I can't feel my fingers, my toes. The image wavers at the edges and I squeeze my eyes shut. Someone comes closer—I can sense them—yet I refuse to check. The moment I open my eyes the illusion will shatter, and I'll be back in the Guild, back in Byron's basement, back in the cage, back on the cross. And I'll never get out. I'll never escape. I'll never be saved.

A hand slaps the floor in front of my face. They do it again, keeping a steady rhythm. My heart syncs with the beat and I match my breathing. When it stops, I open my eyes and Lacey's face floats through the shadows.

"Breathe," she whispers, then shoves something next to my nose. "Does it help?"

I blink the tears away, staring at her. If I answer, I'll throw up. Blood floods my mouth, though I don't know when I bit my tongue.

"What's next?" she murmurs to herself. "Already breathing, scent doesn't work…oh. Focus on one thing. One thing that you can control. It doesn't have to be big, just one tiny thing that's solely within your power."

Minutely I shake my head. There's nothing I can control. Every decision is made for me. And every time I've deviated, I've paid the price. I'm so tired—of waiting, of hurting, of living. My lungs seize, choking off what little breath I was able to find seconds before.

"Shit," she mutters, then Dante's face replaces hers.

Blood streaks down his cheeks, a bullet hole piercing his temple. Tears blur my vision and I bite my cheek to keep from screaming.

"You have choices, Aelia. You chose to trust me. You chose to befriend Avery. You chose to be with me. You chose to stand up for yourself." His dark eyes plead with me to listen. To believe him. "What can you control right now?"

I shake my head again. He may believe what he's saying, but I've lived in a world of lies. Every time I've trusted someone, they've failed me. Whatever they can squeeze out of me, they will. And once I'm used and dried up, they leave me behind to pick up the pieces of my self-worth alone. No one stays. No one cares. No one loves.

"I'm going to pick you up," he whispers. "I'm not going to hurt you."

I tense, fighting the urge to recoil as he slides his arms around my body and lifts me. I cringe away from his heat, my mind at war with itself. The rational half knows he won't hurt me. The other half is terrified I'll emerge from this dream and find Grant or Byron or Jenkins holding me instead.

"Hold on, angel," he murmurs. "Hold on."

"Eat," Dante grunts even as he ignores his own food in front of him.

I pick up the spoon, dip it into the soup, and take a single bite. It's more of a struggle than I want to admit. The comforting taste explodes in my mouth, transporting me back to a time I can't fully recall. Another spoonful and another set of memories dance just out of reach.

Leaning over my bowl, I breathe in the aroma of cream and potatoes and celery. My eyes fall closed as I continue to eat until Dante's fingers wrap around my wrist.

"Easy or you'll ruin it." He gives me a look as I glare at him. "You won't want to eat it again if you puke it up. Believe me. Plus, we've got a vat of it in the kitchen. Ren isn't used to cooking for such a large group and went overboard."

"Ren made this?" I ask softly, staring at the carrots floating on the surface.

"Don't act so surprised," Ren mutters, setting down a small bowl.

I glance from Dante to Ren, wondering what the hell I'm supposed to do. "Thanks for…this."

Ren sighs, grabbing the tiny bowl and dumping some of what I think is bacon bits into my soup. He snatches my spoon and mixes them in before sitting down next to me. He stiffens, glancing at me.

"You're not a vegetarian, are you? Dante said you weren't."

"No, I'm not. This is good. Thank you." The words feel weird in my mouth. Whether it's because I spent most of the day melting down or because I haven't said thank you in a long time, I don't know.

"You're welcome. Don't fill up. There's cheesecake." He leans over his bowl, digging into his own soup.

I nod, not that he's paying attention. I concentrate on eating, even though my eyes fill with tears. Crying about cheesecake shouldn't be a thing. Dante brought me a lot of food I hadn't had since I was a kid, but he never brought me dessert. Apparently, it's harder to stuff a piece of cake in his pocket than a cheeseburger.

Ren clears his throat, eyes fixed on his bowl, and mutters, "Did the shower help?"

"Yeah. Must have shocked my system or something." I shovel another bite in, nerves dancing in my stomach.

"Sometimes it takes a while. Find something that works and do that. Good to find other things that work too, especially since you won't always have a shower available." Ren glances at me from the corner of his eye. "We've all been there at one point or another. It's why Lacey was trying a bunch of tactics."

I nod, going back to my food. Blocking out the other conversations, I finish, then grip the sides of the bowl. Ren holds his hand out and I jolt. He takes it from me, careful not to touch me. I wonder if he knows I wouldn't be able to handle another person's skin on mine. The only one who's gotten close to me since I spiraled is Dante. The others are avoiding me. Even hours later, they've taken seats at the other tables, except for Ren.

A piece of cheesecake appears in front of me, and I blink. Ren sets a fork next to the plate, then presents a can of whipped cream.

"I don't...I..." I shake my head, my mind a muddled mess.

"Do you want it on the side?" he asks softly and I nod. "Any glaze?"

"Plain is fine," I murmur, peeking at Dante.

He meets my gaze, raising an eyebrow. "Is it fine because you don't want to bother Ren or because you don't want to offend him?"

I straighten in my chair, tipping my chin up. "I like plain cheesecake. I prefer my dessert to actually be dessert, not masked as healthy because it's got sugar fruit on it. Plus, the consistency of fruit glaze is nasty. It coats your mouth and then you can't even taste what's underneath."

The corner of his mouth twitches as he dips his head. Then he takes a large dollop of strawberry goop and plops it on top of his piece. He smears it around until the whole thing is coated. I look away, holding back the urge to gag. When I glance back, he's grinning with a mouth full of cheesecake and goo.

"It looks like you murdered a breast implant," Ren says, taking his seat again.

Lacey drops next to me, taking the chair between us. Ren nudges the dessert plate toward her and she waves him off.

"Listen, I know you've had a hard day and this should probably keep, but I've got news. And we can't wait on shit anymore or we'll lose the momentum we gained with the multi-hit." She laces her fingers together and fixes her gaze on me.

I point with my fork at my plate. "Can it wait until I'm done with this? It's the first dessert I've had in like ten years."

She nods, then turns to Ren. They start muttering about syntax and arrays, all of which go over my head. Dante's fingers brush mine as he switches seats closer to me. I assume he was trying to give me space. I should have told him it was okay, but I was still struggling with forming sentences. Now that I've been infused with food and sweets, I feel more like myself. Or at least who I think I am. It's hard to tell being on the outside.

"I should have brought you dessert," he murmurs.

"Actually, I think this is perfect. I wouldn't have enjoyed it as much if I ate it while my life still belonged to the Guild."

He nods, then stuffs the last piece in his mouth. He scrapes the plate, scooping up all the glaze, and I wrinkle my nose.

"It's really not that bad," he says around the mouthful.

"Manners, Raines," Lacey snaps.

He actually has the good grace to look sorry, and I giggle. Lacey waves the others over and I stiffen as they pull up more chairs and plop down. Dante's hand lands on my thigh. The move should probably ground me, but instead it sends electric shocks through my system.

"From what I've gathered, Anders is missing again. I'm not entirely sure where he is, but I'd put money on the fact he's not in Rima. I'm assuming you two think he'll go back to Synd?" She gestures to Dante and me.

"It's likely. He's obsessed with Synd's downfall. Are they prepared to handle it there?" Dante asks even as his fingers brush higher.

"They'll be fine. Hawk can handle things. We'll see about the other," Lacey sneers.

I have no idea who the other one is. In fact, I don't really understand any of their dynamics or how they interact with one another. I assumed all mafia and MC families kept to themselves. Anders always said it was every man for himself, though he's not the best model to emulate.

Lacey leans forward, catching my eye. "Aelia?"

"The last time I saw him, my hands were around his throat so…I'm not entirely sure where he went after that."

Wide eyes blink at me from around the table. I shrug, not sure why they're so surprised. I thought they'd all killed people before. Hearing about me trying to commit patricide shouldn't be that shocking.

I clear my throat. "To be fair, he was selling me at the time. Again. After having me tortured, so he kind of deserved it."

Sam's mouth drops open. "Kind of? Fuck, that man should have died years ago. Ten years, to be exact. Hell, even better, twenty when our father's pushed him out of Synd in the first place."

Something flashes in Lacey's eyes, a recognition or some sort. She ducks her head before I can truly decipher it. And I'm too tired to ask what she just figured out.

"Well, if he comes back, I plan on putting a bullet in his head. Or strangling him with his own intestines, so hopefully I can rectify that." I smile sweetly.

"So bloodthirsty," Dante growls in my ear. "I fucking love it."

Pride rolls through me, extinguishing the last vestiges of my hallucinations from earlier. My muscles ease and I sit back, listening to the conversation flow around me. For once, I don't feel so alone.

THIRTY ONE

Dante

"I can walk, Dante," she mumbles while cuddling closer.

I breathe in her scent as I head toward our room. "Doesn't mean you have to. Are you tired?"

"Is content a thing? I could sleep, but I don't want to. I feel like that's all I've been doing. And I napped earlier." Her voice turns whiny the longer she talks.

"Of course content is a thing. If you want to stay up, you can. You've been healing, which means more sleep. And napping doesn't mean you can't nap again." I lower her onto the bed, and she unwinds her arms from my neck.

"You certainly have an answer for everything, huh?"

Digging through the wardrobe, I grab a pair of sweatpants. Thankfully, my driver picked up several more and dropped them off. Mac delivered more of my clothes, knowing I wouldn't leave Aelia. Before she showed up, I'd just stop by my house every day to change. This is easier, but I almost wish I'd moved her over there.

"You want me to grab you another piece of cheesecake? You can eat it in bed…" My mouth goes dry when I face her.

She stretches her arms above her head and her shirt rides up, exposing a strip of skin. Her bruises have faded, thank fuck. Even the scars on her back are better. She blinks sleepily at me, a soft smile playing on her face.

"If I eat anything else I might explode. Do people actually explode? I mean, like if they eat too much?" She stares at the ceiling as if the answers will magically appear.

I shake my head, silently arguing with my cock about why it would be a terrible idea to fuck her right now. She's been through a lot today.

We spent a good hour in the shower. She shivered on my lap even with the water as hot as I could get it. It took hours for our skin to return to normal. At one point, Aelia couldn't stop laughing about it. The stress I'd been carrying since she spiraled drained away then. At least some of it.

"That's a question for Alex when he gets back."

She rolls her eyes, then pulls the hem of her shirt higher, scratching her rib. I lick my lips and avert my eyes. After she falls asleep, I may need to take a cold shower. I toss the sweatpants on the end of the bed, then grab the hem of my shirt and pull it over my head. I ignore her eyes traveling down my body. It only serves to make me harder. I wonder if she's doing it on purpose, knowing the effect she has on me.

I reach for my belt, and she scrambles toward me. Her hands land on my stomach and she leans forward and bites me. I grunt, jerking away as she giggles.

"What the hell was that for?" I cry, rubbing the spot. It didn't hurt, but I can still feel her teeth sinking into me.

She shrugs, glancing away. Shit. Now I hurt her feelings. I step toward her, intending on saying something—anything to ease her mind. Then she glances at me from the corner of her eye, a smirk forming on her lips, and I scowl.

"Don't blame me that you're bitable." She shrugs again, sitting on her heels.

She folds her hands in her lap and ducks her head. I can't tell if she's put herself in the position on purpose or if it's habit. I slip my knuckle under her chin and tip her face up. Her eyes meet mine, her lip between her teeth. I pull the flesh from her mouth, brushing my thumb over the plumpness.

"Are you doing this on purpose?" I murmur, gripping her jaw lightly.

The corner of her mouth twitches. "I wasn't at first. Then I wondered if I'd still like it when it wasn't a part we were playing."

"And do you?" A blush stains her cheeks, and she tries to look away. "Don't hide from me. Answer the question."

Her gaze meets mine again, desire lining her dark eyes. Her chin trembles in my grasp and I wonder if I've pushed her too far. I'm terrified I'll set her off again without warning or even the knowledge of what I said to hurt her. Earlier it was a simple comment about her profession. I had no idea it mirrored Byron's words when he had her. I don't want her to go through it again if I can help it.

"I'm afraid to say yes," she mumbles, and my brows pull low as I try to read her. "If I say I enjoy *this*…"

"Being submissive isn't a bad thing, Aelia. Enjoying when you give over control…you remember we talked about this?"

She rolls her eyes. "It was a lot easier when it was expected of me. I had to wear the collar and play the part of your bit. Now, I don't know what I like."

I drop to my knees and cup her face, staring up at her. "We've got time. Even with everything else going on, you can take all the time you need."

"You like this, don't you?" There's no accusation in her voice, merely curiosity.

I run my hands down her arms before lacing my fingers with hers. "I liked watching you take control when you had the collar on. I liked that you could let go and not worry."

"I wasn't worried. Because I knew you wouldn't hurt me. At least that's what I thought. Maybe it's more. I just don't know how to find out what that *more* is." She tips her head back, pulling from my hands.

With a groan, she slips to the side and sprawls on the bed. I run my hand up her leg and goosebumps scatter across her skin. She shivers, then arches her back.

"If you keep doing that, we're not going to get to sleep anytime soon," I murmur. Skating my fingers past her hip and over her stomach, I'm fascinated by the way her muscles jump.

She rolls to her side to face me. "Don't threaten me with a good time, Mr. Raines."

I chuckle, shaking my head. "I don't think anyone has ever called me Mr. Raines. Not entirely sure how I feel about that."

"Well, what do they call you then?"

"Usually Prez. That's my title."

She sniffs, nostrils flaring. "I knew that. I feel like I've forgotten a lot of things from my childhood."

"Stick around and it'll all come back to you eventually." The words pop out before I think about them. Holding my breath, I avoid her eyes as I continue my quest to map every dip and groove of her body.

She grips my chin, turning my face to hers before she whispers, "Don't do that. Don't hide because you're afraid of how I'll react."

I drop my forehead to the mattress and she scratches her nails across my scalp. It's fucking incredible, but I swallow a moan. We're having a serious conversation. Inviting my dick to the chat won't be productive.

She sighs, scooting closer to me. "I know what I want right now. And that's to stay with you. I don't think I could handle being alone or watching you go off on some secret mission to bring down the Guild."

I grin and lift my head. "I'm not a secret assassin or a spy."

She snorts as she pushes up, swinging her legs on either side of me. Pulling my head into her lap, she runs her fingers through my hair. I breathe her in, smirking.

"You smell fucking delicious," I murmur, then sink my teeth into her inner thigh.

She grips my hair, tugging at the strands. "And you scolded *me* for biting."

I run my nose along her flesh, then bury my face between her legs and suck in a deep breath. Only a thin strip of fabric separates me from her exquisite cunt. Her underwear is already damp, her body begging me to nudge them aside and devour her.

Sliding my hands down her thighs, I grip her knees and shove her legs apart. Her gasp echoes around the room as I suck her through the fabric. Her hips buck as she writhes under my ministrations. Pulling back, I gaze up at her glazed eyes.

"Would you like me to stop?"

Her eyes widen and she shakes her head. I nip at her thigh, then the other, as I dig my fingers into her flesh. Her hands find my hair again and grip the strands, sending a delicious burn through me. She attempts to tug my head back to her cunt, but I don't move.

"I'm going to need your words, angel."

"Shit. P–please," she stutters, yanking at my hair again.

I lean in, grazing my nose across her clit. "Please what?"

"Dammit, Dante. Please fuck me." It's not even a question, more of an ultimatum. Her hands fall away as she sits back, her legs widening even more.

"So demanding," I murmur, then press my lips to her clit before pulling away.

A low whine leaves her, and she collapses onto her back. Her legs snap shut, and she glares at me as I stand. Leaning over her, I place my hands on either side of her head and my cock drags against her cunt through my jeans. The determination in her eyes not to show how this affects her, while admirable, is unnecessary. The flush on her cheeks, her chest rising and falling rapidly, the subtle shifting of her hips, all point to the pleasure coursing through her body.

I brush my lips against hers. "Something wrong?"

"Why do you ask?" Her breathless voice catches on the last word, and I nip at her bottom lip.

"You're acting like a brat. Teasing me with your pretty little cunt and then pulling away." I tilt my head as I stare into her eyes.

"*I'm* the one teasing? You're the one who's making me beg to be fucked," she huffs.

I cover her mouth with mine, sweeping my tongue against hers as I grind my hips against her. She whimpers, clinging to my arms. When I pull away, a soft sigh leaves her, melting parts of me I'd long since forgotten.

"I think you like begging, but you're embarrassed to do it. It's just us here, angel. Show me how well you can beg for my cock. Tell me how much you want to come all over my face," I growl, rolling my hips again.

Her nostrils flare even as her lips part, inviting me to devour her again. Her nails dig into my skin and I shudder, dropping my head, and my hair brushes her shirt.

"Please, Dante. I need you," she whispers.

It's not what I was expecting. Nor did I anticipate the effect her words would have on me. I push myself up and grab the waistband of her underwear. For a split second I think of ripping them, but reason takes over. Something like that will have to wait until she's more comfortable. Instead, I yank them down her legs, then toss them to the floor.

She reaches for the hem of her shirt, but I grip her wrist to stop her. Leaning down again, I pull one of her nipples into my mouth through the fabric, then do the same to the other.

I drop to my knees and hook my hands behind her own to slide her until her ass is hanging off. Throwing her legs over my shoulders, I kiss my way down her soft flesh.

"I'm going to worship this pretty little cunt of yours, angel." I lick up her center, then swirl my tongue around her clit, and she whimpers. "I'm going to make you come so hard you see stars." I lick her again, relishing the taste once more. "And then I'm going to do it again and again."

"Dante," she gasps, my name both a plea and a prayer on her lips.

I give into her silent demand, latching onto her clit as I drag my finger to her core. Slipping one inside her, her cunt spasms, pulling me in deeper. I add a second finger and bury them into her.

My tongue circles in time to my thrusts, building her up. Her orgasm takes me by surprise. Her body stiffens, her back arches, and her cunt pulses in time with my heartbeat. I glance at her, tracking the bliss as it spreads across her face.

I press a kiss to her pussy as I pull my fingers from her and stand, her legs falling away. Her hooded eyes watch me as I pop them in my mouth, closing my eyes as I lick them clean.

"Where do you want me?" she asks, her voice barely above a whisper, and I raise an eyebrow.

Her lips pull into a smirk as she sits up, then whips her shirt over her head. My mouth waters as I scan her body, her tits still heaving as she catches her breath. A choking noise leaves me when she cups them and rolls her nipples.

Her head tips back, creating a portrait of wanton beauty. I don't know what I did in life to deserve to watch this woman, to taste her, to fuck her, but I'll spend the rest of my life thanking whatever deity deemed me worthy.

"Am I going to have to fuck myself, then? I thought you were going to make me see stars?"

I slide off my belt and push my pants and underwear to the floor before kicking them off. "Are you saying you didn't already?"

Her gaze is fixed on my cock, and she licks her lips. I wrap my hand around the base and stroke to the tip and back down. Her eyes follow my movements, even as I step closer to her.

"My eyes are up here, angel," I murmur, and her head whips up. "Do you want to suck my cock? Is that why you can't stop staring at it?"

She doesn't even have a response, at least not one readily available. Her eyes dart down again, fascination on her face as I twist at the tip. I don't need her mouth on me. At least not tonight. But as she leans forward and her tongue darts out, I can't hold back a groan.

I hold my cock at the base as her breath coasts across the head. I don't know how long I'll be able to last while she explores. Her lips wrap around the tip and I groan, resisting the urge to thrust into her mouth. Just the thought of me hitting the back of her throat has me hardening even more. She pulls back, and my cock throbs with need.

"Now that I have your attention. Please answer my question." She smirks as she purses her lips.

"What exactly was your question?" I try to sound cocky, but it comes out as a wheeze as she licks her lips.

"I asked where you wanted me."

Anywhere. Everywhere. My mind blanks as I imagine the many positions I could put her in, watching her climax again and again. My cock twitches with each new scene, and I close my eyes as I grip myself harder. Her hands run up the back of my thighs and I gaze down at her.

"I could get on my hands and knees. Unless you don't want to see…"

I slide my hand into her hair and tip her head back. "Do it. Facing me," I growl.

I release her and stalk to the wardrobe to open the door. The mirror isn't big, but at least I'll be able to watch her tits sway as I fuck her. And the ecstasy exploding across her face. When I turn back, she's on her hands and knees, watching me as she wiggles her hips in anticipation of what's to come.

Slowly, I walk around the bed as she tracks me. When I crawl behind her, I let out a shuddering breath. She pushes back as I brush my palms across her ass.

"You're going to be the death of me, angel. And I'll gladly accept my place in hell."

Her cunt drips with desire, coating both her thighs and my fingers as I stroke her. She whines, whispering something I can't hear.

I drag my cock over her wetness, holding back the urge to embed my length into her. "You're going to have to speak up."

"Fuck me," she wails.

I push into her slowly, then ease out again. Her fingers dig into the sheets as needy sounds fall from her lips. I do it again, just to hear how much she craves this. I thrust into her fully, and she cries out in pleasure.

Gripping her hips, I hold her still, letting her adjust to this new position. I lean forward, slipping my hand into her hair and tug her head up. Her eyes meet mine in the reflection.

"Keep your head up. I want you to watch what you do to me. How beautiful you look while being fucked. How exquisite you are when you come."

When I'm sure she's heard what I've said, I pull out until just the tip remains, then plunge into her again. Her heat wraps around me, sucking me in with every thrust. I'm already close to coming, but I never want this to end. I could spend the rest of my life buried in her cunt. She pushes back with every surge.

Wrapping my arm around her waist, I circle around her clit, and she explodes. Her pussy quivers around me, pushing me closer to the edge. I plunge into her harder, my eyes fixed on our reflection as she climaxes.

Her lips part and her eyes fall closed, her entire face going lax. I drag out her orgasm until her head drops to the mattress. Grasping her hips again, my moves become desperate, until I come with her name on my lips. Nothing will ever compare to this.

I cover her body with my own, whispering my love for her into her damp skin.

THIRTY TWO

Aelia

"What do you mean, they're gone?" Dante demands, slamming his hands on the table, and I jolt.

I'm not afraid of him, but I've also never seen him this upset unless it was in defense of me. He shoots me an apologetic look before pacing away. Lacey drops into the chair next to me, then pats my hand.

Being woken up in the middle of the night isn't exactly ideal, especially since I have no idea what's going on. Dante was rushing out the door before I even had pants on.

I've never been to the restaurant—Nico's—since I've been here. It's like stepping into a seedier world than I'm used to. I half expect someone to start throwing Molotov cocktails through the windows like in the movies.

"Do you think I should go back to headquarters?" I mutter to Lacey, and she shakes her head.

"You need to know what's going on. And they're going to need your help once Raines calms down enough to stand still for more than two seconds." She tracks him as he paces back and forth, then winces as he kicks a chair. "And stops trying to destroy the restaurant."

Jag steps in front of Dante, stopping him in his tracks. "Shane and Sam said they needed to find Alex. They've been scouring the labs, but there's no sign of him. They need to make sure he's not dead."

Mason scowls as he drops into the chair next to Lacey. He nods to me, and I give him a small smile. We'll never be best friends, but at least he's polite now. I don't blame him for thinking I was a mole. I lived with the Guild long enough to understand how hard it is to trust others. Being in the mafia doesn't make it any easier, I imagine.

"At what point do we assume they're dead, too? And where the hell is Helms?" Dante's nostrils flare as his fingers flex by his sides.

Jag sighs, tipping his head back. "They can take care of themselves. They'll be back when they're back. Helms and Mac went—"

"Mac? You let my sister go off to fuck knows where and didn't fucking tell me?"

Avery slides into the chair on the other side of me and grimaces. "You think he's going to punch Jag? Because if so, I'm going to need to borrow someone's phone."

"For blackmail or embarrassment?" I smirk, then sober when Dante grips the back of his neck.

Lacey leans close, and I resist the urge to put more space between us. "He'll get it out of his system soon. And Jag's capable of taking his vitriol. Don't worry, hon."

"I wasn't worried. I am, however, wondering if you've found my father." I fix my eyes on Lacey and confusion floods her face.

Mason glances at me, the same lost look on his own face. I don't know what they're so perplexed about. Lacey was the one who told us Anders was missing in the first place. My eyes dart to Dante, who's still raging while Jag listens impatiently. A vein in Jag's jaw is pulsing as he grinds his teeth. Maybe Dante didn't tell me something. I don't think he'd purposely hide things from me. Unless he thought he was protecting me. In that case, he probably would.

"What aren't you telling me?" I ask, glancing at the others.

Lacey clears her throat as she exchanges a look with Mason. "Aelia, we don't know who your father is. I didn't realize we were supposed to be searching for him. Can you give me his name?"

Her tone is gentle as if I'll bolt under the slightest bit of duress. This isn't funny, but part of me wants to laugh. The corner of my mouth twitches as I fight against the feeling. I'm sure they'd stare at me like I'd grown two heads if I did.

"Dante didn't tell you? My father is Anders Drake." My words are met with wide eyes, and someone behind me drops a curse. Lacey mutters something under her breath, but I don't catch it.

Glancing over my shoulder, I spot a man from the night I showed up unannounced. I assume this is Helms. Dante's been trying to catch me up on how they're all connected. When he described Helms as his best friend, my heart hurt, crying out for Ember. It got even worse when he said they were like brothers.

I swallow hard and turn back around. The scowl on his face doesn't bode well for us getting along. I wonder if Helms would be able to convince Dante to drop me off at the nearest bus station. With the way Dante spoke about him, I wouldn't be surprised.

"Let me get this straight," Helms mutters, though his voice still echoes around the room. "Your name is Aelia Drake. And your father's name is Anders Drake?"

"I thought you all knew. Dante's known for a while now. Since Anders is the one who sold me. I mean the first time, and the second time I suppose."

"Holy shit," Lacey breathes. "That's what I was missing."

I bite my lip, not sure what I'm supposed to say. These people all went through different trials, but they usually had others with them. I've survived so long by myself, I don't know how to react or respond.

Mason mumbles something in her ear and she nods her head, eyes still fixed on me. Avery's fingers find mine under the table and she squeezes. I'm grateful for the support, but I still don't know what to say.

A tall woman busts through the front doors, long, dark hair streaming behind her. With panic awash on her face, she scans the area. No one moves, all staring at her with mouths agape. The heavy wood slams shut behind her and the noise seems to snap her out of whatever trance she was in.

"They're coming," she whispers. Her eyes find Helms. "Run."

A beat later and chaos erupts. Chairs are knocked out of the way. Mason grabs Lacey's arm, dragging her to the back door while she struggles to break free. I wonder what information she's left on her tablet for them to find. I snatch it up, then sprint to Dante.

This isn't some lowly gang coming for the Vipers. No, this is the Guild. I didn't think they'd ever do something like this. The men the Guild employs don't have the skills to launch an attack. Unless Jenkins hired mercenaries. Or maybe he found the remnants of the Night Slayers and paid them to take the Vipers out.

Avery's hand is ripped from mine as Jag throws her over his shoulder and takes off for the side door. Everyone scatters as if this was planned. I'm not surprised, but I am frozen in place. I don't run. I don't scream. My fight or flight is broken. Probably from years of trauma. If I don't move, no one will see me. No one will hurt me. No one will care about me if I just don't move.

Dante wraps a hand around my arm and hauls me to my feet. I shake myself out of my stupor. I'm no longer in the Guild. I don't need to hide in plain sight. I'm capable of fighting too. Maybe not skilled enough, but definitely able.

Dante tugs me toward the back as Helms rushes around us and the table. I glance over my shoulder and watch as Mac mouths something to Helms, and he roars as he shoves chairs out of his way.

Mac spins and rushes out the door. Helms jumps over a fallen table as a fiery bottle flies through the front windows. He trips as he avoids the ball of flame. The breaking of glass fills the air seconds before there's a whoosh and a wall of fire separates Helms from the door. Dante drops my arm and takes off for his friend.

"Go, Aelia," Dante bellows as the old curtains go up in the blaze.

I hesitate, then sprint for the back door. The cold air slaps me in the face as I emerge into the alley. Mason and Lacey are long gone, expecting the others to get themselves out. I wait for Mac to come around the corner any second, but she doesn't.

The revving of engines takes over the night, along with an orange glow emanating from the front of the building. I bounce from foot to foot, counting the seconds, with my eyes fixed on the back door. Dante probably wanted me to run to headquarters. In fact, I know that's what he expected me to do. I won't leave him behind, though.

Helms bursts through the side door, dropping on his hands and knees with the force of his coughing. I rush to his side and crouch in front of him.

"Where is he?" I whisper harshly. Peeking up the alley, I try to see if the men are still here, but my view is blocked.

Helms just points to the door, then retches. I scramble away from him, terror slicing through me. I drop the tablet, hoping it doesn't break. Swallowing down my nausea and fear, I skirt around his still-heaving body and burst through the exit. Smoke billows out into the night and I cover my face with my arm before ducking inside.

"Dante!" I duck, trying to stay under the haze obscuring my vision.

My eyes water as I search for him. I only make it a few feet in when I find him lying on his stomach, his head turned to the side and a gash on his forehead. I roll him over, a sob catching in my throat.

Hooking my hands underneath his arms, I try to slide him to safety. Between the smoke and the terror coursing through me, he barely budges. I adjust my grip and yank him as hard as I can, and we finally make progress.

My lungs burn with each breath, but I finally make it to the door. It swings open, and an arm wraps around my waist and pulls me off my feet. I shriek, trying to hold on to Dante. I thrash around, attempting to fight off whoever has hold of me.

"Calm down, for fuck's sake," Helms growls, dropping me in a heap on the concrete.

He rushes back to grab Dante and throw him over his shoulder like a sack of potatoes. He makes it look easy, which I suppose under normal circumstances, it is.

"We have to move. Can you walk?"

I nod, jumping up to follow him into the shadows. I swing back and snatch up the tablet before I rush after him. "Shouldn't we call the fire department?"

"Either they'll come or they won't. Calling them only attracts more attention to us. Since the Vipers don't control them or the police yet, they're better off just pretending they don't have anything to do with it." Helms pulls his phone from his pocket and shoves it at me. "Call Kenzie."

I unlock the phone and scroll through the contacts until I find the right one. "It's going straight to voicemail. Do you want me to keep calling?"

"No. She'll call when she gets where she's going."

I glance behind us after several blocks, finding the flames licking high into the sky. "We should check that he's okay."

The adrenaline is the only thing keeping me from breaking down. My heart races in my chest and my fingers tremble as I grip Helms's phone and Lacey's tablet.

"He's fine. Just bonked his head too soon after the last time." His words are short and clipped.

Being in a high-intense situation with someone who clearly doesn't like me makes my skin itch. Usually I'd keep quiet, fade into the background. I doubt anyone would notice if I slipped off into the dark. Dante will when he wakes up, though, and I won't abandon him.

We've already had the discussion. We won't leave each other behind anymore. It made sense when I was locked up. But things have changed. Everything has changed.

"Call her again," he says gruffly as the Viper headquarters comes into view.

I almost drop the phone as I scramble to obey. "Straight to voicemail."

He sighs, glancing around the quiet night. "Shit is falling apart. We'll be lucky if we make it out of this alive."

His words send a chill down my spine. I don't say it, but I think he's right.

THIRTY THREE

Dante

One week. Seven fucking days of nothing. The first several I was laid up, healing from a head injury that was brought about through my own stupidity. Which Helms hasn't let me forget. His texts are stacking up—an ever-present annoyance.

My sister's disappearance wears on Helms a little more every day. I don't blame him, but I wish he'd stick around long enough to talk to me. I haven't seen him for days.

The rest of the time we've been subtly trying to find the others. They've all vanished into thin air. Shane and Sam being gone hasn't helped either. No matter how much we all express that each of them can take care of themselves, a constant tension hangs in the air.

"Maybe you should try to go back into the Guild. They still probably don't realize you're the one behind all this," Aelia says for the fifth time today.

"We made a deal," I respond through gritted teeth. It's the same thing I say every time she brings it up.

She sighs, setting the tablet Lacey gave her on the table. They haven't interacted much with Lacey since Nico's was hit. She's been firmly entrenched in her office at headquarters.

I've moved us into my house since I'm not willing to risk us sleeping at Viper's headquarters. Not with all the activity coming in and out. No one has tried to attack us there, but I'm not taking any chances. I won't risk Aelia's safety. The others don't have the same fears. At least it's given us the chance to reconnect without them constantly interrupting.

She spends most of her time wandering around the house. I keep waiting for her to break down again. It never comes, but I'm constantly on edge. I wish I could remember the shit that happened before Nico's was hit, but the memories are murky at best.

Her finger taps against the table, her mind a million miles away. She shoves out of her chair and meanders to the basement door.

"Why do you keep poking around?" My tone is sharper than I intended, and she jerks her hand away from the handle.

"I didn't realize you cared. I'm going to go take a shower." She attempts to walk past me, but I grab her wrist and haul her into my lap.

Her body stiffens and she leans away from me. I let her go and she pops up, shuffling back.

"I don't care that you're exploring, Aelia. I just want to know why." I drop my elbows on the table and cover my face with my hands.

She hums and I peek at her. "I was looking for places to hide. Just in case. And while we're on the topic, I would like to know why you won't hear me out."

"I have heard you out, Aelia. It's too much of a risk. Especially now that they're coming after us. They might have gotten the wrong places a lot at first, but burning down Nico's was spot on. The chances of them getting lucky again are better now than they were before. I'm not going to waltz back into the Guild unless there's a guarantee I won't leave in a body bag."

She snorts, smothering the sound behind her hand. "Sorry. That's not funny. It just…never mind. I do think we should call a meeting. Jag said Helms is about to climb the walls if he has to keep hanging around Viper territory. At some point I'd like to get to know Helms seeing as how he's your best friend and all. Our frantic conversation wasn't exactly a great impression."

"You will. We're going out to search some places Mac might have gone. We're dropping you off at headquarters with Lacey and Avery."

"Fine, but you're keeping your phone on or else we can't track you. And we're not going to risk losing you two as well." She tips her chin up, daring me to challenge her.

I hold out my hand and she comes, sinking into my lap again. This time she melts into me, her warmth seeping in.

"One of these days I'm going to wake you up with an orgasm," I mumble, burying my face into her neck.

"I'm looking forward to it. I've had to take care of things myself since you've been conked out for the last however-many days."

I rear back, pouting. "When the hell have you been doing that?"

She giggles, then presses a kiss to my lips. "Why do you think I've been taking so many fucking showers?"

"Fucking showers." I grin and nip at her bottom lip. "We need more of them, too."

"Time to go, Raines. Sorry, Aelia," Helms calls from the front door.

She kisses me one last time, then climbs off my lap. My palms itch to reel her back in. Sleeping next to her every night isn't enough. I can't wait for the day that the worst thing we have to worry about is what we'll have for dinner. We've avoided all talks of the future, dancing around the subject. There's no point until we know we'll both survive—until we know we're safe.

I shove from my chair and follow Helms out the door as Aelia trails behind. I lace our fingers together as we make our way to headquarters. Helms keeps his head buried in his phone, sending text after text to everyone who's missing. Lacey hasn't been able to track any of them, much to her dismay.

"We don't have time for a long goodbye, so get your instructions out now, Raines." Helms leans against the building, eyes still glued to his phone.

"I feel bad for him," Aelia whispers as we make our way to Lacey's office.

"We all do, but that's why I'm going with him. We'll find Mac. And the others." I infuse my tone with a confidence I no longer feel.

"If I hadn't been in there—"

I swing her around, gripping her arms as I stare at her. "Don't. We're not going to start assigning blame and wondering about the what ifs. It doesn't change the here and now. None of this is your fault. This all would have happened sooner or later. Anders would have gone back to Synd. Or Jenkins would have been swayed. Or Rima would have been put in jeopardy. This rests solely at the Guild's feet. Don't start taking ownership of their guilt, Aelia."

She nods, tears filling her eyes, and I pull her into my arms. She trembles as she clings to me. I press a kiss to her head, then gently push her away. I nod my chin toward Lacey, who's stepped out of the office, waiting until Aelia is safe inside before I pivot and walk back out the door. Lacey will probably spend her time behind her computers like every other night.

"Let's go. I don't want to leave them for too long," I growl as I pass Helms.

"She didn't go back to Synd. At least according to Hawk. My guess is she's lying low while they circle the city." He runs his fingers through his hair. "Byrns said the Guild has been hitting random places. Plus, three of their labs blew up. Another gambling hall started in the water district."

"What the fuck is the water district?" I've lived in Rima my whole life and we never had names for the different quadrants of the city.

He waves away my question as we make our way down the dark streets. I suggested we search closer to home. Both so I'm not leaving Aelia completely unprotected, but also because I don't know where else to look. Unless we start putting up flyers, I doubt we'll just run smack dab into her. Mac will come home when she can. I don't blame Helms for his urgency, though.

"You take this side of the line and I'll take the other," he says, slipping his phone into his pocket.

"I thought the whole point was to stick together?" I grab his arm before he can rush off and he snarls at me.

"We'll cover more ground this way." He deflates before my eyes. "I have to find her, Dante. I can't lose her again. I can't fail her again."

"We're gonna find her, Ryker."

He shakes his head, in a completely different world. "I wasn't strong enough for her."

"Search the abandoned houses first. I doubt she'd hole up in one that is occupied."

He nods, shaking off my hand before disappearing into the dark. I convince myself that he'll be fine. The next hour is torturous. I'm constantly checking my phone with no results.

I keep waiting for Helms to text me that he's found her. That he's back at headquarters with her. That he has a lead. Every time it's a punch to the gut when nothing's there.

As I step between two houses, the flickering of a fire from inside one of them catches my eye. Peeking through the window, I can't see anything other than a small blaze in a fireplace. The rest of the space is hidden in shadows, but it doesn't look like someone is squatting there. No furniture, no supplies, nothing other than that small fire.

I doubt Mac would do something like this. If she thought she was being followed, she wouldn't attract attention to herself like this. Especially in Viper territory. It's too risky. Searching the house wouldn't be smart. Then again, I don't want someone squatting in a house and accidentally burning it down. Especially if they need help.

Prowling around the back, I survey the small overgrown lawn. The only thing able to hide back there would be a bunny. Sneaking onto the back stoop, I peer through the tiny window, but nothing moves. I reach for my gun as my pulse ticks up a notch. A dead leaf crunches behind me, and I tense.

"Finally," a voice hisses.

I duck as I spin around, bringing my gun up. It's knocked from my hand and thuds into the overgrown grass. Slamming into the railing, I crash through the wood and tumble into the bushes. Thank fuck the wood is rotted or that would have hurt.

The man laughs manically, stalking toward me and I leap to my feet. I have a knife on me, but it's tucked away at my ankle. I squint into the dark at the figure. Clouds shuffle through the sky and finally the moon appears, illuminating his face.

"Grant," I sneer as I straighten.

"Cruz. Or should I say Raines?"

I smirk, not even the slightest bit concerned. Grant may have talked a big game, but he was only as important as the Guild allowed him to be. Rage simmers in my gut as I remember all he did to Aelia. He'll pay, but his death doesn't belong to me.

"Look at how smart you are, Grant. Glad to see someone figured it out. When did you get ousted from your shitty home?"

He slashes his hand through the air, gritting his teeth. "I'm not here for small talk, asshole. Where's the bitch?"

I snort, crossing my arms. The jackass doesn't even have a weapon. I'm not worried about him overpowering me. Allowing him to get under my skin will only put me in danger. I'll shove the anger aside and wait for retribution to hit him.

"Lost her, did you? I told you I'd torture you the same way you abused her. Looks like your time has come." I drop my hands to my sides, waiting for him to come at me.

Grant never could keep his anger in check. Just a few choice words and he'll charge like a raging bull. He tips his head back and laughs. I take advantage of his distraction and dive at him. A high-pitched shriek echoes through the night as his body hits the ground. I scramble off him, standing as he writhes on the ground.

He rolls and I snicker as blood seeps from a wound on his back and stains his light shirt. I don't know what he fell on, but as he continues to flop around, I search for my gun. It takes a hot minute to find it. By the time I pick up my weapon, he's staggered to his feet. He holds up his fists as if we're going to box, and I chuckle.

He lurches toward me, swinging erratically. I easily dodge him. Skipping back a few steps, I slide my gun into the holster. When he comes at me again, I punch him in the face. Blood splatters from his nose and he reels away, covering his face.

He drops his hands, fury etched in every line of his body. He rushes me again, running his stomach straight into my knee, and my knuckles split as I crack him across the jaw.

His eyes glaze over, and I catch him before he crumples to the ground. I'll drag his ass back to headquarters and let Aelia decide his fate. Latching onto the back of his neck, I march him around the house.

He stumbles along, not even bothering to resist anymore. We're not terribly far, but I don't relish the idea of carrying his limp body. I'd rather tie him to the back of my bike and take a little joy ride.

As headquarters comes into view, he struggles in my grasp, twisting to break free. Tossing him to the ground, I kick him in the side, hopefully breaking a few ribs. Based on the wheezing noise that leaves him, I accomplished my goal.

He rolls onto his back, and I stomp on his hand, bones crushing under the force. My hits are purposeful and calculated. It's as if my mind has shut off, leaving the desire for vengeance behind.

"Stop," he gasps, and I pause, heaving as my fingers flex by my sides.

"Stop? You think you deserve any mercy? You're a worthless sack of shit. You deserve nothing," I spit.

Seizing his wrist, I drag him the last block and bust through the doors of headquarters. When I drop him, he rolls onto his hands and knees, attempting to crawl away. I slam my heel into the small of his back and he collapses again.

Gripping his hair, I yank his head back and an anguished cry leaves him. "Fucking coward."

I shove his face into the floor, grinning when there's a crunch. If my hit from earlier didn't break his nose, that certainly did. Feet rush from the hallway and I straighten. Spreading my arms wide, I beam at Aelia as she stutters to a stop, eyes darting between the prone man groaning at my feet and me.

"Honey, I'm home. And I brought you a gift."

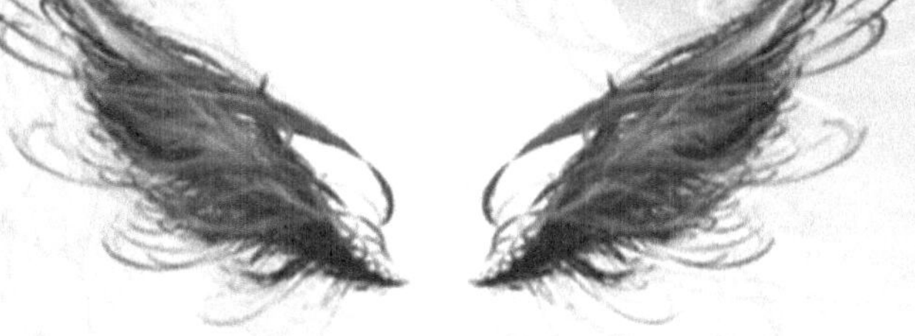

Thirty Four

Aelia

"Holy shit," Lacey breathes behind me, snapping me out of my stupor.

"Uh, Dante? What exactly did you do?" I ask as I slowly approach him.

I'm ten feet away when I realize the injured man is Grant. His bloody face turns to me, eyes almost swollen shut, and I'm pretty sure there are a few teeth littering the floor. I thought he was with my father. Or at the very least, still with the Guild.

Instead, he looks like he's been running into someone's fist. Glancing at Dante, it's not hard to guess *whose* fist. He slips his phone back in his pocket before glancing at me.

"It's a gift. Figured you'd want to deal with him. Although, I can if you want. Hell, we could make it a *Choose Your Own Adventure*." The giddiness in his voice and plastered across his face is almost too much.

"A what?" Lacey squawks, laughter lacing her tone.

Dante skips to the side like he's in a line dance and grins again. "She chooses what happens to him and I act it out. I mean, I wouldn't be acting. I'd actually be cutting his intestines from his body and strangling him with them, but she'd still be the one making the decisions."

My mouth drops open as he smirks at me. "We can't strangle him with his intestines. We already decided that wouldn't work."

"Au contraire," Ren says, appearing from the back door. He's been disappearing for days at a time, never telling anyone where he's going, but Lacey told us not to worry about it. At least he's keeping someone in the loop, even if it isn't Dante.

Ren clears his throat. "It is possible to strangle someone with their own intestines, given that you're able to keep them alive while you extract the organs and are able to keep them from slipping from your grasp while strangling them."

"I'm not even going to ask how you know that," Mason mutters as he presses into Lacey's back, wrapping his arm around her waist.

Dante grabs Grant's ankle and yanks him back, leaving streaks of blood behind. "Where do you think you're going?" he snarls.

I glance at the others as they argue about intestines and their many uses. This is the side of the mafia I've never seen before. Most of my childhood consisted of witnessing the raging of a man possessed by revenge, but being left out of many of the horrors. There wasn't time for laughter or good-natured bickering. This is a dynamic I don't fully understand, but it heals my soul in a way I never expected.

Dante sidles up next to me and whispers, "You don't have to make a decision now. We've got holding cells below."

"You got me a gift." Tears fill my eyes and I sniff.

"Dante fucking Raines. What the fuck did you do?" Helms bellows from the front door.

He stares at the man who's attempting to escape again. He rests his foot against Grant's forehead and shoves. Grant grasps at Helms's ankle, clinging to him. Dante stalks to them and grips Grant's hair, then hauls him away. As Dante systematically beats him, I expect to be afraid, or sickened, something other than relief.

"It's strange, isn't it? Watching them go into protective mode. Knowing they're willing to kill for you." Lacey sighs as she gazes at Byrns, who tracks Dante's movements. "I always expected to feel guilty. Might be fucked up, but it gives me the warm fuzzies that he's willing to take out various threats for me."

She smiles, love shining from her eyes. I'm not ready to admit out loud that she's right, but to myself I can. The idea that someone cares enough for me to go to the extremes to keep me safe. Watching him exact justice on Grant for hurting me mends the ache that's rested in my heart since we were separated.

I don't blame him for leaving me. I'm sure it wasn't easy. It still stung, though. He's been attempting to make up for it ever since I came here. Eventually we'll need to talk about it, but not tonight. Tonight he got me a gift.

Dante's chest heaves as he faces me, blood splattering his clothes. The glint of rage in his eyes disappears and his lop-sided grin returns. He sobers as I approach, each step measured. Stopping in front of him, I smile and a shaky breath leaves him. Sliding my hands around his neck, I pull him down until his lips touch mine with barely a whisper.

His arm slips around my waist, hauling me into him as he deepens the kiss. When he pulls back, he searches my face, probably for regret. He won't find it.

"Thank you for my gift. You shouldn't have," I murmur against his lips, and he chuckles. "How can I ever repay you?"

"I'd love to throw you on this table and fuck you senseless." He nips at my bottom lip. "I'll settle for watching you kill him."

I bite my tongue, leaning back to study him. He raises his eyebrows as I struggle to decide. He'd take care of Grant if I asked him to and relish in exacting justice on my behalf. Killing Grant may be the ending I need after years of abuse at his hands. I don't want to go through another episode like I did after I killed Molly, though. The nightmares are less frequent, but I'm far from over what she did to me.

Memories of the humiliation Grant put me through flood my mind, and I close my eyes. Every time he hit me, every time he starved me, every time he threatened me, every time he touched me. All of it meshes together, feeding the wrath inside of me. Unraveling my arms from Dante's neck, I slip my hand around his back and grab his weapon.

It's been a long time since I've held a gun, much less shot one. With Grant thrashing around not five feet from me, I doubt I'll miss. The worst that will happen is leaving several bullet holes in his body before I get it right. With the damage Dante inflicted on him, he'll probably die if we just leave him.

What's the fun in that? I snort at the voice in my head that suspiciously sounds like Rachel. My heart clenches and I pull in a deep breath.

Dante's eyes meet mine and I stand on my tiptoes, pressing my lips to his. He tilts his head, deepening the kiss, and his tongue sweeps against mine. A thrill runs down my spine and heat gathers between my legs. I pull away and he groans, tipping his head back. I slip from his arms and approach Grant.

I kick at his shoulder, and he moans as he lands on his back. I don't even think he can see me anymore through his swollen eyes. Several teeth are missing and blood paints his skin. I crouch and Dante steps toward me. Grant can't hurt me anymore. Dante doesn't have to worry. He still will, which sends another burst of warmth through me.

"Hello Grant," I say.

His head turns, trying to find where I am. I stand, pulling in a deep, calming breath.

"Goodbye Grant."

"You missed a spot." I point behind Dante's ear. Not that he can see it.

I grab the cloth from the rack and wet down a corner, pointing him toward the bench next to the shower. He sits and his towel gapes open, revealing everything. He wanted me to join him, but with both of us covered in blood, I knew we'd never get clean if I got in with him.

Dante's dark eyes track me as I make my way over, the knot of my own towel holding on for dear life. It falls when I climb onto him, straddling his lap. His hands grip my waist, holding me still as I tilt his head to the side and wipe away the last of Grant's blood.

"All done," I say in a singsong voice as I attempt to stand again.

He holds me in place, a growl rumbling through his chest as his eyes drag down my body. A shiver rolls through me, and I throw the cloth over my shoulder.

"Do I get my thank you now?" he asks, sliding his hands up my sides until his thumbs rest under my breasts.

Gripping his shoulders, I shiver as he brushes my nipples back and forth while heat gathers between my legs. I grind into him, seeking any type of friction I can. His towel unravels and I shove it aside. Gripping his cock, I lift onto my knees, then sink onto him. My pussy stretches, a delicious burn shooting through me.

He groans, then dips his head to capture a nipple in his mouth. Pleasure courses through me as I sway. Every move sends another bolt of lightning through me. He releases the bud with a pop before seizing the back of my neck and slamming his mouth to mine. This isn't the slow lovemaking we've had before. His moves aren't hesitant, wondering if I can handle his intensity. He's no longer holding back, thank fuck.

"I should have gotten a wider bench," he mutters against my lips.

I tip my head back as he nips at my skin, then latches onto the sensitive flesh of my neck, sinking his teeth in. "Then fuck me against the wall."

His growl is the only warning I have before he grips my ass and stands. I cling to him and he slams my back against the door and it rattles on its hinges. Winding my legs around his waist, I moan as he slips deeper.

"Hold on to me, angel. I'm going to fuck you hard and fast."

"Yes, please," I gasp.

He thrusts into me, true to his word. The wood behind me shakes as he pounds into me and my climax builds quickly. His head dips again, and his tongue flicks at my nipple. When he sucks the sensitive bud into his mouth, I sail over the edge, sobbing with the intensity. Pleasure floods my body, engulfing my senses. He doesn't slow. If anything, he surges into me harder.

"You're fucking perfect. Such a good girl coming around my cock," he hisses through gritted teeth.

The veins in his neck stand out with the strain as he holds me up. A weightlessness overtakes me, and I lean forward to bite his shoulder. He groans, his pace faltering the slightest bit, and my pussy spasms around him. His chest heaves, sweat dotting his skin as he slows and pulls out of me before slamming back in.

"Tell me how much you love my cock taking this wet little cunt of yours." His forehead lands on mine and he stares into my eyes. I smirk and he grins back at me.

"Fuck me harder, Raines."

He groans, burying his face into my neck. "Little fucking devil."

He thrusts into me harder with each stroke, igniting the flame within me once more. My breasts bounce from the force, but I'm too focused on his cock disappearing into me to notice, really.

"Play with your clit. Make me come for you," he growls.

My hand drops between my legs, obeying him without a thought. I've gotten better at figuring out what I like. He fixes his eyes on my fingers, watching as I circle them around my clit.

It's been a while since he's watched me pleasure myself, and it sends a surge of desire through me. I whimper as he embeds himself into me over and over. My orgasm catches me by surprise, flaming up within me, and I cry out as my pussy shudders around him. Dante grunts, then tips his head back and groans my name as he follows me.

Pressing his body into mine, he holds me up while I tremble in his grasp, never wanting to come back down to earth. The stars flashing behind my lids are brighter. The flames licking across my skin are laced with pleasure. The feel of his skin against mine is more comforting. I'd spend forever here if I could.

He straightens too soon, and I whine as I cling to him. He chuckles, pressing a kiss to my neck.

"Don't worry, angel. I'm not leaving you," he murmurs.

He grabs a robe I didn't notice before and drapes it over me. He doesn't even bother covering up as he steps into the hallway. I shiver, my pussy quivering around him with every step he takes. His cock hardens again, and a moan slips from my lips.

"Just a bit farther and then I'll fuck you again."

I hug him closer, knowing neither of us is going to get much sleep tonight.

Thirty Five

Dante

Collapsing into a chair, I stare off into space. I drop my elbows onto the table as Jag takes the one across from me. The last week has been a shitshow filled with massive amounts of nothing. Half of our crew is still missing. The ones who are left are disappearing left and right. Thankfully, we know where they're going this time, but we can't afford to lose anyone else if we want to take out the Guild.

"So he just left a fucking note?" Jag grumbles, crossing his arms.

"Helms knows what he's doing. He'll take care of Mac. Plus, he said he'd come when we call and not a minute sooner. I don't know where the Guild got all this manpower from unless they're pulling guards from the embassy." I scrub my hands over my face as frustration flutters in my chest. I may understand why Helms left, but I don't have to like it.

"They've postponed the Auction again. At least according to Raven."

Aelia appears from the hallway, smiling when she spots me, yet there's an edge in her eyes. I've kept her away from most of the operations. I've kept her in the loop, though. She keeps pushing us to figure out a timeline. We don't have enough people to hit them right now.

"Where the fuck has Raven been?"

"She says she's working on the lower gangs. Whether she's luring them to our side or taking them out, I don't know. You heard from Shane or Sam?"

I shake my head, then hold my hand out for Aelia. She slips onto my lap, curling up against my body, and I hold her close. Something's been bothering her, but she won't say what. I'm not about to push her. She's been through enough without having me badger her to share. She'll tell me when she's ready.

"Helms is convinced Alex is dead. I'm not so sure." I press a kiss to Aelia's temple, breathing in her scent to center myself. "He probably slipped off somewhere. But the others aren't as convinced."

Jag tips his head back and stares at the ceiling. "I gotta get Avery out of here. I don't want her around when this shit blows. And it will. Soon. I can smell it in the air."

"Fat chance of that happening," Avery sneers as she drops into the chair next to him.

He scowls at her. "Your brother will be here in a fucking week. You really want to be lurking around when he shows?"

"I can handle my brother. Question is, can you?" Her eyebrow pops up, taunting him.

Aelia's shoulders shake and she buries her face in my chest. She's still convinced those two will get together. Apparently there's too much banter between them to lead anywhere else. Personally, I think Jag is too fucking stubborn and noble for him to make a move.

"You realize you're going to get us both killed, don't you?" he snaps, glancing toward the front door.

She pats his arm and his head whips back around. "Don't you worry, kitty cat. I'll protect you from the scary monsters."

He scoffs, glancing away again. Avery's face falls for a split second before her mask slides over her features again. I wonder if Jag realizes how hard she's trying to remain unaffected.

Watching Mac grow up in an MC was difficult, especially since I never felt like I could help her. If I did, the others would view her as weak. Plus, our father was an asshole. I may not know Ghost very well, but he's nothing like my father. He runs his MC the way Helms and I always said we would. Looking around my empty headquarters, I wonder if I'll ever get that chance.

"Byrns said we need to get Lacey into the embassy."

Aelia straightens, wide eyes finding mine. "She can't go in there."

I rub small circles on her back. "He means when we attack them. She needs to tap into their main network for something. And she has to do it before we burn their headquarters to the ground."

Her brows pull low, deep grooves appearing between her eyes. "I don't like it. We need to take Jenkins out. No one else is qualified to take over for him. He doesn't trust anyone enough to shoulder the burden of running the organization. Which helps our cause, obviously, but I bet he's got a ton of security around him now."

"I know, Aelia. We've got a plan, remember?" I say softly, and she nods. I fix my gaze on Jag again. "Did Byrns and Lacey tell you where they were going?"

"Just closer to the embassy. Said the less we know, the better."

I nod, even though I don't like it. Everyone else is either missing or scattered. Ren still disappears for days, searching for his family. I can't blame him. It's what I would do too.

As if I've manifested him, Ren shoves through the back door, shaking off the rain from his hair. It's been pouring for the last three days. The streets are starting to flood. Not that anyone is doing anything about it.

"Can't stay long. I've got a lead I'm chasing down. However, I believe I found where Anders went." Ren rests his hands on the back of a chair.

Aelia shoots upright, tension flooding her body. When he doesn't continue, she glares at him. His eyes narrow on hers, but it's more like he's working something out in his brain. I can practically hear the gears turning in his head.

"Well?" she snarls.

He slips his hands in his pockets. "He's in Synd, as we expected. Trying to exact revenge."

"But everyone he wanted to take out is in Rima. Are you sure he's not wanting to take over now that you're all here?" My chest tightens as I notice his eyes darting to Aelia every few seconds. He knows something. And it will change her in some way. I can feel it in my bones. I hold her a bit tighter.

"We're not all here. You remember we left someone in charge in our stead?" His gaze fixes on Aelia. "I believe Roman Drake will be perfectly capable of taking out his father."

She blinks, a blank mask sliding over her features. "That's not possible."

Ren tucks his chin to his chest. None of us move, waiting for his response. I'm not surprised I missed the connection. Aelia never used her brother's name, just calling him her brother. If she did, I don't remember. None of the others said anything about him being related to Anders. They talked around the subject, assuming the older man has scuttled back to the Guild for good. Drake isn't exactly an uncommon name, either.

"It's true. Your brother is in Synd right now."

Aelia is already shaking her head, her entire body trembling. She staggers to her feet, holding her hands out as if she can ward off the truth. Slowly, I stand and reach for her. The last thing I want is for her to run.

"Roman is dead. He died. I don't know h-how…" A choked sob leaves her. "Roman was killed years ago. If he was a-alive, he would have come for me. He would have s-saved me."

Ren picks his head up, compassion lacing his eyes. "He was told you were dead. That both you and Anders were dead. When Anders showed up in Synd, he tried to kill Roman."

Aelia's eyes dart between us, never fully settling on anyone. When I reach for her, she jerks away, and my heart cracks. I've been through trauma before. I've been through betrayal. But nothing could prepare me to help her deal with something like this. To find out her brother has been less than four hours from her for almost a year…

"Maybe you should call him." Ren sets a burner phone on the table, sliding it closer to her.

Aelia collapses into a heap, sobs racking her body. I crouch next to her, wishing I could ease her pain. Jag signals to me and I nod while he grabs Avery's arm and marches her out the back door. My touch is gentle as I rub her back. At least she doesn't pull away again. I glance at Ren over my shoulder, and his mouth pulls into a frown.

"Thank you," I murmur and he nods before turning on his heel and following the other two.

It takes a while for her to sort through her feelings. Eventually, her sobs subside and she ends up curled in my lap again. Gently, I lift her and settle us into a chair. She sniffs, wiping her face.

"Sorry," she whispers as she scrubs away her tears.

I wrap my fingers around her wrists and pry them away from her face. "You have nothing to apologize for. You never have to say you're sorry for crying. It makes you human, Aelia."

She rolls her eyes, more as a defense mechanism than anything. "I don't see you bursting into tears when shit way worse than this happens."

The corner of my mouth twitches. "You know what I did when I got Avery back here? I dropped to my knees and sobbed. Because I knew I'd left you behind. And I regretted it every fucking second. Then when Mac showed up and told me what happened to her, I bawled. Everywhere I looked was another glaring example of how I failed."

"You didn't fail me, Dante. If I wanted to be saved, I would have stayed with Avery. But we both know you wouldn't have been able to get both of us out. And I never would have let you choose me over Avery."

I shake my head. Regret is something that I'll always live with. Every time I see her scars, every time she wakes from a nightmare, every time she cries, I'll regret my decisions. Maybe one day I'll learn to live with it, but not today.

"You need to call him, Aelia. He deserves to hear your voice. To know you're alive." I press the phone into her hands. "And if you want to go to Synd, I'll take you there myself. You can be with your brother."

The words burn as they come out. As much as I hate it, she deserves to be with Roman. He's her family—one she thought lost long ago. Not many people get the second chance resting in her hands. At least if she's in Synd, I know she'll be safe. I may not know Roman, but from what the others have said, she'll be safe with him. And if she chooses to stay, so be it.

She pulls her gaze away from the phone to stare at me. "What about you?"

I sigh before sliding her into the chair next to me. I won't manipulate her into staying. This is her decision and hers alone.

"I have to stay here." I suck in a deep breath. "Even after the Guild is dealt with, I have to stay here. Someone needs to rebuild Rima."

"So my choices are to go to my brother in Synd and hope my life will be okay or stay with you and never find him again?" Anguish colors her tone and tears fill her eyes again.

"What? No, angel. This isn't black and white. And you don't have to decide anything right now. But if you want to go there, I'll take you." I try to keep my face blank, to not let her see the pain this conversation is causing me.

"Do you want me to stay?" Her voice cracks along with my heart.

"I want you to be happy. I want you to live, Aelia. Whatever you decide, that's what I want for you. And I'll do anything to make it happen. Even if that means letting you go."

"What if I don't want you to let go?" she whispers, tears cascading down her face.

I cup her cheeks, resting my forehead against hers. "Then I never will. No one will ever take you from me again. I'd tear the world apart with my bare hands before I let them."

"Don't make me leave."

"Never." I brush her lips with my own and she shudders.

"Being with you makes me happy. Loving you makes me feel alive. I don't want to lose that."

My breath catches in my throat, and I pull back, scanning her face. Too many emotions swirl in her eyes to decipher them all. I'm terrified that her admission was merely a slip of the tongue, spoken in the heat of an emotionally charged moment.

"Say it," she whispers, eyes finding mine again.

I open my mouth, then snap it shut again. "You'll never lose me, Aelia."

She's shaking her head before I've even finished. "No. Say it."

I brush her hair behind her ear. "I love you."

She pulls in a shuddering breath, a soft smile tugging at her lips.

"Do you want me to stay while you call him?" I ask, brushing her tears away with my thumbs.

"Go talk to Jag. The sooner we get this done, the sooner we can visit Roman. But will you wait until he answers?"

I kiss her gently. "Of course."

She swipes at the screen, then presses the phone to her ear. I can barely make out the ringing, then a man's voice echoes through.

"Drake."

Aelia shoves her fist in her mouth, silent sobs taking over her body. She curls into herself, and I wonder if she's going to be able to speak. The line goes dead, and she whimpers, dialing again.

"Don't fuck with me—"

"Roman?" she whispers. Her eyes find mine, concern lining them. "Hello? Are you there?"

He clears his throat and she sniffs. I wonder if anyone told him she was alive. Maybe Ren thought it would be better coming from her directly.

"Roro, please say something," she pleads softly. She slides from the chair, dropping to her knees.

"Aelia?"

THIRTY SIX

Aelia

I shake myself from my thoughts, concentrating on the scene in front of me. I should be excited, or afraid—something. Instead I feel detached from reality. My phone call with Roman was too short. Too draining. Too much.

I spent the rest of the night crying while Dante held me. He brought me back to the shower, hoping it would help like when I spiraled. I don't know if it did or not. I didn't have the energy or heart to tell Dante, though.

Four days isn't enough to process everything. I thought about calling him again, but I don't want to bother him while he deals with our father. At least, that's what I assume he's doing. Mostly he wanted to know where I'd been. He barely spoke, only to ask another question. I wonder how much he actually heard.

"Aelia, we need to move," Avery hisses, latching onto my upper arm.

"Dante said to stay on this side. They'll be coming out of that door," I mutter, gesturing vaguely at the warehouse across the street.

"Except there's like seven guys hanging around. They're going to spot us any second now." Avery bounces from one foot to the other, her gaze fixed on the guards taking a smoke break.

"If you keep jumping around like you have to pee, it'll probably be even sooner."

She plops down next to me, leaning against the building. Jag and Dante have been inside for ten minutes, but it feels like forever. My palms are itchy and my stomach rolls with every noise that emanates through the night. The warehouse doesn't look much different from the ones I passed while I was running from the Guild. I was always too scared to go in them, preferring to find tiny alcoves. I'm glad I listened to my gut.

"Where's Raven's gang again?"

I sigh, checking the burner phone Ren gave me for the seventh time. I may be calm on the outside, but it's all an act. One I spent years perfecting. Avery didn't have nearly as much time to learn how to hide her nerves.

"They're two blocks down and three blocks over. They've got trucks to transport the people who come out alive." I narrow my eyes at the flashing red light in one of the windows. It's gone before I can mention it to Avery.

"How many women are inside?"

The guards filter back into the building, laughing and clapping each other on the back. One trails behind the rest, turning when he reaches the door and our eyes meet through the shadows. He taps his wrist, and I suck in a breath. I didn't realize any on our side would be out here. I assumed they were all still at the embassy, creating chaos on the inside.

"It's not just women, and we don't know. Get up. It's time," I murmur, scrambling to my feet.

"How do you know?" She shoves upright, anyway. Avery might want answers to everything, but she follows directions at least.

The top of the building explodes, and glass shatters onto the concrete two stories below. Avery curses, covering her head. We're too far away to feel anything but a gust of heat. The rumbling makes it seem worse than it actually is. Small fires flicker from the open windows and shouts echo through the night.

I step from the shadows, pulling the flashlight Dante gave me from the front pocket of my black hoodie. I'm pretty sure it's one Sam left in her room. The worn fabric wraps around me, heating me to the point where I'm boiling. It's too hot now for a sweatshirt, but I needed something that would hide me.

Now I'm the one bouncing from one foot to the other, whispering prayers under my breath. I'm not religious, but if one of them is listening, all the better. Guards spill from the front of the building, smoke trailing after them. Several of them take off into the dark. Others collapse to their hands and knees, retching onto the pavement. How Jag was able to get ahold of tear gas, I don't know. The victims will be affected as well. It was our best chance at getting them to safety.

"Where are they?"

She hasn't even finished her question before the side door pops open and figures stumble as they exit. I flash the light, clicking it on and off to get their attention. One woman stops short, then races toward me.

I skip to the middle of the street, trying to keep an eye on the guards as well as the people. Avery whisper-shouts at them, her voice still carrying. She takes off, the crowd of women following. I have no idea where the men are. Usually there's several stuffed in with the women.

I lose count of how many stream past me. I urge them onward. Dante told me to follow them, but I won't leave him behind. The guard from before shoos the last of the women from the building, then charges at me. I tense, gripping the gun Jag slipped me before we left. I stashed it in my hoodie since I didn't have a holster. It probably would have gotten stuck as I tried to pull it out, anyway.

He skitters to a stop in front of me. I recognize him. "You're the one who slipped me the list."

"Yes. They moved me here two weeks ago. They're trying to move to another city. There's another holding center five blocks that way." He points the opposite way from where Avery has taken the women.

"Did you see Dante? Did you tell him?"

He shakes his head. "They were clearing out the back rooms, but there's no one there. I couldn't warn them since I wanted to stay with the women. I killed the guard who was leading them out, at least."

He drops his hands to his knees as a coughing fit overtakes him. I scan the area, trying to find the rest of the Guild's men. They've all disappeared.

My hand drops to the guard's arm. "Are they going to the embassy or the other holding center?"

"Protocol is to go to the holding center and move the assets. Sorry," he wheezes, but I wave away his apology. We all got used to the lingo the Guild uses. "Half of them move the people, the others go back to the embassy. Unless there's another hit."

"Go," I command, shoving him past me. "Two blocks down and three blocks over. Tell them I sent you. Stay with the women until they're safe."

He nods before staggering off. I'm surprised he's able to move at all without keeling over. I hope he makes it. I take off for the building, intent on getting Dante and Jag out.

The door busts open before I reach it, smoke pouring from the opening. They step out, gas masks covering their face. Dante's hand wraps around my upper arm and drags me back.

He rips his mask off and slams it against his leg. "Too many got away."

Jag tears his own mask from his face, and they mutter back and forth while I attempt to grab Dante's arm. They're too absorbed to pay attention to me and frustration sets my blood on fire. It races through my veins until I step between them.

"Shut the fuck up," I snap, and they finally stop. "I know where they're going. One of the guards is on our side and told me they're going to another holding center five blocks away. They'll move the assets and then half of them will break off for the embassy. If we hurry, we can free more people. And hopefully take a few more out."

"Shit," Jag mutters, then grabs his phone.

"Tell Raven to move the trucks five blocks south and get more here if she can. Otherwise, we'll get them to headquarters. Go find her, Jag." Dante grabs my hand and drags me down the street before he answers.

We shouldn't go alone, but Jag will catch up. We don't have enough people to enact a large show of force. It's why we targeted the holding centers. Getting them out before they could be shipped off to one of the satellite cities or transported to wherever the Guild is trying to move is the best chance they have. We won't be able to follow them. We won't be able to save them if they leave Rima.

Dante drops my hand and shoves his phone at me. "Call the others. Leave messages if you can. Then text them the message. Hopefully, someone will get it and come help. Call Ghost. Maybe he left early."

Trying to keep up with him while doing everything isn't easy, but I manage to send out a mass text. No one answers, though I'm not surprised. None of their voicemails pick up either. I'm out of breath by the time we careen around the last corner. Mason's text comes in, promising to be there as soon as he secures Lacey.

Dante shoves me back into the shadows of the alley, blocking my view with his body. "Lots of activity out front. No trucks yet, but some guards."

"Do we sneak around back?"

I peek around him and my jaw drops. "Some" doesn't adequately describe the crowd milling about. I can't tell if they're with the Guild or not. Most of them are arguing with one another. A fistfight breaks out and others rush in to break them up. I grip Dante's arm, shaking him when I see it.

"Dante, they're dressed differently."

"What?" He pulls his eyes away from his phone to scan the area. "They look like they're from the lower gangs. They're helping us, even if they don't mean to."

"It's chaos," I breathe, watching as another fight breaks out.

Dante grunts, burying his face in his phone again. At some point, we'll need to intervene. In fact, we should take advantage of the distraction. My stomach flips, and I wrap my hand around my gun. I'm not qualified to be carrying this thing, but it certainly makes me feel safe. I'm counting on muscle memory to take over if need be. Roman made sure I knew how to shoot. He also taught Ember and me to defend ourselves. Not that I used it very often.

"Let's go around back. We can slip in while they're fighting and get the others out," I say as his fingers fly across the screen. "Dante. We need to go now."

I smack him and he jolts. "You're supposed to be the lookout, Aelia. So, keep an eye out while I sort this shit out. We can't get them out if we don't have anywhere for them to go."

"*Anywhere* is better than there." I gesture toward the warehouse.

Shouts ring out and I stumble forward a few steps. Dante yanks me back, snarling. I give him a look and inch forward again. The two factions are in a standoff, waving their guns around and threatening each other.

"We'll go around the back and see what's going on. Do not go in without me, no matter what happens. We have to stick together."

I nod, then slip toward the wall and peek around the corner. No one is coming, but that doesn't mean there aren't others lying in wait. Dante laces our fingers together and tugs. His other hand slides around my neck and he slams his mouth on mine. It's hard and fast and feels more like a goodbye than anything. I swallow my tears and glance away. He doesn't need to see me cry again.

We slide along the shadows, Dante watching behind me. But my eyes are fixed on the group still screaming at each other. It's almost like a play instead of an actual showdown. No one is shooting. Other than a few punches, no one is beating each other. It's as if they're all playing a part.

I pull Dante to a stop, tilting my head as I narrow my eyes on the scene. "Does it feel like they're acting?"

He glances over his shoulder. "The lower gangs are working for the Guild. This may just be a display of force. Most of the time, the group with less power does a lot of posturing, but they don't actually want to start a war. Shit."

"Who's tha—Oh shit."

THIRTY SEVEN

Dante

Sam, decked out in head-to-toe black, skips forward into the lights. She twirls her daggers, I'm sure with a smirk plastered on her face.

"Where the fuck is Shane?" I snarl. Not that Aelia could answer me. She doesn't know any more than I do.

"Maybe they found Alex?" Aelia whispers, hope tinging her tone.

She never got to meet him, but she's seen Ren's slow spiral into frustration and rage. With all of his family missing, he's been on edge. I don't blame him. I've been the same way since Mac vanished. Now with Helms gone, it's too much.

We can't lose all of them. And yet here's Sam, standing in front of a gang, probably intent on taking them all out by herself. Being the Wraith might help, but not enough to take on thirty men—fifty if they join forces.

The warm night wind carries her voice as she yells at them to give up now. As if they'll listen. One man steps forward, tipping his head back and laughing. Sam cocks her head, twirls her knife one more time and then flips it around. It flies through the air and embeds itself into the guard's throat.

Chaos. That's the only way to describe moments following her blade. The guard falls to his knees, then tips to the side, dead before he hits the ground. Trying to decipher the lower gangs from the guards is impossible as they attack each other.

Aelia takes off, heading for Sam, and I dash after her. Wrapping my arm around her waist, I pull her clean off her feet. She shrieks, pounding on me to loosen my grip.

"Stop, Aelia. We can't get in the middle. Sam knows what she's doing," I growl in her ear.

She deflates, and I set her feet on the ground. Sam crouches, a gun in one hand and a knife in the other. How does she think she's going to take on the remaining group, even with the lower gangs getting in the way?

Both sides have fled, lining the opposite sides of an invisible demarcation line. The lower gangs hide behind whatever they can find—dumpsters, concrete barriers, and even the abandoned store perpendicular to the warehouse. The guards retreat to the holding center, setting up their defense behind the windows. I wonder how many of them will get shards of glass embedded in their eyes when it shatters from the bullets.

Sam is stuck in no-man's-land, a single bastion against the might of the Guild.

"Fuck. Reynolds," I spit.

Jenkins's right-hand man steps from the warehouse in a three-piece suit. He's so out of place among the dirt and grime it's almost laughable. All he needs is a flat cap and he'll look like he stepped out of a 1920s gangster movie. It'd be funny if he wasn't palming a gun.

I spin Aelia around. "Stay here. No matter what you see, do not come after me."

I dash away before she can respond. I don't make it far before a gunshot rings out and I freeze. Alex fucking King saunters from the darkness, his usual grin in place. He wraps his arm around Sam, tucking her behind him. Reynolds steps forward, gun pointed at Alex's head. Aelia's hands press into my sides, and I shuffle us back toward safety.

"So you two are the ones fucking with the Guild?" Reynolds calls.

Alex grins, shoving Sam behind him again when she tries to scoot around. "Good to see we've done our job."

"Hardly. Because now I'm going to kill you. And then where will your shitty little operation be? The Guild will live on, just as it always has."

Sam steps next to Alex, who sidles in front of her. They're in a subtle dance, each trying to protect the other.

Alex growls at Sam, then turns to Reynolds. "See now, I don't believe you. Maybe you should say it with more gusto. Put your back into it."

Reynolds sneers at him even as he glances around. I'm surprised he didn't shoot Alex as soon as he showed up. Actually, I'm surprised he didn't shoot Sam first. Then again, Reynolds is just like Jenkins, believing all women are inferior. They'd never be able to stand up to him.

"He's posturing. He doesn't know what Alex has done, so he'll try to get it out of him," I mutter as I pull Aelia past the alley. There's nothing I can do for those two, so I'll try to get the victims out instead.

"How do you know?"

"Because it's what I would do."

Seconds later, Reynolds proves me right as he questions Alex and what he could possibly have to fight the Guild. Alex laughs as his hand slides to Sam's back and grips her shirt. He forces them both back a step.

"We could shoot him. Then they could run." Aelia pulls the gun from her hoodie, and I shove it down.

"You'll set off a chain reaction and they'll be caught in the crossfire."

"Good fucking luck dealing with the rest of us," Alex booms out.

Pandemonium erupts at the sound of another gunshot. Alex whips around, knocking Sam to the ground as he covers her with his body. Sam's scream cuts through the chaos. The two factions rage around their prone figures, creating a background of war. She rolls Alex's body from hers, crouching over him. Aelia runs for them again, and I shove her to the ground.

"Go," I bellow, charging for them.

The scene is even worse than before as I try to decipher the lower gangs from the guards. They charge at each other, and I dodge the masses. Sam screams again, allowing me to pinpoint where she is in the crowd. I'm surprised I haven't gotten shot yet.

A Molotov cocktail sails through the air, exploding against the warehouse. Two more follow and smoke billows up, clouding the scene. Assholes put tar in them.

A guard barrels into me, and we crash to the ground. His knife swipes at my face, and I throw my arm up. The blade sinks into my skin, burning as he yanks it out. I punch him in the jaw, and he snarls. Then he jerks and tumbles off me.

Shane looms over me, gun clutched in his hand. He shoots the man again, then holds out his hand.

"Where are they?" he snaps, scanning the chaos.

"Over there." I take off, shoving men aside.

Sam screams again, her terrified voice echoing off the buildings. I've never heard a more gut-wrenching sound. Sirens blare in the distance, and the crowd scatters. The police in Rima might be shit, but no one wants to deal with them. They're corrupt to the core. Most of these men would disappear before morning if they were brought in.

The crowd parts and I freeze. Reynolds drags Sam toward an SUV as she struggles to break free. Pure, unadulterated terror paints her face, her eyes fixed on Alex's lifeless body. Shane shoves past me, charging for her. Sam's screams are abruptly cut off as Reynolds smashes the butt of his gun into the back of her head. She goes limp as Shane roars.

The world slows when Reynolds grins, lifting his gun, and squeezes the trigger. Shane's body jerks, his steps faltering, and he falls. Reynolds throws Sam into the SUV and dives in after her. I shoot at the tires as they squeal off into the dark.

My head swims and my vision darkens. The smoke from the bombs infiltrates my lungs, and I cover my face with my arm. Staggering to my feet, I fight the nausea in my stomach. Between one blink and another, Ren appears, crouching over Alex's body. His hands move in a steady rhythm.

Even from here, I can tell his efforts are in vain. I lurch to Shane and roll him over. Ripping off his shirt, I sigh in relief when his chest rises and falls. Blood seeps from his shoulder and he gasps, his eyes flying open.

"Don't fucking move," I growl.

Aelia drops next to me, tears streaming down her face, and she whips off her sweatshirt. She presses the fabric to his wound.

"Go. Help Ren," she chokes out.

The sirens cut off several blocks away, the flashing strobes piercing the sky. Maybe Jag's and my diversion threw them off. I crawl to Ren, who's still pumping Alex's chest.

"Come on, you son of a bitch. Fucking breathe," he grits out.

Sweat drips down his face, mingling with his tears. I press my fingers to Alex's neck, but I can't feel a pulse. Leaning over his body, I hold up my hand to stop Ren's attempts. Nothing. Gazing up at him, I shake my head.

His hands drop to his sides. He tips his head back and screams, his anguish given life. It wraps around me, piercing into my body.

"Save him," Shane yells. "Fucking save him, Ren."

Ren's breath heaves out of him, and he positions his hands on Alex's sternum. His body trembles as he begins again. I glance back at Shane, though I have no words of comfort for him.

"Where the hell is Aelia?" I snarl, and Shane's eyes dart to mine.

He glances behind him, then back at me, eyes widening. "She went after Sam."

"Fuck," I bellow, shoving to my feet.

I'll storm the Guild myself if need be. I won't fail her again. I take off toward the embassy, praying I get there before she does.

THIRTY EIGHT

Aelia

This is not my smartest decision. Chasing after the SUV carrying Sam might have been a mistake. I couldn't let her suffer the same fate I did. I've stood by long enough while others succumbed to the whims of the Guild.

I'm wheezing by the time I step onto a street filled with night clubs. Music bleeds into the air, pounding in my head. I flag down a cab and slide in the back. I don't have any money. Rubbing my palms along my leg, I meet the driver's gaze in the rearview mirror. She turns around and her smile falls. She scans me, eyes catching on the flecks of Shane's blood on the backs of my hands. Thankfully, my black shirt hides the rest of it.

"You okay? Are we running from a boyfriend?"

I swallow hard. "I need to go to the old embassy on the south side of town."

Her eyes widen and she whips back around. "Can't. Get out."

I push back on the seat, the gun digging into my back as my body trembles. "I have to. Don't make me…"

Our eyes meet again in the reflection, and she sighs. "You don't want to go there."

"I don't have a choice." I dig my nails into my thighs and wait.

"You going to shoot me if I don't?"

Fuck. This isn't me. I'm not my father, and this is something he'd do. Forcing people to do his bidding without regard merely because he commanded it was his specialty. I refuse to be like him.

"I'm sorry," I whisper. I scoot across the seat and reach for the handle.

"Wait," she snaps, and I glance at her. "You realize what you're getting into?"

I snort. "All too well."

"Don't come for me if you get yourself killed."

She eases into traffic, then weaves around a standstill before taking off for the embassy. I bounce in my seat, staring out the window as the buildings thin. I can feel her eyes darting to me every few seconds.

When the city lights fall away, she hits the gas. Hopefully we're not speeding toward my death. As the glow from the embassy takes over the horizon, I bite my lip as I attempt to control the anxiety rolling through me.

"Don't go around front," I say softly.

"Duh. I'm taking you around back." She snaps, shaking her head. "Did they knock out all the lights on purpose?"

I shrug, not that she notices. "Probably. They're not exactly keen on neighbors. I think they cleared the buildings around them so no one could spy. Wouldn't want people learning their secrets."

The bitterness is clear in my voice. Goosebumps scatter on my bare arms, and I rub them. I left Sam's sweatshirt with Shane. Dante is going to fucking kill me if the Guild doesn't beat him to it. I should have said something, but he would have stopped me. Or he would have insisted he come with. The longer I sit here, though, the less sure I am about going alone.

"Where you want me to drop you?" She breaks through my thoughts, and I jolt.

"Take a right. There's an alley about two blocks down. You can just pull in there. There's an exit out the back."

"You're not going to be able to pay, are you?" She doesn't sound upset, but fuck do I feel bad. She's helping me when she didn't have to.

"If you go to Viper territory, someone at headquarters can. Might want to wait a bit, though. We're kind of dealing with some things," I mumble.

She snorts, flipping her hair over her shoulder. "No shit, honey. Just don't get yourself killed, or I'll probably be held liable for it."

"They wouldn't do that. Don't worry."

She cuts the lights as she pulls into the alley and comes to a stop. I shove open the door and get out, bracing myself as best I can. It takes me a minute to get my breathing under control. The last time I was here, I was staring at Rachel's lifeless eyes. She died because of me. I wasn't strong enough, quick enough. I wasn't enough to save her.

I duck my head back into the car. "Thank you."

She nods, sorrow lining her eyes. She doesn't respond since there's nothing much to say.

You're welcome for shuttling you to your death, doesn't exactly send hope shooting through anyone. I could use an infusion of hope right about now.

This was a really bad decision. My stomach clenches tighter with each step. They haven't repaired the garage door. I sneak along the building, searching for cameras. Nothing moves, nothing flashes through the dark, and I breathe a sigh of relief.

Ducking, I peek into the hole. There are no guards inside, and the silence is overwhelming. It presses down on me, threatening to crush me under the weight. I'm terrified the minute I start to wiggle through, they'll seize me and throw me back in the cage. I survived it once. I can do so again if need be.

I drop to my stomach and peek into the garage again. The hole is larger now that there's not a tire blocking the way. Hopefully I won't fuck up my other leg in the process. Scooting forward, I hold my breath. The lights flicker, sending pulses of pain through my head. I haven't had enough time to heal with everything going on. If I get out of this, I'm taking a week long nap. I fucking deserve it.

My feet clear the metal and I pop up. I fix my eyes on the door to the rest of the building and take one step before I'm plunged into darkness.

"Shit," I breathe. If Lacey is fucking with the lights, she picked a very bad time to do it.

I shuffle forward, my hands spread out in front of me. Waving them back and forth in an attempt not to run into anything, I'm sure I look ridiculous. Maybe I'll give Lacey a good laugh. I hold up my middle finger, just in case she's watching.

After an eternity, my fingers connect with cold concrete. Trailing my hand along the wall, I search for the door. My palm brushes metal, and a sob catches in my throat. The handle gives easily, which only makes me more uneasy. Too much is going right. Nothing ever goes my way in the Guild. I'm not a particularly lucky person.

I slip through the door anyway, closing it quietly in case someone else is around. The lights flash on, though the ones back here are dim and far apart. I sprint through the dark, then slow as I approach each beam. My heart pounds in my ears, making it hard to hear if someone approaches.

Another door, a set of stairs, then another, and I'm finally on the right floor. Whoever designed this building should be shot. It's convoluted, probably set up to disorient people. I doubt they thought people would be down here often. They still deserve to at least get throat punched.

A guard leans against the door leading to the cages I was held in not too long ago. I peek up the stairs and around the hallway for more people, but I'm pretty sure he's alone. From what the others have said, I'm sure Sam could save herself. She seems the most capable of doing so. Unless they drugged her. Or hit her hard enough. I doubt I'll be able to carry her out of here.

When the guard peers away from me, I dash to the stairwell, trying to keep my feet quiet. Pressing my back against the wall, I hold my breath.

No scuffle of shoes or curses erupt from him, thank fuck. I peer around the corner, finding his attention still fixed on the opposite end of the hallway.

I grip my gun, then let go to wipe my sweaty hand on my leggings. Grabbing it again, I pull in a deep breath and duck around the corner. Fate must be smiling down on me. He doesn't move until I'm pressing the barrel to the back of his neck, and even then he only tenses.

"Open the door," I hiss as his hands shoot into the air.

He reaches for his pocket, but I dig the metal into his skin. He freezes as his jaw trembles. I swear he's about to cry.

"Slow. Wouldn't want my finger to slip." I sound like I'm in a bad gangster movie, parroting lines I read five minutes before I went on screen.

His head turns slightly, and I flinch.

"Aelia?" He turns, his bright blue eyes piercing mine.

"Benjamin? What the fuck are you doing?"

"Thank fuck you're here. Some guard came and told me to stand here. And not to let anyone in. Said they'd hurt her." He still has that boyish look to him, like he'll charm or trick me from one moment to the next.

"Where the fuck did you go? Wait, we don't have time for this. Open the door." I gesture to the metal with the gun, and his eyes widen. "Sorry, Ben, but I don't trust anyone right now. Open the door and you can come with us. But if you turn on me, I'll shoot you without a second thought."

He nods, then dives his hand into his pocket. I'm surprised they gave him regular clothes. Either the Guild enlisted him and I'm making a big mistake, or a rogue guard really did spring him loose.

"They brought her about thirty minutes ago. She was unconscious, but breathing. Guard said they were using her as bait."

I bounce on the balls of my feet as he fumbles with the lock. Finally, he gets the key in and rips the door open. The familiar red light bathes the rank space. I rush forward, checking the cages one-by-one.

A small cry of triumph leaves me when I find Sam's prone form in the last one. I wave Benjamin to me and point to the door. It takes him twice as long to find the right key, but eventually it pops open.

"I can't carry her." I'm loath to trust him, but I don't have a choice. Now that I'm back in the Guild, I wonder if I can do more damage while I'm inside. "Can I trust you to take her out of here?"

His eyes harden, and I lift the gun slightly. "Where's Rachel?"

Tears fill my eyes and my chin quivers. "She's…dead. She died while getting me out. It's my fault."

His jaw twitches as he grinds his teeth before he nods. "Rachel always wanted to go out doing some good. I can carry her. Just tell me where to go and I'll get her there."

I glance between Sam's prone figure and Benjamin. "I don't think I have a choice, but if you fuck with her, believe me, she's scarier than me and she'll torture you for it. And then you'll have her boyfriends to deal with."

He rolls his eyes, then sobers when he catches the seriousness on my face. Shane may be shot and Alex is probably dead, but Ren would systematically take this man apart bit by bit if he hurts her. And that's after Sam has her turn. Their loyalty to each other is something I've never experienced before. And I doubt I ever will again.

"How do I get out?" he asks as he gathers Sam in his arms. She moans, but doesn't wake.

"Underground parking garage. There wasn't anyone down there when I came through."

"Here's hoping our luck holds out then," he mutters.

With each turn of a corner, my muscles tense. I don't know what the hell is going on, but I'm not going to complain. It's not until I'm passing Sam through the jagged hole that I wonder what the hell I'm doing.

I could go with them. I could show Benjamin where the others are. I could find Dante and we could come back together. There's a slew of other decisions I could make. None of them gets me as close to Jenkins as I am right now, though.

Benjamin's face appears. "You sure about doing this?"

I grab the burner phone Ren handed me not even a week ago. He takes it, brows pulling low. "Call Dante. Tell him I'm taking care of things. And tell him to come pick you up."

"You don't have to do this, Aelia."

I give him a small smile. "Yes, I do."

He nods, then disappears. I wonder if he's the last friendly face I'll see. I straighten, throwing my shoulders back and pivot. No use second-guessing myself now. Jenkins needs to die for us to succeed. I can't think of a better way to go than if I take him with me.

THIRTY NINE

Dante

"Who the fuck is this?" I snarl into the phone.

Heavy breathing on the other end of the line sets my nerves on edge. As if tonight wasn't shit enough. Now someone has Aelia's phone, too. Image after image of her being taken, beaten, and tortured runs through my mind.

"Cruz, it's Benjamin. Shit. That's probably not your name. Aelia helped me get out. And I've got some chick with me."

My eyes dart to Ren sitting with his elbows on his knees, his head in his hands. He's been frozen like that for a good ten minutes, numbness bleeding from him. It pools around his feet, refusing to evaporate into the hot night.

"Where is she? Where are you?"

I barely recall Benjamin, though I remember he was in the Pit. Too many things are going to shit at once. We're scattered, broken, and in no condition to storm the Guild. This shit wasn't supposed to happen yet. Ghost was supposed to be here. Raven's crew should have been put in place. The others were supposed to be here, not bleeding out on a dirty street in Rima. No one was supposed to die.

"We're about ten blocks north of the embassy."

"We're on our way." I hang up, then seize Ren's arm and haul him to his feet.

I'm practically dragging him to the SUV that conveniently pulls up just then. The driver's head dips as we approach, and I shove Ren inside. Sliding into the passenger's seat, I tell him the address and slam the door as he takes off.

Ten minutes is too long. My body buzzes with pent-up energy. I need to do something. Sitting around waiting for someone to show up so I can go after Aelia wasn't what I wanted to do. I couldn't leave Ren, though. He was practically catatonic.

The silent ride is almost too much. I keep checking on Ren, waiting for him to pass out or start screaming again. It's as if all the emotions he's bottled up all these years came spilling out in one guttural cry. It's a sound I never want to hear again. The tires squeal as we round a corner and the driver slams on the brakes. We skid, bumping onto the curb.

I'm out before it stops, dashing down the sidewalk when someone calls my name from the shadows. Ren's out of the vehicle, sprinting toward Benjamin, who's holding an unconscious Sam. I jump between them and Ren snarls.

"He's not the enemy," I snap, then step aside.

Ren gathers her in his arms with a gentleness I've rarely seen from him. She sighs, curling closer to his body, and I think he might break. Instead, he pivots, marching back to the SUV. I expect him to leave me here, but he just waits, brushing her hair from her forehead.

"I think she was drugged. She was sort of awake when they brought her in. Then nothing."

"Ren," I call, and the driver rolls down the back window. "Oracle."

He scowls, cradling Sam's body to his. They never did find a way to combat the side effects. At least she won't remember what happened to her. I wonder if that will be worse, though.

"Did they do anything else?" I ask, turning back to Benjamin.

He shakes his head. "Not as far as I know. Got a nasty bump on her head. Said she was bait."

I nod, biting my cheek as the question burns on my tongue. "Why didn't Aelia come with you?"

He runs his fingers through his hair, grimacing as he glances at his hand. "She's going after Jenkins. If anyone can get close enough to him, she can."

My heart skips a beat, and a tingling starts in my fingers before rolling up my arms. I must have heard him wrong. I shake my head and my palms burn. There's no way she did it again. We promised we wouldn't split up again. She almost didn't survive the first time. And she still chose to go back.

She broke every whispered promise she made, all because she thought she could save us. Because she didn't think I could find a way. There's no other explanation.

"Go get in the car. They'll take you back to my headquarters." He blanches and I hold up my hand. "I'm the president of an MC. Not with them."

"Don't know if that makes it better," he mutters as he passes.

Ren's eyes meet mine, grief resting within their grey depths. "I'll send who I can."

I nod, watching them drive off. I've never felt more alone than I do right now.

"Don't go in without us. They're waiting for you to fuck up. They know we'll come either because of Sam or Aelia. Either way, you can't do it alone, Raines." Jag's voice rings through the phone, and I grip the device tighter as frustration bombards me.

"They're all out front. If I go around back, I can—"

"No. Aelia knew what she was doing. We're almost there. Just stay fucking put." Jag hangs up, and I fight the urge to ram my fist into the wall next to me.

I peer around the corner, squinting in the night. The embassy is dark, no lights shining from the windows. The moon illuminates the guards stationed out front. They probably have more than the ridiculous batons Jenkins allowed them to have. Jag's right—I can't take them on by myself. I don't even care anymore. All I want is to get Aelia out. Again.

I scrub my palms down my legs, trying to alleviate the pinpricks scattering across my skin. Our plans lay in ruins at my feet with no hope of recovery. They broke like waves cresting along a shore, receding to the sea before our eyes. If I engage with the guards, I'll be swept away. Logically, I understand the reasons I need to wait, but it doesn't stop the frantic energy pushing me to do something.

Engines rev in the distance and I whip around. Dozens of bikes, from the sound of it. Maybe Raven's crew is coming. At least I'll have some cover, although Raven hasn't exactly wanted to fight the Guild directly. Ushering innocents away is all she volunteered for. Hopefully the sounds echoing from the city hide their approach from the men gathered around the embassy.

A sigh of relief leaves me when I spot Raven's dark hair streaming behind her. She stops feet from me, cutting the engine off as maybe two dozen others pull up next to her. The alley isn't quite big enough for all of them. I crane my neck, trying to count them. Nova pulls her helmet off, setting it on her seat.

"Heard you needed more help. Not that we haven't done enough," Raven says, peering over her shoulder.

"Knock it off, Rae. We've got enough to deal with without you being an asshole," Nova snaps.

Raven scowls, then mutters, "Well, we have."

"So, Aelia went back in?" Nova asks, stepping next to me, and I nod. "Well, if it was just us, I'd be worried. But we found a few others who will even the numbers a bit."

Ghost appears around the corner, cutting off my view of the Guild. The silver peppering his black hair is a spotlight in the dark. Rumor is he dyes the strands to seem more phantom-like. I didn't have the balls to question him. Ghost has an air of unhinged chaos about him. Shaking my head, I turn back to Raven, who's scowling at Ghost now instead of Nova.

"Who the fuck are you?" Raven snaps, crossing her arms.

"Wait, you didn't bring Ghost?" I ask as he tilts his head. He turns, surveying the force we're up against, effectively dismissing us.

"I've never seen this man before in my life. I brought *them.*" She throws her thumb over her shoulder, and I spin.

Hawk weaves around the bikes, tugging a blonde woman—Willow—behind him. She smiles at me, and I swear there's something different about her. The last time I saw her she was nervous, waiting for the other shoe to drop. Now she looks confident as Hawk tucks her under his arm. Hawk nods to Ghost as he steps next to me.

"Helms called. Said he'd be here." Hawk peers over the others gathered about.

"He's not here yet. Who's watching Synd?" The more people who show up, the less my palms itch and my nerves settle.

"Doc's got Reaper territory handled. Drake and Ember can take care of the rest for a bit. With Anders dead—"

I straighten, the words sticking in my throat. I clamp him on the shoulder, swinging him to face me. His eyebrow pops up as I gape at him. My lungs can't seem to pull in enough air.

"Oh, that's not good," Willow murmurs.

She untangles from Hawk's arm, then grabs my hand and tugs me down. She forces my head between my legs as she scolds Hawk.

"Did you maybe think he didn't realize Anders was dead?" she hisses.

I grab her wrist, and she whips her head around. "Ember?"

She nods slowly and Hawk crouches in front of me. "You're going through some shit, but if you don't get your fucking hands off my woman, we're going to have problems."

I unlock my fingers from her skin and shake my head. Willow doesn't seem to mind, but I'm not about to piss off Hawk. I have to get to Aelia and tell her. Not only is her father dead, but her best friend is hours away.

I stagger to my feet, closing my eyes. I'd never keep this revelation from her even if it gives her more reasons to leave Rima. Selfish. That's what I want to be with her. I want to tell her to stay.

"Is this all we have, then?" Ghost asks impassively. He always did have a single-minded focus, letting others deal with their personal bullshit without his interference.

I clear my throat, pushing my thoughts aside. "Other than Jag and Avery? Yeah. Which is more than I thought we'd have."

Annoyance flashes across his face. "There's at least a hundred guys down there. Your woman is on the inside. Half your people are missing or killed. And your members abandoned you. And we're supposed to just be cool with that?"

"No one forced you to be here, asshole," Raven snaps, but I wave her away.

"Once Jenkins and the council are dead, the others will scatter. Jenkins has made it impossible to run the Guild without him. Cut off the head—"

"And three more will take its place," he says through gritted teeth.

I shake my head. "Not with this. He doesn't run it like an MC or mafia family. There's no one *to* take his place. Even the satellite cities rely on headquarters to send them more assets."

"People." Raven glares at me. She's been pissed ever since Nova was rescued, blaming me for her being taken in the first place.

Nova grabs Raven's hand, tugging her into the throng of others gathered behind us. I track them until they disappear, the crowd swallowing them up. Raven can be pissed at me all she likes. As long as she helps us get to Jenkins. She probably won't help me ever again, but so be it.

"Your woman capable of taking out Jenkins?" Ghost's low voice has me turning back.

"Yes. As long as he hasn't set a trap for her."

"Which is likely. I've dealt with a lot of shitty human beings over the years, but he might take the cake," he mutters, staring across the space separating us.

"Which is why I called you. Did you bring some members with you?"

"All of the Phantoms."

I blink, not fully comprehending his words. "You brought…fuck."

He dips his chin. "I gave them the option. They all took it. Some of the women stayed behind to make sure no one fucked with our territory, but the rest came. They've set up a perimeter. Most of them are in the forest, since there isn't much cover otherwise."

Hawk grips the back of his neck. "How many?"

Ghost shrugs as he glances away. "About two hundred. Enough to overpower the Guild's forces."

I didn't realize they'd grown that much. The last time Jag mentioned anything, they had barely a hundred. And most of those members were from different factions. Ghost always ran his MC more like the Kings run their territory, with lower gangs rather than a traditional MC like us.

"We don't have a lot of time before they get restless, so let's get our shit together. You have a way to communicate with them?" I ask, my mind scrambling to figure out a plan.

He lifts his phone. "The beauty of mass texting. I want this over with as soon as possible."

The corner of Hawk's mouth tips up. "Got a hot date?"

Ghost scowls, nostrils flaring. "Family business. My sister seems to think it's 'no big deal' to get kidnapped."

"Personally, I've been kidnapped several times and I'm perfectly fine." Willow smirks, wiggling her eyebrows at Hawk.

"That's not a thing to be proud of, *mo dóchais*." Hawk pushes her behind him as he grimaces at Ghost. "Don't worry. I'll keep them away from each other so she doesn't influence your sister."

"Appreciate it," Ghost mumbles, some of his stoicism cracking.

I pinch the bridge of my nose. We're wildly off-track now. We have a limited amount of time before shit goes sideways.

"Twenty minutes. That's all I'm willing to wait or I'm going in by myself."

The others nod, forming a circle to strategize. Glancing at the embassy, I search the windows, as if her silhouette will magically appear. The building stays dark, though. I sigh, hoping I won't be too late.

FORTY

Aelia

I've never seen the embassy so empty. Or so quiet. Or so dark. I keep expecting a ghost to float out of a wall or a masked murderer to chase me with an axe. Actually, I'd take either at this point.

Searching for Jenkins went from anxiety-ridden to boring. He might not even be here. I started in the Pit, wondering if I could help them get out first, but the place was empty as well.

Systematically sweeping the lower levels was a fruitless endeavor. Once I got to the main level, I found deserted card games, half-poured drinks, and in one room, various articles of clothing strewn about. It's as if they were all abducted by aliens in the middle of whatever they were doing. The longer I trudge through this place, the more I wish aliens would beam me up.

I thought this would be more like a spy movie, with me ducking in and out of dark passageways and silently slicing bad guy's throats. Not that I have a knife on me. But imagining me pulling some badass moves helped with the nerves. Now I'm left with pent-up energy and no way to expel it other than tap-dancing my way through the halls. My default setting of apathy in intense situations has fled. I wonder if this is me finding myself or if I'm spiraling again.

"Jenkins," I sing as I climb the stairs to the VIP rooms.

Should I be advertising I'm here? No. Do I particularly care? Not really.

I stop halfway up and stare at nothing. I didn't think about what I would do once I found him. That seems like something I should know. I don't have a plan at all. When Dante and I talked about this moment, it was more of a wing and a prayer kind of thing. And Dante was convinced he would be the one to end Jenkins. I never told him that Jenkins's death was mine.

I plop onto the stairs and lean against the wall, stretching my legs out. They're wide enough I don't have to worry about tumbling to the bottom. Eyeing the landing, I attempt to dredge up the math I learned in high school to figure out if he would die if I pushed him from the top. This particular staircase is long…tall? Whatever. It's enough to break his neck if he hit right.

Shaking my head, I push to my feet. Maybe I've been around the others too much. Or just the right amount if it leads to the Guild's dismantling.

The more time I spend in here, the more I just don't give a shit. As long as Jenkins dies. As long as the Guild blows up. As long as everything I went through wasn't in vain. If I escaped, yet the Guild went on stealing more people's lives, their futures, their sanity, my freedom wouldn't mean anything. I'd spend the rest of my life regretting that I didn't do more.

Before I was surviving. Now I don't care if I live or die. I just want to take them with me to the depths of hell. I'm sure the devil will have plenty to punish me for, but I'll kneel at his feet and beg. Not for mercy, but for the pleasure of torturing Jenkins the way he did me all these years. I can only hope he'll grant that one request. Then I'll wait patiently for Dante to join me.

I skip up the stairs, peeking around the corner. I attempt to curl into a ball and roll across the landing and instead hit my hand on a chair. I was not built to be an assassin. If I walk out of here, maybe Sam will train me. Lacey told me not to ask her for lessons, shuddering as the warning left her. I think I'll do it anyway. Just because I can. I've spent so long existing, I'm ready to live. And if that means getting my ass handed to me by a scary-ass woman, so be it.

Another staircase and I slow to a stop, sobering. A familiar door is just a few feet away, mocking me. All thoughts of hurrying to Jenkins's office flees. I don't even register moving, but my hand presses against the wood.

The door swings open with the slightest push and I hold my breath. Clouds cover the moon, casting the room in shadows. My pulse races, fire filling my veins. I expect to be thrown back into a hallucination and for Byron to step out of the darkness. Instead, I'm met with destruction.

Someone stabbed the mattress, the fluff from the comforter scattered across the floor like tufts of clouds. I step inside, scanning the space. One of the lamps lies on the bathroom floor, the mirror shattered. Who was willing to risk the bad luck that comes from that? Maybe Grant before he fled. Or Jenkins. Neither of them would care about the superstitions.

The clothes Dante left behind create a mountain spilling out of the closet. If I had more time, I'd search for my pajamas. From the tattered remains of the dress at my feet, they probably disintegrated under their rage.

I avoid the scraps of wood from the chair that used to sit next to the bed. Spiderwebs of glass rest in the window frame as if one slight touch will make it explode. They were reinforced before we moved here. No amount of violence will allow access to the outside world. I'm surprised this one fractured as much as it did.

As terrible as it was to be stuck in this room, it holds so many memories. My eyes dart from one spot to the next. That was the first bed I slept in after years of blankets on the floor. That was the first closet that held my own clothes. That was the first shower I took by myself. This place helped shape me into someone new.

Sure, Dante nudged me along, but I took the steps with the help of this room. To see it reduced to this is heartbreaking in a way that doesn't fully make sense.

I step back into the hallway, shutting the door softly behind me, and close my eyes. It's ridiculous to mourn a space, but something drives me to wrap up that grief so I can let it go. Rage takes its place, bubbling up from deep within.

This is what I was missing when I skipped through the hallways. It doesn't matter who destroyed the first place I felt safe after years of abuse. I'll wrap my vengeance in a nice little package and place it at Jenkins's feet. He'll pay for his sins one by one.

Red splashes across my vision as I open my eyes. I stalk down the halls, a new sense of purpose filling me. As I prowl onward, a plan forms in my head. I have a gun with seven bullets. One is reserved for his head, although I doubt it will be as easy to shoot him as it was Grant. He'll flop around more. Asshole.

Taking the back stairwell, I slip into the darkness. I move the gun to my back, shoving it in my waistband and covering it with my shirt. Dante told me I'd probably shoot myself in the ass if I kept my weapon there, but it can't be helped. When I reach the top, I shake out my limbs. Digging deep, I find the woman I was before, meek and terrified. The perfect little bit. Exactly what Jenkins craved all these years.

Tucking my chin to my chest, I force my feet to move. The closer I get to the office, the more I sink into her, sheathing myself in her skin until only my eyes are mine, staring at the floor as I glide forward. The door hangs open, a small strip of light spilling out. My fingers tremble as I wrap them around the edge and slip inside.

A single lamp sits on his desk, casting shadows around the room. My own desk hasn't been touched, a thin layer of dust covering my computer. It's as if the moment I left, I ceased to exist. And now I've walked right back in.

I study his back as I tiptoe toward him. White peppers his hair, a new addition in the several weeks I've been gone. I didn't feel like we were making any progress on the outside. I assumed we were pesky gnats

Jenkins would swat away before long. The slump of his shoulders, the grey in his hair, the silence pressing around us, all points to the downfall of the Guild.

It takes everything in me to sink to my knees and I focus on the hard floor grinding into my bone. I clear my throat, tucking my chin to my chest. His chair squeaks as he turns, and his sudden intake of breath tells me everything I need to know.

He didn't think I'd show. He expected to lose. He doesn't know how to proceed. His heels click against the floor as he slowly rounds the desk, and a shiver rolls up my spine.

I jolt when his palm appears in front of my face. Swallowing hard, I place my hand in his and he lifts me up, leading me around the desk again. He drops my fingers and sinks into his chair. He points to the ground and my knees give out, cracking against the floor as they hit. Pain radiates through my body and my head spins.

Jenkins sighs, leaning forward and tucking his knuckle under my chin. When our eyes meet, I force tears into my own. He tilts his head, studying me. I don't have to pretend to be frightened. Terror slides down my body and tears slip down my cheeks. He brushes away one, then another.

"So afraid, little bit. Don't worry. We'll find somewhere new and start again," he murmurs. I'd almost believe him if it wasn't for the throbbing vein in his forehead and the twitch in his jaw.

"Where did everyone go?"

He waves away my question. "They're gone. I'm sure they'll be returned soon. I'm going to keep you close until we find a new city."

"We don't have one yet?" I force a concerned look to flash across my face before I drop my head again. "Sorry, sir."

His fingers brush my hair, then trail down my neck, and I suppress a shiver. "Oh Aelia. We've been through a lot. We'll recover, just like we always do. Once we find Dante."

My body reacts without warning, jerking in his light hold, and he chuckles.

He grips my chin, forcing my eyes to his. "Missing your handler, are you?"

"No, sir." I'm not lying. How can I miss him when I have him with me? How can I mourn someone who's waiting for me to return?

"He'll be back. He's loyal to the Guild. He proved himself." He sighs, sitting back in his chair.

Dark rings circle his eyes and his hand trembles as he runs it through his hair and then rubs his jaw. I don't understand why he changed every single rule he had in place. He had a foolproof strategy. The orders Jenkins handed down were strict, and the consequences were swift and deadly. The fact he broke every single one for Dante doesn't compute.

"How?" I whisper, and his brows pull low.

"What do you mean?"

I clear my throat. "How did he prove himself? How did you know he was loyal enough to do what you did?"

He scans my face, traveling down my body and up again. "I suppose it wouldn't hurt to tell you. Seeing as how you came back when you broke free. We were hemorrhaging money. Synd bled us dry. Anders didn't help—always disappearing."

He pushes to his feet and steps over to the window. I don't know what he can see since it's pitch black out now. Maybe he just likes to seem contemplative and regal. I slip the gun from my waistband, my eyes fixed on his back. Hiding it between my legs, I hope he doesn't notice. He shakes his head as he faces me.

"Cruz had what others didn't. Vision. Everything he touched came back to him—to us—tenfold. I knew if I didn't give him some leeway, he'd be able to go off and start his own version of the Guild. Or he'd overthrow me. He seemed content where he was, though."

He saunters over to me, some of the arrogance I'm used to bleeding back into his walk.

"And then what?" I don't want to ask what his plan was for after Dante was no longer useful. He had one, even if he won't admit it.

"Once he's no longer useful, I'll merely dispose of him. Men like him never see it coming." He smirks, stopping in front of me.

I lift my head as my eyes harden. "They certainly don't."

He only has time to tilt his head before I lift the gun and shoot him in the kneecap. The kickback has my arm aching, but at least I hit him. I expect a scream, or a stumble—something, but he just groans.

Pointing at the other knee, I pull the trigger. And miss. Of course I fucking miss. Because I'm not trained for this shit. I thought two feet was close enough, but apparently not. The bullet embeds itself into his thigh, and he sways. One more shot and he falls onto the desk, then slides to the floor.

I scramble backward, the weapon wavering in my hand. He silently screams, clutching the wounds I've inflicted. I shake my head, realizing there's a ringing in my ears. The gun tumbles from my numb fingers. When my vision tilts, it hits me how fucked I am.

When I killed Molly, it was a crime of passion. I think that's what they call it. I blacked out, not fully understanding what I was doing. With Byron, it was self-defense. I didn't even mean to kill him. Not really, even though I set his house on fire. He technically could have already been dead by the time the blaze consumed his body. Grant's death was definitely intentional, but he was already so badly beaten, he wouldn't have lived regardless.

This, though. This is premeditated. This was purposeful and torturous. I'd love to lie and say I didn't know how much it would hurt, but I've seen the aftereffects of a wound like this. This was my father's signature move.

Shoot them in the kneecaps, Roman. Then they can't run away. You can take them apart piece by piece and learn all the secrets they think to withhold. Often they bury them deep, which means you'll have to go digging.

I shudder as his words echo through my mind. It's as if he's standing behind me, reciting his lesson to my brother, who couldn't have been more than twelve at the time. Too young to be learning such things. And I shouldn't have been hiding in the shadows, upset I wasn't invited.

I knew what I was doing when I walked in here. When in doubt, fall back to your roots, I suppose. I think the worst is I don't regret it at all. As soon as the numbness fades away, all that's left is grim satisfaction. His screams filter through the ringing as that fades, too.

Scooping up the gun, I grip it tightly before standing. "Shut the fuck up. You're so fucking whiny. Three bullets and you're already writhing around like a fucking baby."

He gapes at me, his cries finally subsiding. His pale face flushes as blood seeps from his wounds.

"What the hell," he bites out through gritted teeth. He's not even asking. It's a statement, just like every other time he speaks to me.

I roll my eyes. "For years, I sat in that chair and did your bidding. I let you harass me. I let you steal my life. You saw me as weak because that's what I was. And then I wasn't. But you didn't notice. Which worked out perfectly for me, but still. Men like you never learn. And you never see it coming."

"You are weak. You're a worthless bit who got lucky. You'll be dead before you leave this building."

I stare at him impassively. His insults never did hurt. Words can't hurt if they aren't true. Jenkins wouldn't know the truth if it reached up and slapped him in the face. Crouching in front of him, I keep a healthy distance between us. I may think he's incapacitated, but a wounded animal is more vicious—more willing to attack. I won't give him the opportunity.

"And therein lies your problem, Nolan." He flinches at the use of his given name. "You see women as property, but also something worth less than you. You throw threats around like candy. After a while, they no longer hold weight."

"You'll never kill me. You don't have it in you."

"Taunting the person with the gun is not your smartest move, Nolan. Would you like a little insight into what *I've* been doing? I killed the one who whipped me with her own stiletto heel. I kicked Byron in the balls so many times he fell and hit his head." I grin as I straighten. "And then I set his house on fire. Oh, and Grant?" I drop my grin. "I shot him in the head. After Dante beat the shit out of him, of course. Because he loves me enough to leave Grant's death for me."

He pales again, but not from my question. He's losing blood faster than I thought he would. And I've heard getting shot in the knee is excruciating. So much for my taunting diatribe I had prepared.

"I'll take your silence as a plea for me to end your suffering. Dying with the realization that it's by my hand…" I tsked. "That must be harsh. But to know that your precious Guild will end with my bullet? That must be worse. If I didn't think you'd somehow crawl out of the grave, I'd leave you alive and burn this place down around you. You should be thanking me."

He gags, sagging as he practically flops to the floor. I don't have time to force him to do something that won't make a difference in the long run. I've provoked him enough. Any more and I'll start to question my own resolve. Or maybe how deeply the darkness has charmed me with its wicked ways.

"Don't," he wheezes, and I tilt my head.

"At some point, you're going to have to give in, Jenkins. How does it feel to be broken?"

I don't give him time to answer. I aim for his head, but the bullet lodges in his shoulder. I grit my teeth, struggling to keep my face blank.

He still moans. I'm surprised he hasn't passed out yet. Maybe he's been dipping into his own supply. I've heard Oracle makes users feel invincible. Apparently, that doesn't apply to leg injuries like I've given him.

I give up on his forehead since I don't want to get any closer to him, and I shoot him in the chest. I want to empty the clip into him, yet I hold back. Leaving myself without a weapon if I come across someone else wouldn't be smart.

"Enjoy your last moments, Jenkins. I'll send your regards to Dante."

I walk out of the office one last time, closing the door softly behind me. I make it ten feet before I drop to my hands and knees and empty my stomach. Curling into a ball, I don't fight the tears. They're not for Jenkins, nor for myself. They're for the girl I was and the woman I became in that room. It's a long time before I move again.

FORTY ONE

Dante

"There's at least a hundred yards of open space," Ghost says as he points beyond our hiding spot.

The buildings surrounding the embassy abruptly fall away as if the Guild carved out its own little dystopian paradise on the edge of the city. The only coverage we'll have before we're exposed to the guards still milling about the circle driveway is a low wall and some trimmed bushes. I'm surprised Jenkins didn't install a fence, or a fucking moat, to keep others out. Maybe there just wasn't enough time.

"Any word on how many are in the back?" I murmur, squinting into the dark and spotting more men stationed at the grand entrance. Several more shadows line the building. There's more than I thought there were.

"Bunch on the patio. There's more coverage back there once they get across the lawn. The east and west sides are going to be the easiest part. Buildings butt right up against the embassy." Ghost shakes his head.

"Whoever laid this city out must have been high on Oracle while they did it," Raven mutters. Nova seemed to get her in line, but she's still glaring at Ghost every now and then.

"I imagine the embassy was here long before the rest of it. The alley on the east side has a door that leads inside, though it's locked now. Only way in will be to blast it open. The west side is where the parking garage is. I'd guess that's Jenkins's escape route. Don't know how many men will be around there." I run my hands through my hair, gripping the strands roughly. This whole thing sets me on edge.

"Willow and I will take the east side. Lure them to us so they'll funnel in." Hawk doesn't look happy about it, but it's the safest place for Willow.

Raven huffs, but I hold up my hand. "Raven and Nova, take some of your crew and set up on the west side. Try to cut them off if they attempt an escape. If you can take Jenkins alive, do it."

"So you can kill him later?" Raven snorts.

"Jenkins's death belongs to Aelia," I snarl.

She rears back as if I've slapped her. She averts her eyes as silence falls over the group. The restless crews keep stealing glances at us. They're all depending on me—on us—to pull this off.

Our plan is to sneak as close as we can and use the element of surprise. It was one of the strategies Byrns suggested that I didn't think would work. Joke's on me. It's the only one any of us could come up with that didn't involve a whole helluva lot of us dying in the first wave. We never would have survived. We still might not with our current plan.

I wish I could do this alone. The truth is, this is my responsibility and I'm foisting it off on others. They shouldn't have to die because of something I started. Most of Ghost's men will die. The sheer numbers he brought with him will help, but they won't go home. I can't imagine they fully understood that when they volunteered.

"Knock it the fuck off," Ghost growls at me.

"What exactly am I knocking off?" I ask as I follow Hawk the few blocks to a "surprise" he brought. Only massive amounts of weapons will be an appropriate surprise in my book.

"You're fucking blaming yourself for us being here. You called for help—we came. That's how it fucking works. Each of these men were told the risks. They understand what they're getting into."

"Doubt you told them most of them will die. Or that their families would starve once they're gone," I grunt as I run my fingers through my hair.

Destroying one family in order to save another isn't a call I ever wanted to make. Anxiety and stress have mixed in my stomach, and I'm pretty sure I'm going to vomit before the night is over.

"Actually, I did. We have protocols in place to help their families should that happen. Not that it's any of your concern. We take care of our own. Just because your woman is inside doesn't make this your fault, and it's fucking annoying to watch you mope around when you should be pulling your head out of your ass and leading." He stalks toward Jag, who leans against a car with the trunk open.

"He's right, you know. I mean, I wouldn't have phrased it that way, but you really shouldn't blame yourself." Willow steps up next to me. "The Kings...hell, everyone in Synd, kind of dropped the ball. They should have done what you did, but it was one damn thing after another. We haven't really had a chance to catch our breath, much less go after the Guild. And I wasn't even there for half of it."

"Mac told me a bit about what happened to you. Merrick..." I don't know how to finish the sentence. I don't have proof that he's dead. Just an assumption. Giving her false hope could lead to her death.

Her hand flits around before brushing her hair over her shoulder. "I killed him. He's definitely dead."

"I'm sorry. What?"

She giggles, a little of the woman I met years ago shining through. "It's a long story, and I almost got myself killed. *But* I did stab him. Several times, actually. Mostly because the first few didn't take. It's actually very hard to stab someone in the heart. I slashed his throat for good measure, though. And I don't feel bad about it. Took a while to get there. I'm still not the best at standing up for myself, but I'm getting there."

Her eyes fix on Hawk sauntering toward us, and I press my fist to my chest over the ache. "I'm guessing Hawk helped with that?"

She sighs, turning to me. "He gave me the safe space I needed to become who I was meant to be. Who I was hiding behind for fear of breaking free. Once we finish this…just be her safe place. Be the one she can fall back on when the world gets too scary and hard."

Willow pats me on the arm, giving me a soft smile before meeting Hawk halfway. He raises his eyebrow over her head at me and I nod. I didn't exactly think I'd be getting relationship advice while we were walking to our deaths, but here we are. I also didn't think it'd be coming from Willow St. James. She fell in with the Reapers even after I protected her from the world of the Vipers as well as I knew how. Maybe fate really does exist.

As I make my way to the car, my eyebrows climb up my forehead. "Is that a fucking flamethrower?"

Hawk turns to me, grinning. "Courtesy of Alex. He raided the King's weapon room when he popped into Synd and brought you back some goodies."

I don't have the heart to tell him I left Alex bleeding out in the back of a car. I've successfully convinced myself he could still pull through. It doesn't matter that he didn't have a pulse. It doesn't matter that Ren stopped screaming. It doesn't matter that the world went silent as Shane stared at his brother's lifeless body. None of that matters because he could still wake up. In another time, in another world, he could be okay.

Ghost pokes around in the trunk until he finds a crossbow and holds it up. "What the hell was he thinking with this?"

"Probably that it'd look cool to shoot someone with a crossbow." Hawk shrugs as if it's a perfectly reasonable thing for someone to want to do.

We divvy up the weapons to Raven's crew. Ghost's crew has enough of their own, thank fuck. Willow approaches the other car tucked away in the shadows. Hawk wanders over to her as she digs in the backseat, then throws a backpack on along with various other bags. He murmurs to her, and she shakes her head before heading my direction.

"So, I've got my own plan. I promise I'm not going after Jenkins. I'm sure Aelia has that figured out. But Hawk is going to get me inside the building and I'm going to start setting these things up." She opens one of the bags, revealing brick after brick of C-4. "I'll find Aelia and we'll finish setting them and then blow the sucker."

She honestly looks like a kid in a candy store, practically bouncing on the balls of her feet with a giddy expression plastered across her face.

"We don't know who's all inside, though. If someone catches you…"

She waves away my concerns. "Sam's taught me a lot of tricks. But I can always just throw a brick at them and run while they freak out."

Hawk's jaw is set, the vein in his neck pulsing. He doesn't like this plan any more than I do. Then again, there's not much he can do to dissuade her. Once these women set their mind to something, they rarely listen to us.

According to Sam, we're too overprotective. Making sure they don't blow themselves up strikes me as a good thing, but apparently it means we're smothering them.

"How are you getting inside?" I ask as Hawk paces away in a huff. I'm sure he was expecting me to talk her out of it. If she didn't listen to him, she sure as hell won't entertain anything I have to say.

"Well, I was going to have Hawk smuggle me to one of the side doors, but you know the place better." She bites her lip, twisting her fingers together in front of her.

"Better tell Hawk. You slip off without a word and he'll die a little inside."

Pity lines her blue eyes, and I glance away. I don't have time to reassure her. Focusing on the battle ahead of us is more important than regretting my decisions. I won't be able to function if I'm constantly worrying about Aelia. I have to trust she can handle herself.

Ghost materializes from the dark, and my muscles tense. He nods and I check the time. The others scatter to their various positions as silently as a large group can. A flare shoots into the sky, hanging over the building, and the guards turn around.

Small groups race across the large lawn. There isn't much coverage between us and the low wall separating everyone. What I didn't expect was a whole lot of nothing. The guards don't make a sound. None of them move other than facing forward again. I don't know what they're waiting for, which only puts me more on edge.

I adjust my grip on my gun, checking my pistols one last time, then take off. Ghost trails me. He wasn't too keen on going up the gut, but we'll need a distraction, and I'm not about to put anyone else in that position. For some reason, Ghost refuses to leave my side.

Maybe Alex anticipated this, since a bulletproof vest now covers Ghost's and my chests. There weren't enough of them to go around, but we did the best we could. I thought Willow would tip over under the weight. She just laughed when the straps settled on her shoulders.

"Sauntering into a potential firefight isn't the smartest idea," Ghost mutters, and I shrug.

I'm still hoping I can bluff my way through this. "Here's hoping they don't aim for the head."

As gravel crunches under our feet, and we stop twenty feet from the line of guards blocking our way. I grind my teeth together and grip my gun tighter as Reynolds forces his way past the others to confront us.

I hardly paid him any attention when I was inside. He was barely a blip on my radar. Jenkins didn't give two shits about relying on him. It might have rankled Reynolds, but he was too dense to do anything about it.

"Cruz, I'd like to say I'm surprised, but I'm not. Something was always off about you. Jenkins will be happy to know I took care of the threat."

"You talk too much," I growl, raising my pistol and shooting him in the head.

"Fuck," Ghost mumbles, then dives for the bushes to his right.

Chaos erupts with men shouting and running, but there are no gunshots. Most of the men in the back run for the front doors. The last thing I thought would happen was the guards between us turning on the others and revealing their weapons. It's a slaughter, with screams piercing the air. Another flare flashes overhead, raining sparks down on the scene and giving it a surreal appearance.

I'm frozen, watching the moment unfold in slow motion. Bodies fall, tumbling down the steps to be trampled by the oncoming horde. The darkness swallows their cries, the night lapping at their suffering with glee.

Ghost grabs my arm, shaking me from my dazed state. He yanks me around the building, and I catch sight of Willow's blonde hair streaming behind her as she dashes toward the alley. Hawk is nowhere to be found. He's probably caught up in the scuffle farther away. When I attempt to follow her, though, Ghost drags me along.

"What the fuck?"

"Problems out back. They're going to blow the back of the building, but the connection cut out. We have to warn my men." He drops his hold on me and sprints.

I take off after him, hoping the place doesn't blow with us in front of it. I've been through that before, I'd rather not experience it again. My back might be healed, but my skin still pulls awkwardly at times. And now it's itching just imaging the shitshow that we might get caught up in.

Ghost bursts around the back, revealing a whole other shitshow I wasn't expecting. The guards are running for the trees, zigzagging across the dark lawn.

"Why aren't they shooting?" I wheeze, trying to catch my breath.

"Some of my guys are probably mixed in. Wouldn't want to hit our own." He jumps over the garden wall, leaving me to scramble after him.

"Why the fuck are you going inside, exactly?"

He crouches, then peeks in the window. "Does it look like I'm going inside? Now shut the fuck up. It's hard enough to see without listening to you prattle on."

I shake my head, scanning the area for more guards. They all abandoned Jenkins. I'm not surprised. Even those who didn't care what the Guild was doing didn't have loyalty. I'm shocked they agreed to be here in the first place. If Jenkins sets up somewhere else, he'll have to find new men to work for him. How he plans on paying for that is beyond me, since Aelia basically bankrupted them before she left.

I freeze, staring off into nothing. Jenkins wouldn't be able to set up a whole new operation. Those guards probably travel with them, which means they're not fighting for the Guild. I wonder how many of them have already rendezvoused in the other city. I won't be surprised if Willow doesn't find anyone in the Pit. The Guild would have moved them long before in anticipation of this.

"Would you pay the fuck attention?" Ghost hisses and my head snaps up.

Nothing makes sense. And I can't keep everything straight in my head. I shouldn't be focusing on any of this shit, anyway. It's not until I wipe the sweat from my forehead that I realize I'm stalling. The longer I sit here, the more likely Aelia will walk by. I reach for the handle and Ghost flies out of nowhere, shoving me away.

"The doors are rigged." His arms wrap around me, wrestling me away.

"Aelia's in there," I yell.

"Then hope she's smart enough to get the fuck out."

I strain against his hold, and we tumble backward. My head hits his chin and his teeth clank together. Rolling off him, it hits me how quiet it is. The guards have fled, disappearing into the night. Ghost's men are sequestered in the forest, no sounds but the low rumble of thunder in the distance. Even the gunshots from the front of the building have subsided.

"Shit," Ghost wheezes, pushing to his hands and knees. "We have to go."

He scrambles to his feet, then hauls me up.

"I'm not leaving her behind."

"She's probably already out. I'm not getting you fucking killed. This isn't fucking Shakespeare, asshole."

My confusion is all it takes for him to drag me along. Halfway across the lawn, it doesn't matter, anyway. The back of the embassy explodes, along with my hopes of finding Aelia.

FORTY TWO

Aelia

"Fuck. Fuck. Fuck," I spit out, slamming another brick of C-4 to the wall.

"Good thing these things aren't touchy, huh?" Willow asks, side-eyeing me.

"I hate being in here when they're out there fighting," I snap.

I shouldn't take my frustrations out on her. I don't even know her. She just showed up like a little cherub angel and gleefully shoved a bag full of explosives in my arms. I'd barely gotten my shit together not even five minutes before she appeared.

I wonder what she would have done had she found me frozen outside of the office with blood splattered all over me. Based on who she hangs around with, she probably would have handled it just fine.

"Actually, I don't think they're fighting anymore. And I'm pretty sure they weren't really in the first place. There a reason all the guards would run away like chickens with their heads cut off?" She skips around the corner, and I stomp after her.

"What do you mean, the guards fled?" I didn't see anything from the windows. Not that I was paying attention.

She grabs my arm and drags me to the nearest one. Nothing moves, not even a whisper from the trees. Pressing against the glass, I try to peer at the patio below. Usually there are heaters and lights and music and men pulling resisting partners into the shrubs. Those bushes are merely dark splotches now.

Willow tugs on my arm. "We have to keep going. We still have another floor to get to if we want to blow up the foundation."

I jerk away, fixing my eyes on the lawn. Something is out of place. My eyes dart back and forth, starting at the tree line and working my way closer.

"Oh shit," I breathe.

Time slows as I spin before latching onto Willow's backpack. I haul her with me as I sprint toward the stairs. I don't know what Dante was running from or who was with him, but if they're moving, then so should we. I'm not wasting time trying to figure out what the hell is going on.

"Faster," I whisper, my breath heaving in and out of my lungs.

The only sound is our gasps and the taps of our feet down the stairs. I swear we're flying by the end. I'm tempted to check if we've sprouted wings, and I swallow down the manic laugh crawling up my throat.

Extreme meltdown. That's the only explanation why giddiness is worming its way through my body. Eventually the terror will take over, and I'll be a quivering mess on the floor again.

The air shivers, and a rumble echoes through the building. I've never been in an earthquake, but I saw a movie once. I imagine this is as close as I'll get to one. The floor vibrates, not enough to send us tumbling, thank fuck.

Another giggle bubbles up when I realize how much Dante has influenced me. I can't say I'm upset about it. Especially because thank fuck is a perfect way to express gratitude to the universe.

"Why are you smiling?" Willow rasps as we slow to a stop and lean against a wall.

"Nothing. Or something. Rollercoaster." Each word is punctuated by another deep inhale, and she gapes at me. "Sorry."

She glances back the way we came, and I follow her gaze. "You think it's done?"

"No idea. Are those flames?"

She shakes her head. "I'm pretty sure it's just your eyes. Let's empty this shit and get the fuck out of here."

We don't have many left. She passes me the detonator, giving me a look, and I raise my hand. She already scolded me when I grabbed it the first time.

"Two minutes and then we blast out the front door," I say, and she scowls.

"Let's not use words like blast, mmkay? You take that wing, I'll take this one. Meet at the front doors." She takes off, slapping bricks to anything they'll stick to.

By the time I reach the main room, I'm just tossing the explosives on the floor, hoping it works the same. Half a dozen at the bottom get upended at the door and they tumble farther inside the space. My muscles tense as I wait for them to go boom, but they don't. Of course they don't. That's not how they work, apparently.

I race back to the entrance, bouncing on the balls of my feet. I keep expecting Willow to appear, but the quiet persists. Now that I'm no longer moving, the nerves hit me hard. My stomach flops, and I wrap my hand around my waist. The pounding in my temples travels to the back of my head, and I close my eyes as pressure builds in my ears.

"Don't fucking squeeze that shit," Willow hisses, and my eyes fly open. I ease my grip on the detonator and pull in a calming breath.

"We're going to have to run. We don't know who's out there. Ready?" I rest my hand on the handle and wait until she nods before I rip it open.

We take off, the dark night wrapping around us like a warm blanket. Willow stumbles over a body and I reach for her, but she rights herself before I can catch her. Small groups of men seem to be fighting by the driveway. I don't know who's on our side. Screaming at them to run might be the only choice I have and hope Dante can deal with the men the Guild left behind.

Willow apparently has the same idea, and she screams bomb over and over. The men scatter, heading the same way we are. I glance over my shoulder and lift the detonator and squeeze. Nothing happens and I skid to a stop. Willow practically flips ass over end to race back to me.

Her head whips back and forth as the men stream around us, not bothering to ask what the hell we're doing. "What's wrong?"

"It's not working. Are we too far away?" My lungs burn and my legs are jelly. I don't know how much more running I can take before my body gives out completely.

"Like hell am I going back there. We put enough in there to take out the building and the surrounding lawns. In fact, we're not far enough," she snaps. She seizes my arm and tugs me back. "Did you flip the clip?"

"Is that a sex thing? Because I've been a little isolated for the last ten years," I croak as we approach the nearest buildings. I feel like we've been running for miles.

"For fuck's sake. The clip. Get the clip out of the way," she screams.

I stop once more, doubling over as I stare at the device. A flash of silver catches the light before clouds cover the moon. I flip it back with my thumb and glance up, my eyes meeting Dante's as I squeeze it again and the night explodes.

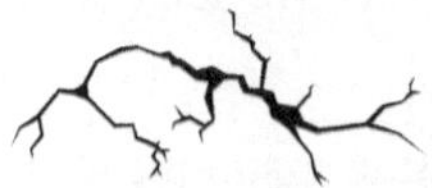

"Stop fussing," I pant as I lean my head back against the seat.

We're stuffed into an SUV, a familiar driver taking us…somewhere. I haven't asked. I don't particularly care. Jenkins is dead. The Guild was blown up. And not many people died.

Actually, I have no idea if anyone on our side was lost. There were so many people, most of them on motorcycles, my mind shut down. Thankfully, Willow stepped in and forced me into the backseat where it was blissfully quiet.

Dante hasn't stopped scanning me for injuries. He's not convinced that none of the blood is mine. I don't blame him, especially after I screamed at him when I saw his singed hair. I expected us to have a reunion like they do in the movies with running and jumping and the raining of kisses. Instead, we yelled at each other, then stared at one another, and eventually walked away.

Secretly, I'm glad he didn't touch me. I think I'd shatter into a million pieces if he did. I'm waiting for the moment my body stitches itself back together enough to function like a human being. Every time he tries to ask me questions, Willow hushes him from the front seat. There's so much we need to talk about. I just don't have the capacity to process everything at once.

He pushes a water bottle into my hand and our fingers brush. His touch sends a shockwave through my system, and I implode. Curling into myself, I tuck my body into a tight ball, sobs pouring out of me.

Dante curses softly and then his arms are around me, hauling me into his lap. I cling to him, terror pouring out of me. We're pulling up to a brightly lit building by the time I calm down. My face feels swollen and my eyes are itchy, but at least I got some of the pain out.

"Are you ready, angel?" Dante whispers, then kisses the top of my head.

"Where are we?" I rasp, and he grabs the water bottle again. I take a long drink before he stops me.

"Don't want to overfill your stomach. We're at the hospital. We can stay out here if you want, though." His voice is so gentle tears fill my eyes again, and I swipe them away angrily. I'm sick of crying.

Sniffing, I tuck my head under his chin again and he holds me close. The doors slam shut. Willow rushes for Hawk and they hurry inside. I just need another minute in his arms. Then I'll feel safe. Then I'll feel whole again.

"Where's everyone else?"

"Depends on who you're talking about. Everyone from Synd is inside. The rest are at Vipers headquarters."

"I want to go inside," I murmur. No matter what I'm going through, they've been through worse. I can set my own feelings aside to be there for them.

He helps me out of the car, and I glance down, grimacing. At least my black shirt hides the blood. We both look like we've been through hell and back. I wonder if the staff will say anything.

I don't know how it is here, but in Westmont we never went to hospitals. If the doctor on staff wasn't able to help, my father just let them die. His men were expendable.

"Before we go in, you need to know something." He tugs me to a stop and faces me. "Your brother killed your father. Anders is dead."

I blink at him, waiting for something to click. I'm a husk, all my emotions left on the seat of the car behind us. I nod, then tilt my head.

"Is Roman okay?"

"I'm sure he's fine. There's more, but it can wait."

"I don't think I can put more in my brain right now."

He nods, then wraps his arm around my waist and guides me inside. I barely register the twists and turns we take. At one point, we're in an elevator and a nurse is eyeing me with concern.

Dante smiles, explaining to him that it's been a long night. I can feel the man's gaze following me as we step out. I think about reassuring him, but the doors close before I muster up the energy.

Raised voices beckon us onward, and I bite my lip as we round the corner. Shane's shouts echo through an open door. The others crowd the hallway, almost as if they're guarding the two rooms across from each other. Mac races for us, and I step away from Dante. I may need the support, but I'm not going to get in between siblings. Instead, she beelines for me, wrapping her arms around me and I freeze.

"Sorry," she whispers in my ear. "I just needed you to be okay."

"Me?" I squeak and she squeezes.

"If you had died, he wouldn't have survived. You didn't see him before. He just…I'm glad you're alive."

She lets go just as quickly as she embraced me and turns to her brother for a hug. I wave to the others, suddenly feeling very awkward. I shouldn't be here. This is a family thing and then there's me—the random girl who got their cousin or whatever into trouble. I shake my head, wondering where the hell that thought came from.

Shane yells again, and a nurse finally comes out of the room, huffing. "I don't know which one of you is going to control that man, but you'd better speak now or I'm going to wallop him."

Sam pushes from the floor. I didn't even see her hiding behind Ren's legs. She wobbles, and Ren slides his arm around her waist. Her eyes meet mine, and I swear she's staring into my soul. Dante isn't the only one I need to talk to, apparently.

"If you put him in the same room as Alex, he'll stop bellyaching. We all just want to make sure he's okay," she says, her voice much softer than I've heard before.

"Alright," the nurse sighs, then leans into Shane's room. "Fine, you can get your ass out of bed, but so help me if you pull those stitches, I'm making the blonde woman sew you back up."

Willow scrunches her nose, then shakes her head. I step back when the others file forward, crowding around Alex's door. The nurse pushes her way through and holds up her hands. When she starts listing rules, more than a few of them scoff softly, but at least they're listening. Dante moves to Helms and they have a whispered conversation. Leaning against the wall, I close my eyes. Maybe I should have stayed in the car.

"Sam wants you in there," Willow mumbles, glancing over her shoulder. "Come on."

I'm not about to piss off Sam, especially if she's still feeling the effects of Oracle. High and deadly isn't exactly something I want to mess with. Everyone files in, huddling in the room that's probably the biggest they have, but doesn't fit all of us. I stop by the door, still not wanting to intrude on their time.

I've never met Alex, but even I can tell he's pale. Wires poke out of his hospital gown, connecting him to machines that whoosh and beep at random intervals. I don't know much about hospitals and I'm suddenly very glad I haven't had to spend any time in one of these rooms.

Sam brushes Alex's hair from his forehead, tears splashing down her face, and I avert my gaze. Her sob has me glancing back and relief floods me when his eyes blink open. Slowly, he lifts his hand and she captures it in both of her own.

"What's—" He coughs, and Shane stumbles forward. "What's the difference between a joke and three cocks?"

Ren's eyes pull low and glares at the nurse as if it's her fault he's talking about cocks when he just woke up. Alex clears his throat again.

"Shane can't take a joke," he wheezes.

There's a collective groan even as Alex grimaces as he chuckles. The nurse shoos everyone but Sam back, glaring at Shane until he drops into the chair next to the bed.

"No more jokes, Mr. King, or you'll collapse your lung again. And I sure as shit ain't giving you any more drugs to combat the pain that'll come from that." She glares at him until he nods, then spins around. "Alright, other than immediate family, the rest of you out."

I'm out the door before she's finished her sentence. Mason and Lacey aren't far behind. I wait for Dante at the end of the hallway, giving everyone their space. Helms and Mac, along with Hawk and Willow, are next. Helms claps Dante on the back as he passes.

Dante makes his way to me and slips his arm around my waist. My stomach flutters, the first sign of anything other than numbness filtering through.

"Where are we going?" I ask as he guides me away.

"Home. We both need a shower and sleep. The others will be back soon. I have to meet with Jag and Ghost, but it'll wait until the morning."

We're climbing into the SUV before his words register. "Where will they stay? And what about the people in the Pit?"

"We've got everything sorted. And we're staying at my house. It's over, angel. All that's left is the talking."

Exhaustion crests over me, and I sag against him as we take off into the night. At some point I fall asleep, only waking when Dante gathers me in his arms to take me inside. I need to tell him what happened, but not now. Everything can wait until tomorrow. It's been a long time since I've let myself hope for tomorrow. He tucks me into his soft bed and kisses my forehead.

"Don't leave me," I whisper, clinging to him.

He slides in next to me and I curl into his warmth. "Never, angel. Never."

FORTY THREE

Dante

"It's been a week, Dante. I'm getting out of bed today," Aelia grumbles as if I'm the one who's been keeping her here.

I stretch my arms over my head, the sheets sliding to my hips. Aelia cuddles against my side, and I tug her closer. Brushing the hair off her forehead, she sighs. If we lie here much longer, she'll fall asleep again.

She's been waking up at random times, crying before she's even opened her eyes. No one cared about doing the meetings in my dining room. I wasn't about to leave her, even if someone else was sitting in here.

I thought once we'd figured out what happened with everyone else, they'd trickle from Rima back to their respective cities. Instead, they've been hanging around. Helms finally told me they were waiting for Aelia. I don't understand why, but apparently it's important. Ghost just grunted when I told him he could leave. Most of his men went back to Harris, at least. I can't imagine having to feed all those bikers.

"If you're ready to get out of bed, then go ahead, Aelia. Or we can stay right here if you want."

She hums in response, her lips brushing my skin, and I shiver. We haven't talked about anything other than her telling me Jenkins was dead. She went quiet after that, and I wasn't about to push her.

She gazes up at me with hooded eyes. "You said there was something else to tell me."

"I think you should hear it from your brother…" I couldn't wait to tell her about Ember, but the more I think about it, the more I wonder if I should.

"You already told me Anders is dead," she murmurs.

"It's about Ember." Her body tenses and I hold her closer. "She's in Synd. With Roman."

Her body melts into mine, and she clears her throat. I tip her chin up, then wipe the tear from her cheek. A smile blooms across her face, easing the ache in my chest. Light flickers in her eyes, and I let out a sigh of relief.

"Are they together? I always knew they'd get together if they just got out of their own way."

"I don't know, but there's a lot you three need to catch up on."

"I don't want to worry about that now. It'll happen when it happens. I just want to be here with you," she murmurs.

I press a kiss to her head. "You won't hear me complaining about that."

She crawls on top of me, straddles my hips and plops her hands on my chest. "Are you trying to keep me in bed for nefarious reasons, Raines? Because I'll have you know that I have absolutely no problem with that."

When I grip her waist, she inhales sharply, and I grin. Her eyes widen a split second before I roll us. She squeals, wiggling beneath me.

"Keep that up, angel, and we *definitely* won't be leaving the bed today." I lean down and nibble her neck.

Her head tilts, giving me more access to her delicious skin. I groan, sinking my teeth into her soft flesh. Her nails scrape down my chest, leaving red lines in their wake. Her thumbs hook on my waistband, then she pushes them past my hips. She makes a frustrated noise in the back of her throat.

"Need some help there?" I murmur before pulling her earlobe into my mouth and she shivers.

"If you'd lift your hips, we wouldn't have any problems. But you *have* to make things difficult," she mumbles, and her lip slips between her teeth as she keeps trying to shove my sweatpants down.

I push to my knees, and she takes full advantage. The fabric ends up around my thighs, trapping my legs. My cock hardens when her hand brushes against me through my boxer briefs. She winces, staring at my pants as if they'll burst into flames.

"Didn't work how you wanted, did it, angel?" I grin as she flushes.

Her eyes narrow and her lips purse. "If you didn't want to fuck me, you could have just said that."

"Fucking hell, Aelia." I lean down, brushing my lips against hers. "I always want to fuck you. Every minute of every goddamn day."

She smiles and wraps her arms around my neck. "That's a lot of sex, Dante. I don't know if you could accomplish that feat."

"Challenge accepted," I grunt, then seal my lips to hers.

Desire blazes through me as she opens for me. My limbs tremble as I strive to stop myself from crushing her. She's not fully recovered. Neither am I, actually. We both need this—a connection. Her fingers slide through my hair, gripping the strands as I devour her.

Pulling my mouth from hers, I gasp at the emotions she elicits in me. I drop my forehead to her chest, and she slides her arms around my back.

"Are you okay?" she whispers, concern lining her tone, and I pick up my head.

I grind my cock into her, and she whimpers, clinging to me. "I'd be better if I was buried deep inside this wet little cunt of yours."

"I thought I'd hurt you, asshole."

I gather the hem of her shirt and tug it over her head, leaving her in just a thong. Peppering kisses across her chest, I soak in her essence. It's something that's completely her and can't be replicated. I cup her tit, pulling her nipple into my mouth. She moans, arching her back, and the sound resonates through me. I move to the other one, giving the small bud the attention it deserves.

"Dante," she gasps, and I release her nipple with a pop. "I need you."

I grin, then roll off her. She makes a noise of protest as I kick off my pants and underwear. She rolls to her side, the scars on her back on full display. My heart skips a beat as I trace one with the tip of my finger. She shivers and curls into herself. I press a kiss to one, then another.

"What are you doing?" she asks in a strangled voice.

"Worshiping you." I slip my arm around her waist.

I brush my thumb along the waistband of her thong as I continue mapping her scars with my mouth. Rage used to engulf me every time I spotted them. Now they remind me of how strong she is—how she survived the unthinkable. The guilt still rides me, though, knowing I wasn't there to save her from the pain.

"You don't have to do that," she whispers.

"Angel, these are a part of you. They show me how strong you are. I wouldn't change a single thing about you, but especially not these."

I pull her close to my chest and run my hand across her skin. She shudders, snuggling closer to me. I kiss her, my hand drifting to her stomach. Her muscles jump under my palm, and I nuzzle her neck. She throws her leg over my hip. I groan as I graze my fingers along her thigh. A smile curls my lips as she trembles under my touch.

Slipping my thumb under her thong, I chuckle. "So wet for me, angel. Should I take care of this for you?"

"P-please," she stutters as I grind the heel of my hand into her clit.

I hum as I push her thong aside, then slide the tip of my cock against her wet core. She whimpers, pressing her ass into me. I slip inside her warm cunt and grit my teeth as I try not to thrust into her. Aelia doesn't have the same worries. Her leg flexes and I surge into her hard. She flutters around me, and pleasure floods my body.

"Fuck, you're intoxicating."

"Faster," she breathes. "Harder."

I freeze, holding my breath as I tip my head back. She whines, grinding her ass into me, and my resolve slips. I push her leg from mine and roll us. Her muffled shrieks have me grinning as I straighten.

Digging my fingers into her hips, I yank her onto her knees. Her cries of indignation turn to ones of pleasure as I plunge into her, harder and faster, just as she asked. I lean over her body and my fingers find her clit. She jolts under me as I circle the bud. She meets my thrusts, urging me onward.

"Come for me, Aelia. Show me how much you love my cock pounding into your greedy little cunt," I growl.

She shudders, a strangled sob leaving her as she spasms around my length. It almost sends me over the edge myself, but I grit my teeth, never slowing. Her fingers claw at the sheets as I straighten. Gripping her ass, my thumbs spread her cheeks as her cunt clings to me.

"One day, angel. You'll let me in here too, won't you?" I brush my finger against the tight hole, and she squirms.

I slow my movements and tuck my chin to my chest as images of fucking her ass dance across my eyelids. She's not ready for something like that and I won't push her. Still, the idea takes root as she writhes underneath me.

"Do it," she gasps, pushing back, and the tip of my finger presses into her.

I skim my palm across her skin. She whimpers and her hand flies back to latch onto my wrist. She tries to push my hand back to her ass, and she lets out a grunt when she fails. I chuckle, wrapping an arm around her waist and hauling her against me. With her back pressed to my chest, my fingers find her clit again.

"You're not ready for that, angel," I whisper in her ear as I bury my cock into her.

"I trust you," she wheezes.

Her pussy spasms around me, her cries of pleasure echoing through the room. Her arousal drenches my cock. Each surge into her sends sparks through my body. I won't last much longer, especially with the needy noises falling from her lips.

She goes limp, my arm the only thing holding her up. I ease her onto her hands and knees, still grinding into her. Her body twitches each time I hit that spot deep inside her.

She glances over her shoulder, face still doused in ecstasy. "Fuck me, Dante."

I growl, plunging into her over and over. My stomach tightens and I give into the sensations flowing through me.

"Mine," I grunt, again and again.

"Yours," she moans, and I explode, black spots dancing in my vision.

Nothing compares to this—to her. I bask in the afterglow, curling my body around hers. She's everything I never knew I needed. I'll do anything for her, give her whatever she wants, if she'll let me. Whatever I yearned for has shifted. All I want is her by my side. My future only means something if she's in it.

I tip us, slipping out of her, and she quivers in my hold. Gliding my palm across her skin, I soak in the peace swirling around us. She turns in my arms, nuzzling into my chest, and I sigh.

"I missed you," she mumbles, then brushes her lips across my skin.

"I missed you too."

She tips her head back, smiling wickedly. "Did you miss me or my cunt?"

Gripping her chin, I nip at her bottom lip. "Watch it, angel. That filthy mouth of yours is going to get you into trouble."

She wiggles away from me and slides off the bed. Crouching, her mischievous eyes peek over the mattress. I prop myself up on my elbow and raise my eyebrow. She snatches up my shirt and pulls it over her head. My boxers are next, and a surge of lust hits me as she tugs them on.

"Going somewhere?"

"If you catch me, maybe I'll get on my knees for you."

She blows me a kiss before launching up and dashing from the room. I grab my pants, struggling to put them on while chasing after her. Giggling, she skips down the stairs, and I follow.

I growl as I grab her around the waist and pick her up. This moment has lived in my dreams for so long I never thought it would come true. Her peals of laughter echo through the house, filling the hole in my chest. Nothing can compare to her being here, safe and whole.

Setting her on her feet, she gasps, clinging to my arm. I nuzzle her neck, whispering promises into her skin. I freeze as someone knocks on the door. Her muscles tense, and I push her behind me.

It's probably one of the Kings, or maybe Mac, wanting to discuss the topics for the meeting later. There's no reason to worry, yet I can't convince my body we're safe.

"An enemy wouldn't knock, Dante."

I glance over my shoulder, taking in her soft smile and nod. "Go upstairs anyways."

"How about I just stand back here in the shadows? Then they won't be able to see me until we know it's safe." The fact she's willing to appease my paranoia hits me hard.

"Fuck, you're perfect," I breathe.

She shakes her head with that sweet smile still gracing her lips. She slides into the shadows cast by the staircase. It's not enough to hide her completely, but it'll give her plenty of time to slip away if need be.

The knock comes again, and I square my shoulders before opening the door. A man about my age glares from my front porch, mussed blond hair falling across his forehead. A woman bounces from one foot to another behind him, attempting to gaze into the house.

I wish I was wearing a shirt right now. I open my mouth to ask who the fuck he is, but Aelia lets out a strangled cry from behind me. Spinning, I catch her as she stumbles into my arms.

She utters a choked sob as tears spring to her eyes. "Roman?"

FORTY FOUR

Aelia

I didn't think I would break down completely when I came face to face with Roman again. Yet that's exactly what I did for an embarrassingly long time. Having Ember pop up didn't help, either. It just sent me into another tailspin.

Now Dante is forcing a drink into my hand while my brother and my best friend sit across from me. They're not touching, but I can tell they want to. Something happened between them. I can feel it in my bones, in the current in the air, in the flutter of her hands.

There are too many things we need to catch up on it's rendering me speechless. I open my mouth, then hurriedly take a sip. The liquor burns as it slides down my throat, and I struggle to keep my shit together. I choke, then cough, and Dante rubs my back as I catch my breath. Roman leans forward as if he'll save me from myself but sinks back when Ember's hand lands on his arm.

I pass the glass to Dante and clear my throat. "You grew up."

As soon as the words are out of my mouth, I'm kicking myself. Out of all the shit I could have picked, I chose to comment on him being grown as if we haven't lost ten years. I should ask what he's been doing, if he's okay, why he's here—anything but commenting on him becoming an adult while I was gone.

"I think that's supposed to be my line," Roman says, his deep voice forcing tears to spring to my eyes again. "Shit. I didn't…" He glances at Ember and her hand flutters.

I gesture between them. "You two, huh?"

They exchange another look before Roman fixes his gaze on me. "We don't have to get into that right now."

"Why not? What else are we going to talk about?" My stomach clenches and he sighs. "You want to catch up on the last ten fucking years? Great. Fine. Let's do that."

"Aelia, we don't have to—"

I slam my hand on the coffee table between us. "No. We obviously do. Well, after I ran off after Chad, I stepped into a war zone. Anders was nowhere to be found, and there were bodies everywhere. Half the city was on fire and I'm pretty sure most of the leaders were dead. Someone snatched me, brought me right to Anders. He didn't even give a shit. And neither did Chad. Of course they didn't care, because I wasn't useful yet.

"Anders shot Chad, then faked his own death, and we ran. I didn't understand why he was keeping me with him until I realized he was searching for the Guild. He'd heard about them but couldn't find them. Once he did, I became his ticket in. And there I stayed. For fucking years."

My lip curls as I remember how emotionless my father was when he was negotiating my sale. I knew he didn't care about me, but I didn't realize I was no more than a pawn to him. I wonder what would have happened had I been born a boy. If I had a dick swinging between my legs, perhaps he would have treated me better.

"Aelia," Ember whispers, and I shake my head.

"So, I spent about seven years inside the Guild. I survived until Dante came. I survived until he saved me." I tip my chin up as Dante's hand folds around mine.

He leans in, whispering in my ear. "You saved yourself, angel."

Roman swallows hard, his throat bobbing. "Ember never gave up. She kept searching. Every fucking day."

Ember flushes, dropping her head and swiping the tears from her face. I wait until she lifts her head and search her eyes for the truth. It's not surprising. Ember was always there, sticking by me no matter what.

I bite my cheek, willing the tears away. I've cried enough. An understanding passes between us. We'll talk later when we're not so emotional and surrounded by men. Some discussions have to be just between us.

I turn back to Roman. "And you?"

"What about me?" He runs his fingers through his hair, knowing exactly what I'm asking. Bastard always did avoid shit like this. He never wanted to be called out or held accountable by me.

Dante stands, then drops a kiss on my head. "Ember, why don't we get something to eat? I'm sure you're hungry."

Roman and I stare at each other while they shuffle away, their soft conversation floating back to us. Thankfully, the kitchen is far enough away they won't overhear anything as long as I don't start yelling. Which isn't a guarantee. Rage courses through me, making my hands tremble. I lace my fingers together and tuck them between my legs.

"You're obviously pissed at me, so go ahead," he grumbles, running his fingers through his hair again.

"What the fuck, Roman. I don't need your goddamn permission to…" I can't even finish my sentence I'm so frustrated.

I close my eyes, attempting to center myself. It takes me a minute, but I finally get my breathing under control.

"I'm not pissed. I'm hurt. I *know* I fucked up all those years ago. But I was sixteen, Roman. I made a mistake and it cost me a decade of my life. It cost me everything. I don't regret it. All those choices and heartache led me here. And what did you do? You gave up on me. And I don't know if you're trying to ride Ember's coattails—"

"I'm not. You're right, Aelia. I was convinced you were…gone. Even after Anders miraculously rose from the dead, I still told myself you couldn't be alive. Because if you were, that meant I failed. Over and over, every day, I failed you. And then Ember showed up in Synd, still chasing your ghost, and I just…" He deflates, whatever fight he had in him draining away.

"Did she give you shit for it? Please tell me she was a bitch to you." I press my lips together as his jaw twitches.

I'm exhausted. I'm so tired of being numb and scared and angry and whatever other emotions decide to blindside me throughout the day. I understand why Roman did what he did, at least as much as I can.

"I'm still working on making it up to her," he mumbles as he averts his eyes.

"Seriously?" His head whips at my tone. "You two didn't even keep in touch?"

"I blamed her. She got you the car to go to Synd, and I needed somewhere for the anger to go. And she took it. Don't worry. She gave it right back to me, but I fucked up when I blamed her for your death."

My eyes find Dante, seated at the table chatting away with Ember. "How did you forgive her?"

He sighs, dropping his elbows on his knees. "I was blaming the wrong person. Anders was the source of all our problems. From the beginning, he was the one. Yet even when I knew he was alive—even when Hawk told me that Helms met a woman—you. Helms met you. And I still couldn't accept it. If they were wrong…I couldn't live through that again."

I nod, even if I don't fully understand. "Do you love her?"

"Yes." He drops the word at my feet with no hesitation.

I don't know what I expected to feel—maybe relief or happiness—but I didn't think I'd be jealous. "You could have had years together. And you threw that away for what? Some silly misplaced anger? Did you even care where she was? Or that she was searching for me? What the hell was so fucking important that you couldn't have helped her? That you couldn't have loved her sooner?"

Devastation and guilt march their way across his face in succession. No one ever told me what happened in Synd. No one thought I could handle the truth. They said it was Roman's story to tell, and we had plenty of other shit to deal with, but it was clear they thought I was too fragile. Whatever Roman was doing, it wasn't helping them.

"When you died—"

"Allegedly," I murmur.

He nods. "After that, I pushed Ember away. She went off the grid looking for you. I'm sure she'll tell you all about it. But I decided the new leaders of Synd needed to pay."

"Wait. Just…wait." I press my thumbs into my temples. "Are you telling me you took up Father's cause? You thought I'd died, and you followed in his goddamn footsteps? What the hell is wrong with you?"

"I wasn't exactly thinking right, Aelia. Anders was dead. And you were too. I didn't know what the fuck happened. I didn't have a plan or direction. So, I did the only thing I'd ever been taught. I got revenge. Except I didn't care. Nothing mattered anymore. And I didn't abandon Ember. I kept tabs on her—made sure she was okay. You have no idea what it was like to live with the knowledge that my family was gone in the blink of an eye."

My mouth drops open. Immediately, he knows he fucked up. His face flushes, and he opens his mouth to take it back, but I hold up my hand to stop him. Snapping at each other isn't getting us anywhere.

"So your heart wasn't in it. Fine. How the hell did you end up running shit when you were actively trying to kill them?"

"They didn't tell you?" He glances over his shoulder at Dante, then back at me.

"No one tells me anything," I say bitterly. "Then again, I have spent most of my time exacting my own vengeance on the people who've wronged me over the years. I was a little busy. Or they'd use the excuse that it wasn't their story to tell."

"Anders came back to Synd. A lot. Fucking cockroach wouldn't die. You're not the only one who realized I wasn't committed to our father's plan. Eventually, we worked shit out." He clears his throat. "I killed him. He's dead."

"I heard. You really did it?"

"In the end, yes. Alex helped. So did Ember. I thought I could use our father to get to you. No one was calling me or Hawk. We didn't know you were out. You called and then Hawk heard you went back in. Nothing made sense and no one would answer their fucking phone."

I'm sure there's more to the story, but the full version will have to wait. I'm sick of waiting. My entire life, I've been shoved to the side or ignored. Just once, I'd like to know what the hell is going on. I want my opinions to matter. Dante tried, but I didn't have much power. I still don't. I swallow as my gut turns.

"Aelia, we don't have to figure this out today. I just had to see you with my own eyes. After our conversation, it took everything in me not to drive here and get you. We knew Anders was out there. I didn't want to lead him back to you. Now he's gone and can't hurt either of us. You can come home to Synd, and we'll figure it out."

My head whips up at his pleading tone. "Home?"

"Ember and I talked about staying in Synd. We can help them rebuild and learn how to not be whoever we were. We can be a family again. Just the three of us like it used to be." Pain lines his eyes. Pain and guilt. He blames himself and probably always will.

My mouth parts as I stare at Dante over my brother's shoulder. Do either of them understand the impossible position they've put me in? I don't want to choose between the two people I love. Either way, I'll break someone's heart. I'll break my own.

Not going with Roman and Ember will widen the crack that already resides in my heart. Leaving Dante, though, will shatter me. How do I live with only half a heart? I can't. I'll wither away, neither of them being enough to heal me.

To hell with cobbling together the pieces of myself the Guild didn't steal from me. Maybe I was never meant to escape the hellhole. Fate needed me to die, and this is the final battle. One I can't win and will ultimately be my demise.

"Aelia? Are you okay?" Roman's voice, thick with emotion, snaps me back to the present.

"I'm fine," I whisper. "You're staying in Synd?"

"It's as good a place as any. Neither of us wants to go back to Westmont. And we can do some good in Synd. I have money, so you won't have to worry about that. I'll take care of everything." He pushes to his feet, then rounds the coffee table to settle next to me.

His arm wraps around my shoulders hesitantly as if I'll explode if he moves too quickly. Dante's eyes meet mine and he raises an eyebrow. I nod, tears filling my eyes. I duck my head to hide them, and Roman's other arm pulls me into a hug.

A sob escapes me, and I give in to the emotions flowing through my body. Roman's embrace feels foreign. It's no longer the comforting safety it once was. And that may be the worst part.

Forty Five

Dante

It's been a long time since Vipers headquarters has held this many people. Within the last week, the others have seemed to have formed a bond of their own. They're laughing, arguing, and mingling as if this is a family reunion of some sorts.

Even Roman showing up hasn't thrown them. I wonder if he called to warn them. Would have been nice had someone given Aelia a heads up.

"Is this weird for you?" Aelia whispers, gripping my hand.

"A little. I haven't spent a lot of time with anyone but Helms. Every time we're around each other lately, shit is going sideways," I mumble as I scan the room.

"Well, now that the Guild is gone, we won't have to worry about that, right?" There's so much hope in her eyes, I don't have it in me to smother it just yet.

Running an MC isn't sunshine and roses all the time. Especially in Rima. My father never established the Vipers as a force to be reckoned with. He basically moved into an unoccupied area, and that was it. Most of the connections we made were because of me, and that wasn't until after he died.

The back door swings open and Blaze walks in, waving to Alex. I didn't realize they were back. Mac made him interim president in my absence, but I sent him off to deal with the clean-up of the lower gangs.

Rebuilding Rima won't be easy, especially with so few of my crew left. I doubt there will be many people rushing to join the Vipers now. I'll have to figure out how to establish things within my club before I can work on taking over Rima.

The way the others run Synd is a great model, but I don't have the resources or the history they do. Asking Aelia to stick with me while I muddle my way through the next few years seems selfish.

Mac sidles up next to us, smiling as she gazes at everyone. "Pretty amazing, isn't it? I didn't think we'd all get along so well, but I guess toppling an organization as big as the Guild really brings people together."

"Who the hell talks like that?" I snap, and she raises her eyebrow at me.

"It's a nice sentiment, asshole. What crawled up your ass and died?" She turns, crossing her arms.

Aelia tugs her hand from mine and heads for Avery, who's hiding in the back of the room. Probably from Ghost, but it could be Jag. She's refusing to go back to Harris, and they're pissed about it. I think as soon as she spends a little time with Aelia, she'll be fine. Not that I'm getting involved in that debacle.

"I'm just a little on edge. We still have loose ends, and none of you are sticking around for that. I'm…"

"Exhausted?" she asks when my sentence trails off and I nod. "What loose ends? Maybe I can help."

I open my mouth to refuse, then snap it closed. I spent a long time shutting her out, thinking I was protecting her. All it accomplished was putting her in more danger. I thought all my insecurities would disappear once the Guild was taken care of. Apparently not.

"Maddox, for one."

She smiles, but there's a tinge of sadness in her eyes. "I took care of Maddox. When I was hiding from those shitheads Jenkins sent after me, he somehow found me. It wasn't a…pleasant conversation. I thought maybe I could talk some sense into him."

Her eyes take on a faraway look and I slip my hand into hers like I used to do when we were kids. "We lost him a long time ago. And I'm pretty sure it's Dad's fault. He was always whispering lies into Maddox's ear. How'd you do it?"

Helms catches my attention and I shake my head. He doesn't need to save her from this conversation. She'll tell me what she wants and keep what she's not ready for to herself. Mac always did. Guess she has Helms to share her secrets with now.

"He actually did it to himself. Apparently, after the Night Slayers were dismantled—thanks for that, by the way." She smirks, but I didn't do anything other than burn their shit to the ground. "He got mixed up with Oracle. He kept coming at me, and I kept pleading with him to just listen. Eventually, he just dropped to the floor. I'm pretty sure it was a heart attack. Then Ryker showed up. We buried him up north. That's why it took us so long to get back."

I nod, shoving my grief aside. I won't mourn Mad, the man who sold my sister. Later I'll grieve the boy he was before he was corrupted. He was just a normal kid growing up in a club like we were. In another world, things would be different. But today isn't the day to worry about it.

Roman steps in front of us, blocking my view of Aelia. I drop Mac's hand and cross my arms over my chest. Aelia can deal with her brother however she sees fit, but that doesn't mean I have to welcome him with open arms. He gave up too easily, in my opinion. Not that I'll share my sentiments with her.

"Raines. Thank you for helping my sister." The words seem to be dragged from him.

Ember stops a few feet away, tapping her foot as she glares at him. I wonder how much of this is her doing. I'm sure he's not happy with Aelia escaping the Guild just to fall in with an MC. From what Aelia said, he tried to protect her from the violence of our world as much as he could. Being with an MC president isn't exactly the life he envisioned for her, I'm sure.

"I would have saved her anyway, but it helps I fell in love with her." My palms itch and I bite my cheek. I really don't want to get into it with him in the middle of this crowd.

His jaw twitches as he glances at Ember, then back to me. "We're going back to Synd. I told Aelia to come with us, but I understand you might feel a certain way about that. I hope we won't have any issues in that regard."

Mac gasps, but I refuse to take my eyes from Roman. A sharp stab of pain hits my temples, and I struggle to keep my face blank. I don't have a place in Synd anymore. And Roman doesn't seem like the type to be okay with me following her.

Convincing Aelia to stay with me…I shouldn't have to convince her. I won't stop her from going with him, but I'm not going to let Roman dictate where she goes and what she does. She's finally free and I won't let him take that from her.

"I'll support Aelia no matter what she decides."

He nods once, though he doesn't look particularly happy about my response. Maybe he's just as frustrated with the situation as I am. He's shit out of luck if he thinks I'll push her either way.

Turning on his heel, he gestures to Ember. To her credit, she rolls her eyes and stomps away from him to join Aelia and Avery. Roman trails behind, shoulders tense. I wonder how hard it is for him to be here.

Mac clears her throat. "That was…interesting. You need to—"

"Don't tell me how to navigate my relationship, Mac. You handle your shit and I'll handle mine."

"Don't snap at me because her brother is a protective asshole," she hisses, smacking me in the arm.

I sigh, then give her a small smile. "I just need things settled. Could use some good news too."

"Well, in that case, you need to hear Alex's story. When he was in with the lower gangs, there was some asshole named Josh trying to lead shit. Once Alex showed up, no one would listen to Josh anymore." She smothers a laugh behind her hand. "Then Josh got it in his head he'd challenge Alex to a duel."

"Wait, what?" My head whips to her, and she presses her lips together, nodding emphatically.

"Slapped him in the face with a glove and everything. Get this, then Alex just looked at him and the guy sneered back, then Alex punched him. Guy flew right back into a vat of Oracle. Except the whole reason everyone was listening to Alex was because Josh kept fucking up the recipe. The shit was toxic. Like acid toxic. Josh just…disintegrated."

"Bullshit," I laugh. "There's no fucking way."

"You callin' me a liar, Raines?" Alex calls from the other side of the room, and I flip him off. "Why the fuck you think I ran? Rumors were flying about it. And it was the perfect opportunity to fuck off back to Synd for a bit."

"You're full of shit, King," I yell.

He shakes his head, grinning. "Alright, I might have just drowned him in it, but the rest is the complete fuckin' truth."

"Could have informed the rest of us what the hell you were up to," Shane growls.

Alex grins, waggling his eyebrows at him. "Good plan though, wasn't it? I always wanted to fake my own death."

Ren slaps the back of his head. "Maybe next time tell the woman who has an affinity for knives?"

Alex sobers, turning wide eyes to Sam. "Sorry, Bug. I'll try not to die again. Or fake die."

Sam scowls at Alex, and he winces. He just got out of the hospital this morning. I'm sure she pushed for him to rest, but I doubt he'll do it until they get home. Here she's distracted by everyone else, so he's getting away with more.

Plus, dying affords him a lot of leeway. In Synd, he's screwed. And he deserves it. He should be laid up in bed. Can't fault the guy for stepping in front of a bullet for his woman, though.

Aelia glides toward me, lighter than I've ever seen her before. She collapses into my arms, giggling as she looks up at me.

"This is fun. There's so many people and eventually I'll probably need to hide, but it's fun now."

"You can hide in my office if you need to," I murmur, then press a kiss to her temple.

She wraps her arms around my waist. "Being with you like this helps. Feels safe. When it gets loud, though…"

"We can go back home whenever you want."

She ducks her head and rests her forehead on my chest.

"What's wrong?"

"Nothing. You just keep calling it home, and it does things to me."

My stomach flips, and I grab her hand to pull her toward the back door. Lacey tries to waylay us, but I ignore her. Once outside, I debate whether or not to just take her home for this conversation.

Standing in an alley isn't ideal and I didn't want to do this now. With Roman's declaration, though, I can't wait. I need to know what she's going to do, if only for my sanity.

"Dante, stop." She pulls from my grip, and I spin to face her.

I bite my cheek, staring into the night. Moonlight filters down, illuminating her face when I glance at her. I don't know how to start.

When we had this conversation before, I thought we'd decided she was going to stay here. With me. After all she's been through, I imagine she wants to see the world. Find herself again. I just wish she'd do that with me. But her brother showed up and nothing feels certain anymore.

"What things?" I ask, and confusion floats across her face. "You said it does things to you. What things?"

"Oh, I don't know." She glances away, tucking her arms around her waist.

I run my hand through my hair, then grip the back of my neck. "If you don't want to stay, just say that, Aelia. I'm not going to keep you here."

"I didn't say that," she huffs, but she still won't look me in the eye.

"It's fun now. Once everyone leaves, it'll be quiet. And lonely. I get why you'd want to leave. You'll want to build your relationship with your brother. Reconnect with Ember. They want you in Synd. Hell, I'm sure you could even go with Avery to Harris when they finally get her there if you want. There's plenty you can do out there." I wave my hand toward nothing, really. There's nothing here except a dirty fucking alley.

"You think I'd be lonely?"

"I'm the only one here, Aelia. It's just me. I was working on establishing our place in Rima, but the Guild destroyed that. I don't have much to offer you."

And there it is. The one thing I didn't want to throw at her feet. If she walks away now…I didn't want to guilt her into this. Manipulating her by showing her how fucking pathetic my life would be without her isn't want I wanted to do. She shouldn't stay because she feels sorry for me.

"Don't—" I clear my throat. "You need to decide what's best for *you,* Aelia. And if that doesn't include me, so be it."

Her cheeks flush and she glares at me. "So be it? So be it? What the hell does that mean?"

I brace myself as my chest tightens. "I'll support—"

"Don't you fucking dare." She pokes me in the chest and I stumble back, not from the force, but in surprise. My back hits the brick wall and I shake my head.

"Aelia—"

She slashes her hand through the air. "No. You got to say your bullshit, so now you're going to listen. I spent *years* wanting a place I belonged. I dreamed of the day that someone wanted me, broken bits and all. And no matter how fucking hard I fought you, you just wouldn't give up. No matter how many times I pushed you away and was afraid to trust you, you kept coming back. And then you told me you loved me and I didn't believe you. I didn't fucking believe you one bit. And what'd you do? You just loved me anyway. And now you want to just set me free? I'm not a damn bird, Dante Raines. I don't need to find my wings and fly to a far-off land to live happily ever after."

She's panting by the time she's done, her chest heaving with each breath. With her flushed cheeks and determination in her brown eyes, she's never been more captivating.

"Fuck, you're exquisite," I breathe.

The anger flows from her and she chuckles. "You're...I don't even know what to do with you."

I grab her hips, yanking her into me. "Stay and we can figure it out. Stay with me."

She shakes her head, then drops her forehead on my chest. Wrapping my arms around her, I breathe her in. I don't want to let her go. None of this will be easy, but I don't care as long as she's by my side.

"My fingers tingle. Butterflies erupt in my stomach. My heart pounds in the best way. I have this overwhelming urge to giggle. When you call this home, when you say you love me, when you hold me—I feel like I'm whole. Like even if bad things happen, it'll be okay because you'll be there. My entire body lights up every time I think about how deep my love for you goes."

I duck my head and whisper into her ear, "Can I keep you, angel?"
She tips her head back and cups my cheeks. "Only if it's forever."
My lips brush hers, imprinting her on my heart. "Done."

EPILOGUE

Dante

Six Months Later

"Why the hell do I need to wear a suit?" I grumble, tugging on the cuffs.

Aelia wraps her arms around my waist, pressing her chest into my back. I haul her in front of me, running my hands down her sides before gripping her hips.

"Because if you don't, you'll stand out. No one else is going to be wearing leathers. Not even Ryker." She stands on her tiptoes to brush her lips against mine, then twirls away.

"I doubt Helms even owns a suit. And this is a fucking barbeque or some shit. The Kings probably aren't going to dress up. Byrns might, but there's no way the others will. I'm calling Sam." I reach for my phone on the bed, and she snatches it up and shoves it down her shirt. "If you think that'll stop me, angel…"

She holds up a hand as if she can ward me off. "We don't have time for this. We have to get going."

I roll my eyes, spinning to finish straightening my tie in the mirror. "Why the hell did we have to stay in a hotel?"

"Maybe because they needed privacy."

I don't bother responding since she's not wrong. I'd rather not have to hear what my sister gets up to. Truthfully, I try not to think about it, which seems to be going just fine so far. Helps that Mac is back here, in Synd, while I stayed in Rima.

Cleaning up the city has taken most of my time the last six months, and Aelia takes up the rest. Whatever is left goes to the Vipers. Some of our members have wandered back in, wondering what they need to do to atone. Aelia put her foot down and told me to just let them come back. It's what I was going to do anyway, but I let her think it was her idea.

"Hurry up or we're going to be late," she calls from the next room.

"Late for what? It's a fucking lawn party, for fuck's sake. There's nothing to be late *for*," I growl as she appears in the doorway.

She leans against the wall, giving me an annoyed look as she pulls on her scarlet heels. I stalk to her, crowding her against the wall. Her breath hitches and I grin.

Rolling her eyes, she glances away. "Did you maybe think I want to get there and hang out with my brother? Or my best friend? Or our friends? We're going back to Rima in two days, and I don't know when we'll be in Synd again."

Dipping my head, I nuzzle her neck, lending her whatever comfort I can. "You realize Roman and Ember will be moving to Rima in a week. Then you can see them whenever you want."

She sighs, tipping her head back to look me in the eye. "And yet I won't be able to hang out with Sam. Or Mac and Willow. Or Lacey. Visiting is nice and all, but I wish we didn't live so far away."

My heart clenches, wondering if she made the right decision. She's said over and over she loves me—loves that we're rebuilding Rima together. Until this trip was planned. Then the doubts crept in during the darkest parts of night while she slept soundly next to me. Maybe she'd be better off in Synd.

"Stop it," she whispers, pulling my attention back to her. "I don't regret staying in Rima. And I sure as hell don't regret choosing you. I never have. I never will. Now that Roman and Ember are moving, it'll be even better. Doesn't mean I can't miss my friends."

I swallow around the lump in my throat. She has friends who would do anything for her. A family who loves her. She has people she can rely on. I'll spend the rest of my life helping her heal from what the Guild did to her, but it's infinitely easier when she has others to turn to. Ones who she knows won't bail on her or hurt her.

"I'm sorry," I murmur, cupping her face and pressing my lips to hers.

"Don't be sorry. I'll keep repeating it until you believe it. I love you Dante Atlas Raines. Now, get your shit together and put on the damn tie so we can go." She pulls away from me and smacks my ass as she slips past me.

"Fine, but I'm taking it off after an hour," I call to her as she glides from the bedroom.

Our hotel is opulent, definitely fancier than I'm used to. There are four rooms, all for us. Why Shane thought we needed this much space is beyond me, but I'm not going to complain. Not with the room service being so damn good.

Aelia wanted to go out last night when we got into town. Sam convinced her to stay in and she came to us. I don't know how late they stayed up talking, but I woke up to her in my arms.

Ten minutes later, we're stuffed in the back of some fancy SUV on our way to the Kings' place. Aelia bounces in her seat, trying to soak in everything passing by. I hide a smirk behind my hand when she points out another landmark, practically squealing with excitement. The closer we get, though, the quieter she becomes. I fold my hand over hers and she laces our fingers together.

"Are you nervous?" I ask softly.

"Yes and no. It's been a while since we've all been in one place, and everyone gets loud."

I nod, though she doesn't notice. I thought before she was just worried about how everyone would accept her. As time wore on, I realized crowds were a no-go for her. Whether it was the loud parties from the Guild or the fact she can't focus on one thing, I have no idea. We've avoided them ever since. Doesn't matter to me since I never enjoyed hanging out at the clubs. I'd rather stay home with Aelia, anyway.

"What the hell is that?" Aelia exclaims. "Is that a gold hippo next to a squirrel riding a duck?"

"Seems it is," I murmur. "Helms told me about the hippo. No idea where the duck came from."

"Oh, don't mention ducks around Sam. She gets a little heated."

She pushes from the vehicle before I can respond. I hurry after her, skipping every other step as she knocks on the front door. It swings open and we're lost in a swirl of hugs and smiles. It feels more like a reunion than I expected. There are no awkward pauses or sideways looks at us. We step into the backyard, and I do a double take.

"Why the hell is there an arch?" I turn, searching for Aelia and find Alex instead.

"No idea. They got something planned, but nobody tells me shit." He doesn't seem put off by that.

Ren steps beside him. "Couldn't be because you're terrible at keeping secrets, could it?"

"You don't know what's going on either, fucker, so I wouldn't gloat too hard. Might pop a blood vessel."

Aelia's hand slips in mine, tugging me back the way we came. I can always tell when she's near, like my body recognizes her presence. She smiles over her shoulder, giddiness dancing in her eyes. She waves off Roman and Ember as we pass them in the kitchen like she wasn't just raving about seeing them on the way over.

"Okay, I'm pretty sure this is the right one. Just go on in," she says as she opens a random door. She pushes me through before slamming it shut, cutting me off from her.

"Raines," Helms calls, and I whip around.

The large bedroom doesn't look lived in, even with the clothes strewn across the bed. Helms leans back, eyeing me from the bathroom. Aelia was right, he is in a suit. I don't think I've ever seen him in one before, much less the fancy shit he has on.

"What the fuck is going on?" I bark, rooted to the spot.

He sighs and I realize his hands are trembling as he attempts to tie his tie. "I need help with this. And I needed to talk to you."

I roll my eyes as I make my way over. He pivots, averting his eyes while I slide it together. "You going to start talking or should I find Mac and ask her instead?"

"She's a bit preoccupied at the moment," he mumbles.

"Oh yeah? Doing what?" I tighten the knot, then meet his eyes.

"She's busy getting ready to marry me."

My hands drop from the fabric, and I step back. I don't know what I was expecting, but it wasn't this. In our world, we rarely marry. Not in the traditional sense. The fact it's Mac, who said she'd never take that step…maybe she was just waiting for him. I watched her avoid making connections. The only person she's let in is Willow. She was always searching for something—for him.

I run my fingers through my hair. "Okay."

"That's it? You're not going to freak out? Or get pissed I didn't talk to you first?" It's like he's searching for the flaw. Like he can't imagine that this is actually his life.

I smirk, shaking my head. "How do you think that would go down? You asking me for permission to marry my sister? I'm pretty sure that's not how you want to start a marriage."

He scowls and turns back to the mirror. "I wouldn't be asking your permission, asshole. Might need to throw your ass out if you're going to object, though."

"As if I would." I step next to him, glancing at the ring box sitting on the counter. "Why didn't you tell me sooner?"

"Wanted to tell you in person," he says gruffly, still fussing with his tie. "She's going to show, right?"

I chuckle, then sober. "I haven't always been the best brother to her. There's a lot of shit I'd do differently if I could. I should have been there when she needed help. She could have gone anywhere, but she came here. She ran to you, Helms. You're her safe space. You really think she wouldn't lock you down given the chance?"

"Guess so. Don't know why she picked me after what I did," he mumbles. He braces his hands on the counter and hangs his head.

"That was over ten years ago, Helms. You have to stop beating yourself up over it. She forgave you. She chose you a long time ago. Are you really going to doubt her now? You have what the rest of us want."

"You have that too. We all do."

I shake my head. "Not the same. You two have been intertwined since we were kids."

"We're going to have kids. We talked about it." He straightens, shaking the nerves from his hands. "Tell me I'm not going to fuck this up."

I clap him on the shoulder. "You're not going to fuck this up."

There's a knock at the door, and he sucks in a deep breath, then nods. I don't know if I helped, but as I swing open the door, I realize we're out of time. Willow grins at me, gesturing us to follow her.

The hallways are empty as we trail behind her, Helms muttering to himself the entire way. It's not until we step outside that he stops, adoration splashed across his face when he spots Mac. She turns toward us, and I swear I've never seen a person look more in love.

The ceremony is short and sweet, with Ren of all people presiding over it. There are no chairs, no music, no flowers—just the two of them standing underneath the arch I'm sure was Willow's doing. It's not until the vows when it hits me how uncommon their connection is. Aelia starts bawling about halfway through Mac's confident words. Sam gets teary-eyed about the time Helms says he'll always be strong for her. And then it's done.

They pledge themselves to one another, then sign a piece of paper. Helms holds the pen out to me, and it takes Aelia shoving me forward before I realize he wants me to sign it as well.

"Need a witness to be official," Helms grumbles, and Mac smacks his arm. "Kenz, I don't need a piece of paper to tell me how much I love you. And I certainly don't need this asshole's signature proving I committed myself to you. It's always been you, even when we didn't have this."

Mac breaks down, and I snatch the paper away. "I'll put this inside so it doesn't get wet."

Usually, Mac would glare at me for a comment like that, but she's too busy kissing my best friend to notice anything else. Hawk falls into step next to me as I make my way across the lawn. I keep waiting for him to say something. Once we're alone in the kitchen, he stops me.

"Helms won't offer, even though he wants to, so I'm doing it instead. If you want VP for the Reapers, it's yours." Hawk shoves his hands in his pockets and rocks back on his heels.

"You're the VP, Hawk. I wouldn't take that away from you. Besides, I've got the Vipers to take care of. I'm going to need all the help I can get from the Reapers to build Rima again. Can't do that if I take your position."

He nods, glancing out the door at the others gathering around the food. I didn't even notice the tables. Apparently it is a barbeque, just with a little extra thrown in for good measure.

I spot a young woman hanging around Sam, practically tripping over her heels. "Who's the girl?"

"Emma, Shane's younger sister."

"No shit. Last time I saw her, she was covered in blood."

He runs his fingers through his hair. "Shane's loosened the reins a little more. Lets her visit Reaper territory sometimes. He's still dead set on her going to college, though."

"Not surprising. This life isn't exactly easy," I mumble as my eyes find Aelia.

"You worried about Aelia?"

I shake my head. "Not anymore. Especially since we found out Aelia and Sam are half sisters. Not going to complain about the Wraith protecting her."

Alex bounces into the kitchen holding a brownie. "You two better get out there and eat, or it'll all be gone."

He stuffs the dessert in his mouth and grins, then flounces back outside. Hawk follows him and wraps his arm around Willow. Two years ago, I never would have thought this was possible. When Helms called for help, I thought we might find a way to work together, but nothing beyond that. Now we're an extended family.

"You hiding in here?" Lacey asks as she slides through the door with an empty tray.

"No. Didn't want the license to get ruined before it's filed." I gesture to the paper, and she nods.

She grabs more dessert and arranges it on the plate. "I've got some information for you on the politicians in Rima. Figured I could help you set up a security system, then map out the best way to infiltrate the upper ranks. Mason said we're coming out in a couple months to wheel and deal—whatever the hell that means."

"Probably a fancy party we put on or something. Drake and Ember found a house on the south side. He's talking about throwing a gala or some shit. But don't call it a gala since the last one he was at, he got shot."

"Good to know. Ember helped Mac pick out her dress, by the way. I'm not a dress person, but it's gorgeous."

"Mac isn't a dress person either. Wait, Ember helped her? So, all you women knew they were getting married today?"

She nods, wide eyes finding mine. Aelia obviously knew since she made me wear this fucking suit. I rip the tie from my neck as I stomp to the backyard. Aelia bites her lip, peeking at the other women clustered around her. I'm sure they were laughing at their ability to keep us in the dark.

Alex tips his chin at me as he shoves another brownie in his mouth. Shane tries to catch my attention, but I'm focused on Helms. I swing him around, and he narrows his eyes.

"What happened?" he growls, slipping his phone from his pocket.

"Did you tell anyone you were getting married today?" I demand, crossing my arms over my chest and glaring at him.

Shock flits across his face before he peers at Mac across the lawn. "Uh, no? I thought the women would have said something."

"Are you for fucking real?" Shane grumbles.

Alex chuckles and we all swing to him. "I just figured it was a joke. Pretty good one. Turns out you're just an asshole, Helms."

Mac stomps over, dress swishing around her legs. I hide behind Ren, who gives me a look. No way am I putting myself in her path. Mac is a force to be reckoned with when she's pissed. It's the reason we didn't fight her too hard when we were younger. Helms never minded her tagging along. Pretty clear why he never put up a fight.

"Ryker Dain Helms, did you honestly not tell any of them we were getting married?" Mac plants her fists on her hips as the other women gather behind her.

Glee. That's the only way to describe the identical looks on all their faces. They certainly did plan this, like Alex suspected, just not in the way he thought. Helms's mouth resembles a fish gasping for air as he glances around for help. The rest of us back away slowly, not wanting to get caught in the crossfire.

Aelia slips next to me, giggling, and I glare at her. "You knew and didn't say a fucking word."

"To be fair, Helms did say he wanted to talk to you in person. The rest, well…that was just a happy accident." Her smile sends warmth flowing through me.

I lace my fingers with hers and tug her toward a secluded spot next to the tree line. Wrapping my arms around her, I tug her close. Her body melts into mine.

"Funny how everything worked out," she murmurs as she gazes at the others.

Laughter floats through the air, probably from a joke Alex cracked. He doesn't seem to have many issues from his injuries. Dying definitely didn't change his personality. If there's an extra layer of gratitude lining his eyes when he watches Sam, it's not surprising.

I brush a lock of her hair behind her ear. "I could have done without the massive number of explosions. Then again, it led me to you, so I'm not complaining."

"Tell me we won't lose this. Tell me we'll keep visiting everyone and we'll stay close to them. Tell me nothing will change."

I sigh, tucking her head under my chin. "Things always change, angel. Doesn't mean it has to be for the worse, though. We lost a lot of years through the actions of our parents. Now that we've found our way back to each other, I doubt there's much that can tear us apart."

"I never thought I'd be someplace like this, surrounded by people who care. I thought I'd waste away bit by bit until there was nothing left.

And instead, I'm here with them—with you." Her words are tinged with sadness, probably remembering all the people who didn't make it out.

"I'm just surprised Shane is smiling. It's a little unnerving," I say, attempting to guide her away from the pain.

She snorts, then spins in my arms and rests her back against my chest. "My brother actually looks like he's having a good time instead of searching for the nearest exit. Sam told me she'll give me a refresher on how to stab someone. Willow won't stop talking about the bike Hawk bought her. Did you hear it's pink?"

She gazes up at me and I drop a kiss on her lips. "I didn't, but I'm sure she'll show us when we're there tomorrow."

"Ryker is taking Mac on a honeymoon to some tropical place for like a week. Lacey is *not* happy about it. Mason made some comment about dirty martinis and pissed her off. She said she changed all his icons on his computer to unicorns. And every time he walks into a room, the security system announces his presence with 'Here comes the asshole. Run for your lives.' I thought it was funny."

"How the hell did you have time to catch up with all of them in the two hours we've been here?"

She rolls her eyes. "Gossip, love muffin. What do you think we were doing while Mac was getting dressed?"

I choke, shaking my head. "Love muffin?"

"Thought I'd try to come up with a cute little pet name for you. I'll keep searching."

"We've got our whole lives for you to find one." As the sun sets over the trees, casting shadows over the yard, I realize we're all right where we belong.

THANK YOU

Thank you so much for reading the final installment of Dante and Aelia's story!
Ready for another adventure?
Check out the other works by Emilia Abraham:
https://emiliaabraham.com

If you'd like to hear about the other stories that have been living in my head, sign up for my newsletter (including extra scenes & a novella), visit my website, or follow me on social media visit:
https://linktr.ee/emiliaabraham

Special Thanks:
K.B. Barrett Designs-Cover Artist and Formatter
Emily Michel-Editor
Emily Renee-Beta Reader
Krysten & Catlyn-Omega Readers

OTHER WORKS

Shadows of Synd:
Under the Shadows-Book 1
Between the Shadows: Novella
Running From Shadows-Book 2
Becoming Shadows-Book 3
Shadows Within Us-Book 4
Beyond the Shadows-Book 5

Ruins of Rima: *Spin-off Series*
Chasing Darkness-Book 1
Charmed by Darkness-Book 2

Available on Newsletter:
Extra Scenes,
Bridging Epilogues (Shadows of Synd-Book 1 & 2)

Also by Emilia Abraham:
Stuck at Sundown
The Cryptid Chronicles: Bewitched by Bigfoot

About the Author

After many years of dreaming of becoming a full-time writer, Emilia Abraham took the leap, bringing her words to print. From sweet contemporary romance to spicy why choose and everything in between, she focuses on the happily ever after.

Emilia lives in the Upper Midwest with her husband (who's probably sick of listening to her expound on fictional men) and three kids (who try to steal her post-it notes). When she's not writing, she enjoys reading, playing video games, and consuming copious amounts of energy drinks.